THE
SIXTH
NIGHT

A Novel

By

SILVIANO C. BARBOSA

Goa Raj Books
Toronto, Canada

GOA RAJ
BOOKS

Goa Raj Books

132 Roselawn Drive, Woodbridge, Ontario, CANADA   L4H 1A5

email: goarajbooks@yahoo.com

First Edition
December 2004

Copyright © 2004 by Silviano C. Barbosa

The cataloguing-in-publication data is on file with the National Library of Canada

ISBN 0-9736200-0-5

Dedicated to:

My late parents: Caetano Maria Barbosa and Joanita Dias,

My family: Serah, Shawn, Lisa and Glenn,

My brother: Prof. Anthony Barbosa Ph.D.

A few words from the author...

Like anyone who has enjoyed an eventful life and has dreams, the urge to collate anecdotes, experiences and memories into a story is as inexplicable as it is undeniable.

This is a labour of love, which took over twelve years. It took a lot out of me emotionally. For, as I recollected and relived so much on those cold wintry nights in Toronto, I found myself smiling sometimes and at other times wiping away a tear.

Silviano C. Barbosa

Toronto, Canada
December 2004.

I would like to thank:

- **Caetano Maria Barbosa and Joanita Dias** my dear parents, who have passed on, for giving me life, love and comfort.
- **Prof. Anthony Barbosa PhD**, my brother for his inspiration, guidance, encouragement and help.
- **Serah**, my ever-accommodating wife for letting me sit and write while she cooked and toiled.
- **Shawn, Lisa and Glenn** for the kind of love and affection only children can give.
- **Joe Fernandes** (Ireland) and **Armando Rodrigues** (Canada), for reading and correcting my manuscript.
- **Ben Antão**, the author for his invaluable suggestions and comments.
- **Prof. Peter Nazareth** who offered a helpful critique.
- **Prof. Jose Pereira** and **Prof. Teotonio De Souza** for their advice and support.
- **Conceição Menino Dias** my late uncle, who was a treasure house of information.
- **Angelina Cardoso** my grandmother (Navelim Mãe) for all her *hachiak* and sweet love for her *natu*. God grant her eternal peace.
- **Ashley Vales** for his support and timely help.
- **Roland Francis, Joe Lobo, David Rampersaud & Kris Mineyko** for going through the manuscript.
- **Elizabeth Thomas,** my editor who did a superb job.
- **Annie Chandy Mathew,** who gave my manuscript the finishing touches.
- **Shawn F. Barbosa,** my son, for the jacket design.
- **Venantius J. Pinto**, my good friend, for the eye-catching cover art.

No matter how hard you try
No matter what you do
What is written on your Sixth Night
Will always come true!

Old Goan belief!

Chapter 1

It was the *Sottvi Raat*, the auspicious sixth night of the child after its birth, on November 1, 1944. According to an age-old native Goan belief, the Goddess of the Sixth Night, the *Sottvi* was to come exactly at midnight to inscribe the destiny of the child on the book of its life. No external events or influence could ever modify these prophecies during the life of that child. The *Sottvi* set the Karma.

Everything was in place for this solemn occasion. To please and welcome the Goddess of the Sixth Night, all preparations had been made.

The quaint little house, with its mud and stone-walls and a roof covered with half-moon terra-cotta tiles, was decorated and cleaned. Delicious food was prepared in the kitchen, with special care taken over the *dall*, the sweet lentil pudding, to be distributed to the entire neighbourhood for good luck and in celebration. Even the mud floor of the entire house was freshly covered with an even layer of cow-dung and tar, which served as a disinfectant. When it was dry, it left five fingered wavy patterns of the hand all over the floor. This would keep the house free of fleas besides giving it a fresh, clean look.

There was incense burning just below the oratory on a long semi-cylindrical tile containing red-hot coals of fire and white ashes. From it emanated white ethereal fumes that spread throughout the house giving it a religious atmosphere and fumigating it at the same time. Just outside the front door, there was a *divli*, a brass lamp containing oil and a wick, which would burn the entire night to welcome the Goddess and guide Her to the child for the inscription of the Sixth Night.

After all the preparations and prayers were done, the family went to sleep. Now there was nothing more they could do, except leave the destiny of the child in the hands of the Goddess of the Sixth Night.

* * * * * *

The next morning dawned, bringing new hopes for the family. The child's parents were awakened by a shrill cry from their baby. The father switched on a flashlight and using a match, lit up the *divo*, a kerosene lamp made from a discarded medicine bottle with a wick.

The mother picked up the baby and changed the cloth diaper. She held the baby to her bosom and the baby stopped crying as she began to feed. Then, she put the baby to her other breast and when she had her fill, burped her and gently returned her to her cot. Both parents looked down at the cherubic face of their baby girl. From now on, they were ready to accept fortune or misfortune and all that befell their child as the will of the Goddess of the Sixth Night. Hoping for the best, they slipped into a daydream about their child's future.

This baby girl, born on the twenty-seventh of October, 1944 in the village of Navelim was the firstborn of Joanita Dias of Navelim and Mário Cardoso of Cuncolim both natives of Goa, a Portuguese colony on the west coast of India.

Joanita had come to live with her mother, Angelina Dias, in Navelim for her first delivery, as was traditionally expected, and had been there for the last four months of her pregnancy. Mário Cardoso, Joanita's husband, had joined her the very day he received news that she had given birth to their first child.

The parents snapped out of their reverie when the clock chimed. There was much to do. This was the seventh day and the day specified for the Baptism of their daughter. A big day was ahead of them for a Christening was always a grand celebration. Angelina had made half the preparations the previous day and had requested relatives and neighbours to help her out with the rest on that day. Joanita was still weak after the delivery. She put out the *divo* and went back to sleep.

At six in the morning, the *pedo*, the church sexton, woke the village for prayers by ringing the church bells, a giant alarm clock for the entire village.

Every morning, they mumbled and swore at the *pedo* for waking them up this early. After shifting around on bamboo mat on the bare floor, they would grope in the dark for a match, and light up the *divo*.

Today, Angelina awakened by the sound of the church bells at six, sat up immediately on the mat, said a short prayer ending with an invocation *Deva Tum Pao,* Please help us, Oh Lord. She stretched, lit up the divo, got up and went to the kitchen silently. Her first task was to fetch some fresh water from the common well, which was a kilometre away from her house.

She carried a coir rope and two empty copper pots, a small *kollso*, and a larger *shidi*, to the well, which had a raised wall around it and a pulley suspended from a beam across two pillars. Angelina carefully passed the knotted end of the rope over through the pulley, tightened the noose of the rope around the neck of the *kollso*, and holding the other end of the rope, she swiftly lowered it into the well with a thump. With an expert flick of her wrist and a pull and a release movement of the rope, she filled it with water. As she pulled it up with the rope, the pulley squeaked in protest at the friction.

Then she poured the water into the larger *shidi*, which had twice the capacity of the *kollso*. After filling both up to the brim, Angelina carried the heavy *shidi*　at her waist on the left, holding it in place with her left hand and carried the *kollso* with her right hand. With the balanced movements resulting from years of experience, the fifty-five year old, quickly headed home.

Angelina went to the kitchen and filled the charred teapot with water. From the unlit fireplace, she picked up some fine charcoal and brushed her teeth with it. She did not have time today to go out and brush her teeth with *tallo*, a branch of a *yucca* plant. She rinsed her mouth with fresh, warm well water and started the fire in the tripod fireplace in the kitchen with dried coconut fronds and some wood to boil water for the morning tea. She poured a cup of tea into a mug, stirred some sugar in it and drank the hot black tea.

Angelina started the household chores. She went outside in the half-light of the morning to release the chickens and pigs except for the fattest pig, which was to be slaughtered later in the day for the party. She wanted the best for the Baptism of her grandchild.

Angelina prepared to feed the pigs with rice water from the previous day together with some rice husk. She served it in an earthen pot, the *codem* and loudly called out, "Yo, yo, yo" and pigs came scrambling, as only hungry swine can. Then she fed raw rice to the chicken, calling out "Bah, bah, bah". She smoked a homemade tobacco *veedi* wrapped in a dry jackfruit leaf and watched them feed while she mulled over the day's tasks. Taking a copper *tambio* filled with water, she went to answer the call of nature and at once the pigs came out of nowhere heading for their morning delicacy.

Soon, the quiet neighbourhood was once again awakened by the *penk-penk* sounds of a rubber horn. It was the *poder* or the baker. While the older *poder* would come walking with a basketful of fresh hot bread produce balanced on his head and a long bamboo stick and bell signalling his arrival, the younger modern *poder* would carry his basket on the back seat of his bicycle and use his horn. Often, he would give out bread free to pretty wenches in return for favours in the dark of the early morn.

The friendly old *poder* Pedro, known to the Dias family for years arrived at the house of Angelina, dressed in his long *kabai*, a one-piece, full-length, cotton gown. He carried the square and round bread, the Portuguese *pão* or *undde,* the crispy bangle shaped bread, the *kanknnam* and the flat pitta bread, the *bhakri*, in a huge bamboo basket perched on his head and covered with a clean white cotton sheet. He came to deliver fresh bread especially made for the grand occasion of the Christening.

Angelina opened the door, acknowledged Pedro, helped him put down the basket, removed the cover sheet and inspected the bread. The *kanknnam*, the *bhakri* and other breads were still hot and fresh from the oven.

Angelina paid the baker, carried the basket inside and placed it on a table, making sure the cat or dog would not get at it.

The day was November 2, 1944 – All Souls Day. Mário and Angelina went to church for the early Mass. Joanita stayed home with the baby. As they walked through the village centre, they saw mounds of pumpkins, bananas, gourds, cucumbers, boxes and chairs stacked one over the other – another local custom on All Souls' Day.

In the name of *Almas do outro mundo*, spirits from another world, high-spirited young men went around the village under the cover of darkness and picked vegetable produce from backyards of the people they did not like. Nothing was missing from Angelina's backyard, as all the neighbours liked the sweet, kindly woman.

At about 7:30, after the Mass, Angelina's helpers arrived at the house. She served them some black tea and they started to work right away. Three men caught the pig, its shrill protests, waking up any in the village who were still sleeping.

The men killed the pig and collected the blood in a clay pot to be used later for the special Goan pork dish, the *sorpotel*, made with the pig's liver, heart, snout and belly. They burned the pig's hair using dried coconut fronds and shaved it, before cutting it open. They pulled out the viscera, separated the liver, the heart, the stomach and the intestines, which they later cleaned, cut and handed over to the women.

The rest of the pig was carved up for the roast pork chops and diced for the *vindalho*, sausage meat or the *chouriço* and *haddmass* the bone meat dish. A few big slices were salted away for future use. The fat was heated in a big pan and the extracted oil was stored in a bottle for cooking while the crispy fried remains, were eagerly eaten by the helpers and children. The men blew air into the pig's bladder and gave it to the children who played with it as if it were a balloon.

At about nine, an impish ten-year old, arrived with two large pots of *soor*, fresh toddy collected from the flowering coconut trees. The boy wore a smile on his face, a white silver *munj*, a chain around his waist, which held in place a red cloth called *kashtty* around his loins. Jose went around the entire village shirtless and barefoot wearing only his *kashtty* like his father, who was the *render,* the toddy-tapper of the village.

Angelina had asked the toddy-tapper the previous day, to deliver some *soor* to be used for making *sannam*, the traditional rice cakes used for special occasions in Goa. The *soor*, with its sweet and sour flavour could be intoxicating if taken in large quantities, but was used as a leavening agent to give the *sannam* a nice spongy texture and an acidic flavour that went well with spicy pork dishes like *sorpotel* and *vindalho* accompanied liberally by the Goan liquor, *fenni*.

Some women began cutting the big pork pieces into small morsels on a *haddolli*, a wooden stool fitted with a sharp curved knife cum coconut grater. The other women started to grind the *sannam* mixture and *masala,* the spice mixture, using a *rogddo*, a two-piece stone grinder.

The grinder had a fixed base piece, which rested on the floor and consisted of a large, semi-spherical marble stone, which had at the centre, a semi-spherical hole of about eight inches in diameter. The other movable piece was a spindle-shaped stone, the lower end of which fitted loosely into the hole while the upper end was conical to fit the palm of the hand.

The mixture of soaked raw rice and coconut pieces for *sannam*, was placed into the hole, the spindle shaped stone lowered into it and with a clockwise motion, and the *sannam* mixture was ground to a fine paste within minutes. The grinding process was repeated with different ingredients like chillies, garlic, ginger, coconut pieces, and other spices to produce various pastes or *masala* for the different dishes.

The fire was lit in three fireplaces outside the house. One fireplace had a copper *baann*, a large pot, to prepare rice *pulau*. On the other, a huge frying pan was placed to fry the pieces for *sorpotel* while the third held a huge pot containing beef bones mixed with onion, spices and water to make *caldo*, the beef soup.

Just before noon, the house and its environs were filled with the mouth-watering aromas of various dishes and all preparations were on time for the grand occasion.

At noon, it was time to take the child to church for the Baptism ceremony. The proud Godparents were *padrinho*, Luciano Sousa, a good friend of Mário from Chinchinim, and *madrinha* Flávia Coutinho, Joanita's best friend from Navelim.

Mário and Joanita were dressed in their finest. Mário wore a white shirt, a pink tie and a black suit and Joanita wore a green silk sari with a matching blouse and gold jewellery. Joanita applied Afghan Snow and powdered her face with Cuticura talcum powder. As a final touch, she rubbed a red-coloured crepe paper on her lips to make them red. She looked like a doll.

Dressing the baby girl in an immaculate white silk dress, they took her to church and the Padre Cura baptized her with Holy water from the *pia*, the fount. The baby was named Linda Antonieta Cardoso after her dead paternal grandfather Antonio Cardoso. The baby's name, her godparents' names and other details were duly entered in the baptismal register. Outside, the pealing of the church bells and firecrackers welcomed a new Christian member into the growing Catholic community of the village.

After the Christening, it was time for the *fest*, the grand celebration at the Dias residence. Angelina lived alone in Navelim. Her husband, Manuel Cirilo Dias worked as a tailor in Kenya, East Africa. He owned a tailor's shop there and he was the President of St. Francis Xavier Association of Nairobi. His two sons and a daughter also lived there with him. One son, Piedade worked for the British Civil Service and the other son, Remedios worked for a British Bank. The widowed daughter, Teresinha Faleiro had two daughters and a son and she worked as a dressmaker for a department store. They had all sent money to Angelina in Goa to celebrate the Christening of her granddaughter in a big way, though they were unable to attend. Everyone from the neighbourhood was invited, especially their landlord, the upper caste *bhattkar.*

The landlord owned tracts of land in the village. Five or six *bhattkars* owned the entire village and natives like the Dias family were tenants on their land.

The *bhattkar* never showed up, but every one else was present sharing the joy of the Cardoso-Dias family. The constant fireworks outside the house disturbed him in his palatial home nearby. He was jealous that his once downtrodden Shudra tenants made a lot of money in East Africa, and could buy his land at any price. He was determined not to sell the land, where they had built their little house in which their ancestors had lived for the last century. He wanted them to be his tenants for eternity.

Little did he know, that unknown to him, Manuel Cirilo Dias and his sons had already purchased three acres of land in Dongorim, just two kilometres from their ancestral home from another rival bhattkar, and were building an even bigger mansion than his own.

After the fireworks, the *ladainha*, the singing of Litany began. Mário tuned his violin, consulted with the two cantors and started playing. The two cantors sang in perfect harmony – one in the first or *primeiro* or the high-pitched voice and the other in the second or low pitched *segundo* voice. The singing was in Latin – *Kyrie Eleison, Christe Eleison, Santa Maria*. Every one responded with a resounding chorus of *Misere re Nobis* and *Ora Pro Nobis*.

After the main Litany was finished, the cantors started on *Salve Rainha* and *Virgem Mãe de Deus* in Portuguese. Half of the time the village people did not know what they were singing, as they did not know much Portuguese. They just memorized the sound of the words like the Latin litany. They knew however that *Ora pro Nobis* meant "Pray for us". They earnestly hoped all *Saibinns*, the Goddesses invoked in the singing of the litany would pray for them.

After the litany was over, the village elder Pedro João Pereira, popularly known as *Copit-tio*, 'Captain Uncle' who had worked on cruise ships as a cook but preferred to call himself Captain, recited some prayers dedicated to the baby girl's good health, welfare, happiness and future. First, he invoked the blessings of Our Lady of Rosary then those of St. Anthony and of Our Lady of Miracles. But before he was finished, Angelina interrupted him.

"Tiva, say an 'Our Father' for my dead *sasu-pai*, Gabriel Dias," Angelina said, thinking about her father-in-law who had built their ancestral home and who she believed, was always present in spirit there.

At this point, the Godfather Luciano Sousa also asked Ped João-tiu to recite a prayer for Mário's dead father from Cuncolim. Ped João got tired of all these instructions and decided to recite a prayer for the repose of the souls of all dead fathers, mothers and relatives of everyone present and included everyone in the world for good measure. He was determined to leave none to languish in Purgatory.

The air of finality in his voice indicated the end of prayers and the commencement of the best part of the celebrations – food and drinks. The children were served first. They sat on bamboo mats on the floor and they were served cool pink *xarope,* the raspberry syrup with soda before their dinner.

Two long tables were joined together and a long white sheet spread on top for the honourable guests and relatives, who were mostly men. The village elder, Ped João-tio said a short thanksgiving prayer before the dinner and raised a toast to the newly christened child, Linda, saying: *"À Saude, Borem Zaum-chem!"*—To her health. May all good things come her way.

The womenfolk served the tables. First they served the *caldo,* the hot beef soup in large bowls with fried onion pieces, tiny pieces of beef and traces of oil floating on top. Small pieces of *kankonn,* the bangle-shaped round bread were dropped in the soup so that when they were soaked completely, the bowl looked extremely full!

The soup bowls were replaced with dinner plates for the *buddoun-khanvchem jevonn,* the 'dip-and-eat' course. This consisted of pork dishes like the *sorpotel*, the *vindalho* and the *chouriço* meat, the beef curry and *verdura* the green and yellow vegetable dish made of green gourd cooked in coconut milk. Bread and *sannam* were placed at strategic places on all tables. This course was eaten with both hands.

Breaking off a small piece of *sannam*, they dipped it with their right in the gravy and ate it with small pieces of *sorpotel*, *vindalho* and some *verdura*.

The third course consisted of Goan *pulau*, made from long-grained basmati rice. There was also plain rice, curry and fish of three types namely curried fish, fried fish and *recheiada* or pomfret stuffed with spicy sweet and sour *masala*.

During the sumptuous dinner, drinks were served. There was Port wine, Macieira brandy and the local potent liquor distilled from coconut toddy, *fenni* or *rossaum*. Soon everyone was in high spirits. After the men finished their dinner, the womenfolk sat at the table and had their dinner. Ladies did not come first here!

After all the tables were cleared and the dishes washed, there was an announcement from Mário in Konkani, the local language.

"Mogall bhavamno ani bhoinamno. Atam aikat ek bori khobor. Amchea baaiecho podon, Luciano ani modon, Flávia, dogaim raji zaliant cazar zaunk veguim. Amchim porbim tankam." Mário informed the guests that the baby's godparents Luciano and Flávia were to be betrothed. Everyone congratulated them with a round of applause.

Luciano was a clerk working for a British firm in Bombay while Flávia attended a local sewing school. This was in preparation to make herself a strong contender in a market for brides aspiring to net a rich groom. And what a catch she had just managed! Luciano was looking for a village belle, who could cook Goan food and was good at household chores, which was what he sorely needed in Bombay. Every one was happy for the pair.

To keep the party mood going, men and women joined in to sing the traditional folk songs, the Manddo. And to wrap up the celebrations, everyone joined in the rendition of a poetic, cheerful song in Konkani, *"Uddon gelem parveanchem zoddem, voiru pavon iskottonu gelem, Bessaum tumcher poddom re, Deva Bapachem..."* This age-old song was to wish the young couple, God's choicest blessings on their forthcoming marriage.

Chapter 2

As days went by, the child began to grow strong on *niss* or rice water, mother's milk and the mandatory coconut oil massage from the *voijinn*, the midwife who helped Joanita with the delivery.

The village physician, Dr Kakoddkar came by regularly, to check on the mother and the baby on his old familiar BMW motorcycle. The rough village terrain of sand, rocks, river and fields had taken its toll on the engine, which made alarming sounds as he rode along. When he did so late at night, it alerted people that there was an emergency.

The doctor's first requirement was to keep boiling water ready in the house before his visit. On his arrival, the patients were asked how they felt, whether they had a change in appetite, if they had their regular bowel movements or constipation. Next, he would check the body temperature by placing the thermometer in the armpit, check the ears, the throat and the pulse and heartbeat. Invariably, he would open his leather bag for his syringe. As soon as he did that, every child would cry: "Mãe, I don't want the *injecção gue*."

But the doctor would get his syringe out and dip the old fashioned re-usable needle completely in boiling hot water in a bowl to disinfect it. Unruffled by the child's protest he would slowly take the appropriate medication from a vial, into the syringe and inject it into the patient. Even babies were not exempted from this habitual ritual. Most of the time the patients recovered, with the odd case being referred to the Hospício in Margão.

Dr Kakoddkar gave Joanita her usual calcium or vitamin injection at every visit, as she felt very weak after the delivery. Joanita did not really like the shots, but she loved to take her daily dose of the Vincarnis wine to get strong.

Mário went back to Aldonã in Bardez, where he worked as a choirmaster. He was lonely and bored. Joanita and Linda still lived with her mother in Navelim. This arrangement suited Joanita, who did nothing but feed the baby and rest, while her mother did everything else in the house.

Joanita went to her husband's place in Cuncolim a few times taking baby Linda with her to show the new baby to neighbours and relatives. Her relationship with her mother-in-law was not very cordial. Francisca always complained about everything and did not show any particular affection towards her daughter-in-law or the baby.

Just as baby Linda completed three months, her father Mário decided to go to Bombay in search of a new job and a new career in British India.

Mário did not have much of an education as a child since his father had died, when he was barely ten years old. The family did not have any savings and as there was no such thing as insurance in those days, they were in dire straits. Mário had to look after his mother, two younger brothers and a sister. His mother Francisca sometimes worked in other people's households, washing and cooking and helping out in the paddy fields to get some food and money to raise the children.

Mário had finished the third grade in the primary school when his father died. Later he joined the free *Escola paroquial de música*, the music school run by the local Catholic Church, and was taught by a capable *mestre*, the choirmaster. There he learnt the basics of music. Barely two years later he could read and write music and play the violin. He had even composed his first song in Konkani writing his own lyrics and music for it.

The kind old *mestre,* impressed with Mário gave him some music assignments and paid him a stipend. Mário sang in the choir at the local church and for a small fee, sang and played for funerals, weddings and *Teatros*, the Konkani plays.

Mário's first investment was a second-hand violin, which he treasured. He played it at *ladainhas* and weddings and baptisms. With the money earned, he made his second big investment – a used bicycle for his transport to the neighbouring villages of Assolna, Velim and Chinchinim on musical engagements. People were very impressed with this young lad's musical talents and he was in great demand for any kind of musical occasion.

By the young age of 25, Mário had become a *mestre*, a church choirmaster in Aldonã, a village in Bardez, North Goa. His salary was only thirty rupees a month, not enough for rent and other expenses. He supplemented his income by playing in the village band and performing for weddings and funerals.

Mário had great dreams in life and a lot of ambition. He wanted to change things around. He wanted a good wife and many children. He would bring up his children in the best way possible. He would give them all the love, affection, education and care that he never got.

Mário had received a proposal, a girl from the nearby village of Navelim through a *soirikar*, the proposal maker. Joanita Dias was just the right type of a girl for him. She was fair, beautiful and cheerful and knew how to read and write in Konkani. They met for the first time in Salcete Restaurant in Margão and instantly knew they were meant for each other. They both consented, and the *soirikar* earned his commission with no delay.

Mário and Joanita were married and they never regretted making this lifetime commitment, though they never knew each other before getting married. They loved every moment together. Mário took Joanita to Aldonã, where he worked. Within a year they had their first child, Linda. With a young wife and a newborn child, things could be pretty tough in the future with a choirmaster's pay of thirty rupees a month. Mário thought about it and made a decision to try his luck in Bombay.

He wrote to his good friend in Bombay, his *coompar*, his baby's *padrinho*, Luciano Sousa, who promised to help him. Mário did not want to leave Goa or his child and young bride of two years. But there was no future in Goa. People went to Bombay and flourished. Some went to East Africa or Karachi, but he did not have the education or profession that would take him there. So he opted for Bombay. If nothing worked, he could always come back to Goa.

On February 5, 1945, Mário left for Bombay on a steamer from Mormugao and reached Bombay's Mazagaon Docks early next morning. His friend Luciano came to meet him.

"Hello *Coompar*! How are you?" Mário saluted Luciano.

"Fine indeed, *Irmão*," returned Luciano and they hugged each other.

"And how is my *Coomarn*, Flávia?" asked Mário.

"Flávia is doing very well. She loves Bombay, now that she is used to it. But she still misses Goa a lot."

They loaded Mário's suitcase on the tram and were on their way to the Principal Club of Cuncolim at Chira Bazaar on Girgaum Road. Mário was impressed with the great city, its gorgeous, majestic buildings, the fast transport – trams, horse carriages, cars and the double-decker buses. It was his first visit to Bombay or indeed any city.

Getting out of a rural Goa for the first time in his life, Mário got all excited. What luxury! Who owned all this wealth? What made Bombay throb with excitement? Indian people owning these chauffeur driven private cars! How did they make so much money? He could understand the Europeans having these kinds of luxuries. Doctors and lawyers could certainly make a lot of money. So could the film stars and the merchants. What about the rest of them? What could they be doing? He wished he knew all the answers. He intended to find out as soon as possible.

They arrived at the village Club at 9/11 Dukerwadi on Girgaum Road at Chira Bazaar in about an hour. The club was an ornate, three-storied building that belonged to the village members of the Principal Club of Cuncolim. Mário entered the building and was at once registered as its member like his father, who was once a member of this club.

Mário freshened up and after the necessary paperwork met some compatriots from his village over tea. Luciano had ordered some tea, *kheema*, a minced meat dish and *samosas* from the Irani corner shop next door. After eating the snacks and promising to see Mário the next day, Luciano went back to Dhobitalao to his *kottrie*, a tiny single room he had rented for himself and his wife, Flávia.

The village Clubs or *kull* as they were commonly called in Bombay were places where expatriate Goan workers, students and the 'shippies' stayed. Most village Clubs were open only to members of a particular village. Some clubs were open to only certain caste members of that village. There were more than four Clubs of the village of Cuncolim and the Principal Club of Cuncolim was the only Goan Club in Bombay to be owned outright by its members, a remarkable feat considering the members belonged to the Shudra caste.

The Principal Club had three floors with large, open dormitories. Every floor had sections belonging to the various *waddos*, the wards of the village. There were strict rules at these Clubs. Only men were allowed to stay at the Club. Each member had certain rights and duties. In return, they were asked to pay a nominal rental fee for the maintenance of the club. Every morning members took turn to wash the tiled floor of each section. Every member had a right to place one trunk on the floor, which served as his settee and a bed for his afternoon nap.

Some members got together and arranged for a chef to cook special meals on the premises, on a primus stove using kerosene, and charged members for the cost of the meal. At lunchtime, the kitchen smelled of basmati rice, pork *vindalho*, fried pomfret, *reichad* fish and beef curry made with coriander. For those who wanted to eat out, there were numerous Goan restaurants like Pedro's in Cavel, St. Francis Xavier's Restaurant in Dhobitalao and others in the neighbourhood. Members recited the rosary at night on the second floor where there was an oratory with a crucifix and a picture of St. Ignatius Loyola, the patron saint of the Shudras of Cuncolim.

The Club had many benefits, one of which was the cooperative mutual fund society, called *comfre*, wherein each member paid a levy on the death of a member, so that the heirs got some type of provident fund out of the treasury. This amount helped in the burial and other services for the deceased member. The excess money in the treasury was advanced as loans to members at a prescribed rate of interest but it usually required some type of security such as gold.

At night, everyone slept on bed-sheets on the cleaned tiled floor – some snoring noisily, some talking, while pursuing their rags-to-riches dreams in Bombay. A few would remain awake all night from being homesick remembering their families in Goa, worrying about their job prospects or their medical test results. Newcomers could not sleep because of the disturbance caused by the noise of the busy city.

Mário however was so tired after an arduous sea voyage from Goa that he went to sleep at once.

The next day Luciano came to take Mário out to see the sights. They went to Dhobitalao first, where Mário met Flávia.

"*Irmão*, how are you? How do you like Bombay?" asked Flávia.

"Very well, indeed Flávia. You look like real *pukka* Bombay-*karn* already?" replied Mário.

"I am getting used to it, thank you *Irmão*," she smiled.

Flávia served them some very hot, flavoured Bombay tea with milk and lot of sugar. Mário sat on the trunk, poured hot tea into the saucer to cool it and slurped it up while Brittannia biscuits arrived on a plate. Mário felt at home immediately.

Luciano had taken the day off in order to be able to take Mário sightseeing. Luciano and Mário bought a pass for the day for unlimited travel. They went to Crawford Market, Boribunder, V.T. Station, the Museum, Fort area, the Gateway of India, Colaba, Mazagaon Dock, Prince's

Dock, Byculla, Chowpatty, Backbay, Churchgate, Cross Maidan and finally returned to Dhobitalao near Metro Cinema.

Flávia had cooked basmati rice and Goan fish curry with coconut juice and her special *recheiad* pomfret. Mário ate to his heart's content and had a short nap on the trunk. When he woke up, they had some tea and biscuits and then they went for the movie "Ten Commandments" at Metro Cinema. After the show, they went to Cross Maidan to catch a Goan soccer game. He met so many Goans all over Khursa Maidan: ayahs, butlers, cooks, shippies and civil servants of the British Empire. A mini Goa, in which Mario found he was quite comfortable.

Later that night Mário went to see a Konkani play, starring the famous Miguel Rod and his troupe. He was introduced to the band and was at once offered a job of a violinist. There was a big Parsi wedding coming up over the weekend and they needed to start practice right away to master some new English tunes. The band also played regularly for a nightclub.

Mário was enthralled with the music. He loved to learn new musical instruments and improvise music. Within three months he bought a saxophone and he practiced it day and night in the Club though Members of the Club covered their ears every time he did. But he soon became a good saxophone player and his music became more than acceptable to their ears.

Mário often played jazz in Bombay's Taj Mahal Hotel. Once he played the grand piano and the patrons were amazed at his versatility. But he still had to pay for the rent, clothes and food and he had to send money home to his mother and wife. So he started to play for the Hindi movie industry.

Meanwhile the bandleader at Taj Mahal was jealous of Mário who got all the accolades and so he fired him. Despite feeling desperate and helpless, Mário continued full-time with the Hindi film industry pioneers like Frank Fernand, Tony Fernandes and Chic Chocolate. But the income from this struggling new industry at that time was not steady.

Within a year, Mário joined the Seamen's Union as a clerk full-time. In the evenings, he still continued with the Hindi film industry as a musician. After six months, through a Parsi acquaintance at the Taj Mahal Hotel, Mário landed a job at Tata Airlines (later to become Air India) as a flight steward.

The salary was good and he felt comfortable. Mário sent for his young wife Joanita and daughter Linda to come and live with him in Bombay. They arrived in Bombay in April 1946. Mário had leased a small *kottrie*, a single room, which served as a living room, dining room, bedroom and kitchen all rolled into one, in Cavel, next to Chira Bazaar.

For a few days, Flávia took Joanita and Linda around the city. Flávia showed Joanita where and how to shop and bargain for the best. She taught her Hindustani, enough to shop around.

"Just add 'hai' at the end of your Konkani sentence, to make it sound like Hindustani," she instructed her.

"You mean like *'Kitle poishe hai'*?" Joanita responded.

"You got it, *Coomarn*," she laughed, "But say *'Iska kitna paisa hai*?'"

Joanita loved Bombay. It was like heaven: tall buildings, broad multi-lane roads, cars, trams, trains, double-decker buses, horse carriages, and the luxury. Mário took Joanita and Linda, who was barely two years old, to see *Rani Bagh*, the Queens's Botanical Gardens and the Zoo. The plants, the trees and flowers were amazingly well kept. They even took a ride on an elephant's back.

Linda liked the panoramic view from Malabar Hill. Frequent rides on the trams, the electric trains, the BEST double-decker buses gave her extreme pleasure. Linda listened to the sound made by the horse's hoofs during her occasional horse carriage rides. Evening walks along the Back Bay Reclamation at Marine Drive were reserved for Sundays. Living in one of those superb high-rise flats overlooking the Back Bay was

Joanita's secret dream.

Mário, Joanita and Linda mingled with the crowds on the sands of the Chowpatty Beach, just next to Back Bay, where they took in strange sights like a Sadhu who lay buried completely in the sand for days.

Joanita too, developed a taste for Bombay. After just three months, she braved Chor Bazaar alone only to discover her purse had been stolen. She did not know to speak Hindustani or English, so she had to walk home ten miles.

Joanita loved to shop. She bought clothes for Linda and a sari for herself, a lipstick, a small perfume bottle and a small make-up set. This cost Mário almost his entire monthly wages. But he let it go this time. This was his only expensive gift to his dear young wife so far.

Joanita's favourite fruits were guavas, oranges and apples. She regularly bought pomfret, which she slit sideways and fried after stuffing it with special *recheiad* masala, which consisted of chillies ground with tamarind, onions, vinegar, garlic, peppercorns and fresh coriander. This was Mario's favourite too while Linda preferred the chocolates that Mario brought for her.

Little Linda, despite being warned about ruining her teeth, lived for chocolates and toffees. She would even wake up in the middle of the night to eat them. He often got back home only to find Linda climbing on a table to get at the hidden can of chocolates in the cupboard.

Joanita liked everything about Bombay. There were the best doctors and hospitals, good entertainment, people of different background and even Goans and Mangaloreans who spoke Konkani. She picked up a few words of Hindustani and English and even a variation of Konkani with Bardez (North Goa) and the Mangalorean accent. On Sundays, she would meet Goans at the Dabul church after Mass.

Everything was going great. The neighbours were very nice and helpful. Joanita could go and watch Konkani *Teatros*, the plays at Princess Theatre, Bhangwaddi at least once a month. She could travel safely anywhere, anytime on the trams and the BEST double-decker buses. In the evenings she could go to Cross Maidan for a stroll, where Goan boys played soccer and women went for a walk or prayed and lit candles around the base of the big Cross of miracles. Life was fast and interesting. There was never a dull moment.

The Indian political scene too was far from dull. It was the year 1947. The Indian nationalists were waging a war for India's independence. Mahatma Gandhi, Nehru and other Indian leaders were employing non-violent tactics that had escalated to non-co-operation and civil disobedience to force Britain to quit India. The whole world wanted India to be independent.

There were riots and violence in small sections of Bombay now and then. Independence was only a matter of time and already Hindu-Moslem riots in some pockets of India were making headlines.

After the British left, Mário figured, there would be no security for the minority communities in Bombay, especially Catholic Goans in a predominant Hindu India. Mário decided that Joanita and their baby Linda should move back to Goa.

One day, Mário's flight from Delhi to Bombay was really late, late by five hours.

The next day, Mário seemed pensive and did not want to say much. Joanita handed him his coffee and said, "What happened yesterday? Why were you so late?"

"The plane was delayed because of the strike at the airport, " replied Mário quietly.

"I want you to quit this job right away. It is too risky. It is not worth the worry," said Joanita.

"But what will I do then?" asked Mário.

"You have worked at the Seamen's Union. See if you can work on board a ship," suggested Joanita.

Over the next few days Mário made inquiries at the Seamen's Office and also conferred with his friends working on the ships. One of his village friends, Josinho Fernandes, who was an officer on a ship, used his influence to get Mário a job as a musician on a passenger ship.

Mário handed in his resignation at Tata Airlines and joined a passenger ship as a musician for an orchestra on board. Within a week Joanita and baby Linda bid goodbye to Mário and Bombay and left for Goa in May 1947.

Sure enough, on August 15 1947, India got its independence from Britain. The former British India was now split into India and Pakistan. There was chaos in Bombay and all over India and Pakistan. It was terrible for all the minorities, the Moslems in India and Hindus and Sikhs in Pakistan. There were Hindu-Moslem riots all over and millions died in the massive exodus of refugees from both India and Pakistan. The papers were full of atrocities such as the world had never known.

But in idyllic Goa, it was still peaceful as always and no one seemed to be affected. There were a few places where the nationalist sympathizers raised the Indian flag, held small meetings and called for the total liberation of India, including freedom for Goa, Damão and Diu from Portugal, and freedom for Pondicherry from France. But the Portuguese militia soon clamped down on these minor rallies.

Chapter 3

One of the villages in Goa that sympathized with the total liberation of India was Cuncolim, the village of the Cardoso family. Situated about some twenty kilometres South of the city of Margão in Goa, it was always in the forefront of the liberation movement since the Portuguese first claimed it for the Velha Conquista in the sixteenth century. This village had a history of rebellions against the Portuguese.

Soon after Afonso de Albuquerque conquered Goa in 1510 by defeating Adil Shah and established a strong Portuguese presence there, controlling the sea routes of the West Coast of India, Portugal began mass conversions of the local populace to Christianity around 1540. Missionaries from Portugal and Spain came to Goa in droves to convert the whole of Goa to Christianity.

The Christian missionaries, among other things, preached equality in the eyes of God and many of the low caste Shudras voluntarily converted to Christianity wanting to be, free of the despised Hindu Caste System. The Portuguese encouraged the conversions. The mass conversions were progressing in full swing in Salcete, South of Goa.

But when the missionaries arrived in Cuncolim, there was massive resistance from the local Hindus. The Portuguese desecrated and destroyed the Hindu temple at Tollebhatt. In retaliation, the Kshatriya caste members including the famous Dessai clan of Cuncolim used force and violence to stop the desecration of their temples and mass conversions by murdering the missionaries.

The five murdered Catholic martyrs from Portugal and Spain were Rodolfo Aquaviva, Afonso Pacheco, Antonio Avelino, Pedro Berno and Avelino Aranha – all later beatified, by the Pope. There is a chapel dedicated to these martyrs in Tollebhatt, Cuncolim, called the "Capela dos Beatos Martires de Cuncolim" and their relics are kept in Sé Cathedral in Old Goa.

The place Tolle-Bhatt is so named because there was a *Tolli*, a big tank or a pond of water next to the Hindu temple, to wash away the sins of the bathers, and *Bhatt* refers to the estate or property. Before the temple was completely destroyed by the Portuguese, the Hindu faithful spirited away the statue of their Goddess, Xri ShantaDurga Cuncollkarin in a palanquin through the hills to Fatorpa in Quepem district, outside the jurisdiction of the Portuguese.

******

This flight is commemorated even today by celebrating the annual *Sontrio*, the *Festival of Umbrellas* in Cuncolim. The deity Durga's statue is brought from a temple in Fatorpa to Tollebhatt in Cuncolim on a *machila* or palanquin, and then taken back to Fatorpa the same way it was taken from Cuncolim in the sixteenth century.

This parade stops in Tollebhatt, Cuncolim for more than an hour and then passes in front of the Cardoso residence on its way back to Fatorpa. Thousands of people from all over Salcete witness this display in a festive mood, showering *gulal*, a red powder, over men's faces and clothes as in *holi,* and dancing on the streets with huge coloured tall umbrellas around Mhamai Saibinn's statue to the deafening beats of *dhols*, the drums.

Little kids enjoy watermelons, *bhoje*, *chonnem* and ice-fruit from the various stalls at the fair. Busloads of people from all over Salcete swarm into Tollebhatt on this day. Women and girls in saris and dresses add colour to the pageant.

******

The newly converted patriarch of the Cardoso family was. Avelino Cardoso, who descended from a long line of native Shudra Bhanddaris of Cuncolim, who tapped the coconut trees in the region since the millennia. He was the only original toddy-tapper in Mokim, Cuncolim, when the Portuguese arrived. He became the first Portuguese tax-paying *Rendeiro* of Cuncolim, as he paid the Portuguese government the *renda*, (hence the word *rendeiro*) the excise duty for distilling liquor from toddy. The family preserved carefully, the first *fôlha selada*, the signed document with the government seal.

There were no jobs available when some of the refugees from the plague infested area of Old Goa and Carambolim and other places settled in Cuncolim. Toddy-tappers were in high demand since the presence of the Portuguese in Goa made liquor consumption popular. Christians were encouraged to drink and Catholic priests celebrated Mass, using wine.

Avelino was thus the man, the Portuguese missionaries taught how to make the sacramental wine used in the Mass at the newly built churches in the area. The Shudra Bhanddari refugees took to the latest technology to distill alcohol from the coconut toddy and became practicing *rendeiros*, the toddy-tappers once again. Avelino Cardoso hired some of these Bhanddari rendeiros and helped them earn their living in their newly adopted village.

The job of a toddy-tapper was to climb a coconut tree and collect the toddy from a flowering bunch at the top, three times a day. Holding a *kati*, a sharp machete-type scythe in one hand and a container, the *damonnem* in the other, he would climb up, singing all the time. With one foot in a *khamp*, a small angular cut made on the trunk of a coconut tree, he would raise his other foot and place it in the *khamp* above it about three feet apart and effortlessly climb all the way to the top defying the forces of gravity. Thus toddy-tappers came to be known as 'top workers' in Goa.

Once on top of the coconut tree, the toddy-tapper would perch himself on a strong coconut frond and start his daily routine. He would cut a thin fresh transverse section of the *poi*, the heart of the coconut tree containing the flowering bunch, which was tied tightly together. Out of it oozed sweet toddy into the little terracotta pot, held in place by the oblique *poi*. He would then transfer the toddy to his *damonnem* and come down.

Avelino Cardoso would collect coconut toddy from more than hundred coconut trees leased from the Conde. He would make vinegar from some of the toddy after fermenting it for weeks. He would distil the rest of the toddy and produce strong *fenni* with up to 70% alcoholic content for the liquor aficionados of Cuncolim and surrounding areas.

He built a *bhatti*, a local distillery made of a big circular earthen *baann*, where he would pour his daily collection of toddy. Once it was full, he would boil it in the *baann* on a huge fireplace and condense the fumes collected into a distillate, which resulted in the *maddachi fenni – a potent liquor.*

Avelino's *fenni* was very strong, pure, and palatable and therefore very sought after in the surrounding area. Rich Goan *bhattkars* from far off villages would book orders for his *kollso*, an 18 bottle earthen container or carboy, months in advance.

He would improve his distillate with various flavours using skins of local citric fruits such as *maulling* and *torange* and sarsaparilla roots, which were thought to have some medicinal values.

Avelino made good money from this venture and built a nice home for his family. He was a devout man and became the first president of the reorganized (Christian) Mokim *comfre*, a co-op society headed by *dha zonn*, the ten elders, who looked after the interests of its members in times of need.

The *comfre* built an enclosed chapel of the Holy Cross in Mokim and held an annual feast in May. His extended family went to church regularly. In short, he was highly respected among his peers. Avelino was musical-minded, and inclined towards theatre too. He started teaching his group of toddy-tappers how to act and sing in their spare time. The toddy-tappers would practice their songs while climbing the coconut trees. This way, they practised their skills and at the same time became confident public performers. Thus was born an art form of the Portuguese era – Konkani folk-plays, the *khells*, which they performed in all the neighbouring villages during the Carnival and Easter seasons.

Avelino Cardoso's family eventually multiplied as years and centuries passed by. Linda Cardoso was a direct descendant of that tax-paying original Shudra-Rendeiro family of Cuncolim.

Chapter 4

As Linda grew up, her world seemed alive with colour. Everything and everybody seemed good to her innocent joyful eyes. To her the earth seemed paradise enough. The green trees, the blue sky, the fresh breeze blowing from the nearby lake, the chirping of the birds in the trees, the golden sunrise over the eastern hills, the vibrant sunset over the Arabian sea, the coconut tree plantations, the mango trees, the jackfruit trees and the tamarind trees were all part of this, her paradise on earth.

People were very good to her – young children, neighbours, teachers, old people, priests, nuns, merchants, beggars, domestic workers, Kunnbi tribal women who sold dry wood to her mother, labourers who cut large trunks of wood into smaller pieces used for firewood, fisherwomen who sold fish door to door. Everyone just adored her and made her feel very special.

Linda felt happiness everywhere. Right from the kindergarten, where she learnt to write those big letters – ABC with a *pedra kaddi*, to grade one of *aula*, the primary school, where she learnt calligraphy, design, arithmetic and dictation in the Portuguese language, she found school life very exciting and interesting. The new knowledge was soaked up by her eager, young mind. She memorized her favourite Portuguese nursery rhymes like:

"*A Mana toca o piano.*" The elder sister plays the piano.

"*O Papagaio, canta, berra. Diz o Papagaio real. Nossa Terra, Linda Terra. É Filha de Portugal.*" The parrot sings and shrills. Says the royal parrot, "Our Land, Beautiful Land, Is the daughter of Portugal."

Linda topped her class and could answer any question from her *professora*. Arithmetic was her favourite – she learned her *tabuadas* or tables from one to five in grade one. A keen student of the Portuguese language, she always got *sem erros* (without errors) for dictation, although her not so bright friend Olga, thought she received *cem erros* (hundred errors). Linda was the envy of her class.

Linda's father Mário was doing very well on board the ship. He was now promoted to *boatler*, a chief steward or butler in charge of catering in the saloon department, overseeing cooks, pantry-men, waiters and kitchen help. This meant the Cardoso family's income doubled and Linda and her family had a relatively prestigious and privileged life in Cuncolim. There were only six or seven other *boatlers* in the village.

Even though the Cardosos belonged to the low Shudra caste, no one showed them any disrespect, not even the higher caste Chaddo women who came to Joanita's house to request her to write letters to their husbands on board the ship. Joanita was the only one in the ward educated enough to write letters in Konkani using the Roman script. They trusted her enough to reveal their innermost feelings and secrets, to be written in the letters they sent to their husbands.

Linda's favourite pastime was to hitch a ride on a *boil-gaddy* cart, which moved slowly on its two large wooden wheels, pulled by two tired-looking bulls. The cart was covered with red dust, as it was mostly used to carry red laterite stones to the construction sites. A kind, old Dessai farmer, Shenkor would allow Linda to sit at the back of the cart on his way back. She chuckled when the farmer muttered obscenities at the wayward bulls. Shenkor supplied milk to Linda's household. Linda's mom always complained that Shenkor added too much water to the milk, but he denied it, saying it must have rained while he was milking the cow. Linda loved to eat the *saai,* the layer of cream that formed when the hot milk cooled down.

Linda was raised to believe in love as the redeeming grace of humanity. Whenever beggars came to her door they would always call out for alms saying: *Oh gara, ilem ismol galiai go baaie"* and start 'Our Father'- *Amche Bapa, Tum sorgar assa, Tuje naum.* Linda would run to the storeroom, collect raw rice from inside the earthen pot, the *baann,* in both her hands and give it to the beggar.

Then putting her palms together she would accept the blessing from the beggar *"Bapachem, Putrachem ani Espirit Santachem Bessaum tujer poddom baai..."* She was told the blessing from a beggar was equivalent to a blessing from Jesus Himself. Sometimes she imagined that the beggar, especially if it was an old man with a long beard, was the real Jesus Christ Himself in disguise.

Linda was very inquisitive. She always asked her mother questions, especially when her mother, would pick out the lice in her hair sitting on the *balcão* in the verandah with Linda on a stool, with her back to her mother. Then Joanita would part and tousle her hair up to look for lice and nits on her head. When she found any, she would kill them using her two thumbnails, pursing her lips to make a hissing sound.

This was the perfect time for Linda to satisfy her insatiable curiosity. She asked her mother about their house in Cuncolim. She wanted to know who built it and when. She was surprised to know the house was not built by her father or grandfather.

Joanita told her the house belonged to her grandfather's sister, Regina who was married and had no children. After the death of Regina's husband, Regina died too and according to Portuguese civil law, the house was inherited by Regina's next of kin, the eldest son of her brother, Mário Cardoso, Linda's father.

Even though the house legally belonged to them, an absentee landlord called Magdalena Fernandes owned the land. She had bought this land for five hundred rupees taking a loan from Mário himself years ago. Joanita later bought the land from Magdalena who sold it to her for five thousand rupees. But since the interest and principal on the loan amounted to nearly two thousand rupees, Joanita had to pay only three thousand. Joanita wanted to buy the land because she wanted to settle down there and plant coconut trees watered by a well in her own backyard. This they did within a year.

Linda liked the location of her house, which was just two kilometres east of the Cuncolim village market centre in a ward called Moddemaddem.

Her primary school was only a kilometre away and she could come home during the break for snacks like the *pez*.

The road in front of her house was always busy. Every morning, the Dessai herdsmen would graze their water buffaloes and cattle by the road. So there would always be fresh cow dung in heaps, which made things messy if one was not careful. The Hindu students would go to their Marathi *shalla* primary school, reciting *Shri Ganesha, Oh Na Ma Ha. Oh Saraswati, Namana Tujia Podok Mati.* Catholic children would also pass by her house every morning to go to the Portuguese primary school, the *aula*, which Linda attended too.

The neighbourhood had about ten houses scattered about a hundred feet apart. The best view was from the front of her house. There, lay a vast open field, where rice paddy was cultivated in the monsoon season. The rest of the year, part of it was inundated with water diverted from a river to form a small lake and another part was used as a soccer field and for grazing cattle.

Beyond this vast field, all one could see was a huge mountain, the Chandranath Parvat, almost touching the sky and on its highest peak, there was a historic Hindu temple, the Chandranath Temple, which was lit every night during the famous *Zatra* festival.

In the monsoon when it rained heavily the rain clouds hit the mountain hiding it from view. Linda was always intrigued by this strange phenomenon. Her parents said that if the mountain was covered with clouds, there was a definite possibility of rain sometime soon and sure enough this weather warning system always worked. Later, when her father bought her a pair of binoculars, Linda could see the temple more clearly on a sunny day.

Her mother told Linda there were quite a few houses and even a Marathi school up there. Lot of people lived there, including Hindu priests, the *kolvontam*, the temple dancers, workers and musicians. Her father once told her there were a few Indian classical musicians and dancers known as Parvatkars, living in Bombay, originating from the Parvat.

Linda's house in Cuncolim was fairly big but the bare unpainted walls of laterite stone were not very charming to the eye. It was constructed with large stones with some portions in mud. There were still holes in the walls used during the construction days fifty years earlier.

Unfortunately, the crevices in the laterite stones became homes to flying cockroaches and lizards, which looked like mini crocodiles when they crawled all over the walls. There were spiders and webs all over the roof. Once in a while, her mother took a long bamboo pole fitted with coconut leaves, which served as a brush and cleared the webs on the ceiling and walls. There were mice, which came out at night wandering all over the roof covered with curved half-moon clay tiles. The floor of the house was made of mud and it was covered with a mixture of cow dung and tar every three months to make it tidy and clean.

The house had a main entrance with two *balcão* seats and two cement benches on either side. One side of the open balcão was covered by a siding, made of woven bamboo sections and painted with tar to protect it from wind and torrential rains. There was a large main hall with a ceiling fourteen feet high supported on solid wood beams and trusses. This hall, the *vossro*, had an oratory high on the back wall, which housed a statue of Our Lady of Miracles in the centre with a large crucifix on top, flanked by two framed pictures of the Heart of Jesus (Coração de Jesus) and Mary on either side.

There were chairs all along the hall and a large teak table, which was used by Linda to do her homework. Adjoining this hall there were two rooms. The one in front was the bedroom with a big iron bed, a showcase, an armoire full of dresses with a hidden drawer underneath for valuables, and two trunks full of other clothes and blankets.

The room in the back was a storeroom, where they stored rice, seasonal fruits such as bananas, mangoes and other things. Linda's dad's bicycle was put in the attic whenever he went to sea. At the back of the hall, there was a small dining room with table and chairs and at the window was a *pia*, a wash-stand, on which rested a copper *tambio* and soap to wash one's hands and face.

Next to the storeroom, another room housed pots and pans, pickles, cans and jars. There was also a cellar on top of this storeroom, where they kept big copper utensils like the *chondro*, the water bath, the pot to make *sannam*, and other things that they would use only occasionally. Linda loved to climb the ladder to the cellar to check on some antiques hidden there. These were heirlooms. Linda's mom also hid green bananas and mangoes in the cellar primarily to speed the ripening and to make sure Linda would not find them and finish them all at once.

And finally, there was the kitchen at the back with a bathroom and three fireplaces and a place for storing all earthen cooking utensils and a bamboo pole hung from the roof by ropes, used for hanging clusters of onions and *chouriços*, where they would get smoke dried. Below the fireplace, there was a place for storage of *chuttam*, the dried coconut fronds and *kottio*, the shells and *zoddou*, the dried wood to start the fire. Here, there was another *pia* to wash utensils and a place to store the copper pots used to fetch and store water. Spices, salt and sugar were stored in clay jars or tins. The ants always invaded the sugar jar. When Linda complained of ants in her tea, her mother would tell her that the ants were good for her eyesight. No wonder she never needed eye glasses even later in life.

On one stone of a fireplace, Linda's mother kept a tin containing matches and a kerosene lamp to start the fire. Just close to the fireplace, there was a grinding stone on an elevated pedestal for grinding masala for the curry. Behind it there was a rectangular wooden stand designed to hold the tilted covered pot containing cooked rice. The starchy rice water would drain into an earthen pot below.

The kitchen had a thatched roof made of woven, dry coconut leaves. And during the heavy monsoon rain, the kitchen floor would be flooded with water. Linda hated this so much that she hoped it would catch fire, so they could have a new roof.

One day, when Linda was five years old, her mother had gone out to the neighbour's well to fetch water, while Linda and two other children were playing outside behind the kitchen. They were planning to cook rice in their little toy pot. Linda lit a match to make fire and somehow it spread to the thatched roof of the kitchen. The neighbours came running to extinguish the fire, but they could not save the kitchen. Miraculously the rest of the house was in good shape, except that the cement wall of the kitchen was charred.

Linda felt terrible. She had saved some coins in her piggy bank and she offered them to her mother to buy new Mangalore tiles for the new kitchen. Joanita appreciated Linda's guilty offer, but declined it since it would not pay for even one tile. Within three months they had a new kitchen roof and the kitchen never flooded again. Linda's wish had come true.

Outside the house there was a latrine, a sty for the pig, a coop for chickens and a storeroom for wood. The wood was dried and cut in preparation for the monsoon season. In the backyard, her mother grew banana trees, bamboo, a few coconut trees and sometimes gourds, cucumbers and okra.

In front of the house there was a little garden with rose bushes, crotons, bougainvillea and other flowering plants. There was a huge old mango tree whose fruits were plentiful but not very tasty. During the monsoon, branches of the mango tree often fell on the roof and damaged the tiles. The entire backyard was fenced with bamboo and sticks.

At the back of the house there was a stretch of low-lying land belonging to an absentee landlord. Here, garbage and drain water formed a stagnant pond below. This was home to water snakes and frogs. There was a little pathway for the pigs and hens to go down there. Adjacent to this was another large paddy field that was cultivated twice a year.

This field was a paradise for predators. Sometimes a mongoose would appear from a bush and attack a snake. The colourful kingfisher would hover around the pond for a couple minutes, scanning the water for fish, then dive vertically down to catch the fish and fly off. Some water snakes would sneak by and catch little frogs. Linda just loved to watch and learn nature's lessons on survival.

Once in a while at night, they would hear eerie sounds from *reez*, a nocturnal bird. This was considered a bad omen and was said to bring bad luck to the household. At times they would hear a hyena's shrill cries or a den of foxes howling out aloud. One fox would begin and the rest of them would follow in unison. Sometimes they would hear chickens in the coop clucking in alarm. The next morning Linda's mom would realize some had been snatched away by foxes.

Once the young rice was planted in the fields, the farmers would erect fences around their perimeter. But somehow, pigs and cows would gatecrash and destroy the growing plants. The farmers would warn the owners of the pigs at first. But subsequent violations provoked the farmers to shoot the pigs or poison them.

Linda was wary of snakes hiding in the firewood. Camouflaged green and yellow *erbel* snakes were seen hanging from trees at times.

Linda had heard an unbelievable story from some children about a mongoose that attacked a snake, drank its blood, and then quite out character, decided to let it live and even applied rare herbs on its wounds to save it!

When she ventured out in the field, Linda sometimes spotted an eagle, circling high above descending swiftly to lift its victim leaving the earthbound mother hen helpless and bereft.

The Dessai farmers often left dead cattle in the field. This would attract a gang of huge scavenging birds, like vultures, locally called *gid*. They had a sort of captain among them, who led all the others in their systematic attack on the big animal. Within a day or two they would reduce it to just a pile of bare bones. Linda's mom told her that the Parsis in Bombay hung their dead for vultures to feed on. Linda just could not believe it, but her mom said it was true.

Linda loved fruits. In the backyard, there were two guava trees, a custard apple tree and a lot of banana trees as well. Linda would climb the guava trees and pick the ripe guavas almost every day. They were sweet and red inside. She did not like custard apples much as she had to spit out the seeds. But she loved papayas, jackfruits and bananas, especially the tiny variety.

One night, Linda heard a thud in the backyard. She woke her mother up and told her. Her mother was too scared to open the door at night. The next morning they found a bunch of bananas had been stolen and the tree hacked down. The thief probably sold it to a shopkeeper in the bazaar to buy some *fenni* to drink.

Linda loved to explore the field in front of the house with other kids who were too poor to go to school. Linda would go with them to peer into the shallow pools of stagnant, slimy water to look for frogs, fish and snakes. They would play hide-and-seek. Cows disturbed by their play, often chased them. Linda often walked around barefoot and sometimes her mom would have to remove pieces of thorns and shards of glass from her feet with a safety pin. Her mother would then wash the foot, and smear it with some iodine. Later, when fashionable Japanese rubber slippers came into the market, everybody bought these 'bathroom' slippers and wore them everywhere... at school and even to church!

On Sunday afternoons, Linda would go to church for Catechism classes, the *doutrina*, with other kids in preparation for the sacraments. She received her sacraments of Confession and First Holy Communion, when she was in grade two in 1953. It was a most solemn and memorable day for her.

Wearing a spotless white silk dress, with a crown of white crepe paper flowers on her head, Linda carried a large decorated white candle and joined a long parade of boys and girls. She received her First Holy Communion from the Vicar. Having partaken of Christ's body, she was filled with awe. Then she felt more Christ-like, a real Christian.

The Vicar gave the children a party upstairs at his Parish quarters. There they sat at a table and had their first café au lait in a fine china cup and saucer. They also tasted their first cream biscuit and Kraft cheese sandwiches.

After the party, Linda's mother took her to the city of Margão to a professional photographer and had her picture taken in the studio. The large framed picture depicted Jesus giving little Linda the host. In the picture, she knelt and looked up, anxious to receive it. Linda really treasured this picture.

Chapter 5

In 1953, when Linda was about nine years old, she accompanied her mother to their village church for *Santos Passos*, the Passion Service, held on Tuesday of the Holy Week. The church was almost half-full even though they arrived an hour before the service so as to get a place to sit in the pews. It was an unwritten rule that the pews were reserved only for the *gaunvkars*, who came from the Chaddo upper caste. As the Passion Service was about four hours long, Joanita and Linda seated themselves on an unoccupied bench at the far end.

The preparations were still afoot. Soon more people streamed in and the church was ful half an hour before the service. Many of the non-practicing Catholics, who never came to the church all year long, made sure they came to the church for the Holy Week services. The church was packed and people stood outside as well.

In front of the altar, stood a serene statue of Jesus the Nazarene, with a crown of thorns on His head and blood dripping down His face. His hands were tied in front and there was a red robe on His back. Linda looked at the statue and was filled with awe. She prayed to Jesus and asked for forgiveness, because He had to die for her sins and the sins of all mankind. She also prayed to Him to protect her father on the high seas.

The sacristan came through the door by the altar and started to light the tall wax candles on stands on either side of the statue of Jesus, with his long stick that had a small flame at one end. There were fifteen minutes to go before the service began. The *confrade vermelha*, men from the Chaddo caste, in red vestments stood before the statue of Jesus but outside the altar area. These were followed by the *confrade azul*, men from the Shudra caste in blue vestments who stood behind.

Soon the sacristan rang the wooden clamp-like bell used especially during the grieving Holy Week, instead of the normal brass bells, signalling the beginning of the service. The devotees stood up and three priests dressed in dark purple signifying mourning entered the altar area. The Choirmaster started his violin and the head priest started to sing the Passion hymns in Latin. The Choir sang the responses though most of the congregation did not understand Latin.

The Latin singing of the *motetes* continued and the priest got up, sang the hymns and knelt down. The devotees did likewise. This ritual went on for half an hour. Linda's knees began to hurt and she sat down on the bench.

Just then, a tall woman in her thirties dressed in white dress, with a fine black lace mantilla on her head, pushed her way through the crowd from the side entrance. She looked around the church and spotted Joanita and Linda on the bench. With a dour look on her face she aggressively proceeded towards them.

"Hey! Get off the bench and sit on the floor like the rest of your kind. Come on."

Joanita jumped up promptly, relinquishing her seat but Linda continued to sit at the edge of the bench, oblivious of the storm brewing.

"You too little girl. Get up. These benches are not meant for people like you."

"No," Linda retorted, "I won't get up. Why should I? We were here first."

"You Shudras should know your place," the woman continued, looking at Joanita "And you, woman, should teach your child to respect us. Do you expect us, Chaddos to sit on the floor while you low lives sit on our benches?"

"This bench is not yours. It belongs to the church. And this is the House of God, not yours. First come, first served. You should come earlier," Linda responded.

"Keep your big mouth shut, you little girl. Don't try to act smart with me, you Shudra," spat the Chaddo woman as she pushed Linda off the bench.

Linda fell down with a thud. She grimaced with pain and began to cry. Joanita hugged her and tried to calm her down. Everyone around witnessed this incident but no one said or did anything.

"What do the words Shudra and Chaddo mean?" demanded Linda tearfully, "And why did this woman push me?" Linda was inconsolable.

"Let's not make a scene, *Baai*," Joanita pulled Linda towards her, "I will explain everything when we go home. This is the house of God. Just look at those men in blue and red vestments standing in front of the altar," whispered Joanita, in an attempt to divert her attention.

"No! I can't forget about it, Mama," said Linda scowling at the woman who wore a faint victorious smile. Linda's blood boiled. She had to do something.

All of a sudden without any warning, Linda stood up and ran through the crowd shouting, "This is not fair. This is not right. This cannot be allowed in the house of God."

Joanita could not believe her eyes. It was too late to stop her. "Oh my God, what will happen now?" she wondered.

The Church service came to a standstill. All eyes focussed on Linda running towards the altar.

The people who witnessed the incident, knew what had happened, others had no clue. Gradually, whispers spread and the entire congregation was buzzing. The Shudras were happy to see the courage and daring of the little girl and were angry with the Chaddo woman. The Chaddos were furious that the seemingly trivial matter took a serious turn.

Linda reached the altar and the Padre Vigar approached her.

"What's the matter, little girl?"

"Padre, my mother and I were sitting on a bench back there for over an hour. A woman just walked in, made my mother get off the bench and pushed me on to the floor. And she called us names. How could she do this to us in the house of God?"

"Oh God! Not again!" thought Padre Vigar. He had so far steered clear of this caste issue, which every priest knew was a volatile one. The caste issue was a dangerous one. Better left untouched. He did what Pontius Pilate did many centuries ago – he washed his hands and passed on the responsibility to the *Sacristão*.

"Sacristão, go and tell the woman to give up her seat to this girl and her mother and take the child back to her mother." The vicar ordered.

The sacristão, who was himself a Shudra and a lowly servant of the church, hesitantly approached the woman.

"Lady, Pad Vigar has asked you to relinquish your seat," said the sacristão, visibly nervous.

Suddenly, some Chaddo men and women rallied around the woman.

"Don't give the seat to the Shudras, lady," they prompted.

The woman did not move from her seat or say a word to the Sacristão.

The Sacristão quietly went back to the altar and relayed the message to the Vicar.

The Vicar conferred with *Padre Cura*, the curate and decided he had no choice but to confront the woman himself.

"Lady, I kindly request you to get up and give your seat to these people," he pleaded. But the woman did not even look at the priest. She continued sitting on the bench defiantly. The Vicar made his way towards the altar and made a public announcement:

"Dear brothers and sisters in Christ. This is the house of God. We have just seen injustice done to this little girl and her mother, who were forcibly removed from their seats. The Church will not tolerate any caste distinction in the house of God. Since the woman in question will not move from her seat, I can no longer continue the service. If we cannot show some charity, tolerance and equality, there is no reason to continue this farce. Ladies and Gentlemen, if the woman will not concede to my request, the Passion Service is hereby cancelled."

The whole church congregation fell silent momentarily. Then everyone began whispering all at once. The Chaddo men and women remained adamant. The Shudras were afraid.

"They cannot change our age-old traditions. We have to show these people who we are. If we give an inch today, they will take a mile tomorrow. If the priest does not want to continue the Passion Service, so be it," some of the Chaddos declared.

The situation was unprecedented. For the first time in the history of the village, or for that matter in whole of Goa, there would be no Passion Service on Tuesday of the Holy Week. Everyone was preparing to go home. Then some pious, educated Chaddo men and women took a courageous initiative after conferring amongst themselves. They approached the woman, persuading her to acquiesce to the Vicar's demand.

The woman finally conceded and let Joanita and Linda take their seats on the bench. Linda felt sweet taste of victory for the first time in her life. Joanita was proud of Linda. The Vicar was pleased that justice prevailed and that the deadlock was resolved. And the Passion Service was finally resumed.

***

The service went on for another two hours. Finally it was time for the procession.

Two seminarians led with the children in front, the young boys and girls next, followed by women and men. Next came the men in blue, then those in red carrying Jesus' statue, followed by a live band, the nuns and the priests. Each participant carried a lighted wax candle.

The procession paraded through the village Centre, the Hindu market area and passed through the main street, where all traffic was suspended until the procession passed by. The band played mournful Passion music. The boys and girls in the procession started the Rosary. Children had to keep lighting their candles constantly extinguished by the persistent wind. Finally the procession returned to the main portal of the church, by the statue of the Blessed Virgin Mary, *Mater Dolorosa*. By this time it was eight o'clock and pitch dark.

All of a sudden, a soprano voice sang *Veronica* in Latin. Everybody turned to see a little boy on a high stand, dressed in white angelic robes. He held up a towel, symbolic of the one Veronica had used to wipe the Face of Jesus, when she saw him carrying the Cross. Veronica's towel retained a miraculous imprint of His bloodstained Face.

Linda knew the boy. His name was Felix and he went to the same school. The boy's soulful singing moved her and she was close to tears.

Then, the Padre Cura made people cry with his dramatic description of Jesus' suffering. After that, the kissing of the Crucifix began and by the time the whole ceremony was over it was almost ten o'clock.

Linda was really tired and hungry by now. She and her mother walked home. On the way, Linda's mother bought some *bhoje*, little balls of *besan*, gram flour mixed with onion and green chillies and deep-fried in oil wrapped in newspaper. After a quick supper, they went to bed.

******

Next morning, Linda woke up and sat at the table for a spartan breakfast of *pez*, plain rice boiled in water, with hot mango pickle. The experience in church still troubled her.

"Mama, now tell me why that rude woman pushed me off the bench," Linda demanded.

"*Baai*, the woman pushed you off the bench because we belong to the low *Shudra* caste and we are not supposed to use the pews, which are reserved only for the upper *Chaddo* caste. We are supposed to sit on the floor. In olden days, they could kill you for that. Thank God, she only pushed you."

"But Mama, what's a caste? And why can't we belong to the *Chaddo* caste?"

"Let me try and explain my child. In Goa, we have three main social classes or castes: Bamonn (Brahmins) the priestly class, Chaddo (Kshatryias) the warrior class and Shudras the labour class. In our village there are no Bamonns. But we have Chaddos, the next highest caste. We belong to the Shudra caste, which according to them is the lowest caste. One cannot change caste because it is determined by birth. It is hereditary."

"But Mama, I'm no different from the others. Should I suffer for no fault of mine?"

"*Baai*, the only way you fight this is for you to show them you are a better person, excelling in all that you do"

"What about the men in blue and red vestments, in front of the altar yesterday. What was that all about?"

"The ones who wore blue are the Shudras. They cannot carry the statue of Christ or the Blessed Sacrament on Passion Day. They cannot celebrate the feast of the patron saint of the church. They can only celebrate the smaller feast of St Ignatius Loyola. The ones in red are the *Chaddos*. They are the privileged people, the so called *gaunvkars* of this village and only they can celebrate the main feast of the church, which is the feast of Our Lady of Health."

"How awful and demeaning! What a system! It's disgusting," said Linda.

"That's not all. I guess the people who devised this system were quite ignorant. They didn't know that Jesus was the son of a carpenter, and so a Shudra. St Ignatius Loyola was a Spanish nobleman and a soldier – a Chaddo. But the irony is that the lowly Shudras can celebrate the feast of a nobleman Chaddo while the Chaddos celebrate the feast of a Shudra carpenter. Besides I know that in another village, Shudras can celebrate the feast of Our Lady of Rosary, but here we Shudras cannot celebrate the feast of Our Lady of Health. Is it not the same Blessed Virgin Mary after all?"

"Mama, you should have been a teacher, how do you know all these things? I want to be just like you when I grow up," Linda said in admiration.

"*Baai*, this caste system has been followed for thousands of years since our ancestors practiced Hinduism."

"What did you say Mama? Were we Hindus a long time ago?"

"Yes, *baai*, our ancestors converted to Christianity about four hundred years ago when the Portuguese conquered Goa. That means, your great, great, great, great grandparents were Hindus before the year 1540 or so."

"Oh my God, you know so much."

"Listen to me, *baai*, all I ever want you to do, is work hard, study, get to the top and show the world what you are capable of. Put these myths of caste out of your mind." advised her mother. "You'll learn quickly *Baai*. You are smart."

Linda never forgot the incident in the church in the Holy Week of 1953. It shocked her that there could be such discrimination even in the house of God. Life was not as fair or simple as she had imagined. She decided then and there, that she had to be better than the average person to rise above the system.

Shortly after this incident, her father Mário came home to Goa and Linda told him what had happened in the church. Mário explained to her that discrimination existed everywhere. Some think they are superior to others in terms of wealth, looks or ability. He told her the story of Hitler and the reasons for the Second World War.

"This man from Germany called Hitler thought the German race was the supreme race in the world – the Aryan race. Hitler himself was not typical of that race, but felt he had to preserve its purity and do away with the others. He was a dictator with vast armies at his command. He went on a killing spree, attacking people he hated, namely the Jews, the gypsies and the mentally retarded. It took the whole world and a major war to stop him.

"Hitler professed to be a Christian but hated the Jews. Little did he realize that Jesus Christ whom he worshipped was born a Jew. Unfortunately, more Hitlers will be born every day and discrimination among humans will still continue. We must strive to prove that all humans are equal in the eyes of God.

"The only way to fight this inequality is to educate yourself, be a good and exemplary person and show everyone your true worth and exceptional abilities.

"I can tell you the real life story of such an exemplary person from Goa, Cardinal Valerian Gracias. This man was born to a very poor Goan family. His father was a *Shudra*, a poor toddy-tapper from Dramapur, Chinchinim, Goa and his mother was from Navelim. His parents went to Karachi looking for work. His mother worked as a nanny. Young Valerian was registered in a parish school in Karachi.

"This intelligent child later became a priest, a bishop and then an archbishop. A big orator, he could converse in more than seven languages fluently. He became the first Indian Cardinal of the Roman Catholic Church representing India at the Vatican. He never let his caste be a hindrance to his meteoric rise to fame, even though the majority of his competing priest friends in India and in Goa were Bamonns or Chaddos.

"Let me also tell you about a great Indian intellectual, lawyer and architect of the Indian Constitution, the great Dr Ambedkar, who was born an untouchable, the lowest caste in all of India. When he was a child, he was barred from attending school. The ruling maharajah, a good man, decreed that all untouchables could attend school in his state. Ambedkar studied well, went abroad on a scholarship, earned a double Ph. D. and became a renowned lawyer. These great men crossed all hurdles and showed the world what they were made of."

When Linda heard these true stories, she was really inspired and was more determined than ever to excel in everything she could. Now she could put this little episode behind her and look forward to a great future.

Life was wonderful for little Linda, especially when her father came home once in two years. Mário would bring her new dresses, school bags, raincoat, shoes and gumboots.

Mário would pamper Linda taking her for outings to Margão, for feasts, and visits to many friends and relatives. They would have many visitors at home too. People would come to their home to request Mário to play at feasts and weddings. Mário was very busy while in Goa. He never charged anyone for playing music at weddings, feasts and *ladainhas*.

Linda spent most of her free time with her father, as he was on leave for six months at a time before he had to re-join ship. They had a really close relationship. Mário instilled in her a real desire and an ambition to reach great heights of success and achievement in life. He told her about things he had seen in his travels, about European children, how they went to school and how they worked part-time as newspaper carriers to earn extra cash for higher education. He explained that people in different parts of the world lived differently and that some areas were more advanced through the use of science and technology. He told her about some new gadget making its way, in India, called the 'Radio'.

"Papa, what's a Radio?"

"It's a machine which works on batteries and which when turned on lets you hear the voice, the sound, the songs relayed from distant Radio stations."

"Really Papa, is it like the gramophone?"

"Yes, but you don't need to play records, you can hear songs without the gramophone."

"Papa, tell me how does it work?"

"I don't really know how it works, but it's something to do with the sound waves travelling through the air."

"Unbelievable. I wish we can have a Radio some day."

Linda wanted to be like the children in those progressive parts of the world. She had high aspirations and knew she had to train herself for it. Her father was a real inspiration to her.

From every trip, Mário would bring home a new instrument and work on it while vacationing in Goa. He was quite an expert on piano, the violin, the saxophone, the clarinet, the viola and other instruments. Linda never saw her father play the drums, though. They had a big piano, which was brought on a big truck from Bombay. Linda would hit the keys and try to play the piano by ear.

They had a gramophone too, with a big collection of English records, but Linda did not know how to operate it and she could not understand the English songs. Mário had a collection of opera music and compositions by Verdi, Beethoven, Bach and others. Linda would go through his entire collection of various books on music especially, the "Teach Yourself..." kind of books. Mário never taught Linda music, as he thought she should concentrate on her academic subjects. Years later, her father sold the piano to the Jesuits at Loyola School in Margão. The gramophone also stopped working after a couple years.

When Mário went back on board after six months, both Linda and her mother Joanita would feel devastated, lonely and sad. Then they would get used to it and when the next two years passed, the cycle was repeated.

Mário too was tired of going back and forth. The food was plentiful but lacked taste. All those awful cold cuts and frozen food, though the chilled beer and Scotch were good.

There was not much in terms of social life on board the ship. At night, he would pray and think about his beloved wife and daughter. He would wonder what they were doing, finding solace in such thoughts. He would read their letters again and again, drink some more beer or try to conjure up some storyline for the novel he planned to write in Konkani. He would also write lyrics and compose songs and music for his next Teatro for the village Church feast. He was going to produce it when he went home next. This way Mário filled those empty, lonely hours of solitude.

Mário soon grew tired of the unchanging blue ocean all around him – the same routine, same people, same food, same sights and sounds day in and day out. Living alone, without his wife and daughter for two years at a stretch was not his idea of a life. But for him, there was no other alternative.

He did not have the necessary qualifications to work in Goa or in Bombay for a better salary. At least here the pay was good and so he bided his time.

Mário could barely wait for the end of his voyage. He would buy lots of things for his wife and child and be greatly relieved to reach the door of his house in Goa. There his family would wait for him expectantly and smother him with their love, care, affection and attention for the duration of his leave.

Chapter 6

Goa seemed to be prospering and developing economically. The mining of iron and manganese ore and its export to Japanese and German markets brought new wealth to Goa. As radio became popular, the Portuguese Government started *Emissora de Goa* to broadcast programs in Portuguese and Konkani.

⸱But there were problems on the political front. With calls for independence for the colonies in Africa and Asia, there were calls for the liberation of Goa, Damão and Diu in India, especially after the exit of the French from Pondicherry in India.

Goan freedom fighters formed their own groups, such as the Azad Gomantak Dal, the National Congress, the United Front of Goans, the Goa Liberation Council, the Goan People's Party, the Quit Goa Organization and others. Some groups believed in Gandhi's non-violence while others, notably the Azad Gomantak Dal had pledged to fight to rid Goa of Portuguese rule. The Indian Government used their Diplomatic Mission in Lisbon to repeatedly negotiate with the Portuguese Government to give up Goa, Damão and Diu, the way France agreed to give up Pondicherry. But Portugal was not interested.

In 1953, the Indian government in Delhi, under renewed pressure from the Indian National Congress and other Opposition parties mounted strong diplomatic demands with the Portuguese Premier Dr Antonio de Oliveira Salazar to give up their colony, Goa. Salazar however maintained that Goa was not a colony, but a part of Portugal itself, *O Portugal Ultramarino*, Overseas Portugal, and that all Goans were first class Portuguese citizens. He let it be known that while he was still alive he would never cede Goa to India. The Portuguese Government refused to discuss the problem of Goa with the Indian Government.

On June 1, 1953, the Government of India withdrew the Diplomatic

Mission in Lisbon. Nehru maintained he had no other option but to liberate Goa by force. The Indian Government supported all Goan freedom groups especially the United Front of Goans and the Azad Gomantak Dal. The Indian government trained the underground Goan Commandos, who infiltrated Goa and attacked the Portuguese military at border points.

The United Front of Goans took over the Portuguese territory of Dadra in Damão Grande (Big Damão) without any resistance from the small Portuguese force in July, 1954. Soon afterwards, the Azad Gomantak Dal captured the bigger territory of Nagar-Haveli in Damão Grande on August 2, 1954. A corridor belonging to India separated these territories from Damão Pequeno (Little Damão); and Portuguese troops could not get permission to use it to defend their larger territory of Damão Grande.

Portugal felt humiliated and embarrassed at losing its territories in Damão. This was an excuse to send more military aid from Portugal and its African colonies. Soon Portuguese naval ships arrived in Goa with shiploads of white Portuguese and black African Portuguese military.

At the same time, the Goan Liberation Movement got renewed confidence and mounted strong attacks against the Portuguese. Since the famous peaceful march or *'Satyagraha'* of 1946 by Dr Lohia, the Socialist Indian leader, there were more demonstrations and intrusions in 1953 and in 1954 into the Portuguese territory. Many demonstrators were jailed and beaten by the Portuguese.

From 1954 onwards, the Goan Liberation Movement became more violent and redoubled its efforts, attacking Portuguese military barracks, police outposts and strategic points to force the Portuguese out of Goa. But Portugal became all the more adamant and resolved to keep its colony forever bringing in more military might to deal with the threat.

On August 15, 1955, India's Independence Day Anniversary, some 3000 volunteers, under the auspices of the 'All Parties Goa Liberation Committee', including women, entered Goa from different points on the Goa-India borders. The Portuguese military and police beat the peaceful marchers and opened fire on them. About 20 marchers were shot dead and some others seriously hurt. Violent beatings resulted in several deaths on both sides.

The Portuguese had enough of this. They reacted by breaking off diplomatic relations with India, closing the borders and putting severe restrictions on travellers to and from Goa. The sea and rail routes to India were halted. All the tunnels were blocked, buried or destroyed. The only route open was by bus through the South of Goa via Polem in Canacona district to Karwar.

This had a severe impact on Goan economy. All commerce with India was halted. India imposed an embargo on Portuguese Goa. All vegetables and other goods had to be imported from Pakistan. This raised the cost of living and there were big queues to buy rationed commodities.

The Goan *tarvotti* seamen who worked on board the ships and who had to go to Bombay to join them, could not get out of Goa and lost their jobs. Those in India could not go to Goa or send their Indian currency to Goa.

Portugal sent more army, navy and air force reinforcements to Goa. Salazar made military drafting compulsory in Portugal and so every able-bodied man from Portugal had to serve *A Pátria*, the fatherland and protect its interests overseas.

There were *pacle*, the white Portuguese and *khapris*, the blacks from Angola and Mozambique in the Portuguese military in Goa. Everyday in all villages and cities of Goa, the armed forces could be seen marching on the streets, and on military trucks, armed with helmets and the latest machine guns. It was scary for the locals to see the militia with guns drawn, ready for an attack.

On the night of April 13, 1955 Linda heard sound of gunfire coming from the bazaar area. The Azad Gomantak Dal forces, locally called Jaiind (Jai Hind), had raided the Cuncolim Police outpost.

On December 18, 1955 Captain Lino Ferreira, representative of Marquez de Fronteira, the Conde of Cuncolim was shot at by the freedom fighters and wounded in the thigh. He lived just one kilometre from Linda's house. Her mother's friend, Manuelina Pereira knew the Captain well as he lived next door to her. Linda could not understand the political motivation behind the shooting.

Later the police outpost of Cuncolim was re-located and fortified. They built new residences nearby for the Portuguese military with washrooms employing the flush system, never seen before in the villages. The Portuguese built military barracks in Navelim, Ponda, Margão, Bambolim, Canacona, Polem and other places at border points.

A new economy began sprouting around these establishments. There were plenty of new jobs for the locals working for the military in service areas. Poor people got jobs and were happy. At the same time, mining was encouraged in Goa and little known entrepreneurs like Chowgulo, Salgaoncar, Timblo, and Dempo became overnight successes. The Banco Nacional Ultramarino advanced loans for such enterprises.

Goa's minerals comprising of iron and manganese were exported to Japan and Germany in return for goods like Volkswagen, Mercedes, BMW, Opel, Lambretta motorcycles from Germany and Hino trucks of Japan; wines from Portugal like Porto, Vinho Branco, Vinho Verde, Macieira brandy and also other goods from the rest of the world. The goods were quietly smuggled into India where imports were banned and black marketers made huge profits.

Since the labour force in the mining sector was mainly from the Kunnbi or Gauddi class (the aborigines of Goa), they enjoyed higher incomes from the flourishing mining business. The Kunnbi contractors soon bought BMW cars, Lambretta motorcycles and their womenfolk had 22-carat gold jewellery all over their ears, nose and hands. The Kunnbi men wore Raybans and constructed huge homes. Their standard of living rose and this was the only big benefit for the lower caste during the Portuguese rule in Goa.

Other Goans did not do so well. Only Goans who were educated in

Portuguese obtained jobs in the civil service as *empregados*, or teachers or in the military. Other Goans did menial jobs and barely survived.

The Goan *Tarvottis* were a little better off, working on Indian or foreign ships servicing the port of Bombay. But they were paid in Indian Rupees, which when converted to Portuguese escudos in Goa were hugely discounted and did not amount to much. So some of the Goan seamen moved to Belgaum, Karwar and Poona with their families to get a good education and have a better standard of living. There were Goans working in British East Africa and Portuguese Africa. Some of the enterprising Hindu *comerciantes*, the shopkeepers in Margão and other cities thrived on these remittances. They exchanged dollars and pounds for *escudos* and netted huge profits that they used in their mining ventures and became instant *lakhpotis*, millionaires.

Chapter 7

Linda loved her family. She lived with her mother, who took good care of her, advised her on important matters and gave her the best within her reach. Linda never had to do any household chores, as she was required only to study hard and do well.

Her normal daily food consisted of rice and fish curry. Occasionally they would have meat on Sundays. On a feast day, her mother made *pulau* and *sorpotel*. But what Linda liked best was the *paro*, dried fish such as the mackerel or kingfish pickled in *masala* and vinegar. Mango pickle was her favourite but her mother was not very good at making it. Her grandmother, made great pickles and pork sausages, the *chouriços* with the help of her neighbour friend, aunt Libante *ti(a)mãe*, whose touch made any dish, a work of culinary art.

One day, when she was at her grandmother's house in Navelim, freshly made sausages and dried prawns were in the process of being packed and shipped to Linda's uncles and aunt in Nairobi, Kenya in East Africa. Linda who was tired of her leaky fountain pen, wrote a little note to her uncles in Africa asking them to send her a Parker pen. She placed the note in one of the big cans containing dry prawns.

Six months later, there was a parcel from East Africa with three Parker pens from both the uncles and her aunt. When her mother came to know about it, Linda was punished. She had to starve for a day.

Linda loved to be with her grandmother, Angelina, who lived in a grand mansion in Navelim. Linda's two uncles and her grandfather, who lived and worked in Kenya, financed the construction of this big house. But it was her mother Joanita who was instrumental in making critical decisions about the design and construction of the house. Angelina's brother-in-law, Menino Coutinho from Cavorim was the project manager. He looked after the finances and he dealt directly with the excavators, masons, carpenters, painters and other workmen.

The house when completed, was the most beautiful house in the neighbourhood of Dongorim. The land for the new house had been purchased in 1942 when their old landlord would not sell them the land their old ancestral house was built on. The new house was ready in 1954. The entire house was symmetrical and was divided into two sections for the two sons, except for a large common entrance hall, a dining room which had an eighteen foot ceiling and a U-shaped enclosed *razangonn*, a courtyard in the back.

Each side of the house boasted a huge family room, a large bedroom, a big storeroom, a large kitchen with a bathroom and a patio. Adjoining the kitchen there was a raised pedestal for a grinding stone and next to it there was a coop for chickens.

Between the two huge kitchens there was the courtyard, the *razangonn* with a big papaya tree rising high up above the roof, which was covered with large brown Mangalore tiles. The papaya tree was fed by water from the drain attached to the *pia*, the wash-stand in the common dining room. The stairs from both kitchens led down to the high walled deep well. The well had a built-in pulley to draw water from the well with a big rope made of coconut fibre.

The dining room had a large teak dining table with antique colonial chairs. There were two display cases built into the wall on either side of the room containing fine china and sets of plates and glasses. There was also a cupboard below each for storing carafes of wine such as Port, Branco and the *kollso* of *fenni*.

The common entrance hall had a main oratory close to the back wall with a large crucifix and a statue of Our Lady of Hope, flanked on either side by large framed pictures of Sacred Heart of Jesus and Mary. There were also two framed pictures one of St Anthony and the other of St Philomena, later de-canonized by the Pope.

There was a canopy made of bamboo on top of the oratory, which sometimes had spider webs on it. Twice a year, Angelina took the trouble of cleaning the ceiling of this huge mansion with a long bamboo fitted with a coconut leaf brush, the *zaddu.*

There were four antique rocking chairs at four corners and there were six other regular chairs in the entrance hall. Several framed pictures of Princess Margaret, Humphrey Bogart, Cary Grant, Elizabeth Taylor, and other Hollywood stars hung at various intervals on the walls of this hall.

All rooms of the house including the hallway had tiled floors in varying patterns and colours. Most of the walls were painted white both inside and outside. The lower front walls were painted with diagonal squares in white, green, orange and red.

There was a huge verandah with concrete railings in front, custom-designed with the letters 'MCD' for Manuel Cirilo Dias, the patriarch of the family, in the centre of each section. It was painted in blue, green and white. There were two *balcão* seats at the front entrance with two masonry benches on either side. A flight of ten steps led to the entrance.

There were gardens on each side of the entrance with roses, crotons, golmohur trees, bougainvillea and hibiscus. Behind the house, was a veritable forest of trees consisting of five mango trees, twenty cashew-trees, coffee plants, three jackfruit trees, *jambul* trees, a *bimblam* tree, a jujube (*boram*) tree and lots of bamboo.

Linda was always impressed with this house and its surroundings. When she woke up in the morning, she heard the distant sound of the train chugging along the route from Margão to Chandor and watched the coloured light that streamed through the stained glass windows of the bedroom.

She would get up and go outside to hear birds sing the morning symphony. Her grandmother had breakfast ready on the table – *chapattis, bhakris*, freshly fried eggs and tea with condensed milk. Before sitting down to breakfast, Linda would take charcoal, brush her teeth with it and rinse her mouth with water. After a wholesome breakfast, she would eat some plain condensed milk, greedily licking the spoon. Very often the whole tin was finished at one go.

Since she spent most of her days as a child in Navelim, she grew up loving the village and this house. She loved Navelim especially in November, when there was a village feast of Our Lady of Rosary.

Linda would go to Navelim ten days before the feast, so she could celebrate the *Maddi* or the *Fama*, the day before the start of the novena. This would be followed by nine days of novena, with the *salve* every night and the *véspera* on the eve of the big day.

The Navelim church was the biggest in Goa next only to the big cathedrals of Old Goa. The inside of the church was ornate and had a special effect on Linda. As there was no electricity in Goa, they brought in special generators for the occasion and the lighting inside the church was bright and pleasing to the eye.

The statues, the pictures, the architecture and the decorations inside the church were beautiful and when the *pregador*, gave his sermon from the pulpit, his voice reverberated throughout the church, scaring birds nesting in the gaps in the false ceiling. The birds chirped and flew everywhere and Linda watched them. During the novena especially during the *salve* at night, the sight of little boys dressed as angels, replete with wings, lifted Linda's spirits and the pictures of silver angels hanging symmetrically from the high ceiling on both sides venerating the child Jesus filled her with joy.

The only thing she hated was the sound of the fireworks when the *salve* got over, after the priest gave out the blessing of the Blessed Sacrament. As the church bells rang continuously, the village *pedo* fired up the *foznem*, the dynamite petards. The booming sounds would frighten Linda to death. Her heart would almost jump out of her chest, despite shutting off the sound with the palms of her hands.

The day before the feast was a terrible day for the pigs of the village.

On this day hundreds of pigs were slaughtered and pork sold to all Catholic households in the village for the celebration. The village women were busiest on this day cooking *sorpotel, booch (tripe), gaindollio*, pork *vindalho*, roast beef, mutton *xacuti* from goat meat, and fish curry.

On the day of the *vespera*, on the eve of the feast day, Linda looked forward to see the best fireworks in Goa the kind she preferred. The fireworks included grenades, the *pauss*, the 'falling rain' fireworks, the rockets, which would go high up in the sky and explode, and the *kombi*, the 'chicken' fireworks that would simulate the laying of eggs twelve times before the 'chicken' finally exploded.

The next day was the day of the feast. This was the most festive day of the year. Early in the morning at 5 o'clock, the church bells pealed, the *pedo* fired the *foznem*, whose explosive sounds woke up the entire village. This was followed by the welcome sounds of the *alvorada* music played by a live band heralding the feast day.

The womenfolk woke up at five and started preparations for *sannam, pulau* and *sorpotel*. They bought fresh bread like *pão, bhakri* and *kanknnam* from the *poder*, who made home deliveries on his bicycle in the dark. The women went for the earliest mass at 6 o'clock The older women always wore *voli*, a white starched cloth covering the entire body including a veiled piece covering the head, which made them look like tropical penguins going to church. The beautiful Kunnbi women, dressed in their finest multicoloured tribal dresses added to the festive look.

After the mass and prayers were over, everybody went to the fair, bought some *chonnem*, grams and got them blessed at the feet of Our Lady's statue to make them sacred. Then they brought it home to give to those who could not make it to the feast, like very young children and the incapacitated or older folks. When they got home, they would start cooking the *pulau* and *sannam* breads and fry the fish, which had to be cooked fresh for the best taste.

On this day, each household expected relatives and friends from other villages to visit. There were no official invitations. Anyone was welcome and no one would ever be turned away. Goa was famous for such hospitality. Naturally, the food had to be the best and the drink had to include without doubt the local *fenni* and a couple of large bottles of St Pauli Girl beer, some Vinho Branco, Porto and Macieira brandy depending on the status of the host and guest.

It was the year 1955 and eleven year old Linda put on her brand new dress to attend the eight o'clock Mass with her mother, other relatives and friends. She could not stand the High *Cantada* Mass at noon. It would be way too long for her patience and endurance. Besides the church would be packed, there would be no place to sit on the floor, let alone on a bench. She would not understand a word, as the whole Mass would be sung in Latin. The Padre Vigar would start singing, followed by the Padre Cura to be followed and repeated by the Mestre in the Choir.

Sometimes Linda wondered if God would have patience to listen to this Latin mumbo-jumbo. Jesus never went to Latin school! Linda wondered why these priests insisted on singing and saying Mass in Latin.

As she reached the church, a young girl came up to her and pinned a paper flower on the lapel of her dress and Linda put a coin in her box as a donation to the church. She attended the Mass, prayed for her father and the rest of the family and for herself. Then she went to the fair with her family. She enjoyed this the most. The fair was bustling with happy children, men and women, young and old merrily eating, drinking, shopping, laughing and wishing each other *Boas Festas*.

Everyone including even the poor had a new dress, custom-made for the feast. There were beggars lined up in front of the church. They received gifts like parboiled rice (uncooked), and money. There were people selling wax moulds of different parts of the body and candles to the worshippers. Those who had made vows to Our Lady of Rosary for miraculous cures offered the moulds in gratitude at her statue. Those who had received favours through her intercession, lit candles or put money down as offerings.

Linda went through the fair, buying roasted *chonnem*, the sweet *laddoos, kaddio-boddio* and other sweets and ice candies. Her mother and her relatives took her to *caremess* and they sat there for a cool *falooda* drink with milk cream and syrup. Later they visited the wooden furniture section shopping for a nice table for the family and an armoire made of teak. They also looked at the utensils section where Linda saw her neighbour *vattlikar* from her village selling copper pots and brass *vattlis*, or plates.

Linda's relative, uncle Domingos gave her one rupee as a gift for the feast and another relative Uncle Patricio gave her half a rupee. She was rich today. Now she could buy a Japanese doll, which she always wanted. She also tried her luck by placing a bet of one *anna* on number 6 at the *goddgoddo* dice game and lost it all. Never again, she said to herself.

Back at her grandmother's home, at noon, the special feast was ready and everything was set on the main table. Everyone sat, except the women-folk, who were supposed to serve the men. There were eleven men and boys as guests. They washed their hands at the *pia*, and sat at the table. The old man, Uncle Xavier from Paroda started a short prayer. Uncle Domingos fired three firecrackers and they raised a toast with a glass of Port in their hands saying loudly, "À *Saude! Boas Festas! Borem Zauchem! Viva!"*

A typical Goan meal of food and drinks began in earnest. There were hot drinks for the adults. Bottles of Port and Branco were uncorked with a popping sound. A bottle of St Pauli Girl beer was opened and poured into two tall 'Orangeboom' glasses for the two visitors from Africa, who did not care too much for the local *fenni*, which was flowing freely for the other guests. For children and women, there was the red *xarope*.

The feast began as usual with *caldo*, soup made of beef bones and macaroni and onion. Then with some bread and *sannam*, they ate morsels of *sorpotel, booch,* beef roast, *xacuti* and *verdura* using meat or vegetable gravy. This was topped with some *pulau* or rice and curry with fried fish. All this food was consumed with a few sips of beer, *fenni* or brandy or wine to wash it down.

At the end of the day, everybody was full and needed a siesta after the fiesta. The African visitors who spoke English lay down on beds and the rest slept on a large bamboo mat, the *attor*. At 4 o'clock the visitors and guests woke up, washed their faces, and had a cup of tea with fruitcake, cream crackers and Kraft cheese even though their food was not digested yet. Later that night the African visitors went for a dance and the rest went to see a Konkani play. And another special feast day at Navelim had ended.

Linda came back to Navelim three months later in February to celebrate three days of *Intruz*, the Carnaval. In Navelim, there were *khells*, theatrical groups from Benaulim, Vernã and other areas parading from village to village on foot with a live band. The groups paraded along playing to the accompaniment of loud drums and performing their plays at the home of anyone who could afford to pay them thirty rupees per play and give them some food and drinks.

Linda would follow these parades to see where they stopped to perform. The group she liked most was known as *Shempia Miguel*, tailcoat Mickey, from Benaulim starring an attractive female impersonator, Shali Baii. These groups challenged each other for the best performance and won trophies in the competition. Since women did not act publicly in those days, men cross-dressed and faked women's voices to play female roles.

There was always a comedian in these groups, a Buster Keaton type or a Laurel and Hardy look-alike. Most of the stories revolved around landlord-tenant problems, love triangles, familial problems and other pertinent issues of the day.

During the three days of *intruz* or Carnaval, young men and boys dressed in various costumes, their faces hidden behind masks, called the *rupnnem*, went from door to door and collected money and gifts from people. They would throw *pacotes,* pouches of talcum powder and perfume on girls' faces and spray coloured water on their blouses using plastic guns during the *khell* in passing. Indeed Carnaval was a time to really let one's hair down.

→⚜◆⊗◆⚜←

Chapter 8

At school, Linda was the top student. She had a sharp memory. The teacher never asked her any questions, as she would know all the answers and she was easily bored when the teacher explained something that was not too challenging.

Sometimes to fool the teacher, Linda would pretend not to know the answer by feigning a puzzled look. But as soon as the question was asked, pat came the answer and the teacher would feel checkmated. Linda got a kick out of this.

She was good at Arithmetic, although there were a couple of Hindu boys who had studied *gonnit* in their Marathi school and were extremely good and fast at it. Linda was as good as they were, but their Portuguese was not as good as Linda's and they had a heavy Marathi accent.

Linda loved Geography; she knew all the rivers of Goa, the mountains, districts, capes and the entire map of Goa, Damão and Diu in grade three. On the map, she would see *União Indiana* outside the border of Goa. She wondered what that country would be like. She only knew her father had to go to Bombay in India to work on board the ship. Beyond that she had no inkling of what was happening in India or the history of India, as she never learnt about that in her school.

But she knew the Geography and History of a country thousands of miles away from Goa – Portugal. She wondered what it would be like to be in Portugal. The four seasons, *Primavera, Verão, Outomno e Inverno*, were quite distinct in Portugal but in Goa there were only two seasons – wet and dry, and hot all over. She wondered how those Portuguese *maçãs*, apples would taste.

She wished she had winter in Goa so she could enjoy all that snow. Maybe, if she mixed snow with sugar and condensed milk, it would probably taste like ice cream, which she'd never tasted. The pictures she saw in the Portuguese textbooks showed various people in Portugal. They wore good clothes and shoes, even the poor ones. She envied them so much. Why was she born in a poor country? Why was she not in Portugal?

Linda remembered when she had gone to the local church to line up to receive Queen's gift to the children of Goa on her Coronation Day. She had received a plastic bag of powdered milk as a gift from the Queen and it tasted very good. It was her first taste of powdered milk and she saved her first plastic bag too. Imagine how good ice cream would taste if just milk powder were this good? She couldn't wait to taste ice cream. So, Linda bought an ice candy, added some powdered milk, two crushed chocolates and some sugar, stirred the whole mixture and drank it. This must be like the ice cream her father had told her about, she convinced herself.

Linda knew how to draw maps of Portugal and its overseas colonies like Angola, Moçambique, Cabo Verde, Guine, São Tome e Principe, Açores, Madeira, Macao and Timor and including Goa, Damão e Diu. She knew there were lots of minerals in Angola and Moçambique and that Macao was famous for its firecrackers. She knew the history of all the colonies of Portugal hardly aware that her own story was inextricably woven with the history of India.

She knew Macao was granted to Portugal by a Chinese emperor for helping him get rid of sea pirates in the Sea of China. She also knew the Portuguese were the pioneers of the seas. Bartolomeu Dias was the first to cross the feared Cape Bojador followed by Vasco de Gama who crossed the Cabo de Boa Esperança (Cape of Good Hope) in South Africa and reached Calicut in modern Kerala eventually discovering India for the West in 1497. She knew of other Portuguese discoverers like Pedro Álvares Cabral who discovered Brazil and Fernão de Magalhães who first circumnavigated.

An avid student of history, Linda knew the history of Portugal in detail. How Viriato first established Lusitania in the Iberian peninsula, to be followed years later by the formation of Portugal's first dynasty led by Dom Afonso Henriques, how a Portuguese Queen, Dona Isabela of Portugal became a saint. How Infante Dom Henrique pioneered the first Naval School, which led to the discoveries overseas, and how the Torre de Belém was erected to commemorate these discoveries. She had even heard of the poet Luis de Camões, who lived in Goa for a while and wrote the epic book of poems, *Os Lusíadas*, celebrating the glory of Portugal and its discoveries worldwide.

She learnt about the Anglo-Portuguese Alliance, the Spanish invasions and their rule over Portugal, the subsequent successful Portuguese revolt against the Spanish, commemorated by erecting the Mosteiro dos Jerónimos. She knew about the Mosteiro de Alcobaça, which marked the victory over the Moors, who also ruled Portugal for a few centuries. She also knew that Portugal took part in the Crusades in the Holy Land and how they had lost some territories during that period.

Closer to home Linda learnt that Bombay (called 'Boa Baia' by the Portuguese and Mumbai by the locals and 'Bomboim' by Goans) once belonged to the Portuguese and that it was gifted to England as a dowry for a Portuguese princess who married an English King. That even today, the East Indian natives of Bombay had Portuguese names and had stone crosses all over Mud Island, Salsete and Bassein. She learnt that Portugal had once been a great empire spanning the globe including Brazil in South America, Ormuz in Middle East, and Malacca in East Indies and that gradually they had lost all these possessions.

She learnt that with the revolution in the early twentieth century the Portuguese royal dynasty ended and Portugal was declared a República and that later a professor from the Universidade de Coímbra became the Prime Minister of Portugal. He was none other than Dr Antonio de Oliveira Salazar.

Linda was a true believer in the Catholic Church and its teachings. She went to the church every Sunday morning with her mother and later attended catechism lessons. She learnt about Adam and Eve, Abel and Cain, Job, Noah, Abraham, Sarah, Joseph and his twelve brothers, Moses and the Old Testament.

From the New Testament she also learnt about blessed Mary and Joseph and the birth of Jesus, about Jesus' teachings and miracles and his eventual death on the cross. But she did not quite understand what happened to Jesus between the ages of twelve and thirty.

In the Old Testament, she found certain events to be irreverent and immoral, like the one when Jacob cheats his old father who was blind by posing as his elder brother Isaac to get his inheritance. She could not understand how we all came from Adam and Eve, who had only two sons, Abel and Cain. These were the few questions she had asked the village priest, but he did not know the answers either and said these were mysteries. The priest told her that her bible of about 30 small pages that she had read was only a condensed version of the real one.

Linda won the first place in catechism exams and received religious gifts such as the figurine of Our Lady of Fátima, which glowed in the dark and was a novelty at the time. One day, she learnt that the nuns, who taught catechism, shaved their heads and were bald. So she joined her neighbour friends and shouted with them at the nuns: *Madrim Khodde* (Bald Nuns), when they took their boarders from the convent for an outing in the village.

Yet when the village Padre went by on his bicycle, Linda at once reverently joined her palms and said *"Padre-tio, Bessão ghal"* and the Padre gave his blessing to her with one hand, holding the bike handle with the other. One day an older priest fell from his bike while giving blessing to Linda, as he could not manoeuvre his bike with his left hand. After that she stopped asking for blessings from priests on bikes. It was hazardous.

A couple years after her First Holy Communion, Linda received her *Crismo*, the sacrament of Confirmation from the Archbishop of Goa, Dom Jose Alvernaz, who preached in Portuguese with a translator who did instant translation in Konkani. She was very proud to be anointed by a foreign priest and she relished this moment very much. She was very impressed with the Archbishop's huge luxury car, a Ford Continental.

Linda liked the church service on Sunday even in Latin because it was short. She knew '*Confiteor Deo Omnipotente*', '*mea culpa, mea culpa, mea maxima culpa...*' and all prayers in Latin and she even knew all responses in Latin, but she felt sorry she could never serve at the altar because only boys were allowed to serve. She hated the long *Missa Cantada* for the feast days, especially during the Holy Week.

After the church service, Linda liked to eat *boram*, the sweet and sour berries with seeds from the *bori* trees next to the cemetery. When someone told her not to eat *boram*, because they grew from the manure caused by human bones of the dead people in the cemetery, she vomited and stopped eating them.

When Linda wanted to go to the nearby hill to pick *boram*, her mother warned her not to go anywhere alone, especially after dark. Her mother informed her that there was word on the street that there were strange men looking for young kids, that they would abduct them and put them in a sack and take them for *dor*, a human sacrificial offering supposedly used in the construction of a big bridge over river Sal in Assolnã, the neighbouring village. She warned her to be careful and come home before sunset and before the church bells rang at 6 o'clock for the *aimori* (Ave Maria) prayers. Linda was afraid to go out alone and always returned home on time.

Chapter 9

Linda helped her mother by going to the bazaar to buy fresh fish. She liked to buy her favourite fish like crabs, shrimps and squids but she hated mackerel and sardines, as they smelt strongly when fried. Her mother was an expert at cooking *recheiado* squids. She would clean out the insides, and stuff it with a hot and sour *masala* containing ground onions, fresh coriander and vinegar and sugar together with tiny pieces of squid tentacles and fry them on a pan.

She also liked stuffed pomfret but they were too expensive. Sometimes the fisherwomen cheated her because she was a young child and gave her spoiled fish or less fish for her money. Linda's mother always cooked fresh rice and she ground fresh *masala* on a big flat stone using grated coconut, chillies, tamarind and all other spices. She also used fresh green mangoes in season.

The rice and curry combination was what Linda enjoyed most when she came home for lunch from school. She also liked the *attoiloli kalchi koddi*, the dried curry from previous day, which she ate as appetizer for her breakfast of *pez* (*canji*).

At night, they ate the freshly prepared rice with reheated curry. Before supper, they had to recite the rosary followed by the litany and her mother used to pray for her daddy, relatives and the dead souls in the family. Linda always wondered how her mother memorized the entire litany in Latin.

After supper they would open the front door overlooking the wide-open fields in front of the house and they could see a myriad *cazules*, glow-worms in the dark of the night and millions of stars in the sky. One or two stars moved in the sky. Linda told her mother that her teacher said those were not the stars but American satellites. And far away, they could see light on the mountaintop coming from a Hindu temple at Chandranath.

Linda always wanted to go up there to see this temple but everyone dissuaded her saying it was a long and steep climb and that it took hours to get there. There was no road up but a small path. There were wild animals like tigers, monkeys, porcupines and snakes and it was very risky to go up there at least from the South side. Hindu people went there on special days of the *zatra* festival.

Her mother said there was a place called *Sat Devllam*, Seven Temples, just at the base of this mountain and people went there to worship and to bathe in the spring waters that cured certain ailments. She said that in the monsoon season, when clouds hit the Chandranath mountain, the resulting rainwater filtered through the mountain, collecting minerals along the way giving healing properties to the spring water at Sat Devllam. That is why her mother said the old *vaids*, the doctors of *ayurveda*, advised people to bathe in these spring waters.

Dessai farmers cultivated rice in the paddy fields in front of their house during the monsoon. At first they ploughed the hard soil with the help of bulls and water buffaloes. Then they flattened the uneven wet soil by standing on a flat and heavy piece of wood, pulled by buffaloes, and if the buffaloes did not comply, the farmer swore at them.

Later when rice seeds were sown and they germinated to form rice plants, you could see a lovely green expanse. But soon the rice plant would flower and it would turn golden yellow. Before long, it would be time to harvest. These fields were most beautiful when a gentle breeze blew, making huge undulating waves over the entire surface of the rice field. It was marvellous to see such a moving wave formation.

The womenfolk would cut the rice sheaves bent double and singing or reciting stories, barefoot in the muddy waters of the field. Sometimes the leeches, the bloodsuckers would cling to their bare legs. Later, the women would thrash the rice and collect grain in a huge mound.

Linda's mother would buy raw un-husked rice in measures of a *khandi* and this filled about two big gunny bags. She boiled it in a big copper pot, mixed with some jackfruit seeds, to eat later. She then dried the rice on a large bamboo mat, watching over it so crows wouldn't eat it, and later took it to a mill in a *vojem*, a bamboo basket, over her head. And after de-husking the rice in the mill, what came out was pure, nutritious, parboiled brown rice.

After the rice cultivation was over, the farmers would flood the field with water diverted from the local river and the field would turn into a small lake. School kids would come and try to swim in this water along with water buffaloes and birds such as cranes and storks. The teenagers used to make a makeshift raft, using banana tree trunks and bamboo sticks and try to float on the lake. Linda was not allowed in the lake. One day when she tried to catch a dragonfly on its banks, she slipped and fell in the lake. Luckily the water was quite shallow there and she was all right.

Linda liked to fish near the lake with her friends using worms and grasshoppers. There was a little boy fishing for the first time with a bamboo rod and a string tied to a worm. No wonder, he did not catch any fish, his fishing rod had no hook attached to the string! Linda had a good laugh. Another time, she saw a neighbour catch a big water snake.

Monsoon was always a fun time for Linda. First of all her mother allowed her to stay outside and take in the first showers of the monsoon, as she said they had healing power. When the first monsoon rains poured in torrents, flooding the fields, she could hear the frogs come out and croak to their mates.

One such morning when her father was home, her mother asked Linda to go out in the field to catch the green and yellow frogs. Linda went there with other kids and caught the frogs. Linda caught about ten frogs that were copulating in pairs but had no idea what they were doing.

Her mother cut the frogs' legs and threw the legless frogs into her backyard pond. Then she de-skinned the legs, sprinkled some salt and pepper and fried them. Linda's father enjoyed the frog legs. He said they tasted like chicken, but Linda never tried them. Linda was dumbstruck to discover that the legless frogs lived for at least three more days in her pond. How inhumane, she thought to herself and since then she never caught another frog in her life.

Linda liked to go out in the wet fields in search of *congue* or snails and she collected a bag full of them. Her mother cooked these the best. She boiled the snails in an earthen *cunnem*, vessel. Then she took them out of the shell with a toothpick, then separated the unwanted things like intestines and only left the edible flesh. She then added lot of roasted burnt masala and cooked them like *xacuti* using roasted ground coconut.

When it rained in torrents, Linda made paper boats, wrote her name on them and sent them floating. The next day she would find them on her way to school. She kept hoping it would rain a lot so they would get a holiday. But she had no such luck while she was at school, not even a political leader even died and she wished that she did not have to go to school all six days of the week.

Another favourite thing to do when it rained heavily and they could not go outdoors was to roast raw cashew nuts with its shell, over red-hot coals of fire. The fire would flare up with the oil contained in these nutshells making a hissing noise. But the roasting had to be just right so as to be able to break them open to get the cashew kernel intact and yet not overly burnt.

The fireplace in Goa was made of three rectangular stones in a square. The fourth side of the square was kept open to allow placing of the firewood inside. The cooking pot was kept over the three stones. Dried coconut leaves were lit with a matchstick to form a flame, which would ignite the firewood. Some coconut husks were also used and air was periodically blown in by mouth to help the flames spread to the firewood. This took lot of time, skill and experience.

The fireplace had many uses. Its by-product, the charcoal was used to brush teeth in the morning. The red-hot coals, especially from the coconut shells were used in the non-electric iron for ironing clothes. The hot ashes were used by Linda's grandmother to roast brinjal, egg-plant to make *bharta*, a dish made from minced roasted egg-plant mixed with onion, coconut, green chilli, oil, coriander and tamarind. The cold ashes were used to clean utensils with the help of *katto*, the coconut shell fibres.

In the evenings, Linda's friends would come to play with five *gulo*, seashells. The idea was to get all five shells face down. If not you had to use two fingers to strike all four shells. If you failed, you lost your turn. There were many variations to this game.

When they tired of the shell game, another game would be played with five stones using both hands. This required a good manual dexterity and skill with hands. And if they were really bored they would play a game of cards like *burro,* the donkey.

When Linda threw stones in the shallow wells in front of her house, her friend Inacinha told her to be careful. She said she had heard of a man, who had thrown a stone at a snake in the field, and the snake had followed him, had bitten him and he died. She told her that a snake never forgets. Since that day, Linda was very scared of the snakes.

Linda had been scared of loud thunder at first, but when she went to school, the teacher said it was the lightning that was quite dangerous and that people could die if they were struck by lightning. From then on, Linda was scared of both. One night, as Linda and her mother were reciting the rosary, they heard some neighbours shouting. They went out to see what happened. There were a lot of people outside the neighbour's house, four houses down the road. A big cobra had been found in their kitchen hiding in a pile of firewood. A man came with a rifle and shot the snake dead.

This man, Mário Piedade Fernandes was a Jack-of-all-trades. He was a hunter who hunted wild boars and porcupine. He had lot of porcupine quills in his house. He had given some to Linda, who tried to use them as a pen using ink, but it did not work very well. They said he even killed a tiger once. He had a license for the rifle. He shot many cranes and storks on the lake. His main profession was to repair copper utensils and on Sundays he slaughtered pigs.

Chapter 10

Linda was always excited when there was a wedding, especially that of a relative or a neighbour.

A Catholic marriage in Goa was a long drawn out process. It started with a *soirikar*, a marriage broker who forever scouted the villages for prospective brides and grooms. He scanned their background, status, caste, pigmentation, occupation, assets, and education, matched the couples and made contact with their parents.

Later the *soirikar* got them together at a pre-arranged meeting place such as a restaurant. If they liked each other, there was a promise of a marriage and the *soirikar* claimed his commission. Then their parents discussed matters such as dowry and *dennem*, the gifts such as furniture and utensils, and a date for the wedding.

Now the real tasks began. They went for catechism to the church to talk to Padre Vigar. He would ask a lot of questions so they really had to brush up on their *doutrina*. Only if he was satisfied that they were thorough would the wedding banns be read in church. Next, you made arrangements for the wedding; the bookings for the live band, the chief cook, the contractor for the chairs, decoration and the *mattou*, and recorded music. Then you got all your *certidãos*, certificates in order for the civil marriage formalities, arranged for a pig, and built a temporary fireplace outside the house to cook *pulau*, *sorpotel*, *caldo* and *doce*. Then you painted your house white, went to the *shetti*, the goldsmith to custom order various items of gold jewellery including seven bangles, two pairs of ear-rings, a set of gold necklaces with stones and rings.

Finally the bride's father would clear all his savings to provide the best dowry he could afford, along with the best furnishings for the *dennem*. If his savings were not enough, he would arrange to get a huge loan for the expenses or go to all his relatives and friends for contributory loans and possibly even the village *bhattkar* to mortgage his ancestral home. The *Bhattkar* would ask for a thumb impression or signature on a sealed paper, as the case maybe. And if he defaulted on the payments, the bhattkar would take over your property. But Goans would do anything to have a big wedding!

The bride looked forward to the day when she would be married. But before that was the *mudi*, the official engagement celebration, when the groom came to bride's place and they exchanged gold rings.

As soon as the bride was officially engaged, *doce* (a sweet made from lentil flour, coconut and sugar in diamond shapes) and *dall* would be distributed throughout the village. A young girl would carry a black earthen pot full of *dall*, at her waist around the neighbourhood and pour a cup filled with *dall* using a *doulo* (coconut shell ladle) into the homeowner's bowl. Her companion would give them a piece of *doce* wrapped in coloured paper from a tray, compliments of the bride to be.

After the engagement, the bride had to go to her *Mamaguer*, maternal uncle's house. Here, she drank ceremonial water from his well and her uncle offered her a *chooddo*, a bunch of coloured glass bangles to be worn on her both hands, a sign that she was engaged and about to be married. The girl would show her bangles to everyone in the village with great pride and the other unmarried girls would envy her.

Preparations for the wedding began immediately. For the bridal dress, the best tailors were hired from far off villages to do a customized bridal gown and other dresses for the bride's trousseau, as well as dresses for the bridesmaids and close relatives. The bridegroom would order a custom-made two-piece suit in the city, usually with Costão or Abel Tailors.

Parents went from door to door in the neighbourhood, giving personal wedding invitations. If no one was home, they stuck a *tallo* (a twig of leaves) in the main door keyhole to leave an implicit invitation. Practically the entire village was invited anyway. There were no cards printed, so there were no gatecrashers; all guests were welcome and no one was ever turned away.

When only a couple days were left, the close relatives from far off villages came under the guise of helping the household with the wedding preparations. They usually came with hordes of children. The bridal house became a camping ground for all, with children running around making noise and having fun because they need not attend school for a week or two. There were daily family meetings to discuss various aspects of the wedding.

A cook was hired to prepare food for the extended family of over twenty guests. The cooking was now done outside on the temporary fireplace using large *burkulo, tizal* and *kunnem* (earthen pots and pans). A big *kollso,* a carboy of *fenni* was always handy. And after the rosary at night, they ate and drank and all slept on a large *ator* spread on the floor of the entrance hall.

The first time, the bride and groom could go anywhere together before the wedding, was for the civil marriage ceremony at the city hall. After the ceremony, together with their respective parents, they went to a restaurant to celebrate, and get to know each other a bit better. There was a lot of talking but no physical contact, no holding hands, nor any touching. Everything else was reserved for the big wedding night. The groom did most of the talking, while the *loje vokol*, the shy bride looked coy, smiled a lot and said very little.

A day before the wedding, friends and relatives gathered to slaughter the pig, cut the meat for *sorpotel*, vindalho, chouriço meat, tripe and other dishes. On the eve of the wedding day, there was the *bhikareamchem jevonn*, a dinner for beggars. It consisted of big chunks of meat, vegetable and fish served on a *potravoli*, a disposable plate made of dried banyan tree leaves. This lunch was in memory of the dearly departed. The local belief was that if the beggars were satisfied with the meal, it would provide relief to the souls of the dead relatives of the household. All beggars were rounded up on this day and were fed with best of food and given *fenni* to their heart's content. No one wanted to displease the spirits.

And on this day, friends and relatives sent *saguades*, gifts of all kinds for the household including *gantonn* and *kellim-guellavo,* baskets of fish and bananas. All gifts were noted down so they could be reciprocated later in equal measure.

Later that night, there was the ceremony of *rôss,* whereby the close relatives ceremoniously bathed the bride or the groom with coconut milk, singing spontaneous verses in Konkani in praise of the bride or the groom and their relatives.

The neighbourhood womenfolk were busy with the cooking and the preparation of *doce.* The men put up a big *mattou,* a makeshift open-air hall for dancing, built from bamboo and coconut tree wood, in front of the house. The *mattou* was draped with white decorated cotton sheets on the ceiling while the sides were decorated with sheets depicting colourful Goan scenes. Chairs were placed along the perimeter of the *mattou.* The contractor set the stage for the band and arranged tables with the help of some volunteers. The dance floor, which was a mixture of earth and sand, was covered with green jackfruit leaves so the dancers would not kick up too much dust.

The *mattou* contractor also arranged for some recorded music to be played on a gramophone and amplified over the two funnel-shaped loud speakers for the entire village to hear. He also set a mike on a stand for the band and the crooner. The bandleader arranged all instruments on the stand including the drums, cymbals, saxophone, violin, clarinet, *rebecão* and guitar.

The village chief cook set up her wares. She estimated and picked the right amount of basmati rice, meat, spices, oil, vinegar and all appropriate raw materials to put the fabulous dishes together. She barked out orders to all her assistants and all she did was to taste the cooking-in-process and rectify the errors. The rented china and cutlery was kept ready, cups and saucers for the soup, small dinner plates for *pulau* and stew. Small pickled mango pieces were already cut and kept ready to put on *pulau* plates, together with the cooked *chouriços.*

The soda machine was set up near the cooking area next to the well. All empty soda bottles with a marble ball in their constricted necks were ready to be processed with carbonated soda for all guests to quench their thirst. Cases of St Pauli Girl *cerveja* beer were purchased for special guests like Padre Vigar and *bhattkar* and other special guests.

When the big day came, the bride was usually nervous. A beautician was hired to fix her hair, and to do her make-up so she would look like a princess for the day. Every one was busy running around to do millions of tasks and as yet no one was ready. Usually the groom's sister and other women came to the bride's place to help dress her up for the wedding and make her comfortable.

A specially decorated car pulled up outside the house to take the bride to the church and the driver honked to catch everyone's attention to start out. The bride usually started wailing and crying because she was now leaving her mother's home for good. The mother joined in to make matters worse and they cried their hearts out at the final parting. When the bride's car left the house, often later than intended, the firecrackers were set off.

The groom wearing his brand new custom-tailored suit went to the church on time with the best man in another car. In fact, it was considered unlucky for the bride and the groom to be seen with each other twenty-four hours before the wedding. At the church, the father gave the bride away and soon the solemn ceremony began.

The bride and the groom both went to the altar and the Mass began in the presence of friends and relatives. They received Holy Communion, exchanged vows and rings but did not kiss, and after signing the register became man and wife forever. Smiling for the crowd, they would step out.

Outside the church bells would ring, the fireworks would explode heralding another union of two young hearts and the celebration began. They were hugged and kissed by all.

Then the newly married couple would go to the groom's house. They would stand outside the front door and would be given a traditional welcome by the groom's mother. She held a *dhumpel*, an urn containing burning incense in one hand, whilst making circular motions around their heads. With her other hand, she helped her new daughter-in-law to step inside her new home, with her right foot first for good luck.

More fireworks signalled the grand entry. And at once the *mestre* struck up his violin for the commencement of the *ladainha*. Snacks and drinks made the rounds and the bride and groom were driven to the city for the official wedding portrait. Then they retired for some time until the wedding reception in the evening.

And later that evening they would be at the reception at the *mattou*, in their honour, where they would be king and queen for a day. The *mattou* in front of the house was crowded with the guests. Young and old were beautifully dressed. Immaculately dressed men in suits escorted women to the *mattou*.

Guests from the bride's side, the *potvor*, came in especially hired buses singing *manddos* on their way, such as *"Tambdde Rosa Tuje Pole"* (Your red rose cheeks). The loud speakers in the *mattou* churned out Konkani songs from Alfred Rose, Remmie Colaco, Miguel Rod and others. The live bands such as Johnson and His Jolly Boys and C. Pereira belted out romantic music that encouraged every young couple to dance. This was a chance for young girls to check out their future grooms and vice-versa. Men approached their ladies to dance. The ladies graciously declined or accepted depending on who the gallant caballero was.

The sound of popping soda bottles and shouts of joy from the children running around with balloons or the constant rumble of conversation did not deter the band or the dancers.

The dancing went on continuously through the night, interrupted only by the intermittent serving of food. Young men held their ladies tight and the girls felt weak in the knees when their caballeros tried something unexpected and caressed them.

Servings of soup, *pulau* and drinks of all kinds were passed around at periodic intervals. Then towards morning, the *bhattkar* or the Padre Vigar or a VIP would raise toasts to the newlywed couple. With a glass of wine in hand, they would all stand up and listen to the toastmaster extol the virtues of both the bride and the groom and everyone drank to their health shouting *Viva*, followed by the singing of the popular Konkani toast *Uddon guelem parveamchem birem. Voiru pavonu viskottonu guelem. Bessaum tumcher poddom re, Deva Bapachem, Viva re viva. Viva marum-yea, Vokol-noureachi Saude korum-yea, Viva re Viva!*

All the guests greeted the bride and groom who cut the wedding cake and distributed pieces of the fruitcake to everyone present and thanked them for attending their big occasion.

At 5 o'clock in the morning, the wedding would be over; every one would be sleepy, exhausted and tipsy. The bride's party, the *potvor* would perform a short border ceremony of *shim* by pouring *fenni* on the ground for the spirit *hapshi* and then they would depart on their buses to their village singing *manddos* all the way back, with no doubt, a few broken hearts left behind.

And for the exhausted, young wedded couple, their honeymoon began!

The next day, when the *mattou* came down, the house was back in order after the chaos of the last couple days and the wedding celebration shifted to the bride's place. Same scenario, may be little less festive, but nevertheless, a double celebration.

Even though the wedding was finally over, the close relatives from distant villages would stay on for about a week after the wedding.

Linda's cousin Irene got married, when Linda was just eleven years old. Soirikar Salu did the honours and got her a handsome young man Martin Fernandes from the neighbouring village of Velim. Martin was a '*shippie*'. Irene was a beautiful young lady. They had never met before. They saw each other for the first time at Longuinhos Restaurant in Margão, as per *soirikar* Salu's previous arrangement. They liked each other and sent word to Salu that they found the match agreeable.

The dowry was set at 5,000 rupees excluding the *dennem* of an armoire, some copper utensils and gold jewellery. Irene used to help Linda's family a lot. So her father contributed 1000 rupees as part of dowry. Linda and her mother stayed at her uncle's house to help out for about a week and the preparations went ahead as planned.

At first there was the engagement. They hired a taxi and a bus and everyone went to Velim where the couple exchanged 22 carat gold rings. After a week, the formalities of *chooddo* and *rôss* were completed. Then followed by a grand Goan wedding. Even Linda danced with two boys her own age for the first time in her life. She felt a vague excitement, a stirring of her senses.

Then they all came back in a bus and celebrated the wedding at the bride's place in Cuncolim the next day. All this time Linda had a great time with her relatives, making new friends from both villages.

Linda began to wonder how women got pregnant once they got married. She figured that if the woman looked at her man's eyes intensely with a smile on her face long enough, she would probably get pregnant. And how was it possible that some women could never get pregnant in their lifetime? Could it be that their eyesight was bad? She definitely needed to learn more about these things!

Chapter 11

Linda did not like to attend funerals. Her *Papa-mãe or,* her paternal grandmother died a year after Irene's wedding. She had a stroke and was completely paralysed. Her family had to provide her with complete home care. The three brothers including Linda's father saw to the old lady's schedule in rotation. She stayed four months at each of their residences.

Linda hoped her grandmother would not die in her house, as she was scared of death. She felt miserable when she died at her younger uncle's house at the age of seventy-six. All the relatives were relieved that her troubles were finally over. When she was alive, they had to feed her, wash her and clean her, and she talked nonsense most of the time. Everyone got depressed hearing her constant crying and trying to meet her impossible demands.

Linda wondered what went on in her Papa-mãe's mind just the second before she died. What was she thinking about? Did she have a will to live a little longer? Could she see them all gathering around her? Did it hurt her when she died? Or did she feel like it was a bad dream? Did she hear some strange voices or her husband or God calling her?

And after her heart stopped beating and she was dead, did she feel her soul leave her, speeding out of her body like a rocket on its way to heaven? Surely her Papa-mãe must have gone to heaven. She had led a simple life and had not committed any grave sins. And how did she go up there? Was it too fast? Could she see all those houses and fields from up there? And what did the gate of heaven look like? Was it nice and cool there? Was the food good? How about the apples? She had always liked apples. What did God and the angels look like? Did God speak to Papa-mãe in Konkani? Or was there some good Goan Konkani translator up there? She couldn't think of any Goan official translators in heaven, as there was no Goan Saint yet. May be Fr Jose Vaz or Fr Agnelo de Souza? Could St Francis Xavier talk in Salcete Konkani so that her Papa-mãe could understand? And St Peter, did he have a huge beard? She only hoped her Papa-mãe wouldn't get the same awful treatment people got when they went to strange places.

Did her Papa-mãe now have time to think about her family back home? Could she ask God for some favours for them? Or could her Papa-mãe be holed up in Purgatory's waiting room? If so, they would have to pray for her for the rest of their lives, especially on November second, All Souls' Day every year. She only hoped her Papa-mãe would safely reach heaven. She wondered who would be in heaven with her, the neighbours or villagers or other Goans or some foreign people. Would heaven be full of white people, or black people or brown people? Who would be the majority there? And how about the Hindu people? The priests had said anyone who had not been baptized in the church and not cleansed of the original sin would go straight to hell. Would that mean that even nice Hindu and Moslem people would go straight to hell? How awful and unfair, she thought, if it were so.

On the day of the funeral, all three daughters-in-law (including her mother) cried out loud and wailed saying; that her *Papa-mãe* was such a nice lady, an angel from heaven; that she was never trouble at all; and why did God have to take the best from amongst them?

The crying and wailing went on for the entire day. The professional mourners were skilled in their singsong wailing performance that would increase in volume every time mourners entered to pay their respects. They would mention the name of that particular person and say the old lady adored them so much and so on. It was unbearable for Linda to see such hypocrisy in action. After the visitors left, all shut up and became their normal selves again as there was no one to impress. Linda tried to mimic their crying for her cousins, but she did not have the right pitch and her wailing was flat Her cousins started laughing as she couldn't even squeeze out a single tear even after using an onion.

When the priest arrived to take the body away for burial, the wailing and crying reached a high crescendo and some women even seemed to faint with grief. Women mussed their hair, blew their noses with the *palov,* the end piece of their sari, and cried out aloud, raising their hands over their heads and exclaiming, *"Avoi Deva Saiba. Avoi Deva Saiba!"* The Padre Cura told them to keep quiet, blessed the body in the open coffin and started prayers in Latin.

The body was taken out of the house and placed on a bench. Immediately all close relatives fixed their hair, stopped crying and posed behind the coffin for the typical funeral photograph. After the picture was taken, the coffin was covered and the women resumed crying even louder until the funeral procession went out of sight towards the church.

Close relatives and friends carried the coffin in a long procession of men and women. Next came the men in blue vestments, followed by a priest and a live band, which played melancholy music all the way to the church.

The priest started the Requiem Mass in the church and blessed the coffin again. Then the body was taken to the cemetery nearby. There the coffin was lowered into the grave. The priest said prayers again and the *pedo*, the gravedigger gave everyone a chance to throw a shovel full of mud on the coffin in the grave, starting with the priest and the relatives.

After the priest left, the womenfolk started wailing again. Linda secretly wished her dead *Papa-mãe* would get up and "shut-up" all these hypocrites. After the service, everyone went back home for café au lait and tea. The men drank their *fenni*, so the dead woman's spirit would rest in peace and they could rest too.

Later that night, as they slept oblivious to the world outside, in the dark a sinister figure moved stealthily in the cemetery. The figure walked towards the fresh grave, uncovered the soft mud, opened the coffin and snatched the pair of glasses from Linda's Papa-mãe's nose and put it in his pocket, covered the coffin and buried it again, this time for good.

A month after her granny's death, as they were shopping in the bazaar area, observant Linda asked her mother to look at the gravedigger's nose. He was wearing Papa-mãe's eyeglasses!

Chapter 12

Linda liked all festivals of Goa. Traditionally men who wore crowns of green ferns on their heads would celebrate the feast of São João Batista. Carrying a solid *piddo or* a coconut leaf stalk in their hands, they would go around the village hitting the *piddo* on the ground and saying *"Oh re São João"*. They would then jump into a well, fishing for bottles of *fenni* thrown into the well by others. The jumping was symbolic of how St John the Baptist jumped with joy in Elizabeth's womb, when the Virgin Mary visited Elizabeth during her pregnancy.

This feast celebrated on the 24th of June was dedicated to all the new sons-in-law of the village, and prayers were said for the fertility of the young married couples as well as the fertility of the rice fields. It was perfectly timed, during the monsoon rains, when the fields as well as the young couples got wet. With the collection of money and coconuts from the various houses in the village, the young men would celebrate the litany, the *ladainha* at night and party.

Linda was shocked to know from her friend Filomena that some imbeciles who jumped into the wells on São João Batista's feast day actually urinated in the well to get back at the neighbours they had a grudge on.

Feasts in Goa are numerous. On January 6th, there was the feast of the Three Kings on Remedios hillock at Cansaulim, where three little boys, dressed as Three Wise Men from the East and mounted on donkeys, slowly climbed the hill on their way to the Chapel at the top; followed by a big procession of men and women to the loud beating of drums, crackers and a live band. Once on top, the devotees kissed the Three Kings and the Mass began. After the Mass, people went to the fair. From this hill, one got a magnificent view of the Arabian Sea and the city of Margão was clearly visible.

Linda loved the feast of St Anthony in Durga, Chinchinim, where her daddy's sister Consolaçao lived, even though Durga was not accessible by public transport. They walked all the way to Viscondi-Arc, and then turned left at Kanknam-Moddi Hill to Durga, a distance of about ten miles. On the way people talked to her mother. At her aunt's magnificent new house, *Casa Fátima*, she had a great time. There was a preacher at the church there who had gone to the Vatican for his doctorate.

He brought back a film that he showed on his small projector. That was exciting. Linda also attended the feast of Mount Mary in Chinchinim Church, which was presided over by her Uncle Pascoal Domingos Fernandes in 1958. There was always a huge fair at every feast.

Going to the feast of Jesus of Nazarene known as '*Jesu Nodren,*' held at Siridão was tedious since the transport was awful. But she liked the *gasolina*, ferry crossing from Cortalim to Agasaim, as it was very pleasant. Then they would take the Panjim bus via Pilar and stop at Siridão.

Linda never missed the chance to visit the caves behind the Chapel overlooking the majestic Zuari River. As usual, they met many friends and relatives from all over Goa at this feast.

Linda's mother once took her to St. André Church in Goa Velha next to Siridão to see a procession of about 40 statues of Saints. This was the historic village, which was once the capital of Goa during the Kadamba rule, long before the Portuguese conquest.

Just next to Goa Velha was the little hill of Pilar, the headquarters of the missionary Society of St. Francis Xavier. It was also the location of the Pilar Seminary for priests doing missionary work in Goa, Damão and Diu and the rest of India. Here lay the remains of a Goan priest, the venerable Fr Agnelo De Souza, one of the priests who established and founded the Society of St Francis Xavier and lived in an old monastery in Pilar next to the old Church.

Linda and her mother went to Pilar to visit the tomb of Father Agnelo in the Pilar church. People went there to take holy water and the earth from his grave, packed in little pouches, and supposed to have miraculous healing powers.

The newly built seminary with numerous halls and classrooms was funded by donations mostly from its German benefactors. From the balcony, a magnificent view of the River Zuari and most of Goa was visible. The Church in the seminary was formidable, with its stained glass windows, elevated domed roof above the altar and the exquisite marble floor. The view of the magnificent gardens in front and fruit trees in the orchard at the back made this visit a very satisfying experience for Linda.

Then there was the feast at Colva known as the *Fama* at the Infant Jesus Church in Colvá, a coastal village west of Margão on the day before the novena of the actual feast.

Devotees from all over Salcete, the southern district of Goa, came to the *Fama*. The little statue of the Child Jesus, *Menino Jesus* had miraculous powers. Linda had a relative in Colvá and after the Mass they went to Agapito and Antonieta's place for a sumptuous dinner.

On December third, Linda and her mother would get up at 4 o'clock in the morning and start early in the day to join the *romaria* to go to Old Goa for the greatest feast in all of Goa, the feast of St. Francis Xavier, the *Goemcho Saib* or the Saint of Goa. Linda particularly liked to go there during the Exposition, which occurred every ten years, so she could see the remains of St. Francis Xavier, that were kept in a silver casket in the Basílica of Bom Jesus for over four centuries, without showing the least sign of decay.

St. Francis Xavier was a Spanish-born noble turned Jesuit priest who came to Goa in 1542 with a mission to convert the locals to Christianity. He accomplished many conversions in and around Goa and on the Malabar Coast in South India. He set sail for Japan in 1549, where he converted some locals and died on the way to China in 1552. He was buried in Sanchian Island.

Later his body was exhumed from the grave and found to be remarkably fresh. Then it was finally brought via Malacca to Goa. He was canonized a Saint in 1622 by Pope Gregory XV. By 1952 the body shrivelled greatly due to numerous expositions. It is said one lady devotee even bit his toe long time ago when it was kept open for veneration. Now it is preserved in a sealed coffin.

Thousands of devotees from Goa and the rest of India made their annual pilgrimage to Old Goa on December 3rd. Linda was scared of the people coming from outside Goa, as she heard many stories about them. There were rumours that some of them came especially to steal gold from the devotees.

She heard a woman snatched a gold chain from a young girl who was walking in the procession, and put it in her mouth and swallowed it. The police could not do anything, as there was no evidence. Linda was very careful, when someone touched her, she checked at once to see if her gold bangles and her earrings and chain were intact.

She would line up impatiently and walk in the long procession to kiss the body of St Francis Xavier. The long walk to the various churches such as the Basílica de Bom Jesus, the Se Cathedral, the church of St Caetano and others tired her out.

At the end of their pilgrimage, they would walk to the northern side under the Viceroy's Gate all the way to the River Mandovi to see the other side at Divar and some part of Bardez from the ferry dock. By the time they came home, from Old Goa to Cuncolim via Ponda and Margão, Linda would be extremely exhausted.

Chapter 13

Strange, unexplainable things happened in the village, when Linda was growing up. She had poor but very interesting neighbours all around.

One of them was a family of ironsmiths just down the road. They had a small hut, where they kept their tools like hammers, an anvil and goatskin bellows, which blew air through a buried pipe leading upward to a fire pit filled with charcoal.

The ironsmith Sebastião, locally known as Bostião, prepared red hot fire in this fire pit and heated the iron implements, needing repair, until they too were red hot and malleable. He then placed them on the anvil and hammered them, to the required shape or size. Then to cool them quickly, he dipped them in a trough of cold water, to retain their newly acquired shape permanently.

Bostião made and repaired machetes, knives, scythes and other iron implements. Linda liked to watch him. His movements were so deft, so fluid and skilled. She liked to see him fit a red-hot pointed end of a machete into a raw wooden handle, to fit perfectly, producing a cloud of smoke.

Bostião was a good man when he was working, but when he went around the village and sold his goods and got some money, he went to the local *taverna*, a pub, and spent all his money on drink. That's when he turned bad. He would come home swearing at everyone and beat up his wife Luiza.

They were very poor. Bostião's wife did odd jobs for the neighbours and ate discarded food or leftovers while their daughter Mena stole food from neighbours, whenever she was hungry. Linda's parents would not allow her to play with Mena, as they were afraid Linda would pick up bad words, habits, and bad manners from her.

Bostião's wife Luiza's neck was swollen with a big goitre in front, a result of a diet deficient in iodine. They had no money to go to the doctor for treatment. Luiza went around the village begging for food. She would go to other villages on feast days walking for miles so she could get some food. Some people would offer her food and uncooked rice, which she would take home wrapped in some old clothes, and feed the family, making it last as long as possible. When Linda's mother felt lonesome and scared, she would ask Luiza to come over to her house to sleep overnight. In return Luiza and Mena would get free supper. Sometimes when Luiza's husband came home late at night drunk, she would come running straight to Linda's home for shelter for the night, to escape his beatings. Linda's mom would willingly accommodate her.

Suddenly, Luiza lost it and had a nervous breakdown. She became mad and started doing strange things and talking nonsense. Linda was studying in grade 4 of the primary school in Portuguese and Luiza who never went to school started speaking in English. Linda was astounded. How was this possible? Then one day, Luiza went running to the field in front of Linda's house and jumped into a well of stagnant water infested with frogs, snakes and insects.

The whole neighbourhood gathered around the well and pulled Luiza out from the slimy well using a ladder. And again, there was no doctor to treat her, as she had no money. After about a month, Luiza recovered. All this time her daughter, Mena, stole food from neighbours and fed her mother.

Luiza and Bostião had three other children, the eldest boy worked as a servant for a Parsi family in Bombay, the elder daughter and younger son worked for Goan families also in Bombay. But whatever the children earned as pocket money was only enough only for their sustenance and they could not send anything to their family in Goa. They worked as bonded labourers, as their father Bostião got some advance money from their employers for their future services.

Another neighbour of theirs was a good-hearted woman called Flora, in her fifties. She was very good to Linda and gave her goodies on special days. One day, she had high fever. The doctor gave her an antibiotic injection. Within eight hours she died, as she was allergic to certain antibiotics and no one knew about it. This was a real shock. Everybody said the doctor was no good, and since that day people boycotted him.

Flora's husband worked on board a ship and their three sons were in a boarding school, Guardian Angel High School in Sanvordem. They came home for the funeral and it was quite tragic to see these motherless kids crying their heart out over their dead mother.

Flora had a daughter who lived in Kenya, East Africa. But they had relatives rather close to Linda's house. These relatives helped them as much they could. But without the mother, the house just could not be managed well. They had no one to cook and wash. The elder son, who was sixteen learnt to cook and wash when they came home for holidays. But life was tough for them.

A year later, the father came home, but he could not cook either. He hired a woman to do the housework, but things were still not the same. For a while, the father thought of getting married again, but he was too old, and the family resisted being wary of stepmothers.

Two years later, a strange thing happened and Linda actually witnessed and heard it herself. Flora's daughter had come from East Africa and she felt something was wrong in their house. She hired a man to bless this house. This man was supposedly under the influence of St Jude.

The man came to the house and started to pray. After the prayers, his voice suddenly changed from a man's to a female nun-like voice and he started speaking in impeccable English. The voice was authoritative; and it commanded the man to move from the main hall to the storeroom; and everyone followed the man, including Linda.

The man asked for a pickaxe and started digging the floor of the storeroom till he unearthed a dried lemon from the floor. And the voice said that someone had performed *jadoo*, a kind of black magic and that this was the cause of Flora's death. The bad luck to the family would go after he undid the jadoo. Strangely, Flora's family began to prosper after that.

Linda also heard a lot about ghosts in the village, but she never saw one. She was scared to go alone anywhere. She wouldn't go alone from one room to the other at night inside her own house even with the *divo* in hand without her mother by her side. She heard that a robber pulled up tiles on the roof, came down a rope and jumped on the stomach of a sleeping young woman, who died soon after due to shock. Since then Linda started to sleep on her side or on her stomach, but never on her back.

Linda heard from one of her schoolmates that people from all over Goa flocked to a house in their village to pray and offer money. It was rumoured that the young boy, in that house, had apparitions of Virgin Mary; and that the family had made a lot of money from the offerings and selling holy water and candles at exorbitant prices. This prayer group finally ended when the bishop's representative found out that it was a hoax.

Another neighbour to the south, Sofia led an interesting life. She was in her early twenties, married and had two kids and her husband David was at sea. Sofia was young, sexy and very attractive – the most beautiful woman in the entire village. But she was also poor and illiterate. If she was elegantly dressed and had make-up on she would certainly look like Madhubala, a gorgeous Hindi film star. Her husband was handsome but short and not very outgoing like her. They had nothing in common except their same low caste. Linda always felt Sofia's parents had forced her to marry him because of his good job.

Sofia had great taste. She always dressed in a tight fitting blouse and a colourful sari, showing her bare midriff and wearing a red hibiscus flower in her hair, which was bundled at the back into a *shenddo*. When she went to the bazaar, she was always the centre of attraction, and every man lusted after her. Her beautiful face with a vibrant smile had a certain charisma, which could attract and captivate even the holiest monk. When her husband David worked aboard the ship, she felt bored and useless, alone at home with the kids. To forget her frustrations, she took to drinking the local *fenni*.

She was not a devoted wife or a mother.

One day she went to Margão to visit her brother for a week. There she met a man, Abdul Qader who showed a deep interest in her. She could not resist the temptation and this butcher from Margão made advances to her repeatedly. She was very hot blooded. She gave up everything, left her kids with her mother and ran away with him.

Days later a lot of people from Cuncolim saw the pair walking hand in hand in Margão near Cine Lata and also at Bombay Café. Someone even saw an intimate photo of Sofia posted at Borcar's photography studio.

Sofia lived with Abdul Qader for about six months, before he dumped her. But Sofia did not give up this life altogether. Soon she made herself available to the *pacle*, the white Portuguese military men, who were looking for sex with local women. While this was going on, her husband David came to Goa and went looking for her in Margão. Finally he tracked her down in Moddkeam Bazaar, a red light area in Margão and he brought her home.

A large crowd including Linda gathered around her home. Sofia felt very embarrassed. She begged for forgiveness and hugged her sons. David told her if she ever did that again, he would shoot her with a gun and promptly forgave her.

After his leave expired in about nine months and he was called back to Bombay to join a ship, David decided to take his wife and kids to Bombay, as he feared she might run away again with *pacle* in Goa. So they went to Bombay and he arranged a small *kottrie* for them before going on board. Within three months, Sofia ran away again with another man from Bombay.

When David came back from the voyage a year later, he looked for Sofia, found her, forgave her once again and brought her back to Goa. Sofia was not herself again after that affair. She had lost all her self-respect. Linda's mother comforted her and convinced her to stay away from that evil life. Sofia resolved never to do that again, but it was too late. She had contracted a venereal disease and died within two years, leaving two orphans, who would have a bleak future.

In the meantime David married again and his new wife was no different from Sofia. She also ran away with someone. This was too much for David and finally he also ran away from his life by committing suicide.

Linda's mother, Joanita began to experience bouts of epilepsy all of a sudden, after she had an appendix operation in Miraj. Probably because she was allergic to anaesthetic, she thought. The first time it happened one night, Linda was very shocked to hear her mother making eerie sounds and having fits and tremors in the middle of the night. Linda struck the match and lit the kerosene lamp to see her mother shaking violently with lot of froth in her mouth.

Linda got scared, cried, unlocked the front door and shouted to the neighbours for help. Within minutes, the neighbours came and her neighbour Josinho went to call the doctor on his bike. Another neighbour, hunter Mário Piedade, asked for *fenni* and a piece of cloth. He burned the cloth and directed the smoke towards Joanita's nostrils. Then he rubbed the alcohol on her chest and soon Joanita was conscious.

The doctor came eventually but he did not say much. He gave her an injection to calm her down and left. Since that night, Linda knew what to do in case her mother had these bouts of epilepsy again. But she was scared for her mother, especially when her mother went to draw water from an open well without protective walls. If she had a fit there, that would be quite dangerous.

Joanita concluded that she got these bouts of epilepsy whenever there was full moon. She went to hundreds of doctors in Margão, Panjim and Karwar, and they prescribed so many medicines that her medicine closet looked like a little pharmacy. But nothing worked. One day, as she was sitting on her *balcão*, she had a bout of epilepsy and she fell down on the front porch and hurt her knee.

At times like this, Linda felt, she should have been a boy. Then, she would have been able to lift her mother up by herself. Not only that, boys seemed to have certain privileges. A lot of current practices were biased against women. She was not able to serve as an altar-girl. Even when there was a soccer match just in front of her house, only boys and men attended these matches. Linda decided to attend these soccer matches, whenever she could, especially the finals of the inter-village tournament. She did not care what others thought.

The soccer final was a spectacle worth watching. Hundreds of spectators came from around the villages for the final deciding game. There was a big stand erected with seats for guests. Trophies were displayed on a table. The biggest trophy went to the winning team. There was a smaller trophy for the losing team and individual trophies for the players. There was even a live band. Firecrackers were ignited whenever someone scored.

Young men in uniform would play soccer for various villages and people from Cuncolim, of course, would cheer their own home team. Linda did not like it when players fought after being awarded a foul by the referee and the fans joined in, sometimes with knives and fists. The soccer players wore no shoes. Only the goalie used kneecaps. Guest players from Bombay playing for Tatas and Burmah Shell wore soccer shoes and put up a big show.

Even for *ladainha,* girls and women were not welcome, unless the litany was in their home and they watched it from behind the curtains of the inner room. In the church, men and women sat separately. As far as the village communities were concerned, women had no say in the management of these organizations. Only men could participate in the rites.

One day Linda had gone for a neighbour's engagement. She was about eleven years old. She had worn a blue dress that fitted her perfectly. An old woman Benedita, stared at her for a long time. Linda observed the woman looking at her continuously. All at once Linda felt unwell and went home before the party was over. She was ill for three days.

The doctor could not find anything wrong with Linda. Finally the local *dishticarn*, a woman who could neutralize the forces of the evil eye was brought in on a Friday night. The woman Kotrin (Catherine) took three dry chillies in her hand and with the sign of the Cross she circled them around Linda's head three times. Then she touched her whole body with them and threw the chillies over red-hot coals and ashes on a tile. Then she repeated this process with salt and *hodki*, alum. All this time she said prayers like, *Our Father, Hail Mary* and *I believe.*

The salt immediately began to crackle on the fire and alum melted. Kotrin auntie said it was the evil-eyed devils making a noise as they left. Then Kotrin *maushi* took some coconut oil in a brass spoon circled it around Linda's head three times and dumped it into a brass plate containing water. The drops of oil when poured on the surface of water created strange images and shapes.

Then Kotrin *maushi* said to Linda: "*Baai*, look at that fat woman, and look at those two evil eyes and that fat stomach."

"It looks like your neighbour, the fat old woman Benedita," continued Kotrin *maushi*.

Linda remembered seeing Benedita looking at her continuously at that engagement party.

"Oh yes, I saw Benedita looking at me for a long time at the engagement party a week ago, *maushi*!" said Linda to aunt Kotrin *maushi*.
"She must have been jealous of your dress and beauty, my child." Kotrin *maushi* responded.

Then Kotrina *maushi* took the tile containing the contaminated chillies and salt and threw the coal and ashes towards Benedita's house making sure no one was looking at her. Linda's mother gave Kotrin *maushi* half a rupee for her troubles and invited her to stay for supper. Kotrin *maushi* ate some rice and curry and drank a peg of *fenni*, thanked them, and told Linda to stay away from Benedita for at least another week. And soon after Kotrin *maushi* left, almost an hour later, Linda felt much better.

Linda found it difficult to believe in the occult, even when she seemed a victim of it. She had heard about the phenomenon of a *jadoo*, which when cast on a family, had devastating consequences on the lives of the family.

According to some believers, if a family had some misfortunes in a row, it was certain that someone had cast a *jadoo* upon that family. They would then advise the victims to avail the sevices of a *ghaddi* to get rid of the ill effects of that *jadoo* and have it neutralized.

The *ghaddi*, who was usually a Hindu soothsayer cum voodoo artist, would charge varying amounts of money depending on the customer to cast out the *jadoo*. The *ghaddi* would explain he needed the money to buy coconuts and roosters to offer as sacrifice to gods to undo the *jadoo*. Other saner people believed *ghaddis* were fake artists who took advantage of the people's misfortunes.

Chapter 14

In 1956 Linda finished her *segundo grau,* the grade two final examinations with distinction. Everybody came to her house and congratulated her.

Her father, Mário had come home too, a month earlier. Linda loved to be with her dad as much as possible. He just spoiled her. He made sure he spent every moment with her and her mother. Together they would go to church and other places to visit. They would go to feasts, weddings and other functions.

Mário gave her a small party, took her to Margão and bought her gifts as a reward for her great performance.

A month after the examination, Linda went to Panjim with her father to write an entrance examination for the *Liceu,* the secondary school system. This was the first time she had ever gone to the big city of Panjim, the capital of Goa.

But when they got there, they could not find any accommodation to stay overnight. They needed to stay in Panjim for at least three days. They went around looking for a place to stay at Patto but could not find any. It reminded them of the plight of Mary and Joseph in Bethlehem. Finally her father got a place in a small lodging at Fontainhas.

The landlady, Dona Lucia Borges of Divar was a nice lady. She felt sorry for the little girl from the village and her father and offered to accommodate them for the duration required. She had no extra space, as she already had boarders from Damão and Diu, but she was prepared to make two spaces in the dormitory.

Linda and her father were tired from the long journey. It took five hours to get to Panjim from Cuncolim via Margão, Cortalim and Agaçaim.

The boarders from Damão and Diu in Gujarat, were young teenagers, six boys and a girl. They went to the Portuguese Lyceum at Altinho and spoke only Portuguese. One of them knew Gujarati and a little English.

Linda's father, Mário knew Portuguese quite well, but he could speak English more fluently. Linda knew written Portuguese very well, but had no practice in spoken Portuguese as she spoke Konkani at home.

Mário made himself at home with the boarders, who started singing. Two of them had guitars. Mário sang his own English compositions called *Cock-a-doodle-do-cluck-cluck* and *On the Moon* and the teenagers accompanied him on their guitars and all of them had a great time. Later they ate and went to sleep.

The next day, Linda and her father got up early, brushed their teeth and got ready for breakfast. That was the first time, Linda ate butter with her bread and she liked it very much. She had coffee with milk. At home she always drank black coffee with homemade *chapatti* or *bhakri*. She experienced Portuguese food in Panjim, for the first time. She also ate cream crackers with Kraft Cheese.

After breakfast, they went to the *Liceu* Nacional Afonso de Albuquerque, a huge complex of buildings on the hillock of Altinho in Panjim, which was the secondary school Institution for Goa, Damão and Diu.

More than a hundred steps had to be climbed to get there. The long climb was good exercise for Linda and her father. Once they were on top, they felt good, as it was cool and windy and after a while their breathing became normal.

This was where the public examination was to be conducted. They finally found the Registration Department in one of the five buildings. Linda admired the beautiful edifice. There were ceramic tiles all over the floor and walls and it was pretty, clean and neat. When they went to the Registration office however, they could not find anyone to help them.

Everyone seemed to be busy. No one came to see them at the window. After all, who cared about some poorly dressed village people? This institution catered to the rich and the powerful, the elite of Goa, who only spoke Portuguese. After a long wait, which seemed to be an eternity, Mário tried to draw someone's attention. No one seemed to care.

Then Mário lost it. His patience reached its limit.

"Is there anyone working here?" he shouted.

A man walked up to him and said, "What is your problem?"

Mário said, "Mind your manners, Mister. I want to see your boss." The man ignored Mário and walked straight back to his chair.

Linda looked at her father and felt sorry for him. These Goans who worked for the Portuguese government seemed to feel they were the masters of this country. They were Goans, not some *pacle*. And they treated her father as if he were some alien. She could not understand the discrimination meted out to simple Goans like her father by the so-called elitist Goans. She wished Goa would be independent soon, so that every Goan regardless of their background got back their respect and dignity on their own soil, rather than being routinely ignored as a worthless entity by these lackeys of the colonial regime.

Just then, Mário saw a gentleman pass by, whose face looked remotely familiar to him. He looked at the familiar face, trying to recollect where and when had he known this person. It clicked!

"Bom dia, Senhor Alberto De Cruz," Mário introduced himself finally approaching the gentleman. "I am Mário Cardoso, the ex-Mestre Capela de Aldonã, remember me? You used to be the *farmaceutico* in Aldonã, right?" he reminded him.

"Oh yes, Senhor Cardoso, I remember very well, I edited your manuscript for your book in Konkani, how could I forget? Anything I can help you with, Senhor?"

Mário explained to him that he had come for his daughter's registration for the admissão examination. Senhor Cruz, who happened to be the Registrar of the Admissão examinations, took them both inside his office and sorted out everything in five minutes.

Linda and her father visited other buildings to check the location of the examination hall. They walked around the complex and when they came out Mário showed Linda the places of interest in and around Panjim. He showed her where the Mandovi river estuary met the Arabian Sea, the Governor's Palace at Cabo, Fort Aguada jail, Reis Magos, the lighthouse of Aguada, the Saligao Seminary on the hill, lighthouse of Betim, Ribandar, Patto, and Santa Cruz. They had a marvellous view of the river Mandovi and the city of Panjim from the top of the Altinho hill.

After coming down from Altinho, Mário took Linda to the picturesque, white, majestic Panjim church of Imaculada Conceição with hundreds of steps in the front. A little further down was the Municipal Garden, where a maestro was conducting a live orchestra on the bandstand. Recorded music was being played on a loud speaker in Portuguese for the listening pleasure of hundreds of young lovers strolling down the *jardim*, which had a variety of flowers and plants of different shades and colours.

Mário took Linda to the *pastelaria* Café Cappuccino for some coffee and pastries. Linda also tasted cola for the first time and it tasted divine. Later they had ice cream with fruit salad at the ice cream parlour. Linda never felt happier. She was very thankful to her father for these nice things in life, that she had never experienced before. Later, they strolled along past the Casa Internacional, and past the Corte towards Hotel Mandovi.

Her father told her the Hotel Mandovi was the tallest building in Goa with its five floors. Linda admired the grandiose, light green Hotel Mandovi with its decorations and statuettes. She was told only the rich and affluent could enter this Hotel. There was a travel agency on the ground floor and richly dressed Portuguese used this Hotel. Linda could only hope to be able to enter this luxury hotel one day.

Mário took Linda across the street towards the river Mandovi. She saw Bardez on the other side of the river and the *farol* or the lighthouse of Betim on the hill opposite. Then they walked along the bank of the river Mandovi all the way to Campal, with a fresh breeze coming in from the river. Linda saw the generating station, which supplied electricity to Panjim. Mário showed her the Escola Médica de Goa, the first medical school in Asia.

They came walking all the way back along the Rua Dom Afonso de Albuquerque. It was getting dark. The sun had just set behind Fort Aguada hill. The brightly lit neon lights of Panjim made it look like a European city. As they walked back, Mário showed Linda the statue of a dark monk-like figure hypnotising a woman.

"This is the statue of an illustrious Goan priest/scientist Abade Faria," Linda's dad explained, "He was an exponent of the modern science of hypnosis. He studied and did research on hypnosis in France. The statue depicts him in the process of inducing a woman to sleep using hypnosis. This was the Abbe Faria in Alexandre Dumas' famous novel, *The Count of Monte Cristo*".

"Oh yes, our professora once said he was nervous on the podium when he was supposed to give a speech in Portuguese and then his father shouted at the top of his lungs in Konkani *Kator re bhaji*, which gave him courage to continue his lecture brilliantly".

"Yes, that's the one."

Mário showed Linda the Palace of Hidalcão, the summer palace of the Moslem ruler Adil Shah (Khan) of Goa, before the Portuguese defeated him in 1510. Then she saw the statue of *peixe mulher*, the mermaid, in a little *jardim* in front of the Navegaçao building on the waterfront. By this time they were hungry, they went to the Hospedaria Venite restaurant for some food. The food smelt good, different and appetizing. This was where

Linda tasted her first cauliflower. It tasted marvellous. Then they went back to the house of Dona Lucia Borges in the Latin quarter of Panjim, Fontainhas.

Linda's examinations began the next day. She walked up to the *Liceu* complex on Altinho and there she saw smartly dressed Portuguese speaking students, mostly Europeans and a few Goans who came from the big cities of Panjim, Margão, Vasco de Gama and Mapuça, who looked quite fair and very polished. She was the only one from a village. She felt very proud of herself to make it here from a very humble village background along with these highly cultured Portuguese-speaking students.

For the first time in her life, Linda felt out of place. The students somehow seemed to ignore her and look down on her. She did not have any make-up on her to change her natural looks. Her dark hair was nicely split in two braids and she wore an ordinary dress, the *vestido*, while all the other girls were dressed in the avant-garde Portuguese fashion.

Linda wondered why she felt hurt, but she did. For God's sake, this was her own land and she should not feel inferior because of their condescending looks. She wished the day would come soon when all true-blooded Goans would feel proud of their own land and send all these aliens and their lackeys back to wherever they came from.

She looked out towards the Arabian Sea, the hills and the green trees in the fertile land beyond and felt proud of her own motherland. But she felt sorry it was in the wrong hands, in the hands of the people who thought they were the masters and common people like her, their god-given slaves. This could not last for too long. Of that she was sure.

In the meantime, Linda had to concentrate on the task at hand, to write the examinations and get the best results. Linda had prepared well but she was nervous, looking at all these students speaking fluent and stylish Portuguese. She went to the assigned classroom and settled down. She quickly made the sign of the Cross and started praying. When the first examination paper was submitted, Linda felt comfortable and wrote the next few examination papers in a relaxed manner.

The next day the results were announced. There was a crowd of students in the main hall to check the results. Linda checked her name and she was proud to see that she had obtained *dispensado*, a distinction in the written examination and so was exempted from appearing for the oral examination. Then she looked at the faces of all those smartly dressed, Portuguese-speaking students. Most of those faces looked extremely cold, pale and dejected now. Maybe they had failed. Linda came out of the hall smiling, with her head held high and felt proud of her performance at her *Admissão* examination.

After the results of Admissão, Linda and her father left Panjim the same day. They stopped in Margão. It was noon, so they went to the Longuinhos restaurant for some delicious food. Then they walked next door to the *Penguim Gelada* house for some more ice cream and fruit-salad. Finally, they came back to Cuncolim, both feeling victorious and proud of her achievement in Panjim.

Linda shared her experience with her mother – all those wonderful things that happened to her and those arrogant looking, Portuguese-speaking students at *Liceu*. Her mother congratulated Linda and advised her to ignore the mean attitudes of some people. She told her to be herself, to study well and prove she was second to none. Some neighbours and her relatives came to felicitate Linda. They had a small party to celebrate her success and everyone was proud of their Linda.

Chapter 15

Dr B.J. Furtado was tall, fair and handsome. Serious and gentle, he dressed smartly, mostly in white clothes and looked elegant with his well-combed oily hair. He always had a smiling face and a perfect set of white teeth. Though in his early forties, he looked much younger.

After passing his matriculation examination in Bombay, Dr BJ could not decide what he wanted to be. He did a lot of reading and pored over books from history, literature, religion, sociology, and world politics. Finally, he graduated in homoeopathic medicine.

He came from a Chaddo family of Cuncolim, although his ancestors, who originally came from Carambolim, had migrated to Cuncolim during the famous plague in old Goa. His mission in life was to help the poor, the uneducated, the under-privileged and the downtrodden.

While he practised in Bombay and was doing quite well, he came under the influence of Mahatma Gandhi and joined the Goa Freedom Movement. Later he came down to Goa to put into practice both homoeopathic medicine and his political beliefs. He lived and practiced in a rented house next door to Linda's.

Dr BJ was a social worker and an educationist. He was very clean and hygienic and he always stressed the essentials of cleanliness, good health and nutrition to his patients. He advised them not to eat too much meat, especially the pork, which he said was harmful.

He liked Linda very much as he always found her quiet, disciplined, diligent, ambitious and intelligent. She asked him interesting questions. Linda never knew much about Dr Furtado's personal life or his dedication to the freedom and the liberation of Goa from Portuguese rule.

Linda often went to his place because he was a very interesting man and very well informed. Dr BJ seemed to know everything that went on in the world. He had all kinds of news, information and anecdotes to share with her from his experience and the various newspapers and magazines that he subscribed to.

Dr BJ had a sister, who lived with him and cooked for him. His homoeopathic practice thrived. He never took money from poor patients. The medicine that he handed out in little *papelina* or paper pouches seemed to work for any kind of ailment. It tasted sweet like glucose powder.

Dr BJ became a complete vegetarian and a true follower of Mahatma Gandhi. He would eat only vegetables and fruits like papaya, mango, melon and orange. He was a complete teetotaller and a non-smoker. He advised Linda not to eat meat too and to eat lots of fruits and vegetables. Dr BJ was not a typical Goan Catholic. He did not like to go for parties, drink *fenni*, eat *sorpotel* or socialize.

Dr BJ opened up an English school where he was the only teacher teaching all subjects himself. Over a hundred students attended his school. In his spare time, Dr BJ wrote articles for some weeklies in Bombay. He always kept himself busy doing repair work, cleaning, reading or doing something around the house. He would go to church for the early morning Mass at six every Sunday.

Dr BJ educated Linda about the World War II, how it started and ended, about Mahatma Gandhi and how he had helped India get its independence, and how Goa was soon to be liberated by India. Linda could not understand much about liberty and freedom, but she slowly learnt about politics, although she was not initially interested in it. Linda admired the courage and determination of Gandhi. But she did not understand why India wanted to take over Portuguese Goa. All this information intrigued Linda.

Linda learnt about the past glory of India, its rich history and the invasions of foreigners like the Aryans, the Moguls, the Portuguese, the English and the French. She learnt from the doctor about the great Mahatma, who was discriminated against by the white regime in South Africa and how he promoted the passive resistance movement using non-violence as an effective weapon to force the British out of India.

Dr B.J. Furtado told her about the great Indian spiritualist Gautama Buddha, who gave up a life of riches in his father's kingdom to seek nirvana by living the life of an ascetic. He told her how he gave this world a different religion called Buddhism, which believed in equality of mankind, non-violence, reincarnation and the middle path.

He told her briefly the stories of the Pandavas and Kauravas from the age-old Indian epic of Mahabharata and the story of Rama and Sita from Ramayana. He was proud of the great Indus Valley civilization at Mohenjo-Daro and the age-old Universities of Taxila and Nalanda. But Dr Furtado never mentioned to her that he was a freedom fighter working for the liberation of Goa.

One day Linda decided to ask Dr BJ a question that was troubling her. After the afternoon tea, Linda knocked on his door.

"Can I come in Doctor?"

"Sure, come right in Linda. Have a seat at the table. I have nice fresh papayas today. Have some."

"Thanks Doctor. I came to ask you about something that bothers me a lot and I know you have the answer. You always do, doctor."

"Go ahead Linda, what's bothering you?"

"I don't know if anyone told you of a little incident that took place in our church years ago, which had something to do with me and my caste. I want to know all about the caste system and its origin, if you don't mind discussing it doctor."

"Not at all, Linda. I know this is a rather sensitive issue, but it's high time you knew all about it."

"And doctor could you also please throw some light on this *gaunvkar* issue as well? Is it related to the caste system?"

"You sure have a lot of tough questions for a girl your age. No, I am not aware of that incident Linda, but I will tell you what I know about the caste system and the *gaunvkar* issue. As a matter of fact, I have an article that I had written long time ago, which I hope will be published some day."

Dr BJ went to his little room where he had a small library and picked up his manuscript.

"Here is the article that I wrote. It is a history of the original people of Goa, according to me. It's not in any of the history books as yet." The doctor handed the manuscript to Linda and said "Go take it home and read it, but please return it to me."

Dr B.J. Furtado's Manuscript.

This article may offend the sensibilities of some closed minds that have a one-sided view of caste, race or religion. It is written solely to foster a clear understanding among peoples of all creeds about certain events in ancient Indian history, which caused untold misery and pain to the sons of the soil, the ancient Shudras and their progeny through the years. I hope and believe that they will once again recover their stolen dignity.

******

Everybody in India today assumes that all non-Hindu Indians converted from one common faith, the Hindu religion. But I beg to differ. According to most historical accounts, the Hindu religion has existed in India only for about 5000 years since the advent of Aryans from the North. Before that, the natives who inhabited India were not Hindus. This document will explain logically the plight of natives in India and what happened to them since.

******

The first people of India, the dark skinned natives lived in huts on their fertile lands. The entire country was made up of small villages. Each village had farmers, cobblers, potters, iron-smiths, copper smiths, builders, carpenters and workers in occupations that were needed to keep a village running smoothly. Everyone contributed their goods and services to society in their own way and exchanged them through the barter system.

The village elders held regular meetings and resolved amicably all social and judicial matters that arose among the villagers. These decisions were binding on both parties. There were no kings, queens, cities or armies, as there was nothing to defend or fight for. The occupations of priests, tax collectors, clerks and warriors never existed. There were no middlemen, agents, brokers or merchants. There was equal status and respect for every occupation. The dignity of hard work was paramount in this form of democracy in pre-historic India. Direct bartering and trade ran the whole economy of the country, benefiting both the producers and consumers of goods and services.

The native people lived in mutual respect and faith and in peace. There were no contracts and no land registration. Everyone had a piece of land and a hut to sleep in. They all lived together in huge communes, each one contributing their individual services in kind towards their community. There were no landlords or landless peasants or tenants. The common public land was available for everyone's benefit in the village.

But this quiet and carefree way of life came to an abrupt end, with the armed invasion of fierce Aryans from the North.

The invaders were tall, fair skinned warriors, armed, dangerous and cruel. They came on horseback, armed with swords and arrows, plundering and killing any natives, who resisted their advance into this new, vast, fertile land. Countless natives bravely gave their lives to protect their territory. The rest were easily overrun and were conquered. The Aryans had better fighting skills, powerful weaponry, cunning tactics and strategy, acquired on their destructive path all the way from Central Asia. The natives on the other hand were a peaceful people to whom fighting was an alien concept.

The conquerors gave a new name to these natives of India. They called them Shudras, the servants. The Aryans razed all villages, defiled their women and banished the remaining natives from the villages to the forests or hills. The poor natives had to take whatever they had of their personal belongings and move out of their land and household with their families, in what was probably the first and worst 'ethnic cleansing' the world has ever known. Hence, though India today has a majority Hindu population, it was not always so.

The Shudras believed in spirits, but did not have an organized religion. The conquering Aryans created an entirely new, reorganized country and called it Bharatvarsh. A new religion was established called Hinduism. The victors forcibly converted the entire Shudra population en masse to Hinduism. This was the first known mass conversion in the history of the world. Of course, the invaders could not venture out into the wild forests and hills and other inaccessible areas. So they left them untouched, unconverted and called them banvasis, the residents of the forest. As a result, these native tribes in the inhospitable areas of India have never heard of Hindu Gods and Goddesses and do not know what Hinduism is even to this day.

The Aryan religion did not include any noteworthy Shudra deities in the Hindu religion or in their epic books. The Aryans forced Shudras to blindly follow the doctrine of the new religion without any concern about their religious preference. Their caste system established the superiority of the fair-skinned Aryans and deliberately subjugated Shudras by curtailing their rights in all matters, social, political and religious. No Shudra could perform religious rites in the Hindu temples, as they could not become Brahmins, and were therefore not eligible.

The Aryans instituted the first racist regime. The real people of India, the Shudras, were classed as the lowest in the hierarchy of the Caste System. The Aryans divided themselves into three higher castes: the Brahmins (Bamonnns or priests), the Kshatriyas (modern Chaddos or warriors) and the Vaishyas (the merchants). The Aryans introduced new occupations – priests, tax collectors, clerks, warriors, merchants and agents and the entire country was commercialised. The products and services of Shudras were exploited to the maximum. Shudras had to serve their Aryan masters as a matter of course. It was the perfect set up to keep the Aryans in total control.

The world's first colony was thus, established in India by the Aryans. The concept of Kings and Queens was developed later after cities were built using Shudra slaves. They were forced to work on the new agricultural farms developed to satisfy new demands from the invaders and their extended families. The master-slave concept was introduced and the Vedic Aryans lived in luxury in their ill-gotten land, by exploiting the native Shudras as their life-long slaves and servants.

Shudras could come into the central village only at mid-day when their shadows were at the minimum because, if any Shudra cast his shadow on an Aryan, even unknowingly, he would be lynched right away for defiling the Aryan. The Aryan would then take a shower to rid himself of such contamination! Such extreme rules served to attach further social stigmas such as being "unclean" to the Shudras.

The Aryans loved life in their new colony. To protect their newfound wealth and lifestyle, they introduced another system, the 'gaunvkaria'.

In Goa, the Shudras, the owners of the land, suddenly became 'munddkars' overnight, tenants on their own land. The newly arrived Aryan Bamonnns and Chaddos became 'bhattkars', the big zamindars. The Brahmins, known as Bamonnns, and the Kshatriyas, some of whom later became Christian Chaddos, took over the entire village lands of Goa from Shudras and established the village co-operative and landlord system, the gaunvkaria or comunidade, and made themselves owners and members of this comunidade. Here it is not the true natives, but the non-native colonials who own the registered lands as 'gaunvkars', or the shareholders of the village community to the deliberate exclusion of the true village natives, the Shudras, whom the comunidade terms 'moradores', the settlers. Even today, only the Aryans, both Brahmin and Kshatriya caste members can become the gaunvkars of village Goa. To top it all, the Shudras who were the exploited workers toiling in the fields and plantations worked without any compensation, except for some nominal produce but the Aryans earned the right to claim the zonn or the dividends.

After de-franchising the Shudras, the Aryans divided the best fertile land amongst themselves and left the excess land to the gaunvkaria, but made sure that the Shudras were excluded from the membership of the gaunvkaria. No Dravidian Shudras had any right to property and were not gaunvkars as per the new Aryan order.

Each Aryan was given a slave family, who was given the task of tending to the newly acquired properties of his Aryan master. These slaves were their servants for life, bonded forever with no compensation, but were given some minimum produce for their sustenance. The entire workforce involved in the gaunkaria came from the unpaid slave Shudra community.

Thus was born a new country called Bharat, later called India by the rest of the world. The conquerors changed all old names and gave Sanskrit names to all places, rivers, lakes, mountains and roads. Five percent of the population of Bharat controlled ninety-five per cent Shudra population then and the same holds true even today. The Vedic Aryans devised all kinds of inhumane systems, to guarantee their lifelong retention of prosperity and property in their new colony. They expected complete reverence and loyalty and respect from Shudras, but never gave them anything in return.

Over the ages, the Shudras were programmed to believe they were the servant class or the subjugated class meant to serve the godly Aryans forever.

It is amazing how there was not even one uprising of Shudras against the tyranny of the cruel upper castes for 5000 years. There have been revolutions throughout the history against tyranny in the rest of the world, but the Shudras in India suffered this slavery and suppression passively. And worse, they adhered to the religion that perpetrated their caste inferiority to such an extent that they were ready to worship the very gods that they were told would not allow them inside their sanctum sanctorum. Would any Shudra in his right mind get converted to such a religion except under duress?

The natives of Australia and Canada have native rights and privileges because the white Europeans signed treaties with them. But in India, the Aryans never bothered about such treaties with native Shudras and made the whole country theirs. Not even the United Nations can reinstate native rights of the Shudras because the people who rule India today are themselves the progeny of that Aryan race which wants to continue with the status quo.

Eventually down the history, some Shudras were used and abused by the invading Moguls who again forced them to build their monuments, roads, and palaces. Some of the Shudras got converted to the Muslim faith, as they abhorred being low caste Hindus. Eventually the Portuguese arrived in Goa and their missionaries offered these Shudras a new kind of hope, wherein they could lose their caste and become equals in the eyes of God by converting to Christianity.

Well, five centuries later, they still remained the low caste members and untouchables even within the Catholic Church in Goa, for the hierarchy of Bishops and Archbishops of the Archdiocese of Goa, were either Brahmins or Chaddos.

Valerian Cardinal Gracias was the sole exception. Young Valerian Gracias, an exceptional Shudra, grew up in Karachi, Pakistan during the British Raj. He became a priest at Kandy in Ceylon and got his doctorate in Rome. He got such an opportunity because the retiring English Archbishop of Bombay, whom he had served well as Secretary recommended him as his replacement. This was possible only outside the control of the Archdiocese of Goa.

The Saraswat Brahmins of Goa are proud to declare that they originally came from the region around the Saraswati River somewhere near Punjab. When the Saraswati River dried up, they migrated and settled in Goa. There is even a legend that says Lord Parshuram brought them to Goa. Whatever the version, every one knows that the Saraswat Bamonns definitely migrated to Goa during that drought and that they could not have taken anything with them to Goa. But we find that when they settled in Goa, all of them became rich landowners. How was this possible?

When the Saraswats (along with their Kshatriya fighting compatriots) arrived in Goa there were already all kinds of indigenous people living in Goa, such as Velips, Gauddis, Kunbis and Shudras. So the Kshatriya fighters either decimated the indigenous natives or they chased them away to the hills, taking over their fertile land.

Therefore, for the slogan, "Goa is for all Goans" to be true and just, all the original Shudra natives from Goa should have at least the same rights and privileges including the zonn, that all the other later immigrants and settlers, who call themselves gaunvkars today, have in Goa. Only then can Goa prosper in peace and harmony to remain the paradise on earth that nature intended it to be.

VIVA GOA!

*** *END* ***

Linda read this article with interest and later commended Dr BJ for his scholarly, deductive and unbiased article. At least now, she understood how the caste system and *gaunvkar* systems came into existence. And if it was really so, then the interest alone on the properties confiscated from them by the Aryans would amount to huge sums of money. The irony was that most of the Shudras did not even own a home or a piece of land. It was shameful.

She hoped the United Nations would take a genuine look at this issue and see if anything could be done to restore these rights to the poor landless Shudras. But for her part, Linda would not wait for anyone else to help her make it; she would stand on her own feet and struggle hard to live the best life she could on this earth. She would not rely on any handouts.

Chapter 16

In June of 1956, Linda started the *Primeiro Ano do Liceu*, the first year of the Portuguese Lyceum, in a private school in Cuncolim, run by Professor Quennim, a Hindu teacher who specialized in giving private tuition classes for the primary school students. Professor Quennim prepared the Lyceum students for the public examinations in the *Segundo Ano*, the second year of Lyceum. There were eleven other students from the surrounding villages, Linda being the lone female student.

Linda bought a *pasta* or a leather bag to carry her books and other equipment. Now that she was in high school, she was very busy with her advanced studies in science, geography and mathematics. She also began to learn French, which was a little different but still close to Portuguese. If she did not know a word in French, she would use a Portuguese word and add *e* to it to make it look like French.

As Linda and her mother were on their way to an early Mass one Sunday, Linda saw a dead body in the ditch off the main road just in front of the Chapel of the Martyrs at Tollebhatt. The man's nose was encrusted with blood and he must have died the night before. He was from Kulwaddo and known to drink a lot. He probably fell into the ditch while walking home. It was a terrible sight to see. The man had a wife and a daughter. They were quite well off and had lot of property in the village.

Linda finished her first year of high school in the summer of 1957. She loved the summer in Goa because there were a lot of fruits, especially several varieties of mangoes available – *mancurado, alfonso, furtado, mergulhão, musrado, fernandinho, ambi, bolo, etc.* Her mother used to buy a dozen of the *musrado* mangoes and store them in the big *baann*, a big earthen container, and cover it with straw, which helped them ripen faster. When there were plenty of mangoes, her mother would make *mangada*, mango jam using lot of sugar.

Linda liked jackfruit too. They had a tree in their backyard. The jackfruit was huge, with a spiky skin and number of fleshy segments oozing sticky latex. The boys used this white sticky substance, called *punk*, to catch birds like parrots and canaries. They wrapped the sticky substance around a long bamboo stick and left it hanging out like the branch of a tree. The birds would perch on it, mistaking it for a branch and get stuck. Then the boys would catch the helpless creatures and put them in a cage and sell them.

Linda loved the succulent soft jackfruit variety that she could suck rather than the harder variety that had to be masticated well. Her mother made *sattam*, a sweet made out of the jackfruit using sugar. The seeds from the fleshy part of the jackfruit, called *biknnam* could be eaten boiled or roasted.

Linda relished the cashew nuts and the succulent cashew fruit. The green tender cashew nuts were easy to slit open, but left abrasive acid marks on the skin of the hands. Teachers would punish students with such marks on their hands. The cashew nuts when mature had hard shells, which had to be roasted before you could break them open and eat the nut inside.

The succulent cashew fruit with the cashew nut at its lower end, is very fleshy and contains juice used by distillers to make *caju fenni*, a potent and popular liquor of Goa, stronger than coconut *fenni*. You can smell the aroma of *caju fenni* from afar.

Rowdy boys filled their plastic guns with the cashew juice or the juice from a banana tree trunk, to spray on unsuspecting young girls. This left permanent stains on their blouses. These pranks were typical of the three days of Carnival.

In summer, most of the English-speaking Bombay Goans came to Goa to spend their holidays. They bossed over the resident Goans, and thought themselves superior to them. Their attitude was similar to the Portuguese-speaking Goans. They thought the local Goans were uncivilized and poor and had no class.

There were other reasons why Linda loved summer. There were feasts of the Holy Cross all over the village. Each ward or community celebrated this feast. They celebrated the *maddi*, the nine days of *novena* with a *ladainha* every night; and a mass on the final feast day.

As summer went by, Linda started her *Segundo Ano do Liceu*, the second year of high school. She studied hard as there were public examinations that would be conducted in Panjim. Soon the monsoon arrived, followed by Natal, the Christmas holidays. Her mother made *vhodde* and *kulkul*, the Goan Christmas sweets. Linda made a crib out of bamboo wood and straw and grew some 'grass' from germinated cereal around it. She placed two small light bulbs inside the crib, connected them by wires to two batteries and lit the inside of the crib. She arranged Joseph, Mary and the Baby Jesus in the manger and decorated the house for Christmas.

Soon they brought in the New Year of 1958. In April, her final examinations were due. Her father also was due to come to Goa after working two long years on board. He promised Linda a trip to Bombay in April, if she did well in her *Segundo Ano* final examinations. He wrote that Linda's godparents in Bombay wanted to see Linda very badly after all these years. Linda looked forward to visiting Bombay and her godparents.

Linda worked hard at school and finally April of 1958 arrived. Her father came home on April 1, April Fool's day. Linda thought her mother was just fooling her, when she said that her father had arrived outside in a taxi, but it was true!

"Hello Papa! How have you been?" Linda hugged him.

"I am fine darling. How is my princess?" Her Papa kissed her.

When he came in, Linda immediately opened his trunks, which smelled of foreign scents. One was full of toffees, cookies, chocolates and clothes for her along with saris for her mother, and some shirts and dresses for her cousins. The other, had cans of condensed milk, sardines, mackerel, salmon, corned beef, Kraft Cheese and Maggi bouillon cubes, together with lots of bars of soap, Intimate perfume, Cutex and lipstick.

Linda did not sleep that night. She talked incessantly to her father finishing all the toffees in a single day. She did not know her mother had already hidden two bags of toffees elsewhere, before she could get her hands on them.

A week later, the local parish priest invited Mário to a meeting of the members of the upper caste fraternity to give a speech about certain reforms that were required. Mario had earlier indicated his willingness to speak on this issue after his daughter told him of her bitter experience at the church. By this time, most of the churches in Goa had equal rights for the lower caste Shudras, except in Cuncolim.

Mário proposed the enactment of new rules whereby Shudras would be able to carry the Statue of Jesus Christ carrying the Cross during the procession on Good Friday, be able to wear the red *opa murça* (opmus) and be able to celebrate the feast of the patron saint just like the upper caste people.

Mário gave a fiery speech about the need for all people of Cuncolim to have equal rights in church affairs.

"In today's world, where people all over the world are demanding equal rights, why should we, in Cuncolim, not open our eyes and make appropriate changes in our thinking, and behaviour, especially in our church affairs?

"God created man in His own image. We all pray to *Our Father* in the same way. Shudras don't say *Their Father*!

"Why can't you, respected members, just for a minute, put yourself in my shoes and imagine the hurt that you would feel if you witnessed this injustice and lack of dignity inflicted on your people instead? Is my flesh and body any different than yours? Is my blood any less red than yours? Do you not breathe the same air and drink the same water? After we die, don't we all share the same worm infested earth in the cemetery? Did Jesus say Shudras could not carry His Statue during the procession? Did Our Lady of Health say Shudras could not celebrate her feast, the feast of the patron saint? Don't we all know that Jesus Christ himself could be a Shudra, being the son of a carpenter, a worker by your definition?

"This caste issue is all man-made. There are no Shudras, no Chaddos and no Brahmins in America, Europe, Africa or Australia or in heaven or in hell. I have travelled the world over. I have never seen caste discrimination among the same people of one nation, except here. If Cardinal Gracias, who is a Shudra, came to the Cuncolim Church, would you not accord him a welcome he deserves?

"So what is wrong in giving us equality in the church? What are you afraid of? Just close your eyes and think it over and answer the questions of your conscience. We are only asking for equality. This is 1958, America and Russia are getting all set with their rockets and satellites to explore and venture into outer space and we in Cuncolim still live in our prehistoric cocoon. It is up to you to open your eyes and face up to reality in our village. Let us all act as true children of one God. Let all Shudras be full members of the fraternity. Equality is the most urgent need of this community if it is to prosper and live in peace!"

There was a dead silence when Mário finished his speech. There was a cold response to his proposal from all members, who were all upper caste Chaddos. Only the priests applauded. Mário could see anger and disbelief in the eyes of everyone present at the meeting. There were no Shudras present at the meeting, except Mário.

That night, while they were sleeping, they were rudely awakened by loud noises from outside. Dogs barked loudly in the background. Someone banged on the front door violently and stones were thrown at the house. Linda was scared for her life. Mário lit the *divo*.

"This must be the result of the speech I gave today at the church." Mário said.

"Mário, please don't get involved with church politics any more. It does not help anyone. They will never accept equality. So why fight for it? I don't want you to get involved in the caste business in the church. We need to live in peace. It's just not worth it. This is not America. No one else fights for our rights, so why should you take all the risk, and for what purpose?" Joanita begged Mário to stop. Mario relented.

The next morning Linda opened their front door and she saw cow dung sprinkled all over the door and something scribbled on a piece of paper stuck on the door "A good Shudra is a dead Shudra. If you talk garbage, you are dead, Mário. Dead! Beware!"

The next two weeks went by fast and Linda was all set for her public examinations. Her father Mário took Linda to Panjim. This time, they found a place to stay easily. They went straight to Dona Lucia Borges at Fontainhas and were given accommodation immediately. The next day Linda went to the *Liceu* Complex at Altinho for her examinations. The students at the *Liceu* still had the same attitude towards the village people. But Linda did not care about them. She even saw a few faces that she had seen two years ago when she had come to Panjim for her *Admissão* examinations.

She went to check the location of her examination room on the notice board and then went straight to the examination hall. She went in, closed her eyes and prayed to Our Lady to help her perform well in the examination. This helped to calm her. She took out her pen, pencil, *burracha* (eraser) and the compass set, and waited for the examiner to hand out the question paper. She found the written examination relatively easy and was glad it was over. She knew she had done well, except for mathematics where she did not have time to complete the last problem.

After the results came in, she saw her name in the distinction category and she was again exempted from the oral examinations. She then went to the Admissions office to register for the third year of *Liceu* in Panjim. Linda and her father went to Miramar and then to Dona Paula to celebrate and to make the best use of the time there.

"Did you know, Linda, that a noble lady by the name of Dona Paula jumped from this big rock as she could not get married to the man she loved, called Gaspar Dias? This place is named after Dona Paula. And what's known as Miramar is actually the Gaspar Dias beach."

"Papa, Is this really true or just a legend?"

"I really don't know. It could be a legend."

From the top of the rock of Dona Paula, Linda could see the port of Mormugao and the city of Vasco de Gama on the other side of river Zuari. Linda could also see the Paço Cabo, the residence of the *Governador Geral de Goa*. Then they went to the main city of Panjim and shopped around. Linda did not see any Goan Hindus in Panjim, wearing a traditional dhoti and a cap, except the grocery shopkeepers in the bazaar area.

The next day, they went to the government office to apply for the *bilhete de identidade*, the travel document Linda needed to travel to Bombay, India. They already had the necessary documents and passport size photos and there was no problem whatsoever. Their *bilhete* would be ready in two weeks. The next day, they went back to Cuncolim, their mission accomplished.

Chapter 17

About three weeks after her examinations, Linda and her father set out on their journey to Bombay. They went by bus from Cuncolim to Pollem, the Southern border of Goa. They could see nothing but trees and hills on the way, except a few houses in Chauri, the capital of Canacona district. When they reached the border at Pollem, they had to walk down a steep hillock and they made their way through the international border through the bushes to *União Indiana*, the Indian Territory.

They went through the Indian customs and boarded a bus to Sadashivgadd. Then they crossed a big river by a ferryboat to Karwar. They stayed in Karwar for the night with a friend. The next morning they took a bus to Hubli, where they took the Western railway train to Poona. On their way, they ate the curried chicken cooked by Joanita and threw the earthen container out of the running train.

Linda tried to look out the window, but she could not see much because the soot from the train's engine kept getting into her eyes. But she could see wide open never ending fields and farms, followed by small towns, hamlets and villages along the way. For the first time, she saw lambs and horses and fields of green beans, peas and lentils. She saw Belgaum, Jalgaon, Miraj and other towns on the way. The train sped along through the day and the night. Linda went to sleep and early next morning, she was awakened by shouts of *chai-chai, bhaji-bhaji, chickee-chickee.*

Linda's father was tired and was still fast asleep with his feet on the bench. During the night some street urchins had come on board the train. The compartment was crowded. It was hard to see who came in and who went out. The ticket collector never showed up. There were many passengers without tickets.

Linda was hungry by now. She wanted to brush her teeth and drink some *chau.* The train was coming to a halt at a small station. She nudged at her father's shoulder to wake him up.

"Good morning, Papa. Wake up?"

"What time is it, *baai*?" Mário woke up and looked at his watch. It was five o'clock in the morning. "What would you like, *baai*?"

"Some *chau* and *bhaji-puri*, Papa." Linda replied.

Linda's father got up and bent down to put his shoes on. But he could not find the shoes. He bent down again and looked under the seat bench. There were no shoes.

"Oh no, my shoes are gone. Those gypsy children who came on the train last night must have stolen my shoes." Mário said exasperated.

Poor Mário had to walk without shoes. They ate their *bhaji-puri* and drank tea. At about eight a.m. they reached Poona, where they had to switch to an electric train. Poona was a huge railway junction, just like Hubli and Miraj. They had to walk about half a mile crossing overhead bridges before they reached the platform for their onward journey to Bombay.

Then her father asked Linda to solve a puzzle.

"Tell me *baai*, if the train from Poona is going west, but the wind is blowing towards the east, which way will the train's smoke travel?"

As Linda was shrewd, she knew this was not a question of resultant force or direction. Without hesitating, she said, "Papa, electric trains don't give out smoke."

The travel from Poona to Bombay was not too boring, as there were lot of villages and towns in between, with lots of houses, buildings and factories along the way.

Finally at noon, they arrived at the V.T. (Victoria Terminus) Station in

Bombay. Linda was impressed with the city of Bombay. She was awed by the architecture of the V.T. Station and the buildings outside, the Boribunder G.P.O (General Post Office) Building, The Times Of India Building, the Bombay Municipal Corporation, Flora Fountain, and the Fort area buildings. Since Linda's father had no shoes, they took a taxicab and headed straight to the Principal Club of Cuncolim building at 9/11 Dukerwaddi at Chira Bazaar, on Girgaum Road via St. Xavier's College.

Once inside the club, Mário introduced Linda to his friends. They relaxed after he borrowed some slippers from a friend and ordered the usual *kheema*, mince meat and tea from the Irani shop at the corner. In the evening they took a horse-drawn carriage to the house of Linda's *padrinho*, Luciano Sousa at Marine Lines, where Linda was to stay for the duration of her holidays in Bombay.

They knocked on the door and rang the bell of the apartment. Linda's *padrinho*, Luciano opened the door and his wife Flávia came running to the door.

"Oh my God, how big have you grown, my little *filhada*, Linda?" Luciano held his godchild and hugged her.

Linda just blushed and smiled a lot, feeling shy.

"Nice to see you Linda. Welcome to Bombay." Flávia said hugging her.

After the hugging and the pleasantries, everyone sat down on the sofa. Linda's *padrinho*, Luciano was very happy to have her and so also his wife, Flávia. She served them Bombay's scented tea, cake and biscuits. Flávia poured some hot water with cold water in a bucket for Linda's bath. She gave her a towel and a new soap.

Linda felt very relaxed after the warm bath. She noticed the rooms in Bombay were small compared to those in Goa. After a long conversation and making sure Linda was quite comfortable now, Linda's father decided to leave.

"She is all yours now Luciano, at least for the next couple of weeks. Take good care of her, I am going back to the club." Mário hugged Linda before bidding goodbye to Luciano and Flávia.

"You have to stay for dinner, *Irmão*. You can't leave now!" Flávia protested to Mário. It was the Goan custom to ask someone to stay for a meal, whether you meant it or not. But Flávia really meant it.

"Thanks, but I have to go now, I have to go to the shipping office tomorrow."

"But it's only six o'clock, we can have our dinner early, at eight, then you can go back to the club." Flávia persuaded him.

"Come on, *coompar*. Linda is here, stay with her on her first day" added Luciano.

"Okay, if you insist, I will stay for dinner. Who can pass up Flávia's tasty cooking?"

After the dinner of basmati rice and *recheiad* pomfret, Mário hugged Linda, bid goodbye and headed for the club. Flávia washed the dishes, and made up a bed for Linda and talked with her for some time before they went to sleep.

Luciano and Flávia had everything but a child of their own, even after trying for over ten years. They made novenas at Mount Mary's Church at Bandra and burned candles at the famous Cross Maidan. They saw the best doctors and did all kind of tests, but to no avail. They had no children, who could inherit their wealth. And wealth they had in plenty.

When he first came to Bombay, Luciano worked for Royal Crispy Biscuits Company, a prestigious firm in Bombay. He worked hard and diligently and his salary went up regularly. Soon Luciano became a supervisor. He developed good contacts outside the Goan community. He had friends who worked for L.I.C. (Life Insurance Corporation of India) and the Bombay Municipal Corporation and had great influence there. He also knew the local politicians.

Luciano was looking to make some extra money. He did not have to look far. The Congress government of Morarji Desai imposed prohibition .in Bombay in the early fifties, which made distilling and selling of liquor illegal in Bombay.

Luciano took advantage of this and since his family of toddy-tappers in Goa had a centuries-old tradition of distilling *fenni*, he started a small cottage industry of distilling alcohol. But even before the first client could taste his liquor, the local policeman sniffed him out and walked in to register his first *hafta*, the payoff.

After that, the sale of liquor was overlooked by the policeman, who got his quota of the *hafta*. There was no shortage of clients in Bombay. Soon everybody came to Dhobitalao at Luciano's place for *desi* country liquor.

The news of this new establishment spread far and wide throughout South Bombay. Soon Bombay's VIPs came to this watering hole. This list included politicians, lawyers, doctors and rich merchants. With this new income, Luciano bought a two-bedroom apartment with a roof garden in Marine Lines just near the Metro Cinema. This is where he lived now.

There he entertained only elite clients at an exorbitant price. It was very private and safe. They hired a cook directly from Goa to cook *xacuti, sorpotel, vindalho, booch*, Goa sausages and other Goan specialties for these special clients. Everybody was satisfied with this arrangement. Among his clientele were some big shots from the Seamen's Tarvotti Union, Bombay Municipal Corporation, the L.I.C. and some members of the Bombay Gymkhana. And he used them to his advantage. He got jobs for many Goan boys on board the ships and in big companies in Bombay using his influence.

But he still had his old *kottrie* in old Dhobitalao, where he employed an assistant to distil and sell liquor. Luciano also had genuine *fenni* smuggled in from Goa. His assistant also made lot of money from his percentage on the sales. Luciano did not mind, as money was coming in plenty. He was not overly ambitious. He did not want to expand the business and he did not want to be involved deeper in crime. He never had a case of anyone dying from drinking his liquor. He made lot of money from his wealthy clientele at Marine Lines rather than from his Dhobitalao regulars, who paid a little more than the cost and *hafta* for the liquor.

Now that Luciano was a big shot in his own right and a philanthropist, the Goan community approached him for many favours. This included the Goan soccer league, Goan Dance committee, the Catholic community, Goan freedom fighters, Goan municipal politicians, and widows of seamen. He even met personally, the Mayor of Bombay and the Archbishop of Bombay.

He obtained a licence as contractor for Goan *Teatros*. Luciano got involved with the Goan Konkani *Teatro,* produced many plays and promoted aspiring new Goan actors and singers. He brought Konkani *Teatro* groups from Goa to Bombay. This way he was able to launder his illicit liquor revenues into a legitimate business.

Some people became jealous of him and Luciano found out that some Goans he had trusted the most, became his worst enemies. He received word from Goa that he was blacklisted and declared *persona non grata* by the Portuguese, as they found out he had helped finance the Goan Freedom Movement in Bombay. Luciano decided there and then, that he had had enough, abruptly terminated his illegal liquor distilling business and became a legitimate contractor for Goan *Teatro* business, devoting his time to Goan causes. He had his own Goan soccer team, Salcete 11 playing at Cross Maidan in Bombay.

Even though Mário did not approve of Luciano's illegal liquor business, he respected the man and gave him credit for his business acumen and popularity in the community. By now Luciano had bought two flats, one in Bandra and the other in Mahim and rented them both. For the rest of his lifetime, Luciano would not have to worry about money.

If only Luciano could visit Goa! He had been too busy before, building his empire. Now that he had ample time and money to visit his homeland, the Portuguese blacklisted him and he could not get permission to enter Goa. And that is why he had invited Linda to Bombay, since he could not visit her in Goa. He was particularly sad that he could not visit his ailing mother.

Luciano had not seen Linda for over twelve years now, since she was a baby. A lot of things had changed in his life since. He was a young man with no dreams then and now he was a man with power and respect. And he had no child. And this godchild of his, Linda, was a brilliant student and would surely be on her way up to the higher echelons of the Goan Portuguese society, when she finished her Lyceum in a few years. He would help her as much as he could. But her father, that idealistic *compadre* of his, Mário would not have anything to do with what he called his ill-gotten and illicit money. So Luciano decided he would take Linda around in Bombay and show her the best and worst of the city.

The next morning Luciano took Linda in his Ambassador car through Princess Street and made a left turn towards Marine Drive. He showed her the big beautiful flats on Marine Drive and drove all the way to Nariman Point. They got a picturesque view of Marine Drive, Chowpatty and Malabar Hill.

Luciano then parked his car and they went to a posh restaurant, The Gaylords where they had a chicken *tandoori*. Linda never tasted a *tandoori* chicken before. It was very tender and delicious. She remembered the time in Panjim, where she had to use a fork and knife to eat. Here in this fancy restaurant, how could she eat the big chicken leg? Luciano told her to use her hands. A smartly dressed waiter saw and helped her out.

After the lovely lunch at Gaylords, Luciano drove her around to Churchgate then turned left towards the University of Bombay at Fort. They went inside and Linda was astonished. It was a magnificent building with various departments. They went to the biology laboratories, where she could see students dissecting frogs, cockroaches and earthworms and use microscopes. Next they went to the chemistry laboratories, where they could smell strange odours and see various colours of precipitates in the test tubes.

They walked to the Convocation Hall and Linda was surprised to see Luciano's name on the list of donors to the University on a brass plaque on the wall. Linda was very proud of her Godfather. A man who had no University education had donated a lot of money to the University to help those with high aspirations.

Next day, Luciano took Linda and his wife Flávia to *Rannie Bag*, and Linda was excited to see the Botanical Gardens and the Zoo and ride on the elephant and camel. She saw many stuffed animals and birds and the whale. At night they took in a Konkani *Teatro* starring Prem Kumar. It was a marvellously decorated *Teatro* stage with different scenes on a revolving stage and projections on the screen. The play had a moralistic story and beautiful songs.

The actresses were real women, not some cross-dressed man like Remmie Colaço or Nelson Afonso as in Goa. This was the time, when Goan actresses like Mohana, Ophelia, Antoneta, Filomena, Betty, Jessie and others dared to come on stage and revolutionize Konkani *Teatro*. She heard the terrific voice of Alfred Rose and she saw the brilliant acting of C Alvares and Prem Kumar and the comedy of M Boyer and Souza Ferrão, the fast songs of Young Menezes and Kid Boxer. Linda met them all after the performance backstage and she had them sign her autograph.

The day after, Luciano took Linda to the Gateway of India at Fort. Later he took her to Apollo Bunder to see a friend, who was the Chief Steward on a big ship, which was anchored on dry dock there. Linda saw a huge ocean going cargo ship for the first time and she loved it. They had a sumptuous lunch at the saloon, where she had her favourite barbecue chicken and soft drinks. The Goan waiters were pleased to serve her.

The following day Luciano took her to Malabar Hill to see the Big Shoe and Old Mother Hubbard. The view from there was just magnificent. The crescent of Marine Drive, the ant-like visitors on the sands of Chowpatty and the tall buildings of Bombay held her in awe. Then they went to Chowpatty, where Linda ate the famous Bombay *bhelpuri* and drank the bottled yellow sweet cold milk from Aarey Milk Colony. Then they went to the Taraporewalla Aquarium and Linda saw various kinds of fish in huge tanks. At Back Bay, Linda drank coconut water and ate the green coconut and barbecued corn laced with spiced lemon.

After taking rest for a whole day, Luciano took Linda to the Museum in Fort and after that they visited the celebrated Jehangir Art Gallery. Then Luciano took her to Collaba Causeway and she saw the historical RC Church and drove by Sachivalaya, the provincial parliament of the State of Maharashtra.

It was dusk when they headed for the Taj Mahal Hotel in Bombay. For Linda this was the climax of her visit to Bombay. What elegance and luxury inside! They proceeded towards the Restaurant. When she saw the prices on the menu just for coffee, Linda wanted to get out of there, but Luciano held her there and they ordered some food. The waiters, elegantly dressed like in some Maharajah's court, were very courteous to Linda and she had a great time with her Godfather who mixed with the rich *lakhpotis* of Bombay.

The next day, Linda went with her aunt Flávia for an evening walk through Dhobitalao. They went to the Bastani Parsi Restaurant to taste their famous pudding. And just to compare and sample Bastani's rival, they went to Kyani's on the other side of the Girgaum Road. They loved the puddings from both restaurants equally with slight preference for Bastani. Just before sunset they went for a walk along Marine Lines and took in the fresh breeze at Back Bay. At night they went to the Metro Cinema to see *Ben Hur* and Linda never saw such a beautiful movie in her life before.

In Bombay, Linda accomplished many firsts in her short stay. She was really in seventh heaven by now.

Luciano had just bought his first 'Sony' transistor radio. They tuned in to Goa Radio, *Emissora de Goa*. Linda listened to the Portuguese program and translated it for them in Konkani. Later there was a program of Konkani *Teatro* by Jacinto Vaz. They listened to the play and songs and this brought back to them old memories of Goa. They also listened to Goa news.

Next day, Flávia took Linda to Crawford Market. There she saw lots of live chicken, ready to be killed and sold, and Alfonso mangoes and vegetables for sale. After shopping they went to the Badshah Restaurant for a fresh cold glass of *falooda* and mango juice.

On Sunday Luciano and Flávia took Linda to Mount Mary's Church in Bandra for Mass, where Linda met many Goans but did not know any one. Luciano introduced her to his many friends. The girls spoke only English, which Linda did not understand at the time.

After the Mass, they went to the bungalow of a Goan professor in Bandra. They had a display cabinet with figurines and a big library. But Linda could not understand English. She saw just one book by Jules Verne in French. Professor Saldanha had a grand piano and his wife played it for them. They had a three-year-old child Schubert and a maid who did the cooking and baby-sitting.

Linda picked up a few Hindustani words while in Bombay, but she couldn't read the Hindi Devanagri script. It was too difficult for her. A neighbour in Bombay, Shilpa Khorgaunvkar was teaching her the basics of Devanagri script. She learnt to write numbers up to ten as they were quite familiar and the primary vowels a, aa i, ii, u, uu, ye, ai, oh, au, am, aaa. She learned to write the shape of number 3 and modify it to derive various sounds from it. She now vaguely recollected Marathi phrases such as *"Xri Ganesha, O Nama ha, Ye Sarasvati, Namana tujea podok mati"* that the Marathi *shalla* students chanted while walking in front of her house years ago.

Shilpa took Linda to see Hindi movies like *Chaudvim ka Chand* and *Mother India* and Linda loved them both. She had never seen Hindi movies before. Linda loved the evocative sound of the Indian sitar instrument and the sentimental sound of a flute. Although the Indian music was different from Portuguese music, it had a soothing effect on her.

Her last visit was to see Ranno Fonddekar, a Hindu friend of the family from Navelim, who lived in Girgaum, Bombay. He had passed Matriculation in Marathi and was working in Sachivalaya in Bombay. Linda took her friend Shilpa Khorgaumkar with her to see Ranno Fonddekar, who was very pleased to see Linda after about five years. And to her surprise, Shilpa Korgaumkar fell in love with Ranno Fonddekar. Linda was honoured to be the go-between *soirikarn*.

Soon it was time to go back to Goa having spent three weeks in Bombay. Linda had to prepare herself for her school life in the Higher Secondary Lyceum at Altinho in Panjim. She had to arrange for accommodation and many other things. This time, she wanted to go to Goa by steamer. Her father Mário, who lived in the Club in Bombay all this time, had his medical examination done and was interviewed for a new job on another ship. He had finished his business in Bombay, had got an offer and had to join in a month. So he decided to go back to Goa with Linda. Luciano and Flávia came to see them off at Bombay's Mazagaon Dock.

Luciano gave Linda a copy of *The Goa Times*, a Konkani weekly published from Bombay by Dr Simon Fernandes, so she could read something on board the ship to pass time.

"Thank you very much, *Padrinho* and *Madrinha* for such a lovely time in Bombay. I will never forget this," Linda hugged them both.

"We will feel lonely without you, Linda, please do come back again," pleaded Flávia hugging Linda.

"Don't forget to write to your godfather, Linda." Luciano hugged her for the last time and both he and Flávia were close to tears.

Linda also felt very sad and her heart felt empty.

"I won't forget to write you ... *Adeus Padrinho e Madrinha*." Linda bid them goodbye and walked away to board the ship along with her father.

The passenger ship was the *Sabarmati* and it was not a big ship like she had just visited in Bombay. The crew were selling coupons for food. Linda was given a plate of rice and curry on a large *tatt*, a platter with a small quantity of pickle and a sardine. There was a game of bingo in progress on board.

Music played on a loud speaker for the entertainment of the travellers. The sea voyage was boring, with nothing but miles and miles of water to see. Linda decided she would never again travel by ship. She wondered how her father spent two years at a time at sea.

Linda opened up *The Goa Times* and pored over its contents. Suddenly her eyes brightened as she saw her father's name in there.

"Daddy, your article is in here, look!"

"Oh that one. I had submitted it a while back. They must have just published it now. Please don't tell mummy about it."

Linda started reading the article. It was about his demand for caste equality in church affairs with special emphasis on the discrimination of Shudras in the Cuncolim Church.

Linda liked the interesting article and she read about some of the leaders of the American Civil Rights Movement. She felt very proud of her father for being part of this social activism.

"Daddy, who is this Martin Luther King Jr, you mentioned in your article?"

"Linda, Mr King is a university-educated, black American preacher, who is fighting for equality for blacks in America together with some other brave men like Mr. Abernathy. One day I am sure they will succeed in their struggle. Martin Luther King Jr is also a fan of Mahatma Gandhi and believes in non-violence."

"What do you do on a ship with your time, Papa?" Linda asked her father changing the subject.

"I am very busy planning the menu of the day, making arrangements for all kinds of dishes and drinks. I supervise the workers in the saloon such as the cooks who prepare the food, the waiters who serve the food, the barmen who serve the drinks, the pantry staff who take care of canned foods and processed food, the cleaners and laundrymen who keep the saloon clean and neat. I have to sort out all the complaints and problems of the workers. It is a job with a lot of responsibility. I also do the accounting, make sure everybody works as per schedule, buy food and other supplies in bulk and store them, check the quality of food and make sure the crew is fed well and on time so everybody is happy."

"That sounds interesting but it is lot of work and responsibility. What else do you do to pass your time, Papa?"

"Oh I write lyrics and music for my own songs. You remember my song 'On the Moon'. I am going to send it to America for recording. Maybe, we will get rich someday."

"Oh I hope so too, Papa. I would love to go to America."

"The rest of the time I practice on my musical instruments and if I have more time I read *Teach Yourself* books in French, Algebra, Music and Song Writing."

While her father explained to her what he did on board the ship, Linda fell asleep. Next morning she could see Ratnagiri on the coastline followed by Devgadd, Vengurla and other smaller ports. People got off at these ports, by disembarking into small canoes. The ship could not touch these ports, as the sea was shallow there.

The Sabarmati passed by Goa through the international waters. Indian ships were not allowed into Portuguese territory, as diplomatic relations between India and Portugal were broken. *The Sabarmati* steamed slowly towards the South of Goa and anchored at Karwar. From there the passengers boarded the canoes and reached ashore.

From Karwar, they crossed the river to Sadashivgadd and then boarded a bus to the Goa border in Pollem. They went through the customs at the border, boarded a bus to Margão and finally reached Cuncolim, tired and haggard. They went home, where her mother prepared a nice hot bath and lunch. They relaxed, ate and went straight to bed.

Next day, the first thing Linda did was to write a letter of thanks to her godparents in Bombay. It took Linda the next five days to describe and relate all her adventures in Bombay to her mother. The part her mother loved most was the hilarious story of her father's shoeless odyssey to Bombay.

Chapter 18

Linda was quite tall in her fourteenth year and had grown into a beautiful girl. It was the first week of June 1958, time to go back to school. She had made all preparations to go and live in the city of Panjim for higher studies. Friends advised her to cut her long hair short; they said she would look smarter, but Linda declined. She would never change her looks. She liked the way she was, a simple and humble village girl with natural looks, whose only objective in going to the big city was to pursue higher education.

Linda had bought some dresses, a scarf and a pair of Bata shoes during her trip to Bombay. A local tailor had sewn a few more dresses for her during her vacation. She packed them all in a trunk together with other necessities of life in a boarding school. Her name was pasted on the trunk to identify it. She had packed a new toothbrush and paste, even though she had never used them before as she always brushed her teeth with charcoal from fireplace. Just in case, she also packed a fork and a spoon. These too, she had never used at home, as she ate food using her right hand out of a brass plate like everyone else in the village.

A priest from the local parish who knew a nun in Panjim had arranged for Linda's accommodation at *Instituto Piedade* in Panjim. Nuns ran this up-scale boarding school for young women, who studied in Panjim. Most of these boarders belonged to elite Goan and Portuguese families. Linda was lucky to have been admitted there, solely on a recommendation by the village priest; otherwise it would have been near impossible to get accommodation for her in Panjim.

Linda's mother Joanita was thankful that her daughter would be under the protective wings of the nuns, who monitored the boarders and raised them in a strict Christian discipline. Linda was excited and looked forward to the day she would be in Panjim. She liked Panjim from her previous visits. Now she would live there at least for the rest of her academic life.

Linda was in two minds. She was curious to venture into the big city on her own. At the same time having lived most of her sheltered life with her mother in the village, she was hesitant to leave her alone. Her father too had gone back to work on board the ship. This was the first time her mother would be left all alone. Normally both of them would hug each other and cry whenever they were alone during the long absence of her father.

Linda was emotional and sensitive. She was also very understanding, cheerful and with a great sense of humour. She cared about people, especially the poor and the helpless. Intelligent and humble, she was curious about everything that went on in the world. She loved her parents dearly and had been taught by them to respect everyone, especially teachers, priests, nuns and the elderly. She knew right from wrong and easily forgave people for their faults, but she could never forget one incident that had affected her deeply. That incident in the church had turned her little world upside down and it was the single most important reason for her fervent desire to take up any challenge.

She wasn't going to show the other cheek to that woman or anyone else while she was alive. It was precisely because her forefathers showed the other cheek for too long that they were oppressed in their little village, and deprived of their rights and dignity. Of this she was sure, she would be rebellious if needed to attain her objective of getting respect and dignity from others. No one could stop her.

It was a Herculean task to achieve it. She would start gradually. And the easiest way to do it right now was excelling in the only thing she knew she was capable of – higher education. Linda had only one ambition in life – to be one of the best. She had to show the world she could do it. She had no immediate role model in mind. She had no access to radio, library books, newspapers or anything else to have decided on anyone to emulate. But she knew she wanted to be the best in her school and had chosen the best school there was in whole of Goa – the *Liceu Nacional Afonso de Albuquerque* in Panjim.

This would mean staying away from her mother, who would be all alone in the house. But Linda decided she had to go through with it.

Linda didn't sleep most of the night before she had to leave, thinking about this. Suddenly she heard the distant village church bell pealing. It must have been six o'clock in the morning. She kissed her mother lightly and got up. Her mother heard her and woke up too. The early birds began chirping.

Her mother said a short prayer, lit the kerosene *divo* with her matchbox kept in an old tin. She made a fire with dry coconut leaves and some wood. Then she went to the well and fetched some water, which was quite warm in the morning fresh air. She fed the pigs and the chicks. Linda brushed her teeth with charcoal from the fireplace and rinsed her mouth with the well water. Her mother made nice hot tea in her black aluminium kettle. They had their breakfast with black tea and *bhakri* and *kanknnam*. Both went through their usual routine like it was any other day. Linda began the last minute preparations for her long trip to Panjim.

The night before, they had cried and hugged and slept the whole night holding each other. The pillows were wet with secret tears they had hidden from each other.

At about ten, Linda's cousins arrived to see her off. Linda went to all the neighbours to personally bid farewell to them and ask them to take care of her mother in her absence. Linda arranged with Saudina, a girl next door to come and keep her mother company every night. She had previously arranged for porter Miguel to carry her trunk to the bus stand. Miguel arrived right on time.

When he was a handsome young man, Miguel Costa was in love with a beautiful young girl. But she left him to marry a young man who worked in East Africa. Since that day, poor Miguel was heart-broken. He gave up his job on board the ship, went crazy with grief, talked to himself all the time, swore at nobody in particular and took to drinking. He became the village idiot.

He had nobody to look after him and was now fifty years old. He had to take a porter's job and run errands for people in the village to make ends meet. He would do odd jobs and visit people in their homes uninvited. They would then offer him some food and *fenni* especially on feast days or other celebrations. Linda always treated him well.

Just before noon, Joanita served lunch to everyone including Miguel. After the lunch Linda was ready to leave. Mother and daughter started to cry. They prayed for the last time in front of the oratory and hugged each other for what seemed to be an eternity.

"Mama I am leaving now, will you be okay?" Linda's heart sank as she said these words.

"I'll be fine. Take care of yourself, *baai*." Her mother said wiping her tears. Joanita never called Linda by name; she was always her little baby, her *baai*.

Linda stepped out of the house and started walking, then from a distance she looked back waving at her mother, who did the same. Her tears could not be contained.

Ahead of her, Miguel carried the heavy metal trunk on his head, supported by a thick weight-absorbing ring of old rugs wrapped together to form a cushion, muttering something to himself. They both walked about four kilometres to the bus stand, Linda waving to all neighbours on her way.

"*Borem korun rau baai,*" everyone waved back, asking her to take good care of herself.

Joanita did not want to create a scene at the bus stand, so she stayed back home. Parting was always so sad. Joanita never stopped crying for the remainder of the day and she had to take sleeping pills to get some sleep that night.

Linda on the other hand sat on an old Ford *carreira* bus, which would take her to Margão. Her luggage was placed on top of the rack of the *carreira* along with loads of baskets of fish, liquor carboys and other heavy goods to be transported to Margão. On the way Linda was pensive, thinking about how lonely her mother would be after she left, how she would cry and worry about her all the time. She must be missing her already. Linda had left her mother alone when she had gone on her trip to Bombay for three weeks as a sort of preparation. She hoped that it had prepared her at least a little, though of course this was for much longer.

When Linda reached Margão, she changed to a *Marlim* bus going to Cortalim. Once she reached Cortalim, she asked a porter to carry her trunk to the ferryboat while she bought a ticket. She ran as fast as she could, as the ferryboat was about to leave with her trunk and she had to hop and jump to it after paying the porter, before the hatch closed and the heavy ropes were untied.

On the ferryboat, which was locally called *gasolina*, she relaxed holding on to the railing behind a car. A cool breeze blew from the big river. She saw a framed picture of St. Francis Xavier on top of the engine room and the name of the ferryboat was *Salvador do Mundo*, 'Saviour of the World'. The ferryboat was swinging wildly from side to side, as the big river was rough. Linda was scared and prayed to the Saviour to preserve her from any calamity. Linda got splashed with saltwater spray. While she was still daydreaming, they crossed the big Zuari River and reached the other side at Agaçaim.

Before the ferryboat landed, the motorcyclists and car drivers started their vehicles and off they went. Linda got her trunk transferred to the Panjim bus. When an hour later, she reached the Panjim bus stand, she hired a porter again to carry her trunk. She walked with him along the bank of River Mandovi on Rua Dom Afonso de Albuquerque all the way past the *Palacio* to the *Instituto Piedade* just before the Hotel Mandovi.

When she entered the *Instituto Piedade*, Linda felt very uncomfortable for the first time. Her mood changed completely. Everybody was speaking in fluent Portuguese, including the servants. A nun passed by her and did not even seem to notice Linda standing there. Linda felt very hurt. She waited for what seemed to be an eternity, before a nun finally came up. Linda at once stood up and smiled.

"Hello Sister, I am Linda Cardoso from Cuncolim," Linda introduced herself.

"Hello Linda, I am Sister Augusta. Welcome to *Instituto Piedade*. We were expecting you." Sister Augusta rang for a boy to carry Linda's trunk to her dormitory. Then she took Linda to her office and had her sign a few papers and told Linda to relax and make herself comfortable. The nun said she would see her later to brief her on the rules and regulations of the house. She rang the bell again and a maid walked in.

"Rosa Maria, take Linda around and show her the bed in the dormitory. I hope you enjoy your stay here, Linda," the nun said as she left.

Rosa Maria and Linda walked out of the office.

"*Baai*, I am RozMari. I work here, you can ask me anything about this place," said the girl by way of introduction.

"Hello RozMari, I am Linda from Cuncolim."

Linda was very happy to talk to someone in her native language, Konkani. Linda soon made friends with Rosa Maria. Both of them really got to know each other. The servant girl said she helped the cook, made beds, and did laundry and other chores at the boarding house. Rosa Maria explained to Linda the time schedules in the boarding house - the time to get up, pray and the timings for meals.

Rosa Maria also explained to Linda the etiquette of fine dining, the proper use of spoons, fork and knife, how to tilt the bowl of soup when eating and what plates to use for what and how to pass dishes around.

"*Baai*, be careful about some of the girls here. Don't mess around with them. They come from some of the illustrious families in Goa. They have great influence in high places. One little slip from you and you will be out the door and out of Panjim altogether," Rosa Maria cautioned.

"Thanks RozMari. I will take note of that. Thanks for your advice."

At suppertime, all boarders were sitting around a huge line of tables in the big dining room. There were white Europeans, Indian Goans and *mestiços*, of mixed race. Linda was the only village girl in the hostel among these sophisticated girls and she looked out of place. She was very nervous, lonely and very uncomfortable. Linda noticed that none of the other girls looked in her direction. It was just like the time she was at the *Liceu* at Altinho, when she went there for her *Admissão* examinations two years ago. She felt they treated her as if she had the plague. She felt like running back to her mother, that very moment.

When the Mother Superior came in, everybody stood up and started a prayer in Portuguese. Linda did not know the prayers in Portuguese, except the words like "*Pai Nosso*", "*Santa Maria*" Our Father and Hail Mary. She did not know what followed. So she just did lip-synching and said "Amen". Linda always said prayers in her mother tongue, Konkani.

After the prayers, the Mother Superior introduced herself, other nuns and the staff at the Institute and asked all the girls to introduce themselves. Linda almost died when she heard this. When her turn came to introduce herself, she meekly stood up and said: "Linda Cardoso." It was barely audible in that large dining room.

"*Deva Saiba*! Thank God, one hurdle is out of the way," She mumbled to herself and wiped the sweat off her brow.

Now, the problem of how to begin eating the supper! Rosa Maria had explained to her the formalities of dining, but when she saw those plates on the table, turned upside down, she was nervous again. Rosa Maria had not explained that. What was going on? She just waited and waited till someone started to eat first. Her hands were shaking under the table. Finally from the corner of her eyes she saw them having soup first. She did the same. She was unable to even taste the soup as she was so preoccupied with this rite of eating right.

She remembered to tilt the bowl of soup at the end. From the corner of her eyes, she observed them turning up the inverted plate for the second course and she did likewise. Linda noticed a nun with a faint smiling expression on her face, looking at her. Could the nun see her predicament, she wondered.

When supper was finally over, Linda's trepidation subsided gradually and she retired to her place in the dormitory to sit on her bed. During the entire supper, no one talked to her, not even the girls next to her on either side. That was so rude and mean, she thought.

Later that night before going to bed, they recited the rosary. Linda decided that by next day or two she had to learn at least the complete 'Our Father' and 'Hail Mary' in Portuguese as each girl took a turn to say a decade. She said her prayers in Konkani in silence and went to bed.

That first night was a real test for her. This was the first time she slept on a bed alone without her mother. She had to be positive, or she couldn't function normally. All her dreams would be shattered. But she had no control over her feelings or thoughts at this moment. She remained awake for three hours thinking and wishing she were at home in the village. She heard some girls groan and some even talked in their sleep in Portuguese, but Linda could not sleep, even though she was dead tired. She prayed and prayed again but still she could not concentrate. Insecurity haunted her until her eyes closed and she eventually fell asleep.

That night Linda dreamt about her mother in Cuncolim and awoke next morning to the strange sound of the morning bell in the uncomfortable surroundings of the *Instituto Piedade* at Panjim.

Chapter 19

Linda got up in the morning, said her prayers, brushed her teeth, changed, had her breakfast and was ready to go to the Lyceum for the registration and the orientation. The Lyceum complex was about four kilometres from her hostel. She walked past the Municipal Garden, passed by the Imaculada Conceição Church and walked up the steep steps of *Liceu Nacional Afonso de Albuquerque.*

Here again she was alone, alienated among the sea of foreigners. The few Goan students there, turned out even worse than the white foreigners. They never once smiled at her or attempted to make her feel at home. How could there be such insensitive people in her own land who could treat their own kind like this, she thought. Linda felt awful. Back home in her neighbourhood she was like a princess, everybody treated her with respect. And here, in Panjim, she felt like an untouchable.

Inwardly Linda resolved to concentrate her energies on her goal of achieving a very good education rather than wasting her time on such useless emotions. Linda finished the paperwork in the registration office, obtained the classroom number and timetable, attended the orientation class and went straight back to the hostel. In the afternoon, she went for a walk along the whitewashed walled bank of the river Mandovi.

At a glance, Linda seemed to be a young girl of medium height, with a beautiful round face, a slightly long nose, large brown eyes, with long jet black hair doused with coconut oil and combed into two braids. She sat on a bench near the wharf. She wore unfashionable clothes, a simple blue skirt and a white cotton blouse and a pair of slippers. She wore no make-up. No one looked at her twice. It was almost as if she didn't exist. She was a non-entity – just another fresh arrival in the big city.

The big majestic river Mandovi ran through the city of Panjim, the capital of India Portuguesa, the Portuguese empire in India; a city lined with Mediterranean style stately homes with white and yellow stucco walls and brown tiles, low buildings, narrow cobbled roads, quaint little boutiques and small alleys. The tallest building was the five storied Hotel Mandovi, fifty yards from where Linda stood.

It was still very hot in Panjim and the monsoon had not set in yet, but Linda felt the cool breeze coming from the river. On the other side of the river to the north, she saw the hill of Betim with lush vegetation and a lighthouse on top. The Betim hill continued towards the estuary of the river to the west, where the sun was setting over Fort Aguada at its westernmost point. And just below the Fort, there was the infamous Aguada Jail, and a little closer she saw the Church of Reis Magos. To her east she could almost see the distant island of Divar, and Ribandar.

Despite the unfriendliness of the people in the city, Linda admired the beauty of Panjim. Presently she saw a barge slowly moving towards the Arabian Sea on its way to the Port of Murmugão with its cargo of iron ore, mined from the hills of North Goa bound for the refineries of Japan.

Linda closed her eyes to imagine how the *caravelles* of Afonso de Albuquerque, must have sailed through this same river as he conquered Goa in 1510, changing the history of this territory. She visualized hordes of Portuguese missionaries navigating the river at about the same time in search of new converts to Christianity in this land.

Linda suddenly came out of her reverie to face reality. Everyone around, except the river, was hostile to her in Panjim. As soon as she had come to Panjim the day before, she had felt unwelcome there. Now she had to go back to that unfriendly hostel. And how would she fare at the first day of school at the *Liceu* tomorrow? These thoughts made her even more uncomfortable. Except for Rosa Maria, Sister Augusta and the registration clerk at the *Liceu*, Linda had not been spoken to by anyone in the city of Panjim for the last twenty-four hours. Wasn't that amazing?

Linda admired the serenity of the river. It was very quiet there, except for the sound of the lashing waves. She felt very close to the river. She felt she could communicate with it, its waves and the cool breeze coming from it. She would disclose all her inner feelings to this mighty river. Amidst the deadly enemies of Panjim, Linda had found an ally.

"Oh River, can I be your friend?"

Linda's whispered words mingled with the cool breeze and the currents in the river.

"I feel so lonely out here. Oh River will you be my friend?"

And immediately she saw a huge rush of waves coming toward her as if the answer was a resounding "Yes". Linda was strangely thrilled as if she had just found a secret friend and she wheeled around in a full circle with excitement. Nature had just accorded her a big welcome. Linda had communed with River Mandovi.

When Linda first found out she was a Shudra, she was determined to overcome that stigma. She did not want to revolve like a satellite around upper caste stars. She wanted to break out of that orbit, never to return to that kind of life. Thousands of years of subservient life had to end. Now was the time for a new and modern order. It was 1958 and she was on her own. It was time to begin breaking free of those shackles.

She had already laid the foundation for this. She was probably the first one from her caste in her village to achieve 19 out of 20 *optimo* marks in her primary school *Segundo Grau* examination and was the first one to have finished the Second Year of Lyceum. Now she was one of the very few from her caste to have obtained admission to the prestigious school of higher learning in all of Goa, the *Liceu* Nacional Afonso de Albuquerque in Panjim. She had to build up on that.

But she had to make some changes in her life first: learn to be thick skinned, learn to speak the Portuguese language fluently and memorize her Portuguese prayers. She had what it took. And she had a great companion to talk to, to whom she could bare her soul – the mighty River Mandovi.

                              ❦◈◈◈❦

Chapter 20

The next day was the first day of school in her Third Year Course at the Lyceum. Linda sat at a desk in the middle of the second row of her classroom. The classes started and the professor welcomed everyone and explained the curriculum and the schedule of the lectures, the practical classes, the tests and the final examinations. He also prescribed some textbooks and other material and he gave them names and locations of stores where those were available.

The first day was a light one, with various professors giving a brief orientation of their courses. By the end of the day the students had introduced themselves to the class in front of their professors. When the school day got over, a shy male student looked at Linda and smiled and Linda smiled back at him. Then he came over to where she was.

"Hello, my name is Rama Naique," he said.

"My name is Linda Cardoso," replied Linda.

"This is my first year at the *Liceu*. Are you also new here?" Rama continued.

"Yes Rama. I am really glad to meet you. I don't know a soul here. Everyone makes me so uncomfortable here. So far you are the only one to talk to me." Linda sighed, relieved that she was no longer alone.

"Don't worry sister, *não é problema*. If we Goans do not help each other, who will?" Rama reassured her.

Both of them instantly became friends. Linda's foreboding disappeared. Very soon they knew a lot about each other. She learnt that Rama Naique was a Hindu Goan from Paroda, a village in South Goa near Quepem and that he had finished his second year Lyceum at Quepem. Like

Linda, he did not speak fluent Portuguese. But both of them had something in common, a will to study hard. They both decided to speak only in Portuguese to get more practice.

They went down the steps of the *Liceu* and walked towards the Livraria Singbal bookstore, where they bought a few books as most were out of stock already. Then they went to Café Tato for some *boje*, *samosas* and tea. Linda felt quite comfortable, as she was no longer alone. Rama was a nice young man and very helpful. All her fears disappeared and she felt she could concentrate on the one thing she came here for, her education. Rama was like a Guardian Angel sent by God. Now she had one more friend in Panjim.

Very soon Linda got used to the rigours of the boarding house and the *Liceu*. She gradually adapted to city life in Panjim. She decided to work hard on her oral Portuguese. And why not? Even the servant Rosa Maria, the cook and other servants could speak Portuguese fluently, even though it was *Tambddi Purtugues*, red Portuguese. It took only a few weeks for Linda to imitate the European accent and master the spoken Portuguese language.

Linda memorized the prayers in Portuguese and took an active part in the rosary. But the girls at the *Instituto* still did not mix freely with her. Even the nuns seemed not to care too much about Linda. That was all right with Linda, she had RozMari to talk to. And who really cared about these rich obnoxious Goan Portuguese pretenders? Linda had time only for studies.

Linda however liked the food very much at *Instituto* Piedade. It was not the typical Goan fare like rice and curry and *pez*. The food was supposed to be pure Portuguese. But the cook, Terezinha was a pure Goan and she could not forget her Goan proclivities for spices and vinegar. She had a superb touch. Her hands could make any dish taste heavenly. Her Goa sausages fried with eggs and potato fries had a divine taste. The *caldo* was tasty and the meat always cooked with a sour and spicy punch to it similar to the pork *chouriço* meat. The breakfast with bread and butter and the afternoon tea with Kraft cheese and cream crackers were Linda's favourites.

But her father had to pay dearly for these. The monthly fee for food and boarding were exorbitant and that is why only the rich got admitted here. But for Mário Cardoso, his daughter Linda was like a princess and therefore he grudged her nothing. He wanted her to have an education he never had.

Since this was her first year in the city, the lifestyle was quite different for Linda and so too the system but she concentrated fully on her studies. After the initial culture shock, Linda adapted to the changes in the ways, customs, etiquette and environment. Her perseverance always paid off.

English was one of the subjects in her Third Year Course and it was quite easy for her. She had picked up certain words while holidaying in Bombay. All she had to master was the grammar and formation of sentences. The rest was easy. Many English words were derived from Latin, so all she had to do was to change the last few letters *ção* to *tion* e.g. *salvação* to salvation and so on. The English grammar was even easier than Portuguese, with verbs like 'eat' -'I eat, you eat, he eats, we eat, you eat, they eat'. In Portuguese the verb changed every time, like - *Eu como, tu comes, ele come, nos comemos, vos comeis, eles comem.*

The rest of the subjects like *matematica, ciências* were getting harder. But she had a great tutor in Rama Naique, who when approached by Linda for help with these difficulties, would only say – *"Não é problema, senhorita"*. Linda would help Rama in English and in Portuguese as he still had difficulty in spoken Portuguese. Both of them again agreed to speak only Portuguese so Rama could improve. But Rama would make her laugh by speaking in a half-Portuguese half-Konkani lingo, all mixed up like the *mix bhaji* they ate at Café Tato after school.

Chapter 21

After the first term examinations were over, Linda went home for her vacation. She had not seen her mother for about five months. But she had written to her regularly. When Linda arrived home with porter Miguel carrying her handbag, the front door was closed. Linda gave Miguel some money and he left.

Linda knocked on the door, but no one answered the door. She figured her mother might have gone out shopping. Linda looked around to make sure no one looked her way, climbed up the *balcão* seat, reached over the beam on the pillar and took out the big iron *chavi*, the key that they always kept hidden there, whenever they went out. She opened the front door with it.

An hour later, her mother came home and Linda went running to open the door for her.

"Oh Mama! How are you? I missed you so much." Linda hugged her mother tight.

"I am fine, *baai*. I missed you too."

"Mama, the whole place looks different here," Linda let go of her after about five minutes.

"You'll get used to it dear. Now you relax. I am going to heat some water for you. You take a bath first. The towel and your change of clothes are in the bathroom."

Linda ran to the back yard. She missed the guava tree and the custard apple tree. She climbed the guava tree and picked the best guavas from it and ate them right away. She was hungry and really loved guavas, with tiny ants running all over them. Then her mother came and gave her some bananas and ripe *antonam*, custard apples, which she had stored in the big earthen pot for ripening.

Linda went to the well and drew water with a copper pot using a rope over the pulley. She fed the chicken and the pigs. Oh how she loved village life! Nature had its own order of things, free from man-made restrictions. She heard the birds chirping on a mango tree nearby. Coconuts hung from atop, a lizard lazily climbed up the kitchen wall and crows cawed on the roof. Nature took its own sweet time here. She ran to the tamarind tree behind her house, and chewed and tasted the sweet and sour tamarinds, and later she sucked lazily on the hard seeds inside them, the *chinchare*.

"*Baai*, when did you come?" She heard a voice calling out to her in front of the house. It was her neighbour.

"Just now, auntie," Linda shouted back.

Oh what a comfortable little place, this village was. With all its shortcomings, it was very dear to her heart. As she came home with Miguel, every one had greeted her along the way. How wonderful this sense of belonging and being cared for!

"Mama, have you received a letter from Papa lately?"

"No *baai*, not for a month or so."

"The letter will arrive today then for sure, Mama. You know what they say when the crow caws on the roof."

"Hope so, *baai*."

"Mama, what's for lunch today? Any *ranchar bangdde*, (stuffed mackerels) today?"

"Better than that, *baai*. I brought your favourite *mannkio*, (squids) for you."

"Ooooh Mama, you are so nice. I just love your cooking."

"*Baai*, those nuns, don't they give you anything tasty to eat in Panjim?"

"Oh Mama, they have nice Portuguese food there, but nothing like our *xit koddi*. I love our hot Goan food the best."

"*Baai*, you better take your hot bath first and change. I'll get the food ready in the meantime."

It took Linda a long time to recite all stories of her life in Panjim to her mother. Linda did write regularly to her mother and father. But she could not write everything on paper. Linda found it a little odd at first to revert to the village life. She ate with her hands again and was glad to taste her mother's rice and coconut curry and *recheiado* fish.

Many of the neighbours came to see Linda and queried her about life in Panjim. How were those *pacle*, the whites in Panjim? Did the police beat her up? Could she show them how she spoke Portuguese like that *Professora*? Did she use lipstick? All these questions drove Linda nuts.

"Did you see my cousin Aleixinho Rodrigues from Betul?" Filomena, her neighbour asked her.

"No auntie. I don't know him."

"He also studies at *Liceu* in Panjim and stays at Lar dos Estudantes in Panjim as a boarder."

"Well auntie, I'll look him up the next time I go to Panjim," Linda assured her.

Linda enjoyed her three weeks of vacation in Cuncolim. One day her grandmother from Navelim visited her. Her grandmother, Angelina a.k.a. Carmina was very proud of her granddaughter. No one from their family or from her village had ever set foot in Panjim, except the landlord *bhattkar's* family.

"*Baai*, our *bhattkar's* son also is studying in Panjim. Do you know him?" Her grandmother asked.

"Navelim mãe, I don't care about any *bhattkar's* son or daughter. I will not have anything to do with these so called illustrious Goans in Panjim and I don't want to get humiliated again with their condescending attitude." Linda said, her disdain for all Goan Portuguese pretenders in Panjim very obvious.

Linda went back to Panjim after her vacation. When the first term results were declared, Linda scored highest marks in all subjects, except in *matematica*, where Rama scored the highest. The name Linda Cardoso was on top of the list of successful candidates for the Third Year Course on the notice board of the *Liceu* building.

On the first day of the second term, when classes resumed, everyone was in class and the Science teacher, Professor Estevão Ribeiro entered and took the attendance and said he had an announcement to make.

"Would Linda Cardoso please come up to the podium?" he said.

Linda got up from her desk and proceeded to the podium.

"It gives me a great pleasure to introduce to you the brightest student in our class. Boys and girls, I present to you Linda Cardoso."

The entire class clapped their hands in unison. Until that time, no one bothered to take notice of Linda or try to know her. They had no idea she would be the best student in the class. After the class, everybody congratulated her on her success. The first one to congratulate her was, of course, her friend Rama Naique. All those students, who distanced themselves from Linda and had avoided her like the plague, were suddenly swarming around her and wanted to strike up conversation with her.

When these students came to know Linda better, they respected her and treated her as their own. But Linda did not let this go to her head, she always remained the same as before and people liked her more because of that. Linda now felt great and confident of her abilities. She left all her misgivings behind and quickly forgot the past.

News of Linda's success at the *Liceu* reached the *Instituto* Piedade. The boarders and nuns congratulated Linda and all those boorish Goan Portuguese girls made an about turn. Many of them approached Linda for help with their studies, even the senior students.

But her success did not distract Linda or make her easy-going. She did not change but concentrated just as much. She became the favourite of nuns and students. Now, the students even introduced Linda to their illustrious parents from Benaulim, Curtorim, Loutolim, Vasco de Gama, Mapusa and Aldona when they visited the *Instituto*.

Linda soon made a new friend at *Instituto* Piedade. So far, she was quite lonesome at the hostel with no real close friends. This girl, was quite fair skinned, and always had a smile on her face.

"Hi, I am Heidi. Pleased to meet you." The new girl introduced herself to Linda.

"I am Linda." she said as they shook hands.

They both had a long conversation and pretty soon found out a lot of things about each other. Heidi was a year senior to Linda. Heidi became Linda's confidante.

Heidi Werner was of mixed parentage, a Eurasian girl, whose father was Gunther Werner, a German and her mother was Rosy Costa from Vasco de Gama, Goa. Heidi was a fair complexioned beautiful girl, who was a loner, as she was neither a full-blooded Goan nor a German. Her father was interned during the World War II at Mormugão Harbour in Goa, where the German ship he worked for, was stationed. He was already married in Germany, but he was in Goa for over three years where he had met Heidi's mother at Vasco and they had a baby girl, Heidi. After the war, Gunther left for Germany, but he kept sending money for Heidi and her mother.

Nobody socialized with Heidi. She kept to herself, almost a recluse. No one at the hostel liked her or talked to her, except Linda, who empathized with her and made friends with her. Linda trusted her completely.

Heidi's mother played upon the solitude of Gunther Werner, Heidi's father and blackmailed him to extract money out of him. Her mother had a brother, Robert who was a smuggler and a pimp. Robert went to Bombay and smuggled Goan goods to India and he was a Portuguese spy in Bombay. That's why he could easily elude the Portuguese customs and have his way. He was also a double agent spying for India, by smuggling out maps of Portuguese sites in Goa and handing them to the Indian authorities. The entire Costa family lacked integrity. They were a bunch that made lots of money, but were never happy or popular. They were suffering from what the locals termed as *pessão* or *birmoti* for what their ancestors did to people by cheating them.

No wonder people looked down on Heidi and her mother in Vasco. They knew the whole story unlike innocent, naive Linda. Heidi felt very lonesome without her father, who regularly sent money to her mother for her sustenance. Heidi's mother was a high-class prostitute from Baina, Vasco and Heidi hated this. So Heidi stayed in Panjim even during the summer holidays. Heidi's mom used to come in a chauffeur-driven car every now and then to see Heidi.

One day as Linda was sitting in her classroom at interval time a boy came up to her. He had a nice young lady with him.

"Senhorita Linda?" The young man said.

"Yes? Senhor, can I help you?"

"Hi, allow me to introduce myself. I am Alfredo Monserrati from Navelim, your grandmother knows my father. Congratulations on your success at the examinations Linda!"

"Oh yes, Senhor Monserrati. I heard so much about you. Thank you.

It was very nice of you to come and see me."

"Linda, meet my girlfriend, Lucinda Gouveia."

"My pleasure Senhorita Lucinda." Linda shook hands with her.

"Likewise, Senhorita Linda."

Linda was taken aback by the visit. A great *bhattkar's* son came asking for her in her classroom. This guy must be something. And pretty Lucinda, the white Eurasian beauty was lucky to have him as her boyfriend. Linda was impressed with Alfredo. He was charming. She found him attractive. Too bad he was already taken. But then, on second thoughts, she knew she had no time for that kind of frivolous pursuit. She had an education to pursue!

Her thoughts were once again directed towards Alfredo. Linda was surprised that he did not seem to be proud at all. He was a nice, tall and handsome young man. Well mannered and friendly, Linda had to admit to herself, that there may be a few good illustrious Goans after all. Linda always respected and admired people of all backgrounds, regardless of their race, caste or creed, so long as they respected her for what she was.

She realized she could not blame all these people, as they did not know anything about her. At the same time, she blamed them for having preconceived ideas about her and for hurting her feelings, when she was quite new to Panjim. Inwardly she forgave everyone who gave her the harsh treatment.

Linda found the boy from Betul, Aleixinho Rodrigues her neighbour's cousin quite by chance. She heard someone call him by that name in the cantina. Linda looked at him and proceeded towards him.

"Are you Aleixinho Rodrigues from Baraddi, Betul?" Linda asked him.

"Yes I am, and who might you be?" Aleixinho was intrigued.

"I am Linda Cardoso from Cuncolim, a neighbour of your cousin, Filomena."

"Oh yes, the scholar. I am glad to meet you, Linda. I have heard of you but I did not know the face."

Aleixinho invited Linda to the Cafeteria for some coffee and they talked for a while.

"I live at Lar dos Estudantes and in my spare time I play soccer for Académica," said Aleixinho.

"I must come and see you play at Campal sometimes. I live at *Instituto Piedade*," added Linda.

"I must take leave now, it's time for practice. May be we will see each other again soon? Bye for now."

"Nice to have met you, Aleixinho. Keep in touch. *Até logo*."

Now Linda knew someone from her neighbouring village that she could talk to sometimes, if she had any problems. Of course Rama Naique was a still a close friend whom she could depend on.

Chapter 22

In December, Linda went home to Cuncolim for the *Natal*, Christmas holidays. Joanita was glad to see her daughter again. This time Linda did not find much difference, as by now she was used to both environments. Her mother had made *vhodde, neureo* and *sorpotel* especially for Christmas.

Linda decorated the *neketr*, the Christmas star with five corners made from bamboo sticks. Then she pasted coloured paper on it, and hung it up from the mango tree outside to be lit daily at night by placing a kerosene lamp inside it. She also arranged and decorated the manger.

Soon the Christmas holidays were over and the New Year arrived. Linda went back to Panjim. Now she was used to her routine. Days and then months passed by and finally Linda's final examinations arrived. She did well as usual and came home for the summer vacation. She relaxed for a week completely after the rigours of her final examinations.

Linda started organizing things. She had forgotten to write to her father for a while during her examinations. She wrote to him, and then realized she had not written to her godfather, Luciano. She wrote to him in English this time. She knew he would be happy to hear from her after a long time.

Linda's mother Joanita went to the seaside at Mobor, Cavelossim for her annual *mudança*, relaxation and rejuvenation. It was a tradition for middle-aged and older women to unwind by taking in some *vharem*, air and sun and salt-water baths, on the beaches of the Arabian Sea, which were supposed to have miraculous medical benefits for the body and soul. If Joanita did not make her annual pilgrimage to Mobor, her body would start aching and her legs would give her nagging pain for the rest of the year. So she was accorded this small annual seaside vacation luxury at Mobor.

Joanita would go there with a few of her women friends from the village. They would get up early in the morning, carry their belongings and food, go to Assolnã, cross the river Sal on a canoe and walk barefoot to Mobor. There they would put their belongings in any of the many huts available nearby. These huts, covered on top with a thatch of dry coconut leaves, gave shelter from the hot sun, and protection at night. There would · be some newly wedded couples too on their honeymoon in the private huts nearby.

They would go to the water on the beach and take dips in the sandy waters early in the morning and late in the evening. This area was dangerous, as there were a few drowning cases in this part of the beach. On Sunday, they would go to the little chapel nearby for Mass. They knew a few people who lived there, as they came here every year.

Most people who lived there were toddy-tappers, as there were numerous coconut groves all over the place belonging to a few *bhattkars*, who lived in towns or other villages. The toddy-tappers would lease the coconut trees from them and eke out a living, collecting the toddy from the coconut trees and distilling the local potent liquor, the *fenni*. There were also a few fisher folk around. Otherwise Mobor was a secluded place with no access to public transport or roads. But Joanita and friends always had a great time, especially at night. Under a moonlit sky with thousands of stars above, and with a cool refreshing breeze coming from the seaside, they would sing *mandde*, the folksongs of Goa, drink a little *fenni*, tell some stories and jokes, smoke *veedies*, enjoy the camp like environment and gossip about the people back home.

They would wake up early in the morning, make some fire and prepare some hot tea. Later they would prepare *pez, the canji,* for breakfast, which they would feast on with a few pieces of mango pickle. Some of them would drink the fresh toddy they would buy from the toddy-tappers or drink sweet water from the *arsoram*, the green raw coconuts. They would make some rice for lunch and supper. They would get fresh fish from the fishermen and barbecue sardines on a slow fire. They would warm the meat curry they had brought from home, eat and relax listening to the sounds of the waves crashing against the shore.

This was an all-woman gathering. Absolutely no men were allowed. The men were only too glad to get away from the constant badgering of their women folk, while the women loved this newfound independence at their yearly get-together away from their bossy men.

In the afternoon, they would lie down for a wonderful siesta and they would get sound and uninterrupted sleep with the undulating sound of the waves acting as a sweet lullaby. There were a lot of cashew trees nearby, they would pick the raw cashew nuts, roast them on a fire and break them up to eat the inner edible kernel. Sipping a little from the coconut *fenni* pint, they would get mildly intoxicated. This would make them feel a little high.

Young children were not allowed to go to Mobor for the *mudança*. So Linda went to visit her grandmother in Navelim instead. This was the time when her grandmother was busy in the paddy field, harvesting the rice crop. Linda visited the fields and it felt good to see the fruit of her grandmother's labour, the bumper crop of golden rice.

It was very peaceful out there, nothing but nature's simple wonders everywhere. A small river ran through the field. Little frogs and grasshoppers jumped about when Linda walked by. Out in the distance, Linda saw two men fishing on the bank of the river. She went to watch them.

"Hello Uncle, can I try fishing please?" Linda asked the older man.

"*Borem baai*. Take this rod and hold it here and don't move. If you get a pull, just yank the rod vertically up and back. Let's see what you can catch. Good luck *baai*." And the man went to smoke a *veedi*.

"Thank you, Uncle."

Linda held on to the fishing rod with a lot of excitement. After a while, she felt a small pull and then it stopped only to be followed by another greater pull and right then Linda yanked the rod high up to reveal a nice catch of a *pintoll*, a kind of mullet. Linda was very excited that she caught a fish for the first time in her life, but she felt pity for the poor fish.

At the end of the day, Linda and her grandmother came home. Linda ate the *ponnos*, the soft jackfruit and mangoes grown in her grandmother's huge orchard in the backyard. Later that night for the sumptuous dinner, Linda had rice and curry with *paró*, the dried and pickled fish, and mango pickle and delicious smelling *chouriços*, the sausages cooked with onion, potatoes and curry sauce.

Next morning, her grandmother made *bhakri*, a bread made of coconut and rice flour, covered with banana leaves and baked on a *koil*, a broken piece of a big earthen pot, kept on the tripod of a hot fireplace.

Linda loved the smell of freshly baked *bhakri*. Her grandmother opened her favourite can of Dutch Girl condensed milk, which Linda finished in a day. She could not control her habit of continuously tasting the sweet condensed milk with a spoon. Each time she would say it would be her last. But then she was tempted to have just a little more. Just like peanuts and sausages and pickle, the temptation for continuously eating such things was just too great for Linda. And her grandmother never said a word, unlike her mother who disciplined her. In the afternoon, her grandmother made *goddshem*, a sweet dessert made of rice and *godd*, molasses from sugarcane.

The next day, Linda got a surprise visit from the village *bhattkar*, Alfredo Monserrati's father.

"Oh! So this is your famous granddaughter, Carmine? What a beautiful piece of God's creation and what a brainy little child you have here!" The old man touched Linda's face and hair with his hand.

"Thank you Senhor Monserrati. You are very kind, like your son Senhor Alfredo," Linda said shyly.

"Yes, Alfred told me all about you, Linda. He said everyone in Panjim knows about you," continued the *bhattkar.*

Linda just gave him one of her sweet smiles.

"Bakar, it is a great honour for us that you came by. Thank you, Bakar." Carmine said to him.

"You are a very lucky woman Carmine, to be blessed with such a beautiful and intelligent grandchild. Good luck, Linda. Someday you will make your family very proud, very proud indeed. I just know it."

"Bakar, can I get you something to drink?" Carmine asked humbly.

"No Carmine, thanks for the offer. Can't stay longer. Just came to see your *morgada*."

And the *bhattkar* walked home with his familiar bamboo stick in his hand, glad that his one-time tenant's child had finally made it in the field of education.

Linda's grandmother was beside herself with joy. She must have been really blessed to have such a smart granddaughter, she thought. Generations of toddy tapping from the coconut trees of the *bhattkars* had finally paid off. She always hoped her future generations would rise to the highest level in society and claim what was rightfully theirs after slaving around for centuries; instead of forever climbing up coconut trees, three times a day, way up in the sky, come rain or shine or heavy winds. Carmine was proud of her grandchild.

After the summer vacation Linda went back to Panjim in June of 1959. Now she was in *Quarto Ano*, the fourth year of *Liceu*. The courses were getting heavier and she was becoming wiser and more mature. Rama and Linda would try to get together often and solve problems if they could, otherwise they would consult their professors. Linda did not take part in any public speaking activities or political discussions. She was basically shy and apolitical.

With liberation movements spreading throughout the world like wild fire, the impending independence of Goa in due course was a grim reality. This subject was the talk of the town especially on campus. Most students at the *Liceu* were against independence, but a few, who dared not discuss it openly, saw the writing on the wall, and knew it could be any time now.

The Mocidade Portuguesa (The Portuguese Youth Group) was very active in Goa and every male Liceista had to join this cadet group and take part in physical fitness exercises, camps, and social work, and attend functions on national days in full ceremonial regalia. Some were chosen to represent Goa in national festivities in Portugal.

The Portuguese Prime Minister Dr Antonio de Oliveira Salazar maintained that Goa was part of Portugal and not its colony, and that Goans were first class citizens of Portugal and as such he vowed never to cede Goa to India in his lifetime. The nursery rhymes in Portuguese carried the following propaganda:

O sangue que corre nas veias é Português
(The blood, which runs through our veins, is Portuguese)

O Papagaio, canta, berra.
(The parrot sings and shouts
Diz o Papagaio real 'Nossa Terra, Linda Terra é Filha de Portugal'
The parrot says: 'Our Land, A Beautiful Land, is the Daughter of Portugal)'

On the other side India would train the militants in guerrilla warfare. These trainees would infiltrate Goa at night at remote border points and mount raids on the Portuguese garrisons and police stations killing Portuguese police officers and Goan informants. Some of these freedom fighters would be caught and sent to the local Aguada jail or to jails in Portugal or Moçambique. Some would be deported to India.

News of these insurrections would fill the local newspapers everyday, but life in Panjim was free from these petty worries. Panjim was removed from these hostilities, which occurred mostly in outlying areas of Pernem,

Ponda, Cuncolim and other rural areas. But the local Portuguese Intelligence Police Agency special branch, P.I.D.E. (*Policia Internacional de Defesa do Estado*) would suspect anyone with links or sympathies to the freedom movement and any such person would be arrested and tried as a traitor.

Blacklisting and political witch-hunting were commonplace especially among the elite in the cities of Panjim, Margão, Vasco de Gama and Mapuça. These suspects were constantly watched and searched.

Aside from these political troubles, Goa enjoyed prosperity in the late fifties. The Portuguese treated all Goans equally, regardless of their caste, although they favoured the educated Catholic Brahmins more, because they acted as their agents and knew the Portuguese language fluently.

The Portuguese loved life in general and they loved Goa in particular with its nice weather, people and food. Although life was not as fast as in Portugal, Goa gave them peace, tranquillity, the best of service and happiness. They were the privileged people with many servants at their disposal. At the same time, the Portuguese treated these servants decently and rewarded them with monetary gifts.

There were a few isolated cases of Portuguese racism, but they were quite insignificant. Naturally they promoted and preferred Europeans to Goans and segregated themselves socially. But there were also a lot of mixed marriages especially among the educated Goans and Europeans.

The local people, except the genuine freedom fighters, did not mind the Portuguese troops, which were concentrated in strategic places like Navelim, Ponda, Cuncolim, Margão and Vasco da Gama. The military personnel did not harm the locals. In fact they socialized with them a lot. In the evenings you could see them riding the bikes and asking *"Cherum borem?"* (Is there a nice girl around?) Soon houses of ill repute cropped up all around these military establishments to satisfy the military personnel.

The locals also got good jobs as cleaners, gardeners and labourers in these establishments. The local economy also depended on the presence of these military establishments. The Portuguese military played soccer games with the local teams and socialized with Goans. Portuguese teams like Independente joined the Taça Goa Soccer League. At times, famous teams from Portugal like Sporting Lisbon and others came to Goa to play exhibition matches against Goa Selection.

Chapter 23

For Linda, life in Panjim was quite fast and exciting. She tried to keep up with it. New styles were in vogue. As she had long hair, she always wore a ponytail. She liked to wear skirts with a belt around her waist. Her father had brought her a nice watch and sunglasses the last time he was in Goa. She started to dress well and use light makeup. She even painted her nails with Cutex, and grew them. Life was going great for her and she was becoming very popular at the *Liceu*, though she was still a little shy.

On 11th of July 1959, Linda was sitting in her classroom attending a lecture, when there was a knock on the door and a peon walked in with a note. The professor took the note and read it.

"Linda Cardoso, there is someone looking for you outside," the professor announced.

Linda got out of the classroom and saw the young man from Betul, Aleixinho Rodrigues, waiting for her. Linda was confused and scared. This was unusual, she thought to herself, something must be wrong.

"Linda, I don't know how to say this. Come and sit on this bench here," he hesitated.

"What is it, Aleixinho? What has happened? Tell me please."

"Listen Linda, your dear Papa just passed away," Aleixinho held Linda by the shoulders and continued, "His ship capsized in the ocean and there are no survivors. Your Mama just received the telegram."

The shocking news of her father's death stunned Linda. She could not comprehend what was happening. Her mind started to spin around. She was petrified and could not believe it at first. She just stood there transfixed without a word. Then slowly it sank in – the terrible truth.

"Oh My God. Oh Papa, why Papa. Why?" Linda hid her face with both her hands and said nothing for a while. Aleixinho hugged her.

After about ten minutes Aleixinho took Linda to the *Instituto* to get her things and he took her home to Cuncolim.

Linda's mother could not contain her sorrow any more. She let out a shrill cry when she saw Linda and both of them hugged and cried their hearts out.

"*Baai*, what shall we do now?" Linda's mom cried and sighed.

"Don't worry Mama, it's going to be alright," Linda consoled her.

But Linda inwardly felt a pang in her heart. She wondered how they would ever be able to manage things now without her father, the sole breadwinner. What would become of them? Who would pay her fees at the *Instituto* in Panjim? Who would look after both of them? There was nobody at home now to give support and directions. All her plans would fall apart. Her aspirations would never bear any fruit now. All these negative thoughts dominated her mind and bothered Linda. She could not think clearly about anything for now.

Linda's mom, Joanita, was devastated and distraught by the loss of her husband. Now she was a widow for life. Her only true love had disappeared from the face of the earth. She would never ever be able to touch him, see him or hear him. How would she face the rest of her life without him, without his support and love? She knew she had to live on for her daughter's sake. But the future looked bleak.

She had waited for months and even years, for her husband's return from the ship whenever he was away; and then they had a great life together for short periods of time during his vacation. Those were the happiest moments of their life together. But now, she could not look forward to his return from the ship. She hoped the news was not true, that it was only a nightmare. But alas! Her husband had really left them for good. Her heart suddenly froze with cold realisation.

Mário had died at sea. His ship had sunk in the Indian Ocean near Karachi, Pakistan. There were no survivors. News of the disaster had just reached their Bombay office and they had wired a telegram to Goa.

Linda was thinking about the last few moments of her dear father just before he left them. What a catastrophic death in the bowels of the ocean with no possibility of a rescue in sight! All that suffocation and pain in that salty ocean water, with not even a chance to think about his family back home. Did her father really have to suffer a lot? She hoped not. This man had sacrificed his life, his family, his everything to make a decent living for his family and now he was gone for good. Linda would never see him again. That thought really hurt her and she lost consciousness for a few seconds. She remembered the happy times she had with him and the strong influence he had on her life. She knew she would miss him sorely. She prayed for the repose of his soul and hoped to meet him in life hereafter.

Relatives and friends came to the house to help and comfort both the mother and daughter. The neighbours brought some food for them. The neighbour, Saudina and Linda's cousin Irene came over to spend the night. Their little world, which had been growing gradually prosperous, had just fallen apart and crumbled to pieces. There was no immediate male left in the family to carry on the name of the Cardoso family. They spent the entire night talking about her father and how they would miss him forever.

The next day they received a telegram from Bombay. It was from Linda's godfather, Luciano. He said he would take care of things at the shipping office in Bombay. He would also settle her father's affairs. Linda was glad that her godfather was in Bombay to look after the formalities in the shipping office there. Two hours later, they received another telegram saying the body of her father had been found and that the body would be dispatched directly to Goa by plane from Karachi, Pakistan.

Arrangements were made with the church for the funeral. The next day, the body was brought from Dabolim airport and a quick funeral took place. They could not keep the coffin open for public display, as the body was starting to stink badly even though the body was well embalmed.

Linda and her mother broke down at their last sight of Mário before the coffin was closed. Just before the funeral, as per the local customs, a widow was supposed to break her glass bangles on the coffin of her husband, a custom descended from the old Hindu rite of Sati, when a woman whose husband died would jump into the funeral pyre and kill herself. Afonso de Albuquerque abolished this custom of Sati, when he conquered Goa in the sixteenth century. Joanita broke her glass bangles over the coffin of her husband, symbolizing that her happiness ended with his death.

The funeral was well attended considering it was at such a short notice. A live band was in attendance. A requiem mass was concelebrated in church by three priests. In the cemetery, Mário was lowered to his final resting place and Linda and her mother were the first to throw mud in his grave assisted by the Vicar. After the last respects and prayers, Linda and her mother went home weeping all the time.

More visitors, friends and relatives from other villages came to their home, when they heard the news. Dr B.J. Furtado walked in to pay his respects too at about 3 p.m. He could not be at the funeral as he was out of station. The doctor hugged Linda and her mother and he conveyed his deep sympathies to the family. Twelve minutes later, without any notice, three uniformed police officers arrived at Linda's house and knocked on her front door.

"Is Dr B.J. Furtado inside this house?" asked one of the officers.

Someone said yes.

And the next thing they knew, the officers had barged inside the house and found Dr. B.J. Furtado talking to Linda. They seized the doctor and beat him mercilessly in front of Linda and her mother without any respect for his rights or for the grieving family. There was a commotion in the house as everyone wondered what had happened. Then putting his hands behind him, they put a pair of handcuffs on him, treating him like a common criminal.

"You are under arrest, Dr B.J. Furtado. You are a traitor to the Nation!" Linda heard the sergeant say to the doctor. Then they took him away.

Linda just watched him leave quietly without saying a word. It was such a terrible incident, right after the death of her father. Dr BJ was like a second father to her. Now he was gone too. Who would give her comfort and advice that she needed so much during this worst time of her life? Linda was desperate and felt deep anguish for Dr BJ whom she loved and admired. It was evident Dr BJ would be sent to Aguada Jail without a trial. Linda prayed desperately but without hope for his release soon.

Later, Linda found out that the Portuguese police had ransacked Dr B.J. Furtado's house looking for secret papers. All they could find was a framed picture of Mahatma Gandhi and that was enough evidence for them to arrest and later prosecute the doctor. They took him to the police station after embarrassing him by beating him up in public for being a traitor to *Patria*, the fatherland, Portugal.

Linda discovered that Dr Furtado had been a freedom fighter. She already knew that he was a great disciple of Mahatma Gandhi, as he even showed her the picture of the Mahatma, hidden in his house. She also learnt that a student in his school had tipped the police that the doctor was a freedom fighter, and that the Portuguese government was sure to incarcerate the good doctor in Aguada jail. Linda mourned the fate of Dr B.J. Furtado, who was not only a great friend, but also an educator and a great inspiration in her own struggle for freedom.

On the night of the burial, Linda and her mother were rudely awakened by a loud banging noise on their front door. Who could this be at this time of the night, they wondered? They heard another banging noise from their window again a minute later. No this was deliberate, they figured, it was not coincidence. This reminded them of that night in April, when Linda's father had given that fiery speech at a meeting about caste equality in the church.

"Oh My God! Do they hate him even after death?" Linda cried out, fear gripping her heart yet again. Mother and daughter held each other tight and went back to bed fearing for their lives.

Early next morning at about 7 a.m., there was a knock on their front door. Linda woke up and opened the door. She saw the *sacristão*, standing with a policeman.

"Linda *baai*, you have to come with me to the church, the Padre Vigar wants to see you as soon as possible," said the sacristan.

"What is it *baai*?" her mother asked from the kitchen.

"I don't know what's going on any more, Mama. But I will be back soon." Linda changed her clothes fast and joined the sacristan in the police jeep.

Strange thoughts were going through her mind now, thinking of the strange sequence of events taking place after the burial. First it was Dr BJ, then, it was that loud banging noise on her door and window at night. Now what? Was there no end to their suffering? Help me God, she prayed.

Soon they reached the church and the jeep stopped just in front of the cemetery gate. Linda got off the jeep and she walked with the police and the sacristan towards a group of onlookers, standing in a circle holding their nose.

What was going on early in the morning, she wondered. When she was almost there, she saw a dead body tied to a cross. The dead body smelt real bad and she could hear flies zooming around. Everyone was holding their nose with fingers and handkerchief. She walked closer to the body through the crowd.

"Oh my God!" she exclaimed and almost passed out. The sacristan held her.

"Papa, Oh Papa! What did they do to you? Is there no peace for you even in death? What are they after? Are they not satisfied that you are dead? How cruel can people be? Is there no God who can see this tyranny? How could they defile a grave? Oh God! This is disgusting." Linda cried out loudly, as she came back to senses.

The Padre Vigar came and hugged her, "God bless you my child. God will help you. Have faith, God will take care of this."

Linda couldn't take it any more. She wept furiously, her eyes flooding with tears. Then she opened her eyes to read what was written on the placard. One line read, "A good Shudra is a dead Shudra". Another line below read, "This Shudra cannot be buried in our *gaunvkar* cemetery."

Linda figured this was the work of those *gaunvkar* Chaddos who could not face the truth in that passionate speech given by her father at that meeting on that April day in 1958.

"Linda, my child, I conferred with the *regedor* and the police. We have to bury your father back in that grave right now and the police will follow up with the case."

The policeman asked Linda to sign a statement. The Padre Vigar and the sacristan said the prayers in Latin and informally re-buried Mário in the same grave. Hopefully he would rest for good this time.

Linda returned home dejected and crying. When she reached home her mother asked what had happened.

"Mama, they desecrated Papa's grave and tied his body to a cross outside the cemetery gate. They wrote on a placard that my Shudra daddy does not deserve to be buried in their cemetery," Linda cried, angry and heartbroken.

Joanita could not believe her ears. She had no more tears left. They had all dried up. There was no point crying any more. They were both sick of these cruel and unbelievable incidents at the worst time of their lives.

A day or two went by, but nothing came out of the investigation by the police. The whole investigation was just a farce engineered by the local village *regedor*, who was a dyed-in-the-wool Chaddo *gaunvkar* himself.

Normally the Portuguese police always investigated all crimes and punished the culprits with corporal punishment. The police station was just behind the cemetery and the police patrolled the bazaar area daily throughout the night looking for freedom fighters. It was unbelievable that the Portuguese police never caught the culprits of this heinous crime.

The startling news did not even make it to any of the local newspapers in Goa. It was really well covered up all the way. That kind of efficiency always existed in the system.

Linda lost faith in the police, administration of justice and the church. They had all failed her. She felt degraded and humiliated once again in the same church for the same reason – her birth in the wrong caste. It infuriated her and made her bolder and stronger in her mission in life. She was determined to show the world her true calibre. Could she ever have a quiet life in this village with such cruel and tyrannical people around her, she wondered.

More days passed, but Linda still felt the hurt. She loved her father very much. He had done so much for her and she had not spent too much time with him, as he was on board the ship most of the time. But she relished those precious moments she spent with him in Panjim during her Admissão examinations and the time they went on a trip to Bombay together. She could always reflect on those times and feel closer to him at least in spirit.

After attending the seventh day Mass for the soul of her father, Linda went back to Panjim, wearing a black dress. Everyone sympathized with Linda. The nuns were a great help and consolation to her at this time. She went to the *Liceu*, and everyone could see that she was grieving.

"Hi Linda. I'm sorry about your father," Rama was the first to console her at the *Liceu*. "Is there anything I can do for you? I made notes for you while you were away," Rama continued.

"Thank you so much, Rama. I don't know what I would do without you. You are a great help – a real brother to me," Linda almost broke down again.

For the first month at least the hurt was still there. The sudden death of her father affected her a lot. She had missed one week's classes, but Rama was there to help her with notes and explanations and the teachers also cooperated.

After about two months, Linda recovered somewhat, and she decided to continue visiting her mother occasionally at least once a month to console her. Linda's mother felt good when Linda went to see her, but reverted to her cocoon, when Linda went back to Panjim.

On 5th October, Linda received a letter from her godfather Luciano. He wrote that the formalities had been taken care of in Bombay but there were some things pending at the shipping office. They had promised that they would attend to them as soon as possible and Linda and her mother would get some financial package from the company. In the meantime, Luciano undertook to pay for Linda's fees at the *Instituto* and the *Liceu*.

Linda felt comfortable when she got that assurance from her godfather. She knew he would do his best to get the best settlement for them from the ship's management. But her mother would have to go to Bombay to sign the papers. Now Linda thought of nothing but working harder at her studies. The mid-term came in December and she did well in her examinations.

She went home for holidays but they did not celebrate Christmas as usual as they were grieving for her father. Then the New Year arrived and she hoped all bad things were behind her. The final examinations were in April and she passed her fourth year *Liceu* with flying colours.

After the examinations, she went back to Cuncolim and stayed with her mother the entire summer. She had to take her mother to Bombay to sign the papers and wind up her father's settlement. They received a sizable package from the shipping company. Her father also had some insurance with Life Insurance of India and they collected the insurance benefits.

As per advice given by Luciano, they bought units of the Unit Trust of India from most of the proceeds. The idea was to get dividends annually which would provide some annual income and the units would provide security. Also since the settlement was in Indian currency, they stood to lose a lot converting it to Portuguese escudos at a low exchange rate. In the meantime, Luciano would send them any extra money they would need for Linda's studies. Having settled the business they left for Goa after staying in Bombay for a week.

The summer of 1960 was not very exciting for Linda and her mother as they were still grieving for Mário. But Linda tried to relax as much as she could and forget about her father's untimely and painful death and the associated cruel incidents. The fact that her father spent most of his time on board the ship, and very little time with them when on leave, helped somewhat. Except that this time he had gone away on leave for eternity and would never ever return. This thought left a stabbing pain in her heart and Linda almost fainted just thinking about it. She would get these sad and disheartening feelings quite often. She tried to overcome them but often had no control over them.

Linda tried to divert her mother's attention. But what could she do? As per local customs, after the death of a close relative, people could not do certain things. For example they could not celebrate feasts such as Christmas, New Year or Easter. They could not even make Christmas cookies and celebrate birthdays. They could not go for weddings and parties. They were expected to wear black at least for a year. But Linda did not believe in these. She believed true love and grief should be in one's heart, and not in the colour of one's dress. She believed in prayers for the soul of the dead person and she remembered her father in her daily prayers.

Linda decided not to wear black when she returned to Panjim. But she dressed in black in the village so she would not upset the village folks and their traditions. Her mother always wore black and would wear it for at least two years. Her mother could not wear her earrings and bangles any more.

Since they did not celebrate the feasts, friends, neighbours and relatives sent them goodies, cookies and food during the festivals. A lot of people visited them after Mário's death. These visits were called *fuddea-kodde*, the consolation visits. People came to sympathize and comfort the family and they brought some gifts such as sweets, chocolates and the like. These visits made them feel good for the moment and the hurt and pain seemed to go away, at least when people were around and they talked about something else. But when the visitors went away, they felt again immersed in a sea of eternal sadness.

Linda was glad when the summer was over and she returned to Panjim. She discarded her black dress, so she would not be reminded of the tragic loss of her father. But she felt bad for her mother. Joanita did not have any life worth living anymore. She would be unhappy and sad for the rest of her life, as in Goa no widow remarried after their husband's death especially if they were middle-aged and not rich or educated. This was an unwritten law at the time, and only the daring, the rich and high-class widows would sometimes remarry.

Linda was now in her *Quinto Ano*, the fifth year of Lyceum, the year of high school graduation. She had to work very hard this year, as it was a very critical year. After this year she could do the *Normal* teaching course and start teaching or continue her Higher Secondary School leading to the *Sétimo Ano*, the seventh year, after which she could go to University in Portugal for professional studies or go to Escola Médica in Panjim to become a doctor.

Linda worked very hard and she still had help from Rama. They teamed up strongly this year. Rama was an expert in mathematics and had set his sights on engineering. Linda had an inclination towards the sciences such as biology and chemistry. Together they formed a team no one could beat at the time.

Linda did not go home until her father's death anniversary for the first anniversary mass for his soul. A lot of people came to the church, there was a high *cantada* singing Mass. They distributed *registos*, holy pictures with her father's photo inside and requesting the reader to recite one Our Father and Hail Mary for the repose of the soul of Mário Cardoso. The local weekly, *Vauraddeancho Ixtt* had carried an advertisement two weeks earlier with the same picture inviting relatives and acquaintances to come to the church for his Anniversary Mass. After the Mass everyone was invited to Linda's home for some tea. The guests helped themselves to some cheese and crackers and snacks and coffee.

Linda fared very well as usual, in the first term examinations. Then for the Christmas of 1960, Linda went home and celebrated in a rather low-key way. It was just a year after her father's death.

Soon they brought in the New Year of 1961, the beginning of a new decade. By now the pain and hurt and memories of her father had almost disappeared for Linda and she wanted to forget the past. She tried to help her mother realize that all was not lost, that they could not do anything to bring her father back to life. But at least they had the security of an annual income and life was not all that bad. After the holidays Linda went back to Panjim once again to devote herself completely to her studies.

Chapter 24

As her final examinations for the Fifth Year of Lyceum approached, Linda put in her best effort, burned the midnight oil and studied hard. She wrote the final examinations and she knew she had done her best ever. After the examinations, Linda went home for the summer holidays.

One day before the results of her examinations, a man arrived at her place on a motorcycle. Linda was sitting outside in the *balcão* trying to clean rice by separating tiny stones and husk from it in an aluminium plate.

"Are you Linda Cardoso?" asked the young man, as he got off his motorcycle.

"Yes I am. How can I help you?" Linda answered him.

"My name is Eurico Silva and I am a reporter for the journal, *A Vida*. Can I have your interview for our newspaper? You have scored the highest marks in Goa for your *Quinto Ano Liceu* examinations. Congratulations!"

"Thanks. I will be most honoured. Please come in." Linda took him to the sitting room and excused herself.

Linda went inside the kitchen to tell the great news to her mother.

"Mama, do you know that your daughter has scored the highest marks at the *Liceu* examinations in the whole of Goa?" Linda whispered with excitement.

"Congratulations, *baai*. I knew it. You were always very smart. Your Papa would have been proud of you today. He must have prayed for you." Her mother hugged Linda and kissed her.

"You know the man who came here on a motorcycle is a reporter for the newspaper, *A Vida*. He is the one who brought the good news and he wants to interview me."

"Go *baai*, talk to the gentleman, I'll get something for him to eat." Joanita let Linda go back to the sitting room to begin the interview.

Then running through the backyard, Joanita went to the neighbours, borrowed some eggs, asked her neighbour Inácio to go on his bicycle to the bazaar and bring her a bottle of cold *cerveja*. She began to prepare an egg omelette and boiled some *chouriços* she always kept in case of emergency. When the cold beer bottle arrived, she set the table for the young man and went to the sitting room.

"Senhor, how are you? I am Linda's mother." Linda's mother introduced herself.

"Nice to meet you, Senhora," said the young man.

"Would you please come and have some snacks?" Linda invited Eurico to the table.

Eurico was very impressed with their hospitality. He savoured the sausages and the omelette with the cold beer in the heat of the day.

"Senhora, you must be very proud of your daughter," Eurico said to Joanita. Then looking at Linda, he continued, "Linda, *parabens!* You have a great future. Keep it up! All the best to you. Adeus!" Eurico took his leave.

"Muitíssimo obrigado, Senhor Eurico Silva, Adeus!" Linda thanked him and said goodbye.

Joanita was indeed proud of her daughter and her achievement.

The next day Linda went to the local *professora*, from her village, who subscribed to the two Portuguese dailies *A Vida* and *O Heraldo*. She quickly opened *A Vida* first. She quickly read the story about her by Eurico Silva. There was a picture of her in it and the accompanying story described how a little-known village girl of humble origin had beaten the odds by coming first in Goa in the *Quinto Ano do Liceu* examinations and had won the coveted Governor's Award. Then she opened *O Heraldo*, which also carried her picture and did a small story on her.

She wondered how *O Heraldo* had got her story. Maybe the nuns at the *Instituto Piedade* hostel or her professors at *Liceu* must have informed them. Linda borrowed the newspapers from the *professora* to show her picture to her friends, neighbours and relatives. Her mother and grandmother were exceedingly happy.

That summer was, in contrast, more exciting and busy for Linda. People came to her house to congratulate her. The Padre Vigário from the local village church, brought her a copy of *O Diário de Noite* with her picture in it and a story about her achievement. The nuns from the local convent came to her house to congratulate her. A lot of people in the surrounding villages had heard about Linda's success. The papers had mentioned that Linda was the winner of the Governor's Award, among many other awards and scholarships. And in June there was going to be a special award ceremony at Hotel Mandovi in Panjim.

Linda spent the next two weeks in Navelim at her maternal grandmother's place. Her mother had gone to Mobor in Cavelossim for her annual *mudança*. Linda went to Margão as often as she could. She would go to Bombay Café for her favourite *masala dosa, samosa, bhaji* and coffee.

One day Linda went to Margão with her grandmother to celebrate her award. They went to Longuinhos for a nice Goan lunch of *pulau, sorpotel* and *xacuti*. Then they went to *O Penguim* next door for dessert of some ice cream and cold fruit salad. Her grandmother had never seen or tasted such fare and the ice cream was very tasty but too cold for her. Linda was proud to go around in Margão with her grandmother who was dressed in a *choli* and *capodd*, a typical rural blouse and sari. Linda was dressed in a smart western dress. Every one looked at and admired the sophisticated young lady who was shopping proudly with her old grandmother.

Linda would sometimes go to the Municipal Garden to listen to the melodious songs in Portuguese and Konkani, broadcast over the loud speakers in the *jardim*. She would see beautiful kids and young couples and lovers strolling in the adjoining garden, named after the famous Aga Khan. There were beautiful varieties of roses and other flowers and plants. She would spend the entire day there alone.

The next day she went to see a movie at Cine Metrópole for an afternoon show of "Gone with the Wind". Another time she visited the Hospital Hospício. But most of the time she went shopping in the bazaar to eat *boram, kandam, morondd* and guavas, which were her favourite fruits.

When her mother came back from the *mudança*, Linda went back to Cuncolim. That summer, she wanted to go everywhere she could. She went to Betul on May third for the feast of the Holy Cross, at the Baraddi Chapel. There on the hillock, she went three times around the miraculous *Khuris*, decked with lit candles and fresh *abolim* flowers, and she prayed in thanksgiving.

From the top of that hill, she could see the Bay of Betul, the coconut tree plantations of Zuvem, the *ogor* saltpans, and the scenic landscape that was pristine Mobor and the calm and beautiful waters of the Arabian Sea to the West. On the other side she could see the village of Velim and river Sal meandering through Assolnã, and she could even see the Mountain of Chandranath, the same one she could see from the front of her house with a temple on top. There were lots of cashew trees around in Baraddi. When she went down the hill, Linda went to see the fair, where she met her *Liceu* mate Aleixinho Rodrigues, who was helping out at one of the church charity stalls. He invited her to his house at Zuvem for the festive dinner.

→〉§◇⊗◇§〈←

Chapter 25

After a long and exciting summer Linda returned to Panjim for her *Sexto Ano*, the sixth year of Lyceum. Now she was very popular and Linda began to feel quite a change in her. She was more confident and sure of herself. The Governor's Award ceremony at Hotel Mandovi in Panjim, was on June 17th 1961. She was getting nervous each day as the big event approached. She had a nice dress already chosen for the occasion.

June 17 finally arrived. This was the first time Linda went inside the majestic Hotel Mandovi the tallest building in Goa at the time with its ornate five floors. She always wanted to see what it would be like inside. This was her moment. She showed the invitation card at the entrance and she was ushered into the 'Lisboa Saloon', where the ceremony was to take place.

As she went in and took her seat all eyes focused on her. People inside this hall had seen her picture on the newspapers and had read her story. This young lady had an air of elegance of a simple village belle, but her abilities, intelligence and her looks were worthy of great respect and admiration from this appreciative elite audience. This young woman had already received several accolades in her young life and she surely would be one of the brightest stars of Goa, they thought.

All winners of the various awards were present and seated right in front. Rama Naique was present too, to claim the Mathematics Award. There was soft music coming from the speakers on the stage. Some people were still filing into the hall. Finally, a retinue of officers arrived followed by His Excellency, the Governador Geral Vassalo e Silva himself. Everybody stood up in deference to the Governor.

The ceremony started with a short introduction from the Director of Education of the *Liceu* Nacional Afonso de Albuquerque. He introduced all winners including Linda, highlighting their achievements. And then came the moment of presenting the Awards. They started with the various awards for the Fifth Year and the Seventh Year Lyceum and finally presented the last two awards – the Governor's Award for the Fifth Year and Seventh Year winners.

Linda's name was called out on the podium. Linda shivered and felt nervous but she got up and gracefully walked towards the podium bowing to the Governor, who shook her hand, congratulated her and presented her . with the coveted Award, with her name inscribed on it. Flashlights from the photographers' cameras almost blinded her.

People lined up to shake hands with her. Except for Rama Naique who congratulated her first, she did not know anyone else. She did not know who was who, even though they all introduced themselves, but she recognized Eurico Silva, the reporter of *A Vida*, who had interviewed her earlier in Cuncolim. Then a young white Portuguese man approached her.

"Excuse me Senhorita Linda, or should I say Linda Senhorita? My name is Carlos Soares." the young man introduced himself to Linda with a disarming smile.

"Nice to meet you Senhor Soares," replied Linda.

"I am a special assistant to the Governador Geral Vassalo e Silva," Carlos continued, "I have read a lot about you in the papers. What a story that was in *A Vida*, Senhorita!"

Then he took a certificate from his folder.

"Here is the Governador's Special Merit Certificate that the Governor General forgot to present to you with your Award. It is a pleasure to present this Certificate to you for your great achievement, *Parabens!*" Carlos shook hands with Linda and presented her with the Certificate.

Linda felt electricity pass through her body. Could it happen with a mere touch? Just at that time, a flashbulb from Eurico Silva's camera exploded and the camera recorded this moment, frozen in time. Linda gave

Carlos her best smile and thanked him *"Muitíssimo obrigado, Senhor Soares."*

And just before he left, Carlos gazed into her eyes and said, "I would like very much to see you again sometimes, Senhorita, maybe at the *Liceu?*" and gave her his business card. His gaze was transfixed on her for a lot longer than necessary.

Linda was taken aback. She did not know what to say. She just smiled back at him. Carlos finally whispered to her *"Adeus Senhorita."* and left with the Governor General.

The next day *A Vida* carried the picture of Carlos presenting the Governor's Special Merit Certificate to Linda. *O Heraldo* and *O Diário de Noite* carried the picture of the Governor presenting the Governor's Award to Linda at Hotel Mandovi on the occasion of the Governor's Awards Presentation.

Since that fateful time Linda met Carlos, something happened to Linda. Was it love at first sight? Linda looked at their picture in *A Vida*, read the caption below the picture and smiled to herself. This was the match of the century, she thought aloud. She had never had a boyfriend before. In fact, she never knew what love was. In all those years, she concentrated on her studies, which helped her ward off any notions of boyfriends from her mind. But now that she had finished high school, she welcomed the possibility of a romantic involvement with a nice young man.

Carlos came to see Linda the next day at the Lyceum complex at Altinho on his BMW motorcycle. He was waiting for her outside, just as Linda finished the last class of the day and was about to leave the building. Linda saw him and stopped abruptly. She was hesitant and nervous at first. She wasn't sure she was stepping in the right direction.

Carlos felt guilty about this very direct approach. What would she think of him? He slowly walked up to her.

"Bom dia, Senhorita!" Carlos saluted her.

"Bom dia, Senhor Soares!" replied Linda.

Both of them did not know what to say after that initial salutation. After some moments of indecision, Carlos asked her "Can we go for a ride?"

"I suppose so." Linda replied.

Carlos Soares was actually born in Ottawa, Canada, when his father was an attaché in the Portuguese Embassy in Canada. He now worked as a special aide to the Portuguese Governador Geral, Vassalo e Silva in Panjim at Cabo Palácio. He was a twenty-five year old Portuguese Architecture graduate from Escola Superior Técnica of Lisbon. This was his first job posting. He was fresh out of school. He was the son of a diplomat, Eustaquio Soares and his wife Dona Elita Borges. As a child he had moved from one Portuguese embassy to another through most of the world, staying the longest in London, Washington and Ottawa. He had spent the last six years studying in Portugal.

Carlos was a young man with a wide vision. He was a free spirit and he believed in the universality of humans on this planet. He was a socialist and a peaceful man growing up in the turbulent fifties. He admired the revolutionaries in South America and the poets and elitists in America, who were trying to change the world. He had read "The Howling", "On the Road" and other similar books and he loved them. He admired the non-violence espoused by The Father of União Indiana, the great Mahatma Gandhi. His newly found taste in the progressive societies of the modern world brought him to the distant Portuguese colony of Goa. He took up his post with the Governor, who had similar beliefs, with great enthusiasm.

Carlos was six feet tall with a clean-shaven face and short black hair. He had blue eyes that matched his fair face. He was tall, fit and handsome and had a carefree attitude. He was charming, attractive, intelligent and jovial with a great sympathy for the downtrodden. He seemed kind and was known for his integrity and devotion to his work. With a progressive Governor, his job was made much easier.

Carlos read the local Portuguese papers daily and he had noticed Linda's picture on the local daily when she was declared winner of the Governor's Special Award. He had read about her in both the dailies. He was curious about her. Now that he had met her in person, he wanted to know her even better.

Carlos liked the people and culture of Goa. The article on Linda on *A Vida* daily sounded very interesting to him. And when he saw Linda in person the first time, he just knew she was the one for him.

Linda hoped no one would see her with Carlos. She would be in trouble if the nuns came to know about her and Carlos. She had never ventured out on a date before. She did not know what was supposed to happen next. Her heart throbbed faster, as she sat on the backseat, with her hands clasping Carlos's shoulders tight and her young body against his. They rode down the Altinho hillock. This was Linda's first ride on a motorcycle.

Carlos took Linda to Clube Tennis Gaspar Dias at Miramar, where he was a member. They sat down on the patio facing the river and relaxed. They had some refreshments and then went on a stroll along the Gaspar Dias (Miramar) beach.

"Tell me about you and your family, Senhorita".

"Please call me Linda, Senhor. That's more informal. I am a simple village girl from down South. My mother is a housewife and my father was a sailor. And what about your family Senhor?"

"All right Linda. Call me Carlos then. My mother is in Lisboa. My father died seven years ago. He was a diplomat overseas and we lived in London, Paris, Washington and Ottawa. I spent only the last six years in Portugal after my father's death. I finished studying Architecture from Escola Superior Técnica from Lisboa. I am twenty-five years old. And this is my first assignment and I have been working for the Governor General in Goa for the past six months now."

"Oh that sounds very interesting, Carlos. I was born and bred in a village as I said and I came to live in Panjim only three years ago. I am sixteen years old and I live in a hostel at *Instituto* Piedade."

Carlos learnt all about Linda, her age, background, her village life, her parents and her aspirations. Carlos told her about his life in Portugal, his mother and his student days in Lisbon. They were very curious about each other. In all too short a time they came to know a lot about each other but the sun was going down, and it was time for Linda to go. However they promised to see each other again. Linda told Carlos to be discreet and not be seen with her near the *Instituto* Piedade. Then Carlos took Linda home and left her near the *Instituto*.

During the night, both of them reviewed what they knew of other mentally and decided they should definitely see more of each other. Carlos liked Linda – she was beautiful, exotic, intelligent and open-minded. But he was concerned that she was only sixteen.

Linda saw her Prince Charming in Carlos. He was her dream man. He seemed to be a sincere, honest, young man. He was well groomed, polished and very likeable.

Carlos did not come to the *Liceu* complex the next day, but he did show up the day after. Linda missed him the previous day. They decided to go on another date. This time they went to Campal. They took a long walk on the beach towards Miramar and talked some more.

"Linda, there is something that bothers me, before we take this any further."

"What is it Carlos?"

"Your age, Linda."

"I am old enough, Carlos."

"But in the eyes of law, you are still a minor."

"All that matters is you and me and the bond that ties us."

Carlos then held Linda for the first time and professed his love for her. He felt her soft body close to his. Linda was excited beyond imagination. She was filled with an ecstasy that she had never experienced before. Then he kissed her right on her full lips. To Linda it seemed like she was in heaven. She trembled and almost passed out. Carlos had to hold her tight in his arms. She had never experienced the touch of any man before. His close embrace, his passionate kiss on her lips, mesmerized her completely. Carlos looked into her eyes. She blushed and smiled.

They sat down on the golden sands of Miramar beach holding each other and wishing this would last for eternity. It was serene and tranquil out there. The only sounds came from the incessant waves of the river Mandovi hitting the sandy shore and the occasional call of the sea gulls.

Linda lay down on the sand, her head on Carlos' lap. She looked up at the beautiful blue sky and sighed with pleasure as Carlos bent down and kissed her. A strong wave sprayed a salty shower on them as if Mother Nature herself had given her assent to their budding love. They exchanged sweet nothings and kissed each other again.

In what seemed like a minute, Linda saw the sun go down and kiss the waters of the Arabian Sea just beyond Fort Aguada. The lighthouse lit up on the hill at Fort Aguada against the dark horizon, the lights came on at the Aguada jail just below the hill and the Reis Magos church across the river. The solemn church bells pealed from the turret of the Imaculada Conceição Church in Panjim to remind Linda it was time to go.

Linda got up, holding on to Carlos, removing any telltale traces of sand from her dress and asked Carlos to take her back to the *Instituto* Piedade, as the nuns at the institute had strict rules about staying out late. Carlos understood and he took Linda to the *Instituto* on his motorbike. Linda again reminded him not to be seen with her near the *Instituto*, as she did not want to be in the bad books of the nuns.

That night, she was restless. Her first kiss stimulated her entire body, which was filled with unbridled passion. In a day, Linda was almost transformed into a new woman. Her face was radiant with love and there was a constant smile on her face. She saw and felt happiness all around. Her mind was elsewhere. She was daydreaming. She would do anything to be with her beloved Carlos and to feel the touch and warmth of his body next to hers.

She could not concentrate on her studies. For the first time in her life, she forgot to review the notes from the previous day's lectures and do her homework. That night, Linda lay awake all night tossing and turning. She barely had some sleep towards morning and even then she dreamt of Carlos. What was happening to her? She had read William Shakespeare's *Romeo and Juliet* in her English class and now she was experiencing the same heavenly love herself and feeling very romantic. She secretly wished her Carlos would appear outside the *Instituto* below the balcony of her window, just like in that scene from Romeo and Juliet. It felt good to fall in love, even though somewhere at the back of her mind something told her to be careful.

The next day, just as her lectures were over, she saw Carlos on his motorbike waiting for her outside the Lyceum. She went running to him, a damsel in love, hopped on his motorbike and away they rode towards Dona Paula.

They climbed the huge romantic rock, hand in hand, a promontory on the South side of Panjim at the mouth of river Zuari known as Dona Paula. They took in the marvellous view all around, from the big ships at Mormugão harbour and Vasco de Gama in the South to the Palace at Cabo to the North and the endless coconut grove all the way to Siridão along the bank of big river Zuari. The cool breeze coming from the sea excited warm embraces and kisses between these young lovers celebrating the feeling that was love.

Or was it?

Linda remembered the legendary love story of two lovers, Dona Paula and Gaspar Dias, who were madly in love but could not get married. They made a deadly pact and ended their lives on that very spot. Linda hoped it wouldn't be the case with their love.

All of a sudden, without any warning a big grey cloud came their way and soaked them with the first rain of the season. It was June of 1961 and the monsoon season seemed to have set in. Linda always stood in the first showers as a yearly rite, but this year it was very special. She had Carlos by her side. She wanted to be there with Carlos till sundown. Climbing down the rock, they went to the bar, *The White Rock* below. Carlos had a *cerveja* and Linda had a soft drink. And when the rain subsided, Carlos took Linda home to the *Instituto*.

The month of June passed by and the monsoon of 1961 was ferocious. There were strong winds and it rained every day. So the young lovers could not see much of each other. But their love brought them together once or twice a week even in such turbulent weather. Linda did not have access to a phone at the *Instituto* so she would call Carlos from a public phone at the Lyceum complex. They managed to continue their love talk over the phone lines whenever they could not meet.

Carlos missed his *querida* darling Linda during the heavy monsoon days. He could not spend a day without her. He felt fortunate to have met this beautiful and intelligent Goan girl. He would do anything to keep her with him for life. She was his one and only love.

Her long black hair, those brown eyes, that beautiful face and her smooth, dark skin were so exotic. He was enamoured of her good looks and her enticing body. She was gorgeous yet innocent; simple yet intelligent. She was only sixteen and a virgin. Carlos was obsessed with her.

And when the incessant rains eased up somewhat in August, their love resumed its torrid pace again. Linda and Carlos were seen regularly on the beaches of Miramar, Dona Paula and Campal.

They went everywhere together on his motorcycle. They went to the Old Goa Basílica for a Sunday mass. They visited the Archbishop's Palace at Altinho. They crossed to Betim on ferry and went to Calangute on Sunday afternoons. Carlos wanted to see all the important and historical places of Goa with her.

Linda took him to Vasco de Gama and Mormugao harbour on a weekend via Dona Paula on a ferryboat across the river Zuari. Vasco was an industrial town. There were a large number of migrant workers from India doing hard labour at the Mormugao harbour and in railways at Vasco. Carlos saw the famous red light area of Baina beach in Vasco de Gama. They saw many European men visiting the brothels of Baina.

They visited Mapuça bazaar on a Friday. They even visited remote inaccessible beaches of Baga and Anjuna in the North and the beautiful beaches of Bogmalo and Colva in the South. One Sunday, they went to see the water supply plant of Opa and the Arvalem Falls in Ponda.

Almost every Sunday, they went to Cine Nacional and the newly opened Cine El Dorado in Panjim and watched movies in the privacy of an enclosed booth just for two.

Every time Linda came back to the hostel after going out with Carlos, Heidi would come to her and ask all about her date. Linda in all her innocence would go through all the fine details with Heidi.

Heidi started feeling jealous of Linda. Each time she would ask Linda to introduce her to Carlos. One day, Linda took Heidi to Café Real and introduced her to Carlos.

"Carlos, this is my best friend Heidi."

"Heidi, this is my darling Carlos."

"Pleased to meet you Senhorita."

"My pleasure Senhor."

Carlos shook hands with Heidi, who was fascinated by him. But Carlos did not feel a thing for Heidi.

How lucky Linda was, Heidi thought. In spite of her background, she has achieved so much in such a short time. Everyone at the *Instituto* loved Linda. She even managed to capture a prized European boyfriend. What did Carlos see in Linda? How such a handsome, young man could fall for Linda, she couldn't fathom.

Heidi looked like a princess. She was really beautiful in a hard, cold sort of way. She was very attractive, had a great figure and could easily capture any man's heart. But instead she picked Carlos, just because it was a challenge. She felt she deserved to be his girlfriend more than Linda. Heidi's jealousy got the better of her and she was bent on breaking up the burgeoning romance and making Carlos hers.

Whenever she could, Heidi tried to capture Carlos's attention but Carlos never showed any interest in her. This bothered Heidi. The fact that Carlos showed so much affection, love and complete devotion to Linda, made Heidi's blood boil. She could take it no longer and Heidi decided to tell Mother Superior all about Linda and Carlos – their blossoming liaison and their frequent dates.

Chapter 26

Carlos wanted to see Linda's mother and her house in the village of Cuncolim. But Linda was sure her mother would not like her involvement with Carlos. So she gave Carlos excuses and delayed the visit. Finally, she ran out of all excuses and Carlos won. She was prepared to take Carlos to meet her mother. She taught him how to say "How do you do?" in Konkani.

Linda took Carlos to Cuncolim one Sunday. This was the first time Linda went on such a long journey of about forty kilometres on a motorbike. They went from Panjim via Santa Cruz, Bambolim, Velha Goa, Pilar, Agaçaim, then crossed the river Zuari on a ferry, rode through Cortalim, Verna, Nuvem and they stopped in Margão. Carlos refuelled his tank at Quennim Motors Gas Station, and then followed the road south to Cuncolim. On the way Linda showed Carlos the location of the house in Navelim, where she was born, then they crossed the Jackni-Bhand, sped through Sirlim and Chinchinim turning left at Bomboikarancho Khuris, all the way to Cuncolim via Danddea-vaddo and Panzorkon.

When she heard the noise of the motorcycle stopping outside her house, Joanita suspiciously peered round the front door and saw Linda with a white man by her side. She wondered what had happened. She saw the neighbours peering through their windows at the pair. Then Linda walked up to her with the white man.

"Mama, how are you? Meet my friend, Carlos. Carlos, this is my mother." Linda introduced Carlos to her mother.

"*Baba, boro assa mure tum?*" Joanita said hello to Carlos in Konkani.

"*Tum kexi assa?*" Carlos asked Joanita how she was doing in Konkani.

Joanita laughed her head off and replied, "*Aum borim assam, baba.*" I am fine, son. She wondered if this white man really understood Konkani.

And within two minutes, all the neighbours came out of their houses, curious. They saw the white Portuguese man with Linda and Joanita. And at once the gossip mills churned out various stories and explanations. One was that Linda had a Portuguese *paclo,* white boyfriend. The entire village got the news faster than a broadcast.

Linda's mother, Joanita liked the young man but could not communicate with him as she did not speak Portuguese. She just smiled and shook his hand and they went inside. Linda and Carlos sat in the sitting room and Joanita went to the kitchen to prepare some snacks for them.

Linda showed Carlos her house and took him outside in the backyard. Joanita served them a cold beer and hot *chouriço* sausages. Carlos wanted to talk with Joanita but he did not know Konkani. He liked the woman and had heard so much about her from Linda.

"Linda, tell your mother she is lucky to have a nice daughter like you." Carlos said to Linda in Portuguese, which Linda translated in Konkani for her mother's benefit.

"*Obrigado Senhor.*" Joanita thanked him in Portuguese, one of the very few Portuguese words she knew.

After some time, Linda excused herself and went to the kitchen where her mother was. "Mama, Carlos is my boyfriend," Linda announced in a low voice.

"What!" Joanita said furiously. "You have chosen a white Portuguese officer as your boyfriend?" asked her mother in utter disbelief. "Linda, how could you do this, putting us all to shame and at this young age? Don't you have any sense left in that brain of yours? And what about school? And those big dreams of yours? Gone down the drain when you met this *paclo*? Oh what a shame and disgrace you have brought to this family!" Her mother went on a verbal rampage whispering loudly and angrily without giving Linda any chance to interrupt.

"Mama, don't get upset. You don't know him yet. He is a very nice man." Linda tried to calm her mother down.

"I am sure he is a very nice young man. But he is not meant for you. He is a foreigner. You are so young and naive. Tomorrow something happens, he will be gone and you will be left all alone." Her mother warned Linda.

"Mama, I know what I am doing, I am in love with that man and I won't ever leave him, come what may. Do you hear?" Linda snapped back indignantly at her mother for the first time in her life.

Joanita knew her daughter well. She knew Linda had made a final decision and was not going to backtrack.

"At least be careful, *baai*, don't be involved with this stranger too seriously. They get what they want from you, use you and then leave you high and dry. If your father was alive today, he would most definitely not approve," Joanita counselled her daughter.

The conversation was getting on Linda's nerves. She was cross with her mother for the first time. "Mama let me live my life the way I want it, and if you don't like it, too bad, I am leaving now. Bye."

Linda came out of the kitchen, picked up her purse, told Carlos it was time to leave and both of them said goodbye to Joanita. Carlos sensed that something was wrong, as Linda looked quite troubled, uptight and pensive.

When they stepped out of the house, Linda could see all neighbours, from the corner of her eyes, looking at them with great interest. Carlos started his motorbike and they were on their way to Panjim, leaving the neighbours with fuel for fresh gossip.

After the visit of Carlos to Linda's house in Cuncolim, Joanita went through a rough time. Neighbours, friends and relatives bombarded her with their concerns for young Linda because of her liaison with her Portuguese *paclo* boyfriend. When Joanita went to the bazaar, people would point fingers at her and tell everyone that this woman's daughter had run away with an European *paclo*. Joanita was humiliated at the church, in the bazaar, on the bus and everywhere.

Joanita went to Navelim to seek advice and she was shocked to know her mother already knew about Linda's scandalous love affair.

"What should I do, *Mãe*?" Joanita cried out to her mother, Angelina.

"*Baai*, don't worry about little Linda. She is very smart. She knows what she is doing. Besides, who are you to control what is in her destiny? Whatever the Sottvi, the Goddess of The Sixth Night, has written in her book of life will come to pass." the elderly Angelina told her daughter.

Joanita was worried. She had already lost her husband, and now she did not want to lose her only daughter, which was bound to happen if she asked her to stay away from Carlos. Joanita decided to listen to her mother's advice. To hell with neighbours and relatives, she was not going to break up the relationship between Linda and Carlos.

Joanita wrote a letter to Linda in Panjim apologizing for spoiling her last visit to Cuncolim and that she would leave it all to Linda to decide what was best for her.

When Linda received this letter, tears rolled down her face and she cried and felt sorry for her mother. She replied to her that she was proud of her mother and asked her not to worry too much about her.

In the October holidays, Linda went home to Cuncolim. She could see the odd look on everybody's faces when she was around.

"Mama, why is everybody turning away from me?" Linda said to her mother.

"*Baai*, since the day you and that *paclo* came over here for a visit, the village people have made my life a living hell. They gossip about you two and point fingers at me in the bazaar area and have humiliated me since." Joanita started to cry.

"Mama, I am so sorry you had to go through all this because of me." Linda was contrite and both of them hugged each other.

"*Baai*, they can't shut their mouths. I can't even show my face in public."

Linda felt angry with the village people for treating her mother like an outcast. But what could she do? These were the simple village people with strong traditions. No young girl could ever venture to go out with a young man without getting married first – especially when that young man was a white foreigner. Linda felt extremely sorry for her mother.

She did not care too much about these village people. Some of them were hypocrites and back-stabbers. How could they treat her like a leper, a pariah? Had she committed a crime? All she had done was fall in love with a foreigner and at a very young age. She understood it was not usual for any young girl to have done what she had. But she was in love for the first time in her life and no one would get in her way. Not the neighbours, certainly. Who were they to control her life? It was just not proper for them to have such narrow views. Did we have to restrict ourselves to a homogenous, same caste, same race and same colour society all the time?

Linda was being philosophical, but who in this village would be open enough to see her point of view? If only they were in her shoes, they might perhaps understand. After a week, Linda returned to Panjim. She was disgusted.

Chapter 27

Linda forgot all about what had happened in Cuncolim. Her love for Carlos grew even stronger. Linda and Carlos were seen going out openly everywhere in Panjim. They were the talk of the town. They went to the best restaurants. Carlos wanted her to have the best time and he knew she enjoyed being with him.

Linda started coming home late to the *Instituto*. One day, the Mother Superior caught Linda coming home late and she was promptly called to the office. Linda knew something bad was going to happen. She had already dealt with her own mother. Now she had to deal with the Mother of all mothers.

Linda went into the office with a large crucifix on the wall. She noticed that the Mother Superior was not her usual sweet-natured self.

"Hello Linda, my child, sit down." The Mother Superior opened the conversation with a pensive and disturbed look on her face. "I have been informed that lately you have been coming home from school late. At your age it is easy to fall prey to temptation, my child." She looked at Linda sombrely. "Only prayers can help fight the devil. I want you to pray everyday at the Chapel and receive Holy Communion daily." She counselled Linda with a stern look.

"You are still too young to fall in love. You know the facts of life, child. When the right time comes, you will fall in love and get married. But now, this could affect your school and your future." she reminded her.

"My child, you are a very smart young lady. But you are actually violating a lot of house rules at the *Instituto*. From now on, I expect you to come home on time and obey all our rules and regulations. Be the role model you used to be." She pleaded.

"Thank you, Mother Superior. I am sorry." Linda responded in a low tone.

Linda consoled herself she got away so lightly. She had expected some sort of reprimand from her like a suspension from the *Instituto*, but none came. She liked and loved the Mother Superior. She was very pious, understanding and forgiving. But her advice and warning did not sway Linda a bit. She could not compromise her love for Carlos.

For a week, Linda came home early. Then her love for Carlos proved to be too strong. She was ready to lose everything for Carlos. The servants at the *Instituto* tried to help Linda escape the watchful eyes of the Mother Superior.

Day by day their love grew bolder. They were in each other's arms even in public. Carlos took Linda to his residence at the Governor's Palace at Cabo, an isolated cape, a hilly piece of land jutting into the Arabian Sea at the mouth of River Mandovi. She was given a tour of the Governor's magnificent residence, the beautiful Chapel and the offices. But she was not allowed into the heavily guarded Governor's sanctum sanctorum for security reasons.

They went to the west end of the Cabo complex, surrounded by beautifully landscaped trees, from where Linda had a panoramic view of the Arabian sea, the Mormugao harbour, Dona Paula, Fort Aguada, Reis Magos, Miramar, Altinho and a glorious sight of Panjim. Linda saw the Governor's beautiful shiny brand new Mercedes-Benz and Cadillac cars, and then she had a tour of the Governor's kitchen and servants' quarters. She spoke to all the Goan cooks and helpers in Konkani and they served her Goan snacks. After the grand tour Carlos took her back to the *Instituto*.

Everything went fine for Linda and Carlos. The month of October was very good, as the monsoon rains had stopped completely by September and they could venture outdoors most of the time.

On 27th of October, 1961 Carlos celebrated Linda's seventeenth birthday. He took her to Hotel Mandovi for a special candle lit dinner. A famous group from Portugal was booked there that evening. They sang *fados* on stage, the Portuguese folk songs mostly about fate. Linda got very emotional listening to the sad love songs with a melancholic strain. Then she heard her favourite song *Cartas de Amor* (Love-letters). Linda knew every word of this beautiful song. She hugged Carlos and they danced the night away to romantic songs from great hits like *Diana, Sweet Sixteen*, O *ABC do Coração* and *Manhã de Carnaval* to the accompaniment of Latin music and Spanish guitars.

They spent the night in a room at Hotel Mandovi. That night was the most romantic for both Linda and Carlos. They were intoxicated with both the wine and love. Linda's blood flowed fast, her whole body was excited beyond comprehension and she lost control. She gave herself to him without restraint. Now she was a woman. Full of ecstasy and complete satisfaction, she could not wait for another day to be with Carlos again. She had tasted the forbidden fruit and she wanted more of it. That night, they did not sleep at all and they were completely exhausted by morning.

From the moment Carlos set his eyes on this beautiful girl, he had only one thing on his mind: to make her, his own – body and soul. He was not disappointed. She was the woman of his dreams and more. She satisfied him beyond imagination. He now loved her even more. The night seemed to have lasted far too short.

Early morning at 6 a.m., Carlos and Linda left the hotel and walked to the *Instituto*. They shivered from the cold breeze coming from River Mandovi. There was no one on the road. Linda tapped on the main door and a servant opened the door for Linda as per the pre-arranged plan. Linda kissed Carlos goodbye, slipped in thanking the servant girl and went to her room on tiptoe. She was tired and half asleep. She did not go to school that day.

The next few days in the month of November proved to be heavenly. Their days in *paraiso* continued. Linda and Carlos had their romantic encounters more frequently. They wished this would never end.

But Linda was falling behind in her studies. Since she started going out with Carlos, Linda saw less and less of Rama Naique, who had always helped her with some difficult academic problems. Carlos was concerned that Linda would ruin her life and career because she spent less time with her studies. He insisted Linda devote Saturday and Sunday mornings to keep up with her studies.

The next weekend, Linda and Carlos tried not to see each other. But Linda could not concentrate on her studies at all and Carlos too missed her more than he had imagined. They started seeing each other again every weekend. They were true lovers, young and reckless. Linda even skipped her usual mid-term vacation to Cuncolim, as she wanted to spend her precious time with her lover, Carlos.

Finally it was the last month of the year, December. Carlos and Linda went to Old Goa on December 3, 1961 for the feast of St. Francis Xavier. The saint's skeletal remains that were more than four hundred years old were open for veneration at a special exposition.

Normally the exposition took place every ten years. But this year was very tumultuous for Goa. The attack from India was quite imminent. This called for special prayers to St. Francis Xavier to protect Goa from the ravages of war. Even the Governor was present and so also thousands of people praying for the safety of Goa.

The freedom fighters were mounting strong guerrilla attacks at border points. Recently the Indian passenger ship from Bombay S S Sabarmati had ventured into the Portuguese territorial waters outside the Anjediva Island, just South of Goa. The Portuguese had responded by warning the ship and then firing a missile at it. This had caused fresh start of hostilities and skirmishes between Indian and Portuguese forces at border points.

After Mass and prayers were over, Linda and Carlos went to the fair and had beer and *chouriço* sandwiches. Linda bought some souvenirs and they rode towards the River Mandovi, crossed it by a ferry and went to the island of Divar, Piedade. They rode around the village and found an isolated and idyllic spot for a romantic sunset picnic. There, with no one in sight, Linda and Carlos made free and passionate love under the wide-open blue sky. And at nightfall, they returned via Ribandar to the beautiful neon lights of Panjim.

Chapter 28

The next day, on December 4, Carlos was appointed a member of the Governor's Special Planning Committee to devise a new strategy to neutralize the insurgency at border points and to provide security in Goa for the Europeans.

That evening, Carlos did not show up as planned to see Linda, who called his office and left a message. The same thing happened the next day and the day after. Carlos was incommunicado. Linda was beginning to get worried.

Finally on December 9th, Carlos made a frantic effort to see Linda. He went straight to the Lyceum complex in Altinho in a jeep with two soldiers. Linda went running to see him.

"*Meu querido* (My dear) Carlos, what happened? I was worried, sick." Linda embraced him and wept in his arms. Carlos held her soft body close to his, kissed her repeatedly and apologized.

"I am sorry, *querida* Linda. Please listen carefully. I don't have much time and I can't talk much, as I am involved in a top-secret mission and I can't divulge any information for obvious reasons. I don't even know when I will see you again."

"Please, darling Carlos, don't say that. You must make time to see me. I can't live without you," Linda entreated him.

"Darling Linda, I am sorry this has to be this way. But this is not my doing. *A minha Pátria*, my fatherland and the safety of our people come first. I will see you as soon as I can, once this threat against our country is dealt with once and for all. Please be patient and have hope." Carlos kissed her for the last time and abruptly left in the waiting jeep.

That night Linda did not sleep. She had nightmares. She did not know what was happening to her. The next day she called his office. The operator gave her the same message that Carlos was not available.

In the meantime the Portuguese Intelligence sent secret coded messages to the Special Planning Committee, that India was ready to strike around December 16, and that the U S reconnaissance planes had confirmed a massive military build-up of Indian armed forces near the Northern, Eastern and Southern borders of Goa. Washington had already been briefed about the impending strike.

The Governor at once decided that the European families belonging to the Portuguese armed forces and other civilians must be evacuated from Goa as soon as possible. They appointed Carlos to be completely responsible for such an evacuation. And this evacuation had to be kept secret, as they did not want to alarm the general population.

The secret evacuation commenced on December 11. Planeloads of Portuguese civilians including children and wives were transported from Goa by Transportes Aerias de India Portuguesa airlines to Karachi in Pakistan and from there they were safely transported to Portugal. A couple of ships too were chartered for this evacuation to Karachi. Arrangements were made to mobilize the shipments of Goan gold and confidential documents from the vaults of the Banco Nacional Ultramarino to Portugal. Because of the nature of this top-secret evacuation, Carlos was deliberately kept away from Linda.

Carlos was very busy preparing schedules and logistics for the evacuation. He had to go through a long list of Portuguese dependents and civilians in Goa. He had to prioritise the list of evacuees. Then he was involved in drawing strategic plans to block the advance of invading Indian forces in case of war. Among his suggestions were plans to destroy the major bridges of Borim and Banastarim and smaller but critical bridges at Pernem, Aldona, Canacona, Sanvordem and other places. With such responsibility, Carlos had neither the time nor the means to communicate with Linda.

Linda cried night after night, and she could not concentrate on her studies during the day. She felt very nervous and uptight and could not function properly and felt stressed out. When she came back from *Liceu*, she would take a shower and go straight to bed, sometimes without eating and drinking. She felt weak and her mind was crowded with strange thoughts. She tried to call Carlos every morning but she would get the same message from the operator. Linda almost gave up all hope. Her health was getting worse. Her whole system seemed to undergo some changes.

It was December 17 and Linda had just come out from her Chemistry class at interval time at the *Liceu* complex, when she saw the same jeep in which Carlos and the two soldiers had come there about two weeks ago to see her. Linda's heart jumped with joy. She hurriedly walked towards the jeep. Then she stopped. Carlos was not there. She recognized the two soldiers. One of them saw Linda. He got out, came over to her and handed her a letter from Carlos and left.

Linda did not open the letter right away. She went straight home to the *Instituto*, showered, sat on her bed and started reading the letter:

> *Carlos Soares*
> *Dec 15, 1961*

Minha querida Linda (My darling Linda)

Darling, I apologize for having kept you in the dark for so long. But as you know this is a top-secret matter of the State. I missed you already for the longest two weeks of my life and I know what you are going through. Please bear with me until this dark cloud passes over and the sun shines once more. When that happens I will be in your arms once again.

In the meantime I am leaving Goa today on my way to Portugal. I have asked my two buddies here to deliver this letter personally to you and I hope you get it

Please write to me at this forwarding address:

"Caixa Postal 34279, Correio de Lisboa, Portugal."

You know I will be thinking of you all the time. There will be no one for me but you. Remember that always!

Take care darling. Adeus!

Your affectionate devotee, worshipper and lover,

Carlos.

By the time Linda finished reading the letter she burst into tears. Her Carlos had already left Goa and now she was all alone and helpless. All of a sudden, she felt some acidity in her stomach and a lump in her throat and she threw up. She went to the bathroom, vomited some more and went back to her bed and started crying out loud again. Other girls came to her and asked her what had happened and ran to call the nuns. When they came Linda turned almost blue and was violently sick. She passed out for a couple minutes and they sprinkled some cold water on her face to revive her. The nuns called the doctor.

When the doctor came, every one was asked to leave the room, except for the Mother Superior, who was sitting next to Linda and comforting her. The doctor asked Linda what her symptoms were, obtained all pertinent information from her and then examined her.

The doctor looked at her and said "You are pregnant, Linda. Go to the Medical lab tomorrow to confirm it." Then he prescribed her some Gravol pills to stop the vomiting and some vitamins to regain her lost strength.

Linda started to cry loudly again and the Mother Superior, shocked though she was, hugged her and said, "It's all right, my daughter. We will take care of you. God will not abandon you. You just go to sleep and we will get you some medicine. You need a lot of rest now." The Superior knew it was too late to admonish her now. It was of utmost importance to keep her calm or she would go out of her mind.

But Linda could not sleep that night. She was awake thinking about the disaster that had just befallen her. It was the worst night of her life. Negative thoughts about her life without Carlos haunted her. And what about this added complication of her pregnancy? How would she handle this extra burden in her life? What about the bright future that she had carved herself in her dreams all these years?

All that hard work and struggle during her formative years seemed to have dwindled into insignificance. All her achievements seemed to have gone down the drain like the water from a leaking pot. Her life seemed over before it began. And now, she was afraid of her mother. How was she going to tell her Mama about her condition and how would she take it?

Linda had no answers and she cried some more. Her pillow was wet and so was the bedsheet. She tossed and turned in her bed and was overcome by nausea.

Chapter 29

The next day, December 18, Linda was still in bed, she felt too ill to go to school. So she went to the clinic at Escola Médica for the pregnancy test. As she was coming back to the *Instituto*, she heard the loud booming sound of a plane towards the eastern sky and soon after, she heard the loud explosive sound of a bomb. This was followed by another similar explosive sound. She walked hurriedly to the *Instituto* and heard more booming sounds all over Goa. When she entered the *Instituto*, everybody was upset and the Radio Emissora de Goa went dead.

Soon word spread around throughout Goa, that a fighter plane from the Indian Air Force had bombarded the radio transmitter of "Emissora de Goa" at Bambolim. Then they heard that the Dabolim Airport also had been bombarded. There were no more telecommunication links operating between Goa and Portugal. The Airport bombing stopped all air traffic in and out of Goa. And Goa had been cut off from the rest of the world.

As Radio Emissora de Goa went dead, the nuns switched to All India Radio and they heard special broadcast designated specifically for Goan listeners. The announcements appealed to all Goans to stay indoors, and not to be afraid. The broadcast stated that their Indian brethren would soon liberate Goa from the tyrannical yoke of the Portuguese rule. The announcements also said that Goa was surrounded on three sides by the Indian Armed Forces, the Indian Navy blockaded the western sea route and that the Portuguese forces had been asked to surrender without resistance.

After these announcements were heard, the *Liceu* Nacional, all schools and businesses throughout Goa closed down. The government offices were deserted. The Indian fighter planes flew very low turning upside down, trying to dodge the Portuguese artillery fire, and threw down fliers.

Children ran and picked up the fliers, which were printed in Konkani and in Portuguese, and gave them to their parents. The fliers read:

Apelo! Apelo! (Appeal)
Please do not be afraid.
Stay indoors.
We are your Indian brethren.
We have come to liberate you from the yoke of Portugal
Goa will be free!
JAI HIND.

When most people read this, they could not comprehend it. They never felt they were slaves of the Portuguese. They had carried on their normal business in their village without any problems. Why liberate them and from what? And what did 'Jai Hind' mean?

They knew this was the end of Portuguese rule in Goa. They had heard rumours of the ensuing war between India and Portugal. But they were the innocent bystanders. They lived in villages without any restriction on their liberty and led peaceful lives. The only violence they had ever witnessed were the occasional killing of Portuguese officers at the police station or at their residence by the freedom fighters and the cruelty meted out by the Portuguese police when dealing with the sympathizers of the freedom movement.

The majority of the ordinary Catholic people of Goa never had any trouble with the Portuguese, except the lack of influence and power. They did not care who ruled Goa as long as they were happy. Currently, they were happy. They did not go around sending letters to the Indian government for help, or complaining they could not work in their villages without facing persecution from the Portuguese. If India could give them the same standards of living without crime, they wouldn't mind if India ruled over Goa. But they knew the standard of living in India was in no way comparable to the one in Goa. The best option for them would be Free Independent Goa.

The ordinary Catholic Goans would be the real losers. Their religion was foreign, so they would be labelled foreigners and anti-nationalists. The common Catholic Goans knew only how to write Konkani in the Roman script. Marathi or Hindi in the Indian Devanagri script was too difficult for them to learn. They were economically backward and would not get any jobs. Their Christian religion and Portuguese names would definitely be a hindrance and a liability in a Hindu India, as they would be discriminated against as a minority anyway. They had already heard about Hindu-Moslem riots in all major cities in India.

The working class Catholic Goans knew, no matter who ruled Goa, it would not be the ordinary village people anyway. This kind of game of politics was good for people aspiring for power in Delhi or Lisbon. They were the common people of this land for thousands of years; and were given no appointments, not even as head of their village, even before the Portuguese arrived. The higher caste always got the plum jobs. If that were going to change, then they would welcome the Indians. But that did not seem to have happened in India after the British left. The higher caste Hindus still always held power in India.

The Indians could have waited, at least for another few years, for the total liberation of Goa, when the majority of village people would have been educated and economically better off and have equal opportunities to rule the land. Right now, Hindus and the higher castes would rule it. The ordinary Goans would still have to struggle and would not be totally liberated until every one of them had equal rights.

The Catholic Brahmins and the landed *bhattkars* were alarmed with this situation. If India took over, they thought, the Socialist government would certainly take away their huge tracts of land and give them away to their tenants. And they did not like it a bit.

Hindus welcomed the good news of India taking over Goa. Now Goa would certainly be theirs for the taking. They figured the days of Ram Raj were finally back. They identified fully with mainland Indians in their religion, customs, Marathi language and Devanagri script.

Hindu Brahmins were elated as they were economically powerful already and the powerful people in Delhi, especially in the Congress Party, were mostly Brahmins.

Moslems, like Christians were alarmed at the situation. But they were economically better off and there were lot of Moslems in India that they could identify with, who spoke Urdu like them and Urdu was rather similar to Hindi.

During the afternoon of December 18, 1961, the Indian *jawans*, young military men, consisting of mostly Sikhs and other Indians and some Goan freedom fighters, in grey helmets and fatigues, entered Goa from all sides. From Pernem through Mapusa in the North, from Belgaum through Sanvordem in the East, from Canacona through Cuncolim in the South and from the West by Indian Navy war ships.

The Indian Forces, which came in a big procession of Renegade jeeps and trucks with their wireless and other equipment, had a very easy advance into Goa. There was practically no resistance from the Portuguese, except in the Anjediva Island, just south of Goa. Here the Portuguese Navy ship, Afonso de Albuquerque, mounted a daring attack against the Indian Navy, but the Indian Navy finally hit the Portuguese ship. Similar resistance was mounted in Diu. There were about forty casualties on both sides.

Even though the Borim Bridge was bombarded and partly demolished, the Indian forces erected a temporary mechanical Bailey bridge to be able to transport the artillery, tractors, jeeps and armoured trucks to the other side of the river Zuari. The same thing was being done at Banastarim Bridge and the Indian forces advanced to the heart of Goa. By the evening of December 18, 1961, Linda could see the Indian forces lined up on the other side of the River Mandovi at Betim, with their artillery targeted to hit the Palacio Hidalcão in the heart of Panjim.

There was commotion in the city and throughout Goa. There were no more explosive sounds, save the Indian Air Force planes disturbing the peace in the sky by flying very low. Later, it was learnt that a well known Goan, Marshall Pinto single handedly commandeered the Indian Air Force plane that bombed the Radio transmitting station at Bambolim and the Dabolim Airport. Nothing happened throughout the night, except at Fort Aguada jail, where the Indian forces mounted an assault to free the freedom fighters, who, had been threatened with executions by the Portuguese.

The Portuguese tried to get reinforcements from Portugal. But the Portuguese war ships were not allowed to enter the Suez Canal by the Egyptian authorities under orders from President Nasser, who was requested to comply as a favour to his friend from the Non-Aligned Movement, Prime Minister Nehru of India.

Portugal knew that even if those ships were allowed to cross the Suez Canal and Portugal had tried to save Goa, India would one day recapture Goa anyway. The attempt to mount resistance against the advancing Indian forces would be futile and result in numerous casualties on both sides.

The Portuguese Governor General Vassalo e Silva was a peaceful man and he loved Goa and Goans. He had given strict orders to the Portuguese military not to open fire. When these orders were passed on to the rank and file, the Portuguese soldiers did not like it since they wanted to defend their colony with whatever means they had at their disposal. But orders were orders. They were helpless. Unwillingly they laid down their arms. At least they were alive and could go back to their wives or mothers in Portugal. They lost the battle, so what? An hour ago they were the masters. Now they were at the mercy of the Indians. What a world!

Overnight the Indian forces crossed the River Zuari at Borim and Agasaim and the River Mandovi at Betim and at Banastarim and soon entered Panjim. The Indian armed forces took over all military installations and the airport and took over Goa without any bloodshed.

And so in the morning of December 19, 1961, the Governador Geral Vassalo e Silva surrendered to the Indian Armed Forces. The Portuguese forces were captured and held as prisoners of war and protected under the Geneva Convention. The *Bandeira Portuguesa*, the Portuguese flag was lowered at Palacio Hidalcão in Panjim and the Indian tricolour was raised to the mast for the first time ever on Goan soil. Goa, Damão and Diu became part of India.

In the meantime, a small minority of extremist Hindu Goans came out of the closet and offended the Catholic population of Goa by branding them foreigners and Portuguese stooges and telling them to go to Portugal. These extremist Hindu thugs invaded the Portuguese barracks and property and looted transistors and other equipment that they could get their hands on. These extremist Hindu goons said Goa now belonged to them and shouted abuse at men, women and children who were Catholic. What the Catholic Goans had feared turned out to be a reality.

On the other hand, many Hindus and a few Catholic freedom fighters set up meetings at City Hall and village plazas to celebrate Goa's freedom, shouting slogans such as *Jai Hind* (Long live India), *Bharat Mata Ki Jai* (Long Live Mother India), *Mahatma Gandhi Ki Jai*, (Victory to Mahatma Gandhi), *Pandit Nehru Zindabad*, (Long Live Pandit Nehru), and *Salazar, Guddia Mar* (Kick out Salazar)!

Most Goan Catholics did not understand the meaning of these slogans as they were quite new to them and were in a foreign Indian language. They were at a loss as to what would happen to them amidst this Hindu euphoria.

There were many rumours floating around among the Catholic population. Some said the Portuguese carried away the body of St Francis Xavier to Portugal. Others said the Americans were going to take over Goa and that Kennedy, being the Catholic president of U.S.A. would definitely execute this plan. Some said many *pacle*, European military personnel who had Goan girlfriends had escaped to the hills. Others said the Goan troops in the Portuguese army had all defected to the Indian army. Another rumour said the Portuguese took all the Goan gold held in the vaults of Banco Nacional Ultramarino to Portugal.

The Indian military was given strict orders by Prime Minister Nehru not to harm the locals, especially Goan Catholics. News spread that some Indian soldiers, the *jawans* had taken some spoils of war for their own personal gains; that a couple of Sikh *jawans* had raped a Goan school teacher on a train while travelling from Chandor to Margão. In another incident in Bogmallo, a *jawan* threw a grenade at a house and killed a young Goan girl, who had spurned his advances. Apart from these and other few incidents, the war was over without too many casualties.

There were also rumours that the Portuguese Governor had not officially signed over Goa to India and that the question of invasion of Goa by India was before the United Nations Security Council. Many diplomats had questioned India's use of force in this takeover; accusing India of ignoring Gandhi's policy of non-violence. Salazar vociferously condemned India for the invasion of Goa. India's Defence minister Krishna Menon defended the action and applauded India's peaceful takeover of Goa without casualties.

The US tried to open up the debate of India's Invasion of Goa at the United Nations, but the USSR used its veto power to remove the resolution from the UN Security Council. Despite these developments, some Catholic Goans still had hopes that the Portuguese would return to reclaim Goa some day.

The next few days were tumultuous for the Goan Catholic community. Now they felt like strangers in their own country. The Church also appealed to them and said that nothing had changed and that they would be able to follow their own religion regardless of the political situation. Catholics, who always considered themselves Portuguese, did not like to be called Indians now. The young teenage Catholic *Liceu* students, the *Liceistas*, angrily lowered and burned the Indian flag at the *Liceu* on Altinho and raised a Portuguese flag instead.

Such minor altercations occurred in the big cities sporadically. Some small bombs and live grenades went off here and there from places mined by the Portuguese. The Indian government installed a military governor in Goa and there was a curfew in place. Slowly things returned to normalcy but there was general displeasure among the Goan Catholic community that would linger for a long time to come.

And Portuguese forces never did return to Goa to reclaim it and the hopes of the Goan Catholic populace died a gradual death. They felt abandoned by the Portuguese. Dr Antonio da Oliveira Salazar had taken it very hard. He never recovered from the shock of losing his most precious colonial jewel, Goa, Damão e Diu.

Chapter 30

The events leading to the liberation/invasion of Goa had a devastating effect on Linda. She was shattered beyond comprehension. She was going to be a mother at the young age of seventeen. The baby's father had gone, she was unmarried and abandoned. What would become of her now?

Oh God! What have I done to deserve this? Why me? Why now? Only four months ago I was having the best time of my life. My aspirations, my hopes and happiness have all ended so suddenly. Is this part of your big plan, prescribed for me on my Sixth Night? Can you not make an exception just once and take it all away from me. Please won't you wake me from this terrifying nightmare?

Linda thought of suicide. Her father had already died and if she died, she figured her mother too would probably die of shock. No, she had to talk to her mother first. But right now the country was in turmoil and she could not even go to her mother and tell her she was pregnant. She did not know what to do.

She was sick most mornings, she vomited most of the time and she had no one to turn to. It was still not safe to travel as most roads were mined and the army had not yet cleared the roads.

She could not wait for long. Pretty soon her stomach would begin to show and she could not go home then. Everyone there would laugh at her, they would tell her mother "See, we told you, these *pacle* make you pregnant and then take off."

There was confusion everywhere. The *Liceu* and all the businesses were closed. The *Instituto* also had to be reorganized because of the situation at hand. Linda decided she had to go and see her mother in Cuncolim, because she would be worried about her because of the war.

Finally when roads were reopened for civilians, Linda went to Cuncolim on December 22. There was the demobilization of the military all over Goa, and she saw the Portuguese military personnel in open trucks being shifted between barracks. It was tragic to see the fallen faces of these captured Portuguese military prisoners of war. At least the Indian forces did not ill-treat them. She was glad Carlos had gone away to Portugal for his sake.

When Linda reached home, she hugged her mother and tears trickled down her cheeks. Her mother did not realize why. Soon the neighbours came to welcome Linda. They asked her what had happened in Panjim on and before the Liberation Day. Linda recounted all incidents and rumours she had heard. After a while, when all neighbours had left, Linda cried and cried as if she could not stop. Her mother came and hugged her. She thought Linda cried because of Carlos.

Linda told her mother everything. She told her how Carlos was involved in the government's top-secret mission and that she had not seen him since December third at Old Goa. She explained how he came to her just once with two soldiers at *Liceu* before going away to Portugal on December 15th. When she came to the end of her story she just looked straight into the eyes of her mother and said, "Mama, I am pregnant." She then hugged her mother and began to cry uncontrollably.

Her mother was shocked and did not know what to do or say for about three minutes. Her mind went blank and she wasn't sure she heard right. She just held Linda and said, "It's all right, *baai*. It's all right. We will think of something," over and over again like a stuck record.

Joanita did not move. Disaster after disaster seemed to hit her family lately. She could not comprehend why these things happened. First, it was the death of her husband and now Linda was pregnant and Carlos was gone! What was she to do with poor Linda now? She felt desperate but her maternal instinct to protect her daughter at any cost forced her to sort out her thoughts and come up with a plan. No point looking back! She analysed her limited options.

Her mother said, "*Baai*, you stay in Panjim for the duration of your pregnancy, and never show up in Cuncolim until after you deliver the child. People here will make my life miserable, if they know you are carrying that *paclo's* white Portuguese baby."

"But mother," Linda said, "How will I be able to deliver the baby and where will I stay?"

"You should have thought about that before you got pregnant. I warned you about Carlos, but you were in love and you did not listen. Where is your love now?" her mother reminded her. "Try to talk to the Mother Superior and explain to her that you cannot go back to the village, carrying this baby," her mother continued.

So it was arranged that after the Christmas holidays, Linda would return to Panjim never to come back again to Cuncolim until after the baby was born.

"What are we going to do about the baby Mama?" Linda asked her mother.

"You are not going to keep the baby. That's for sure. You are only seventeen. You have no husband and our society will not accept this scandal. You better give the baby up for adoption. With the baby, you will have no future. You better talk to the Mother Superior; perhaps she can help you out there. But I do not want you to keep the baby, and that is final," stressed her mother.

After a while, a new thought struck Joanita.

"Wait a minute. I just remembered that the people at the Social Welfare Agency, the *Provedoria Assistência Pública* accept unfortunate children born out of wedlock. They keep them in their crèche and Montessori school in Panjim. I read about it in the Konkani weekly *Vauraddeancho Ixtt*. Please talk to the Mother Superior about it when you go back." Her mother advised Linda.

Linda felt much better now that she had talked to her mother, who had offered her wise advice, and always had solutions to problems. For the first time in a month, Linda slept rather well that night.

On Christmas day, Linda and her mother went to church and celebrated a low key Christmas like every one else in Goa, as there was a curfew in place. There were no Christmas dances anywhere, just the midnight Mass and celebration at home. This year even the annual Christmas night serenade was cancelled.

Joanita made sweets and *sorpotel* for Christmas. Linda could not relish it as much as before. Despite the pills to control her vomiting, she did not do any Christmas visits this time for fear of betraying her condition.

After a week, Linda said goodbye to her mother and cried, as she was not going to see her for a long time at least not until the baby was delivered. Her mother had never been to Panjim before as she felt out of place visiting the *Instituto* where everybody spoke Portuguese. May be now, after liberation, she would be more comfortable visiting Linda in Panjim.

When Linda went to Panjim, she explained everything to the Mother Superior. The head nun said it was her moral duty to keep Linda at the *Instituto* and help her deliver the baby, even if it meant to bend certain rules. And yes, the Mother Superior assured Linda she would talk to the Director at *Provedoria Assistência Publica* to make arrangements for Linda's delivery and the subsequent adoption of the baby. Linda was comforted after that assurance.

The next day, Linda found courage to write a letter to Carlos in Portugal.

Linda was about to go out and mail the letter, when she saw Heidi at the door.

"Hi Linda, you look ill today. Is anything the matter?" asked Heidi.

"Come with me Heidi, I need someone to talk to and I need to mail this letter to Carlos."

"A letter to Carlos? And why? He is in Portugal right now, isn't he?"

"Heidi, I am pregnant with Carlos' baby."

"Oh My God! Then Linda you must abort the baby right away and forget about Carlos."

"No way Heidi. I am not going to abort my baby."

"But how will you bring up the baby alone, Linda?"

"I don't know. Maybe I will give the baby up for adoption or something. But I have decided not to abort my baby."

"So why are you writing to Carlos? What can he do now? He can't come here now to be with you?"

"But he has a right to know. He is the father. Besides he has got to know what I am going through. He truly loves me"

"It's up to you Linda. So what are you going to do now?"

"Probably go back to school. We will see what happens later."

"Good luck Linda. Tell me if I can do anything."

Linda mailed the letter to Carlos and kept herself busy after that. She was waiting to get a reply from Carlos. Anything could happen now. As days and weeks went by, Linda started to have doubts about Carlos. Maybe he did not want to take her to Portugal and get married to her; or by this time, he would have written to her. It was now more than two months after the war in Goa. Carlos should have written to update her about what had happened to him after the war. But no letter arrived. Linda was worried.

Until she received a letter from Carlos, she could not keep up her hopes of going to Portugal to be with Carlos. In the meantime, Linda decided to make alternate plans. She had to concentrate on her future. Now she had to plan her future. As the Portuguese had left, there was no point in continuing her studies at *Liceu*. She had to switch to English. She could get admission to College next June.

In the meantime she registered for the Secondary School Certificate Board Examination (S.S.C.E.) through an affiliated local English High School in Panjim. She attended the school and worked hard to take her mind off her troubles. She obtained distinction in all subjects at the Annual S.S.C. Examinations in April 1962. Linda was ranked in the top ten at the S.S.C. examinations in Goa and won a Merit scholarship at the local Dhempe College, when it opened in June of 1962.

Chapter 31

It was during the second week of December 1961 that Carlos had to leave Linda abruptly. This was because the Portuguese military in Goa had received secret messages from their intelligence sources. The surveillance pictures taken from the reconnaissance planes by Pentagon and NATO indicated that India had its army mobilized all along Goa's borders and was going to invade Goa soon. Carlos was given responsibility to evacuate Portuguese civilians including women and children from Goa to Portugal as soon as possible. And since this was top secret, he was asked not to divulge this information to anyone, including Linda. Carlos had no choice. He was disciplined enough to concentrate on the mission at hand, rather than get distracted by thoughts of Linda.

It was the most hectic time of his life. He had to make frequent trips from the Dabolim Airport in Goa to Karachi, Pakistan and back to Goa. Then from Karachi someone else would take over and escort the Portuguese civilians all the way to Portugal.

He had to make sure all his passengers boarded each of the connecting flights. It was very difficult with children on board. Carlos was exhausted. At nights he could not sleep well. Linda's memories haunted him. What must she be feeling now? She must think that he abandoned her. Thoughts of Linda crying and missing him bothered Carlos. He missed her too. But what could he do? He had devoted his life to his *Pátria*, his Fatherland, which took precedence over anything or anyone else.

Carlos would take Linda's photo from his wallet and feel better just looking at her. "Be patient, *querida*. Be brave, my little Linda." he would mutter to himself. Carlos would think about their intimate last night at Hotel Mandovi on Linda's birthday. How they had made sweet love that night. How romantic it was that night! He wished she were with him now by his side.

On his last trip, which he had made on December 16th, he received word that Goa was definitely going to be invaded by India. Carlos was held directly responsible for carrying all the Goan gold from the Banco Nacional Ultramarino to Portugal. He couldn't even phone Linda and talk to her. That really hurt. Instead he had to leave a letter for her at the last minute.

When he arrived in Portugal on December 19th on the last escape flight, Goa, Damão e Diu had officially become a part of India. He lost his beloved Linda too in the process. His heart broken, his spirits down, he almost lost his sanity.

The whole of Portugal felt as if it had lost a beloved daughter, gloominess reigning everywhere. Portugal had lost its favourite overseas possession, its first since Brazil. There was a huge uproar and lament in Portugal after the loss of Goa, Damão e Diu.

For a few weeks, Carlos stayed with his mother, solitary and lonely and he wouldn't talk to anyone. His mother tried to take him out somewhere for a change, but Carlos wouldn't go anywhere.

Carlos told his mother about his Goan girlfriend, Linda Cardoso. He showed her Linda's picture. He asked her to check his mail in his absence and take particular care of any mail from Linda. His mother liked the girl's photo and she even asked Carlos to marry her as soon as possible.

Carlos wrote this letter to Linda:

Carlos Soares
January 11th, 1962

Darling Linda,

I hope you are doing fine my darling.

I miss you so much. I cannot tell you how much I love you. So many things have happened since I last saw you, my love. I am waiting to hear from you. Please write as soon as possible.

After the war started in Goa, I reached Portugal safely. But those were hectic days for me, making so many trips from Goa to Pakistan. Now that the war is over, the entire country is grieving sadly at losing our favourite possession and I am even more devastated at losing you at this time. There is not one moment when I do not remember you or miss you. I am sitting in my mother's apartment quite alone and desolate and I miss you the most.

I have not gone out of the house since I arrived here. My friends and relatives are trying to comfort me, but I just don't feel I am alive without you by my side. I don't know what's going to happen now.

A letter from you would give me solace in these trying times. Please write to me soon. I love you! I kiss your photo every time and wish you were here.

Waiting eagerly to hear from you soon!

Yours,

Forever in love,

Carlos

After a month, Carlos received orders from the Portuguese Foreign Office to go to Geneva, Switzerland to discuss the issue of Portuguese prisoners of war in India. He was to liaise with International Red Cross office.

Carlos went to Geneva to negotiate and secure the release of Portuguese prisoners of war in Goa. After a lengthy process of sorting out matters with the United Nations and the Red Cross, Carlos was instrumental in securing their early release and ships were sent to Karachi, Pakistan to get all Portuguese military prisoners and civilians back to Portugal from Goa via the Red Cross.

It took the better part of three to four months for these negotiations to take place and with all the red tape connected with the bureaucracy of the international organizations, Carlos had absolutely no time to think about Linda or write to her. By the time he came back to Portugal from Geneva, it was already May of 1962.

In a strange turn of events, Carlos' mother Maria Elena Soares had a stroke in early March. When Carlos went back to Portugal, his mother had been paralysed and she could not talk.

Carlos's mother Maria Elena had received Linda's letter in February 1962 and she had saved the letter in her jewellery box for Carlos, but unfortunately soon after that she had the stroke. Someone notified Carlos that his mother had been very sick. But since Carlos was very busy, he could not go to Portugal right away. Now, his mother could not talk or show any signs where the letter was kept.

Carlos never even thought about the jewellery box, but he checked the tables, drawers, the cabinet and everywhere, but he could not see any mail from Linda. Carlos even went to the post office to check the post box, which was in his mother's name. Still he found no mail from Linda.

Once he was back in Portugal from Geneva, Carlos looked after the welfare of the Goan refugees, servicemen and families affected by the liberation of Goa, Damão e Diu. Carlos had to deal with Goans with Portuguese passports who declared themselves as refugees and who came to Portugal from Goa via Karachi, Pakistan and other parts of the world including Africa. Salazar decreed that the Goan refugees be treated extremely well in Portugal and that they be given priorities for jobs there. But the Portuguese economy was not good at the time. The refugees were given shelter and were offered welfare payments by the state.

Chapter 32

Heidi knew it was about time for a letter to arrive from Carlos to Linda. She was always on the lookout for foreign mail. One day a letter from Carlos, postmarked in Portugal, did arrive at the Institute's office, and Heidi as usual being the first to look at the mail, quickly stole the letter addressed to Linda from the mailbox in the office. She never gave it to Linda. Heidi read the letter but never divulged its contents to Linda.

Linda thought Carlos never sent her any reply to her letter from Portugal. Every day she would look in the mailbox, but she never saw any mail for her, except from her godfather in Bombay. Not a single line from Carlos! Linda could not understand why Carlos had not replied. Did he not love her any more? Was the address he had given her wrong? She did not think so. She knew Carlos well enough. But then what could he do anyway even if he did receive the letter? He could not come back to Goa, as Portugal did not have any diplomatic relations with India. At least he should have replied as a courtesy. She almost gave up on Carlos and concentrated only on her own future. But she would write to him when the baby arrived.

Heidi would ask Linda several times if she had received a reply from Carlos, just to make her feel bad, instead of comforting her. "You see I told you not to write to Carlos in the first place," Heidi reminded Linda.

"Well I won't write to him another letter again until the baby is born."

"Good for you Linda, you can forget about him now."

Linda registered for the First Year of Science studies at Dhempe College, as she had a free scholarship. But she did not attend College when it started in June. Instead she was getting ready for her delivery.

On the fourth of July 1962, Linda was taken to the Goa Medical College Hospital and she delivered a beautiful seven-pound baby girl. Her mother had been informed about Linda's labour pain and she came to see the baby at the hospital in Panjim. They had a photographer take a picture of the baby. The mother and baby were doing fine.

Linda named the baby 'Lusindia', which was meant to be a hybrid of Lusitania (old name for Portugal) and India. She registered the birth of Baby Lusindia naming Carlos Soares as the father.

A representative from the *Provedoria Assistência Pública,* the Social Welfare Agency of the government, arrived promptly along with a nurse and all relevant adoption papers.

The baby looked very cute. The baby looked very fair and beautiful. Linda felt so attached to the baby that she wanted to keep her, but her mother strongly convinced her not to keep the baby, as it was the best for both of them in the circumstances.

Linda could not part with a piece of her heart, a product of her eternal love with Carlos. How could she give away her own flesh and blood?

But then again how could she bring up the baby without her father? Society would frown upon such a scandal. She had no job. How was she going to look after the baby? The new Goa government was looking for candidates with an English education for the civil service. Linda did not have proficiency in English. With the baby around, she could not go for higher education. Her father had already died, and there was no male adult in the family, who could look after them. It was impossible to keep the baby.

Linda had asked the *Provedoria* to prepare a document in triplicate whereby Linda or Carlos retained an option to claim the baby back later, if the baby was still under the care of the *Provedoria.* Linda signed this document in triplicate so she could mail one copy to Carlos in Portugal, should he be interested in the baby later on.

Linda signed all adoption papers and signed away all her rights to the baby over to the *Provedoria*. With tears in her eyes she handed over her precious little Lusindia to the nurse from the *Provedoria*. They took the baby right away, without even letting Linda breastfeed her new baby. Both Linda and her mother cried when the baby was taken away. Linda felt a pang in her heart as she realized she was really an unfortunate and disgraced mother, who couldn't even feed her own baby with milk from her full breasts.

They would not have anything to do with the baby, when she grew up. It would remain a secret for the rest of their lives. For her own good and that of the baby, Linda was discouraged from visiting *Crèche Ninho Infantil*, the infants' shelter of the *Provedoria Assistência Pública* in Panjim, where Lusindia was taken.

Linda returned to the *Instituto*. She would think about the baby day and night and feel guilty. She would dream about breastfeeding the baby, only to wake up alone at night with no baby around, milk dripping from her nipples. She felt desperate and her spirits would be down. This would go on day after day and she would wake up crying in her sleep.

After taking a long rest of two weeks, Linda went to the birth registration department and obtained two birth certificates of the baby. She wrote a letter to Carlos and mailed it to him, enclosing the picture of the baby, the birth certificate and a document from the *Provedoria*.

On August the fourth, when the baby completed one full month, Linda gathered some courage and went to *Crèche Ninho Infantil* at Fontainhas, Panjim to see how the baby was doing. Linda took Heidi along with her to show her the baby. Linda told Heidi that she had just mailed a second letter to Carlos. Heidi made a mental note of the date, so she could watch out for the reply from Carlos to Linda in the foreign mail about two months from now.

The *Provedoria Assistência Pública*, a public assistance organization in Goa, had built this beautiful complex, just outside Fontainhas in Panjim, along the road, Rua de Ourêm leading to Agaçaim. A lottery, private donations and charitable institutions from Europe and the Portuguese government had funded it. This orphanage was established to take care of, aid and adopt the abandoned and handicapped children of Goa. It was run by nuns who were assisted by an efficient support group of nurses, social workers, attendants and two full-time doctors on duty twenty-four hours a day.

Crèche Ninho Infantil was a huge place. It had a Montessori school and a huge park for kids to play. There were swings, slides, a sports ground and other equipment for children's games. There was a beautiful garden with roses and flowers of different varieties to give the place a real homely touch. There were well-dressed little boys and girls, white, black and brown running gleefully around the big compound.

The young Goan women, who had these babies out of wedlock from liaison with the European and African Portuguese military personnel, could not and did not keep such illegitimate babies and raise them themselves. These women wrapped up their newborn babies and left them at the front door of any big house and disappeared. Then the owners of the house would call police, who would take the babies and hand them over to the *Provedoria*. In most cases there were no names of the baby's father and mother. And the society called these innocent kids *filhos de puta*, (sons of a bitch), the bastards.

Linda went inside to the reception. She signed in at the desk and a nurse came to take her to the baby. They went to the children's nursery and the nurse picked up Lusindia and handed her over to Linda and left. Lusindia looked quite different in just a month. She looked fair and beautiful. She had her father's colour and some of his features but she had her mother's jet-black hair, brown eyes and looks.

Lusindia looked very cute and Linda held her and hugged her. She had grown and she was a warm, quiet and happy baby. The baby looked straight into Linda's eyes and held her gaze. Linda felt guilty. She thought the baby seemed to question her. Why had she been left here in this crèche. Didn't she already have a father and a mother? Was it her fault that she was brought into this world?

Tears of guilt rolled down Linda's eyes. She kissed the baby again and again. Linda looked around the infants' nursery. There were more than a hundred babies there, mostly white, about ten black and the rest brown. The babies ranged from just-born infants to about a year in age.

Linda's heart sank when she saw these infants, who would never feel the warmth of their mother and neither would her own darling Lusindia. She could not stand it any longer. She kissed her baby again and again and for an instant Linda saw her baby smile. She hoped it was a smile just for her.

All at once Linda thought of something on instinct. This was a perfect opportunity for her to show her baby she was her real mother. She went to the corner of the room, unhooked her bra and put the baby to her breast. At first the baby did not know what to do. Then Linda squeezed her breast and some milk sprayed in the baby's mouth. Lusindia liked what she tasted and she started to suck the nipple naturally. It was the most delightful moment in Linda's life. Oh how heavenly it felt when her baby sucked at her breast. After a while, Linda shifted her to the other breast.

Linda's breasts had been heavy with milk all this time and they hurt considerably at times. Her baby tasted her mother's milk for the first time and both mother and baby seemed quite satisfied. Lusindia was on infant formula, with which the nuns fed her daily.

While she was feeding the baby, she heard a sound behind her; Linda abruptly stopped feeding. Breastfeeding by mothers who abandoned their babies was strictly against the rules in the crèche, but Linda was determined to fulfil her maternal duty at least once in her life.

Linda tapped the baby lightly on her back and Lusindia burped a little.

Linda took the baby to the sitting room for visitors, where Heidi was waiting.

"Look at my baby, Heidi. Isn't she wonderful?"

"Oh whât a beautiful angel! Hi Lusindia, this is your Aunt Heidi."

"Who do you think she looks like, Heidi?"

"She has your looks Linda and Carlos's skin colour. It's still too early to tell. But she is a perfect baby."

"Thank you Heidi. I only wish I could keep this baby."

"Can I hold the baby, please, Linda?"

"Sure Heidi, here."

"Oh my! Look at her! Coo-chee-coo-chee-coo!" The baby started to cry as soon as Heidi held her.

Linda took the baby back to the crib, planted a kiss on her forehead and with a heavy heart said goodbye to Lusindia and left.

Chapter 33

West Germany wanted to recruit people for their expanding post-war economy. The Portuguese government was only too glad to oblige and Carlos was posted as a special liaison officer with Germany's Manpower and Immigration Office at the Portuguese embassy in Bonn. Carlos went to West Germany in July of 1962 to take up his new post. He helped Portuguese nationals and refugees obtain employment in Germany.

Carlos thought about Linda, but what could he do? He could not go to India, as there were no diplomatic relations between India and Portugal. He wondered where she was and what she was doing. He thought of writing to her, but where? She would not be at *Instituto Piedade* still. He did not have her correct address, even at her village. There was nothing that could be done, unless she came to Germany or Portugal. He did not think her mother would allow her to do that. In any case he wanted to write to her, explaining the situation.

After a month of his arrival in Germany, things were much quieter for Carlos. For the first time, he got some rest in the office. Finally Carlos took time to write this letter to Linda:

Carlos Soares
August 18th, 1962

My Dearest Linda,

I am sure you will be surprised to hear from me after a long time. I hope you received my first letter, which I wrote to you in January of 1962, after I came to Portugal from Goa.

First of all let me apologize for this long delay. I have been too busy since I left Goa. When I went to Portugal, I was given the responsibility to go to Geneva to negotiate the release of Portuguese prisoners of war in Goa with the United Nations and the Red Cross. That took three to four months. Then I came back to Portugal in May 1962 and I was in charge of subsequent resettlement of the Portuguese refugees and ex-servicemen and their families from Goa.

I never received any letter from you in Portugal. My mother has been sick and she is paralysed. Now, I am posted as a Special Liaison Officer in the Portuguese Embassy in Bonn, West Germany.

I always wonder what you are doing presently and I am worried. I am sure you are pursuing a good career in Goa. However if you are keen on coming to Germany, I can help you out as I am still attached to the Portuguese embassy in Bonn, West Germany.

Please let me know if you are interested. It's quite easy for you to get a Portuguese passport and travel to West Germany. We can get married once you are in West Germany.

Please let me know of your decision. Please reply to me at the Portuguese Embassy, Bonn, West Germany. I will be waiting for your reply, darling.

Yours,
Forever in love,
Carlos

Carlos mailed this letter in duplicate on August 18th, 1962 in the official Portuguese Embassy envelope with the embassy address on the front of the envelope without his name on it. Carlos did not know Linda's full address in Cuncolim. He addressed one copy of the letter to: Linda Cardoso, Cuncolim, Goa, India and the other copy to: Linda Cardoso at *Instituto Piedade*, Panjim, Goa, India, without the complete detailed addresses.

The letter sent to Cuncolim came back to Carlos in September after more than a month and the reason given was:

"Address Incomplete. Return to Sender."

The postman in Cuncolim had looked around for Linda Cardoso in the entire village. There were at least three such people in Cuncolim, but when the postman asked them all if they expected a letter from Germany, they all replied in the negative, including Linda's mother Joanita, who had no one in Germany. The postman could not deliver the letter without being sure who the right recipient was, as the address did not mention the exact location of the recipient. The postman returned the letter to the sender in Germany, which was the Portuguese Embassy in Bonn, as per the rules.

Carlos was really sad that Linda did not get his letter. But then again he thought that Linda should have written to him by now. And he had not heard from her. He wondered what had happened to his second letter addressed to Linda in Panjim. She must have received that letter, since it had not come back, unless she had moved out of the *Instituto Piedade*. May be, he thought, she had got married or something. But right now there was nothing he could do. He could not even visit Goa, as Portugal had no diplomatic ties with India. If Linda was really married, he did not want to get in her way. Carlos gave up on his Linda.

Carlos' mother Maria Elena finally died in September 1962. Carlos was too busy in Germany and could not attend her funeral at such short notice. The post office was informed of her death, and her attorney collected all the mail from her post box. Three months after Maria Elena's death, her attorney sold her house and settled the affairs of her estate. He executed her will and handed over her valuable documents, jewellery box, her mail and other papers to Carlos' aunt, Teodora Cabral for safe-keeping, to be given to Carlos whenever he came to Portugal. Linda's second letter to Carlos was in this mail collected from the post box belonging to Carlos' mother, Maria Elena.

Carlos wished Linda were here with him. Too bad, she never got his letter. Where would she be? If only there was some contact with her, he would be at peace knowing her intentions and whereabouts. Their love was true and immortal, but political events and other circumstances had separated them from each other. For hours, he would think about Linda feeling helpless in his inability to contact her.

Chapter 34

In the month of September of 1962, the second letter that Carlos had written to Linda arrived at the *Instituto Piedade*. Again Heidi intercepted this letter before Linda could get it. Heidi was very happy after she read its contents. She was glad Carlos was employed in Germany. Here was her chance!

Heidi hid both the letters from Carlos to Linda, in the inner pocket of her suitcase. She got a passport right away, wrote to her father in Germany about her trip, made all travel arrangements and left for Germany in December of 1962, without even breathing a word about it to her best friend, Linda.

Her father came to welcome her at the Frankfurt airport. She saw her father for the first time, since he had left Goa after she was born.

Heidi's father had arranged a small apartment for her in Frankfurt. He had not yet told his family about Heidi though he had helped Heidi and her mother financially. He asked Heidi not to get in touch with his family for obvious reasons.

Heidi's life was a peculiar one. She had her mother in Goa, but she was ashamed to live with her mother, because she was a prostitute. And here in Germany, she had a father, who was ashamed to call her his daughter, as she was illegitimate. He could not even introduce her to his family. Heidi belonged to no one. She had never experienced true love and affection from anyone and so, was close to no one. She had not learnt to trust. She just lived as well as she could in such insecurity. The only consolation was that her father supported her financially. However, she desperately yearned for a normal family life and a loving relationship. Heidi hoped to find a whole new life.

Now was the time. She had to execute her plan carefully and see if the strategy that she thought of in Goa, would work now in Germany. Heidi got up one fine morning, wore a provocative dress, took a train to Bonn and headed straight to the Portuguese Embassy.

She went to the reception and asked for Carlos Soares. In about ten minutes, Carlos showed up. Carlos could not believe his eyes.

"Heidi! I don't believe it. How are you Heidi?" Carlos hugged her.

"I am fine Carlos. And you?"

"When did you come to Germany?"

"Just last week."

"And how did you know I was stationed here?"

"I didn't." Heidi lied. "I just came here to attest my certificates and I just happened to see your name here on the official list."

"Welcome, Heidi. I am so pleased to see you. Have you heard from Linda, recently?" Carlos asked her right away.

"I am sorry, no. I haven't." She lied again. "The last I heard was that Linda was about to get married to some Goan in East Africa."

"Oh I see. I sent her two letters and I haven't heard from her since I left Goa."

"I am sorry I really can't help you there, Carlos."

"Listen. Can we go out this afternoon and talk some more?"

"Sure. I am not doing anything for now. It will be my pleasure. I just have to leave a little early as I have to get back to my apartment in Frankfurt."

"No problem, Heidi. Meet me here at about 2:30 p.m. We can go for a late lunch, if you don't mind please."

"Of course not, Carlos, I will be waiting for you here."

Heidi murmured to herself "Ah! Just as I had planned."

Later that afternoon, Carlos took Heidi to a fancy Portuguese restaurant. They ordered some food and drinks.

"So tell me more about Linda. What was she doing when you last saw her?"

Carlos was very eager to know more about Linda, but Heidi did not volunteer any information about her. She did not even tell him that Linda had been pregnant with his child and that he was the father of a baby girl, Lusindia. Instead, Heidi concocted stories about Linda.

"She left *Instituto Piedade* a long time ago. I heard the girls talking about her. They said she was about to get married right away to a very rich Goan boy in Nairobi, Kenya, East Africa. She even quit College all of a sudden to get married, which probably means she is in Nairobi right now." Heidi lied convincingly.

Carlos seemed really sad to hear this piece of news about Linda. Now he saw no hope and was dejected. Heidi used this to get close to him.

"Come on Carlos. Cheer up! It's not the end of the world." And she kissed him lightly on his cheeks and hugged him close. Just then the drinks arrived.

"Here's to you Heidi. *Prost!* Welcome to Deutschland," Carlos raised his glass.

They had lunch consisting of soup, rice, bacalhao fish and roast chicken, which they washed down with some cold German beer and wine.

After the lunch was over Heidi asked Carlos for his phone number and address.

"It was nice to see you after a long time, Heidi."

"It was my pleasure, Carlos. Thanks for the great lunch and for your lovely company."

"You are welcome. We must do it again soon."

"Sure. I hope I manage to get a job."

"I will see what I can do."

"*Até logo*, Carlos."

"You take care, Heidi. Call me if you need anything."

Carlos accompanied Heidi to the station, hugged her and they parted company.

The next day, Heidi called Carlos at home. She talked for a long time. Heidi called Carlos almost every day after that.

Carlos began to think about Heidi now. She was not bad after all, he said to himself. And he was quite lonesome. Why not go out with Heidi? He had not heard from Linda since he left Goa in December 1961. It was now more than a year, since they were separated. If Linda really loved him, she would have found him or written to him. May be she was happily married to that man in East Africa. Should he wait for her, when she didn't wait for him?

The next time Heidi called Carlos, she received good news from him.

"Heidi, Congratulations! You got yourself a job. A friend of mine has lined up a job for you as a secretary for a small Portuguese company."

"Oh really? Thank you very much, Carlos, you are wonderful."

"You have to go and see your employer tomorrow. Come to my office at 9 a.m. and I will take you there. Then in the afternoon, we can celebrate."

"Oh Carlos, you are an angel, you think of everything."

"Guess what! I even found an apartment for you right here in Bonn."

"Oh my! Carlos, you are the most thoughtful person in the world. Thanks."

"You are most welcome, Heidi. See you tomorrow."

The next day Heidi received her job offer as expected. Heidi and Carlos celebrated it with a nice dinner at a restaurant.

"Here's to your success, Heidi. *Prost!*" Carlos kissed Heidi on the cheek.

"Thank you Carlos, I will always be grateful to you for the big favour."

Later, Carlos showed Heidi her new apartment. Within a week, Heidi moved into the apartment and began working in Bonn.

Heidi began seeing Carlos more frequently and soon they began dating each other. Carlos, having lost Linda, was lonesome. Heidi played her game well. Soon Heidi moved in with Carlos. In March of 1963, Carlos and Heidi got married.

Heidi's well-planned strategy had worked and she had achieved her objective. Heidi began to think about Linda as she lay beside Carlos, who was in deep slumber. Linda would have been the one to share Carlos's honeymoon bed tonight. Suddenly, guilty thoughts about Linda plagued her and she couldn't sleep. Heidi squeezed Carlos's hand for reassurance, hoping it was not just another dream.

Carlos turned around. Heidi felt good. It was not a dream! They were really married. Heidi smiled. She put her hand across Carlos' chest. Carlos was all hers now. And Heidi finally went to sleep, satisfied with her victory.

Chapter 35

In the meantime, Linda wondered why there was still no reply from Carlos. Linda wondered what had happened. She kept hoping for one, but none came. Eventually, Linda gave up all hopes and she was determined to put it all behind her and start life all over again.

One day at College a girl she knew, Maria do Céu Távora told her that some Portuguese-educated Goans were obtaining Portuguese passports through the Delhi embassies of Mexico and Brazil and were leaving Goa in hordes. Since India and Portugal had broken diplomatic relations, these embassies had volunteered to carry on diplomatic affairs of Portugal and its citizens in Goa. With Portuguese passports, they could travel to Pakistan, Germany or the UK and from there they would proceed to Portugal or its colonies in Africa.

Maria Távora had some blank application forms for passports. Linda thought she would it give it a try and promptly got her birth certificate and other documents in order, filled up the forms and got everything ready. She had hoped that if she had a Portuguese passport, she might someday be able to see her Carlos in Portugal.

A group of Goans was planning to go to Delhi in January of 1963. Linda joined them. Maria do Céu was in this group as well and they all went to Delhi. On the train, the group consisting of about nineteen *Liceu* educated young people pooled their resources together, had many discussions in Portuguese and planned a strategy to get out of India, in secrecy. They all agreed that they were not going to have a future in India with their Portuguese education and that they would be better off in foreign countries.

Once in Delhi they stayed in Goa Sadan, a hostel for Goan visitors. The next day, they went to the Brazilian Embassy and applied for Portuguese passports in person. They signed and filled all necessary documents, paid the fees and were given receipts. They were told they would get their passports in about three months.

The next day, the group visited the Taj Mahal at Agra. They were all very impressed with this beautiful monument of love. It was designed with great artistry and symmetry and built of pure marble and various kinds of decorative coloured tiles from all over the world. The guide said it was built by the Moghul Emperor Shah Jahan for his beloved wife Mumtaz Mahal in memory of his eternal love for her. The legend said the Emperor ordered the hands of the skilled artisans to be cut off so they could not reproduce this work of art anywhere else. But the emperor paid for such cruelty. His own son imprisoned him a few kilometres away in another fort, from where he would gaze with longing at the Taj. The Taj was best seen at night, when it shimmered in the moonlight.

The next day, they went on a tour of Delhi in which they saw the Qutub Minar, Akbar's Court at Sikri, the Rajghat, place where Gandhiji was cremated, the Parliament buildings, Red Fort and other historical places. Most of them did not know anything about India, its rich culture or its history. They began to view India in a new light.

They stayed in Delhi for a week and enjoyed their stay there. They returned to Goa on a train, singing Portuguese folk songs and telling jokes. They also had further discussions about their strategies to get out of India. When they reached Goa they promised to keep in touch, and let every one know of any developments.

Linda went back to College. She had missed a few lectures and practical classes. She would make up for them in the next few days. In April 1963, her examinations were over and she did not do too badly. Two days after her examinations, she received registered mail. Her Portuguese Passport had arrived. There was a message for her the same day from Maria do Céu Távora, who had called for a meeting at Clube Vasco de Gama at 4:00 p.m. the next day.

Linda went to Clube Vasco de Gama the next day and met Maria do Céu at the reception. There were fifteen other people from the group at the meeting. The leader Aurélio Abranches got up, "Senhores e Senhoras, I have very good news for you. Please try to keep it to yourselves. We do not want an exodus of Goans leaving India, all at once. This plan is legal and has been successful. Some Goans are already in England, Germany and France and are ready to help us out there.

"Here is how it works. We fly from Bombay to London or Frankfurt. From there we take another flight to Portugal and declare ourselves as refugees. Once in Portugal, the government will take care of us either by providing us jobs in Portugal or by handing out stipends until we get jobs, or we could go to Angola or Moçambique. We could even get jobs in Germany or job permits in England. There are lots of opportunities out there. In Goa, with our Portuguese education, we would be at a disadvantage. So it would be best to leave India as soon as possible. I wish you all good luck, Viva!"

Abranches concluded and sat down. Everyone there listened intently and asked many questions. At the end of the discussions and clarifications, Abranches concluded.

"You have a legal Portuguese passport and so a legal right to leave India if you choose to do so. Once you land at London's Heathrow Airport you can claim refugee status and insist you want to go to Portugal. If there is any problem, contact the Portuguese embassy there. They cannot send you back to India. We will get you phone numbers of our contacts in London and Frankfurt. Think it over carefully and make your decision, but hurry. The Portuguese government might recall the Refugee statute any time. Don't delay."

Linda and Maria do Céu talked for a while and Linda told her, she needed some time to ponder over this, as she had to discuss it with her mother. Linda thanked Maria and Abranches and left. Two days later Linda went home to Cuncolim, for the first time after the baby was born, to discuss the subject of going to Portugal.

"Mama, I have something to discuss with you." Linda

started cautiously.

"What is it *baai*?" her mother asked.

"I want to go to London and from there to Portugal."

"*Baai*, why do you want to get out of Goa? We do not have relatives in London or in Portugal. Who will help you? Your boyfriend Carlos has not replied. Maybe he does not even want to see you. Maybe he is married already. At least here in Goa, I will take good care of you. We have a steady income and some day you may marry a nice Goan man and have a great future. But if you go to London or Portugal, you would be jumping from the frying pan into the fire." Joanita was vehement about her misgivings.

"But Mama, you know what happened to me here. I can't even think of getting married to anyone else without knowing what happened to my Carlos. And with the baby, it would be criminal to marry someone else without telling the truth. You know I won't ever do that. I have no life left here in Goa. No one will marry me once they know of my affair with Carlos. And how long can I bear the thought that my baby lives in an orphanage, while her mother lives right here in Goa?" Linda laid bare her soul to her mother.

Joanita realized that Linda was more than right. The poor girl would never make it here in Goa, alone, and she was still young and intelligent and could have better future abroad with her education. Joanita changed her mind, the moment she realised it was in her daughter's best interests.

"*Baai*, do what you have to do. My blessings are with you in whatever you choose to do. I will miss you a lot, though. But this is your life. May God be with you and guide you in the right direction." Joanita approved of Linda's decision to leave Goa and supported Linda all the way.

Linda tried to have great time during her summer holidays. She attended weddings and several functions. She visited her grandmother in Navelim. She knew these were her last few days in Goa. She received the results of her examinations. She had passed her First Year Science with flying colours.

They had a *ladainha* one night at her home. Neighbours, and relatives and children came and they had a great time. Linda quietly prayed that her plans would come to fruition. The day after she saw all her neighbours and relatives, she left for Panjim with all her important belongings after receiving her tearful mother's blessing.

In the morning of June 1, 1963 on the eve of her journey to Bombay, Linda had to make two important visits. First, she took the Agaçaim bus to the miraculous Holy Cross at Bambolim. She bought some flowers and lit some candles at the cross, which was in the middle of a cashew plantation, close to the military base. She knelt down, closed her eyes and in deep meditation, prayed to God to for her plans to work out. She would start a new life in a new country, wherever He guided her. She left everything in God's hands.

The second visit was the difficult one, which was to see her child, Lusindia for the last time. She could not bring herself to do it. Finally with a heavy heart, Linda went to the *Crèche Ninho Infantil* for one last time to bid her adieu. Lusindia was not yet a year old. When her first birthday came, Linda wondered where she would be.

Linda took the baby, hugged her and kissed her. Lusindia had grown. She had a smiling face and already had some teeth. Linda put her finger in her mouth and the baby almost bit her finger. The nurse said she was attempting to walk now. Linda had been so busy with college and making arrangements for her travel abroad that she had neglected to visit Lusindia lately. What an unfortunate mother she was! She wouldn't even be around to witness her baby's very first steps.

Lusindia smiled all the time and Linda felt assured that she was happy at *Crèche Ninho Infantil*. She hoped and prayed fervently that her child would be happy. Linda had taken a small doll for Lusindia. She had an impish look of interest in her face when she saw the doll. That was good. The child liked the doll and started to play with it. All too soon, it was time to say goodbye and Linda could not bear to leave. The baby was so cute and loving and Linda felt like dropping all her plans and taking the baby with her.

Linda looked at her baby and wondered what her future would be like, without her parents by her side. When she began to talk, her baby's first words would not be *Mama* and *Papa*. How would her baby feel on the first day of school, when all other loving parents accompanied their kids? Would she take it in her stride, when people callously called her *filha de puta*? Would she ever wonder who and where her real parents were? Would she hate her parents for the predicament she was in or would she forgive them?

Linda felt very depressed as a million such thoughts bothered her. She held baby to her bosom; a bosom that should have nourished her but never did, save one time. How utterly disgraceful and pathetic she was as a mother! With tears in her eyes, Linda slowly put the baby down, asking God and her daughter to forgive her.

Looking straight ahead, she resolutely made for the door. But when she was past the door, Linda could not stop herself from turning for one last glimpse at her baby. On an impulse, she ran back, kissed her one more time. Tears falling on to Lusindia's cheeks, Linda gave her a big, long hug. She looked intently at Lusindia trying to capture her baby's image in her mind, to be etched on her heart for as long as it took to secure a better future for her.

And all this while, the little one looked at her puzzled. Unable to answer the unasked question in her daughter's eyes, Linda abruptly turned away and left Lusindia. She was determined that it would not be forever.

Linda's heart felt like it was torn apart after her visit to Lusindia. She went to see the Mother Superior, drawing comfort from her words of encouragement, thanked her from the bottom of her heart for all her help and went to sleep. She had to have a good night's rest before the big trip.

The next day marked the beginning of an end to a life that she wanted to forget.

She got up early, made all the preparations, packed her suitcase and was ready for her journey to Bombay. She had bought the steamer ticket at the Chowgule booking office as she was travelling by the *Konkan Sewak* from the Panjim dock. She had heard the sound of the ship's signal as it arrived that morning. She went to the Chapel and prayed to the Virgin Mary that everything would go well on her journey to parts unknown.

She arrived in Bombay early the next day. Her godfather Luciano was already there to receive her. He had received her telegram two days ago. They went to his house where her *madrinha*, Flávia awaited her anxiously.

On the evening of June 4, 1963, at Bombay's Santa Cruz International Airport, Linda boarded a plane for the first time in her life. She was excited yet scared, literally and figuratively, to take her first flight.

She looked out the window; it was dark out there, except for a few lights on the runway. Soon the plane taxied on to the runway, took off and rose high up into the sky... soaring with hope, speeding to leave the dark Indian sky in time to catch a new day that was just dawning in the West.

Chapter 36

The plane landed at Heathrow Airport. Linda came out of the airport and called her Portuguese contact in London, who picked her up and took her to a rooming house in Vauxhall. There they met other Goans, who had come to London the same way. Linda had fish and chips and some pale ale for lunch. She liked the chips but the fish she found tasteless. She liked the city of London, but it was too cold for her, even in summer. After talking to others there, Linda changed her mind about going to Portugal as she heard things were not that wonderful in Portugal. Linda decided to stay in London.

Two days later, Linda went to the Portuguese Embassy in London. The personnel at the embassy were most helpful and cooperative. Linda talked to a counsellor. She told her she wanted to stay in London and finish her studies. The counsellor said they could assist her with a student visa and give her some contacts to find a place to live. The counsellor even gave Linda a loan of hundred pounds for immediate expenses and told her she could pay it back anytime. Linda was very grateful.

Linda and her Goan friends went on a tour of London on the double-decker London Transport bus. They saw Buckingham Palace, the Parliament Buildings, the Marble Arch, the Tower of London, Madame Tussaud's Wax Museum and other historical places. Linda admired these places of interest.

On Monday, first thing in the morning, Linda went to the University to check for admissions. The counsellor recommended that she complete advanced courses in Biology, Chemistry, Physics, Mathematics and English before attempting the University Science programme. She recommended a pre-University Grammar School in London that catered to foreign students.

On Tuesday, Linda went to the school and consulted the counsellor, showing her the First Year Science transcript from Bombay University and her Fifth Year Lyceum diploma. Linda received some credits for these and she had to do only six courses to get her advanced level accreditation. She could start her academic year in September, 1963 and finish her 'advance level' courses in one year. Linda also applied for some financial help in the form of a scholarship.

On Wednesday, Linda went to Oxford Circus and was amazed to see the huge shopping malls there. She made her first clumsy ascent on the escalator, saying *"Muj Mãe gue!"* She was thrilled with it and even more taken up with her first roller-coaster ride.

The shopping malls looked inviting but poor Linda could not buy anything. They were too expensive. She could not help converting the Pound into Indian rupees to see if a thing was worth the price. And each time she got a shock. Nothing was affordable.

Linda managed on cheap food and vegetables. She had to save money for school. She had to think about getting a job right away. She called her counsellor at the embassy after a week to see if anything had come up. But there was nothing at the time.

About two days later, Linda got a phone call from the Portuguese counsellor asking her to come to the embassy to talk about an employment offer. Linda went the next day. She was taken to the Portuguese Ambassador, His Excellency Dom Eleuterio Borges who told Linda that he had a part-time vacancy for a nanny to look after his two school-going kids.

Linda told him about her school commitments. The Ambassador said it was all right since the job would require her to take care of his kids when they were not in school and to do a little household work over the weekends. The Ambassador told her that she would get free room and board in his house and she would get a salary that would be enough to pay for her education. Linda could not refuse such a welcome offer and she readily accepted.

The next day Linda took her belongings and went to live at the Borges's residence in Golders Green. It was an upscale residential area, with executive homes and huge driveways. Only the rich and famous lived there. Linda loved the surroundings. The Ambassador's kids were adorable and they took to Linda at once. The Ambassador's wife, Dona Amelia who spoke Portuguese was an elegant woman, and she was extremely warm and courteous to Linda. Dona Amelia showed Linda her quarters and briefed her on her duties at the residence.

Linda thanked God for giving her a nice new home and a wonderful family to work with. She had about a month before she went to school. She prepared for school whenever she could. Her work with the children was interesting. The kids preferred to speak English but the parents wanted them be to be fluent in Portuguese, and so Linda had to keep talking to them in Portuguese. The Ambassador managed to get Linda a work permit from the Home Office as a live-in nanny, who spoke Portuguese.

What Linda liked best in London were the television programmes, especially the comedy. She was convinced that the London comedians were the best in the world. Although at times she could not comprehend the local Cockney accent, she gradually got hooked. For world news and investigative journalism, she thought nobody could beat the BBC. Linda loved the documentaries and reports, the London Palladium shows full of glitter and glamour especially the new talent show, football matches, the Eurovision contest and musical hit parades with beautiful dancers and singers belting out their "Song of the Week" to the delight of millions of viewers.

Linda started her advanced courses in September of 1963. She had to work really hard as the educational system was more comprehensive than in Goa. She divided her time at home efficiently between her household chores and her homework. The weekend was usually the busiest especially when the Ambassador entertained dignitaries and gave lavish parties for diplomats from different parts of the globe. At other times, she was left with the kids, whenever their parents went out for parties. Linda received some extra money for the special parties and managed to pay back the hundred pounds she borrowed from the counsellor at the Portuguese embassy.

Linda celebrated her first Christmas in London. She was surprised that people were busy shopping, buying gifts, decorating their homes and lighting their homes and streets as early as the first week of December. This really made her laugh. Linda saw her first snowfall in the middle of December and she was filled with happiness. She went out and felt the snow, soft and white as cotton. But it had no taste. She remembered her habit of soaking in the first rain in Goa. She thought she would do likewise with the first snow of the season, but it was too cold.

It was a picture-perfect White Christmas that year just like the Christmas cards she used to receive from her relatives in East Africa. They went to the church. But Christmas in London was different. The Mass was a simple service that was over in an hour. No long lines to kiss the Baby Jesus and drop coins at His feet. No long hours of singing a *cantada* Mass. It was like a fast food service that served His body and blood. They sang Christmas carols before the Mass and the actual service was over in an hour. She liked the service in the Westminster Cathedral in London. There were no long sermons here, no Latin quotes. Everyone received Holy Communion, even the men. In Goa you had to go for confession before you received Holy Communion and so men shied away from this except for the mandatory Holy Communion at Easter.

After the Mass there was no Christmas Dance in the church hall. People did not meet outside the church to wish each other "Merry Christmas". It was too cold outside. After the service, they all walked or drove straight back home to open gift boxes kept under the Xmas tree. You did not see anyone dressed up for Christmas here whereas in Goa, they wore the best suits and dresses. Here in London, every one used same old winter coat and you could not see what was worn underneath anyway. She missed home. No Christmas cookies, no *sorpotel* here. If she had the time, she would make some Goan Christmas sweets herself.

Soon, it was New Year's Eve of 1964. There was no dance to attend. Instead, she planned to join her Goan friends, who had arranged a small party. None of them knew how to cook real Goan food. Back home, they had servants and cooks to do the cooking. Linda went to a local Indian store to buy basmati rice, spices and pickles and vegetables. There she met a

Goan lady from East Africa, Mrs Sophie Rebelo.

She told Linda there were some Goans with British passports from East Africa, who had just migrated to England. Sophie said this group was having a New Year's Dance in a church hall in Swansea, London. Linda told her she could not make it at such a short notice but she would love to come the next year. Linda took Sophie's phone number for further contact. Linda prepared some Goan pork *vindalho* and some *pulau* for the New Year's party. They had a great time singing in Portuguese and Konkani.

In June of 1964, Linda finished her advanced level courses, and she did very well as usual. When the results came in, she had straight A's in all subjects. She was offered a scholarship for a four-year course leading to the Bachelor's Degree in Science at the University. She was still living at the Borges residence but not working as a nanny any more. She helped in the household chores sometimes as a favour, and did her own cooking.

Linda had thrown a small party for her Goan friends in London in the summer of 1964 to celebrate her results and admission to the University. All her friends were present at the party. Maria do Céu Távora and Abranches, who had just come to London three weeks ago attended. They were about to leave for Portugal the following week and Linda threw a party in their honour. Linda cooked pulau and pork *vindalho* for the party, as she was now an expert at these two dishes.

They celebrated by drinking and singing. Linda gave Abranches and Maria her phone number at the Ambassador's residence. She asked them to find out about Carlos Soares in Portugal if they could and to let her know if there was any news. Right now, Linda wanted to complete her university studies in London. Later, she could join Carlos if he was located. After the party was over, they all hugged each other and Linda went home.

Linda managed to get a part-time job as a Laboratory Assistant in one of the Medical laboratories attached to the University Hospital in London, and worked the entire weekend. She made good money there. In the summer holidays, she would work full-time.

As months went by, Linda met more Goans in London. She met newly arrived Goans from East Africa, who were just beginning to migrate to England after their colonies in Africa were almost assured of getting their independence. All these Goans had British passports and England became their natural destination because life seemed uncertain for Asians after independence in East Africa.

Linda was well liked by the British. There was not too much discrimination against the Asians, as they were very few and were not considered a threat as job seekers. The Asian people were in demand for their diligent work and quiet, servile nature. Linda had a rather easy time at the University as she received a lot of cooperation and help from her professors.

Linda finished her First Year with straight A's in June 1965. She worked the entire summer and earned a lot of money. It felt good to have cold hard cash in her hands. With her first full pay cheque, she went to the church and offered candles to Our Lady in thanksgiving and sent some money to her mother in Goa. Out of her next pay packet, she kept ten quid for herself and went on a shopping spree at Oxford Circus. She bought some things that were on sale – dresses, lipstick, perfume and toiletries almost exhausting her expense money for a whole month.

Chapter 37

Meanwhile, in Velha Goa, Lusindia grew up in the PAP *Provedoria* building along with the other orphan girls. Most of them were white.

Lusindia was fair and very beautiful. She had many friends there and she was well liked. Some visitors who distributed toys to all the children gave her some. Lusindia collected all these and kept them carefully in her box of valuables. Most of all, Lusindia loved the doll that she had had all her life, ever since she could remember. She faintly remembered a nurse telling her long ago that it was a gift from her mother, whom she had never known. The doll was her most precious possession.

Linda's mom, Joanita wanted to see Lusindia badly, but it was not a good idea to go and visit her in the *Provedoria*. Others would suspect that she had some connection to Lusindia. And if Lusindia came to know about the relationship, it could affect her psychologically. The authorities did not encourage such visits.

Lusindia, like the other children in the orphanage, always wondered about her parents. Why did they abandon her? Who were her mom and dad? Where were they now? Would they come and get her some day? She hoped so and always prayed for this. How could they leave her here in this orphanage, where no one could call anyone mom or dad? She often wondered if both her parents had died in an accident. Then she gave up thinking about them.

Joanita arranged for an official visit of the orphans of the *Provedoria* to her brother's place in Navelim. It was the policy of *Provedoria* to make sure the orphans were allowed occasional visits to various families who were willing to take them to their homes and give them a little bit of real home experience for a day or two.

Then Joanita went to Navelim when Lusindia was brought there.

Joanita embraced her tightly for a long time. This little girl was her own flesh and blood, her granddaughter! Joanita trembled with emotion at this thought. The warm embrace moved Lusindia, as it was the first time anyone outside the *Provedoria* had held her that close. As for Joanita, she felt as if she was embracing her Linda herself when she was younger.

Joanita gave Lusindia chocolates, roasted grams and peppermints to eat and showed her Linda's picture.

"Look at this photo of my daughter Linda."

"She's pretty," said Lusindia, "I wish I can be like her when I grow up." But Joanita never told her the real truth.

Joanita related some anecdotes about Linda, to which Lusindia listened with great interest. Joanita had arranged for Lusindia to come to Navelim, as she knew her own neighbours would suspect something if she had brought her to Cuncolim.

At night, Lusindia slept with Joanita. It was the first time she had slept with anyone else in her bed. Lusindia felt comfortable being held in Joanita's arms while asleep. It was such a warm and affectionate touch, the kind that she had never felt before. Joanita too had not hugged anyone since Linda's departure. Now, she was holding her granddaughter tight. Joanita cried in her sleep the same way she did when Linda was leaving home for Panjim for the first time.

Lusindia wished she had a grandmother just like Joanita. The next day, Lusindia returned to the *Provedoria* with a heavy heart and for the first time, felt bad to go back to *Crèche Ninho Infantil*. That was the first and the last time Lusindia and Joanita were to see each other.

One day a couple came to see Lusindia when she was four and wanted to take her home. The nuns told Lusindia she would have her own home, her own bedroom, lots of toys to play with and even more importantly…her own new mom and dad.

Lusindia wondered what it would mean to have a mom and a dad. She never knew what home meant or what a bedroom was. She slept along with other girls in a huge dormitory, where there was no mom or dad to lay you down to sleep or sing a lullaby. The nun told her that her new mom and dad would come to her bedroom, tell her stories and put her to sleep, just like in a real home. Lusindia felt it would be good and agreed to go with these new parents.

Within a month, the couple came back for her. Lusindia gathered all her toys in the box and took them with her. She went with the couple in a taxi, her first car ride. Her new home seemed far away. Finally, they reached there.

The house was small but nice and she had her own bedroom to sleep in. Their neighbours came to see her. Her new mom served her *pulau* and *sorpotel* and Coca Cola. Lusindia loved the *Coco Cola*, which she had never tasted before. She asked for more and drank two bottles of it! She also got some *godshem*, pudding. She felt very happy. Her new mom gave her a bath and wiped her and combed her hair, like she did for her doll.

They said the rosary together and Lusindia who was tired soon slipped into a deep slumber. In her dream, she dreamt about a big palace where she was the little princess, and her new mom was the Queen.

The next morning, Lusindia woke up and hoped it wouldn't be the orphanage. She was relieved that it was not! She woke up in her own room and saw her new Mom walk in with a toothbrush and paste. Oh! This was the life of a princess, she thought. Nobody to bother you. No loud noises of children fighting for first place in the queue for washrooms, dining room, and showers. This was unbelievable!

This was her very own house! She could run about, play with her own cat, run around the house outside, catch butterflies, throw stones at mangoes or tamarind and eat the fruits all by herself.

Lusindia was very happy in her new home. She almost forgot about the *Provedoria* in a few days. But she still had nightmares that this happy dream would end and she would wake up in the *Provedoria*.

Her new parents, Romaldo and Cassiana gave her a lot of love and affection and treated her very well. She liked that. She prayed for her new parents every morning and at night. They all went together to church and to the market and sometimes to see their relatives. Lusindia played with her neighbours and she enjoyed every moment there.

When Lusindia was ten years old her adopted parents moved to Belgaum. She liked the city, although the house was quite small and she didn't have her own separate bedroom. She made new friends and her school was bigger than the one she had attended. It was St. Joseph's Convent School. She devoted her time to learning new things and everyday was a novelty. Lusindia was nicknamed *Gorie*, a white girl, by her friends.

Chapter 38

Linda started her Second Year of Science at the University. She had chosen Biology, intending to pursue a Medical career. She was good at practical work but found theory a little tough. She was kept busy with many assignments and laboratory work.

For the New Year of 1966, Linda attended the Goan Dance at Swansea, London. She found some of the Goans from East Africa quite friendly, while others would talk only to their compatriots from East Africa. Linda felt neglected and did not quite enjoy the evening on account of this. There was nobody who had come directly from Goa at that dance. She left the dance before it was over.

Linda again worked during the summer of 1966. Her Second Year results were not very good. She got only two 'A's and the rest were all 'B's. This was not good enough for the competitive admission to a Medical college. So Linda decided to pursue a career in Microbiology, a field that was just beginning to develop.

Linda was doing better in the Third Year at the University. There were now fewer students in her class, as most others had pursued Medical, Pharmaceutical or other branches of science. Linda opted for Microbiology mainly because of her skill at laboratory work. She still had her part-time job, but was now promoted as a Lab Technologist, which meant more pay.

After doing her best in her Third Year Science examinations, Linda worked full-time in the summer of 1967. Linda had got A's in every course this time. Finally the fourth and the last year arrived. This is where she had to show her real capabilities. She stopped working part-time and she concentrated fully on her studies.

She wrote the Final Year of Bachelor of Science examinations in May of 1968. When the results came in, she had all A's. This was the crowning glory of her academic life. She was going to work full time now and would never go back to school again.

She was offered a full time job at the same lab. She was now a Microbiologist. She received a good salary, moved out of the Portuguese Ambassador's residence and lived on her own in Vauxhall, London, just south of Thames River. There were a few Goans living in this complex of flats at Bonnington Square. She was very close to the tube and it was very convenient.

On the weekends, she went to Brixton for shopping. She bought fish such as herring and mackerel and fried it. She kept up a regular correspondence with her mother who had even sent her some Goan chouriço sausages when someone came from Goa. She really relished those. When she got her first pay as a Microbiologist Linda decided to throw a party for her friends at her new place on July 4, 1968, her beloved Lusindia's birthday. She wondered where Lusindia was today, on her sixth birthday. She looked at her baby's picture and cried her heart out while praying for her.

Linda bought some Port and Macieira brandy, some Kraft cheese cans and cream crackers and invited her Goan friends to the party. They celebrated her first full-time job and her University graduation by singing, eating and dancing. Sophie Rebelo was invited for the party too.

"Hey Linda, did you know a lot of Goans from East Africa are migrating to Canada these days, since Pierre Trudeau, the Canadian Immigration Minister has opened doors to non-European immigrants now?" asked Sophie.

"Really? That's great! I think I will give it a try. Thanks Sophie for the useful piece of news. I always wanted to go to Canada, a vast unexplored country with lot of potential. Since I am alone, I can move anywhere." Linda said.

The next day, Linda went to the Canadian High Commission. There she talked to an immigration counsellor. The counsellor went through her resume and said she would stand a good chance of getting a landed immigrant visa to Canada, because of her qualifications and experience as a Microbiologist. Linda received the package containing all the information she needed. Within a week, she filled out the application and mailed it to the Canadian High Commission.

Now that Linda was not that busy, she learnt to cook, using trial and error method and from her memory of those dishes from back home and from some recipes from Goan cookbooks.

Linda's mother was glad that Linda had settled in London. She had worked for about four months now and she made good money. She liked London, but was still lonesome. Her mother advised her to get married and wrote that she could arrange for a nice bachelor from Goa and send him to London for her to marry. But Linda did not want to entertain any thoughts of getting married after her fiasco with Carlos.

Linda thought of Carlos now and then. Especially when she was not busy, her idle mind brooded. She wondered where Carlos was now and what had happened to him since she last saw him. He had not replied to any of her letters. Surely, he must have been married by now and may even have kids of his own somewhere in Portugal.

She thought of trying to write to him again after all this time. But his post box number must have been re-assigned by now, she thought. She did not know where he lived. Maria do Céu or Abranches, had not sent any letter from Portugal; perhaps they could find nothing about Carlos in Portugal. She thought about him and dreamt that Carlos was with her in Goa at Miramar beach and she was in his arms again – warm, angelic and secure.

But, she woke up to cold reality in her flat and of course, Carlos was not around. She felt the cold air of London, which brought her to her senses. She had not gone to Goa since she had come to London. She could not even get a visa to go to Goa, as India and Portugal still did not have diplomatic relations and she still had a Portuguese passport.

Two months after she applied for immigration to Canada, Linda received a letter from Canadian High Commission in London that her application had been accepted and that she should come in for a personal interview followed by a Medical examination. Linda went for the interview, and two weeks later, she went for the Medical examination.

About two months later just before the Christmas of 1968, Linda got the best Christmas present. She received her landed immigrant visa to enter Canada. Linda was extremely happy. She made plans to go to Canada in the New Year, gave notice to her employer and got a letter of reference from the lab. They threw her a big send-off party and Linda had one for all her friends too. She gave away most of her furniture and belongings to friends. Linda left for Toronto, Canada on an Air Canada flight on the sixth of January 1969.

Chapter 39

Linda landed at Toronto International Airport on the sixth of January 1969 at about 1:00 p.m. She went through immigration and had her visa stamped. They gave her the necessary forms to fill up. One was for the Social Insurance Card and the other one was for the Ontario Health Insurance Plan (OHIP) Card.

Linda went to the phone booth and dialled a number, which her friend Sophie Rebelo had given her. A woman picked up the phone.

"Hello, can I speak to Rosy Fernandes?" Linda asked.

"Speaking. Who is this?" Rosy wanted to know.

"I am Linda Cardoso and I am Sophie Rebelo's friend from London. I've just arrived at the Toronto International Airport and I was wondering if I could stay with you for a couple of days?"

"Sure, sure. Sophie informed me of your arrival a week ago. Can you come to our house? We do not have a car to pick you up. You could take the airport bus to Islington, then the subway to Royal York and from there, the Royal York TTC bus south. Then take the Queensway bus east and you will be right in front of our door." Rosy gave Linda directions to her house.

"Thank you very much Rosy, I should be there in an hour or so." Linda hung up the phone and was soon on her way.

Linda took the Airport express bus to Islington station and took a taxi to the address on the Queensway. She got out of the taxi and walked upstairs to the residence of Rosy Fernandes, which was an apartment over an electronics store. She rang the bell and Rosy Fernandes opened the door.

"Hi, I am Linda Cardoso."

"I am Rosy Fernandes, come on in. Welcome to Canada!"

"Sorry to have bothered you and at such a short notice."

"No problem. If we Goans don't help each other out, who will?"

"Thank you Rosy, I really appreciate it."

Linda took a shower and freshened up. Rosy served her some tea and cookies and asked her about life in London. They talked for a while until Rosy's kids came home from school. They were glad they had a guest. Later at six, when Rosy's husband, Robert came home they had their dinner. Linda was surprised that Canadians ate so early.

After dinner, Linda got hold of the Toronto Star and scanned the classified section 'Rooms for Rent'. She saw quite a few ads. Linda selected four and called each of them. Two of them were downtown at College and Bathurst. She asked for details and made an appointment to see them. Later they went to bed.

In the morning, Linda studied the T.T.C. (Toronto Transit Corporation) map and found out where College and Bathurst intersection was situated. She went to the Royal York subway station by bus, took the T.T.C. subway from Royal York to Bathurst, took a streetcar south to College and walked west to Euclid Avenue to see the room. She looked at the room. It was nice and airy. She told the landlord, she had to see another room as well and she would let him know her decision by phone.

She went to see the other room at Grace Street. This room was much better and she had her own kitchen and washroom. Besides the owner was one Mr Costa, a Portuguese from Azores. Linda spoke to him in Portuguese and Senhor Costa could not believe that Linda could speak fluent Portuguese. Mr and Mrs Costa were very happy to have a Goan in their house and they even lowered the rent. Linda accepted and said she would move in the next day.

Linda thanked Rosy and her family, called the landlord at Euclid Avenue to say she had found another place to stay, and moved out to Grace Street the next day. She went to Honest Ed's to do her first shopping for utensils. Honest Ed was a great place to shop with all kinds of funny one-liners about Honest Ed written all over the store walls, which made her laugh. Did such a man really exist? She bought all she wanted from this store.

She bought some groceries at the Lombardi store on College Street, and she was all set for her first day in her rented room in Toronto. She filled the fridge in her tiny kitchen with fresh groceries. She quickly fried two pork chops and made some rice. She opened a bottle of homemade red wine offered by Senhor Costa to welcome her. She prayed, thanked God for bringing her to Canada, sipped the wine from a glass and had her first home-cooked dinner in Canada.

The next day she went to visit Canada's Manpower office to make some employment inquiries. Linda filled out a lengthy application form and registered. Then she had a long interview with a counsellor, who went through the available vacancies and dialled a number. He spoke to someone on the phone for a while and hung up.

"Young lady, you are in luck. Can you go to Sunnybrook Hospital and apply for a job there? They are still looking for an Assistant Microbiologist in their laboratory."

"Thank you very much, Sir. I will go right away. Can I have directions to the hospital, please?"

Linda got the address and directions to go by TTC. She thanked the counsellor and was on her way. Linda took the subway to Eglinton station and took a bus to the Sunnybrook Hospital. She went to the Personnel Section, filled out a form, attached her resume, handed it in and waited.

After about an hour, a secretary asked Linda to follow her to a room for an interview. Two men walked in. They introduced themselves, one was the Personnel Manager and the other was the Chief Microbiologist. They read Linda's resume and were impressed with her credentials. They interviewed her for about an hour and offered her the job right away.

Linda could not believe it. Canada, what a country! She had hardly been here a week and they offered her a job right away. She could start next day. The salary was very good; about twice what she made in London. She went home, went to the church of St Francis Assisi, which was just in front of her house. She knelt and prayed and thanked Our Lady for listening to her prayers and giving her such a good job so fast.

The Costas were very happy for her. Senhor Costa joked that he was not afraid to be sick now, as Linda could immediately check out what was wrong, as his personal *emfermeira* or nurse. The next day, Linda started her work in the lab at Sunnybrook Hospital. It was quite a long way to go. She had to take the subway to Eglinton and then the bus. .

The people in the lab were a nice bunch. One microbiologist was East Indian. Of the two lady lab technicians, one was a Pakistani and the other a Filipino. The rest were Canadian born. The Chief Microbiologist welcomed Linda and introduced her to everyone from the lab. Linda felt very comfortable with the job from the very first day.

Linda worked very hard as always and impressed every one with her dedication to work. She became quite friendly with her co-workers. She even visited their homes. On one such visit she happened to be in Thorncliffe Park, a brand new area with new rental apartment buildings. She loved the location. She went to see a vacant apartment and it had a nice view of downtown Toronto and the Don Valley. Linda at once signed the rental agreement and moved in. The Costas were sorry to let her go, but they were happy for her and asked her to keep in touch.

Thorncliffe Park was quite close to Sunnybrook. Now, she did not have to wake up early in the morning and waste her time travelling. She furnished her apartment with elegant furniture and appliances. She could live well, as she could afford it now. She went shopping at Simpsons, Eaton's and Hudson's Bay stores, where she could buy clothes, cosmetics and toiletries that were a little expensive but of good quality and made in Canada.

Linda noticed a few peculiarities in Canada. She had to get used to saying 'washroom' instead of 'bathroom', 'elevator' for 'lift', 'apartment' rather than 'flat' and so on, but it was not a big deal for her. The accent also changed considerably, but she liked the Canadian accent much better and she wondered why she still pronounced English words without the sound of "r", which was well pronounced in Canada. 'Sugar' was pronounced fully as 'sugar' with the 'r' – more like the Indian accent, unlike the British 'suga'.

She noticed people were very quiet on the TTC buses and trains as if someone had died in their family. Back home in Goa, the noise in buses and trains would have woken these people up from their deep trance, she thought. Well, this was their way. People did not say "hi" even in the elevator. The only occasional conversation she would hear was about things like how they looked forward to their weekend skiing on Blue Mountain. Linda almost froze to death when she heard such conversation, as she hated the cold and couldn't understand how they enjoyed it.

She could not figure out why even the next-door neighbour never said "hi" to her. She thought people in Goa would laugh at this. They'd say something was wrong with these people. What kind of neighbours were these? Maybe Linda thought, she had not been in Canada long enough to understand them. Maybe they were cold, like the cold weather they enjoyed.

Linda noticed that at church in Toronto, people came in jeans, a far cry from people back home. In Goa everyone took hours to get ready for church with the best clothes they had, to impress the opposite sex. After the church service, people in Goa would stop outside and talk and gossip before heading home. Here in Toronto, everyone wore coats and jackets so you could not see what they wore inside anyway and people headed straight home after the service just like in London. She guessed it was their culture or the cold weather outside. Back home, priests were better orators and delivered sermons with many interesting anecdotes with lot of ad-libbing, emotion and passion, which she missed terribly in Toronto, where most priests just read from their notes.

There was some noticeable racism in Canada like in all parts of the world. White rowdy kids called her "Stupid Paki" on the subway many times. She wondered why they called her a "Paki" as she was not from Pakistan, but then realised it was a general term for all brown people just like Goans call all whites *'pacle'*. But these rowdies shouted the word 'Paki' as if it was a pejorative word, which it was not. *'Pak'* meant 'holy' in Urdu.

She read in the newspapers about an incident where a *Paki* was pushed off the platform onto the tracks in front of an oncoming subway train on New Year's Day, which horrified her. What a way to celebrate New Year, she thought. This brought back memories of her childhood experience in the Cuncolim church. The Western Guard had painted racist graffiti all over Toronto's buildings and walls and they would advertise a telephone number where they would record 'hate' messages daily. It was despicable to hear voices full of hate for fellow human beings. How could humans be this hateful? She wondered, though she knew that history was indeed filled with instances of hate.

Still, racism in Canada was nothing compared to the caste discrimination practised in India, Linda felt. She was happy that disadvantaged people in Canada could take their cases to the Human Rights Commission if they felt they were treated unfairly because of their colour, race, sex, etc.

Actually, racism in Canada never bothered Linda at all. She took it in her stride as part of human reality the world over. Some people believed in differences, but she liked to celebrate diversity and felt proud of her roots. Except for these minor irritants, she loved Canada. There was no place on Earth that could even come close to it. With just one phone call, she could get things done unlike in India, where corruption reigned supreme, and without paying *hafta* you couldn't get anything done. It was the world's largest bureaucracy that called itself a democracy.

In Canada people were very reliable, honest, conscientious and sincere, which she appreciated. However, her native verdant land of Goa, its people, its climate and natural beauty held a special place in Linda's heart. With the exception of a few, most of the people in Goa, even though quite poor, were very hospitable, generous and caring.

Chapter 40

Once she settled down, Linda threw a big party to celebrate her first anniversary in Canada. She invited Rosy and Robert Fernandes, Senhor and Dona Costa, and her colleagues and friends at Sunnybrook Hospital. There were guests from various backgrounds. After they left and she was alone, she lay on her bed, in a philosophical mood. She thought about life and God.

She always believed in the existence of a Supreme Being, one who created everything including life itself. But who created Him? And what about those different Gods from various religions? She reasoned that if there were many, they would be jealous of each other and fight for supremacy.

So there had to be just one God for all humanity who was known by different names. But why was God so biased? How could He create such disparity? How could He create prosperous, blessed, promised lands for the whites? And why such difficult lives for the blacks and coloureds? Was God racist too? Suddenly she felt God was so unfair. "Where are you, God?" she cried out, "I tried so hard to succeed, to make it somehow, somewhere". She began to weep, feeling very lonely and full of self-pity.

Nights were bad for Linda. She was quite alone in her big apartment with no man by her side. She could sleep well only if she was truly exhausted. Otherwise she would feel quite depressed, thinking of Carlos. Where was he now, leaving her all alone? She couldn't even get into a relationship without knowing anything about him. There were some opportunities for her to get into good relationships, but she never even considered them.

Oh God, what should she do now? How long would she have to wait? These thoughts would trouble her every night. She just couldn't break the oath of love she and Carlos took at Miramar beach – at the sound of church bells that first day when they cemented their love bond as the sun set on the Aguada Fort, that fateful evening. Was it possible Carlos had broken that oath? She had no way of knowing.

Then there was her child Lusindia. Linda knew many single mothers in Toronto. Even the government supported them, by helping out women in the lower economic strata financially. Every time Linda saw these single moms carrying their children in their baby carriages, it would hurt. Why couldn't she have her own child, Lusindia with her? It was acceptable here. She was glad she lived in a country where no one bothered about other people's personal actions or morals. And why should they?

These little worries, frustrations and thoughts always deprived Linda of regular sound sleep. Sometimes, Linda would stay awake all night watching TV, mostly blue movies from the local Cute TV station but this left her even more depressed.

One day during the Diwali festival, Linda's colleague Anil Kamat, the microbiologist, who was a Goan Hindu from Bombay, took her to Gerard Street to show her some East Indian shops and restaurants. They went to Naaz Theatre to see a Hindi movie, Om Prakash's *Das Lakh*. They thoroughly enjoyed it. From then on Linda did all her shopping there. She bought some spices, basmati rice, some green mangoes, fresh coriander and green chilli peppers. After that they went to a South Indian restaurant and had masala dosa and Indian masala tea. There was a lot about Toronto that she did not know.

Linda was doing very well in Toronto and she was content with her situation financially. However, she often felt low emotionally. Maybe, she needed to get around more and see the sights of Toronto. That would probably raise her spirits. So, she decided to learn to drive a car and even buy one. So far, she had not felt the need for a car as she took the TTC bus to work. She failed at her first driving test but passed on second attempt. Linda was now ready for a car.

With Anil's help, she bought a second hand blue Impala for a thousand bucks. The engine was very smooth and noiseless. With power steering and power brakes, the big car felt like a plane. The tape deck, the radio, the heating and its plush seats made this car seem as comfortable as a mobile home.

It was her first car and she loved it, except it was a great gas-guzzler. No wonder it had a big tank. Now she went places and did her shopping very comfortably. She wondered why she had not thought of buying one before this. It was not a luxury like back home, but a very necessary convenience in Canada.

One year in Canada and she had not seen Niagara Falls yet. Her first trip outside of Toronto would be to Niagara Falls. She requested Anil to bring his car too and she followed his car to Niagara Falls. They took the 401 west, then turned South on 427, and turned west on Queen Elizabeth Way, then proceeded via the gigantic Burlington Skyway Bridge in Hamilton and went on to Niagara Falls. Linda admired the recently built Canadian Highways with many lanes, and entry and exit points. After about an hour and a half they reached Niagara Falls. They parked their cars and walked to the Falls.

Linda had never seen anything like this before. It was such a natural wonder! Was it the eighth wonder of the world? Before this, only the Taj Mahal in Agra had impressed her this much. But that was man-made, while this was a natural wonder with a majestic view! She took pictures, bought some souvenirs, and then went down to take a ride on the *Maid of the Mist*. What a perfect name for the boat! She had not enjoyed such a marvellous view anytime before and the view of the Falls, from way down there was surely a sight never to be missed. It was well worth the trip. Then, they went around the town and returned home in the evening. She was proud to be part of this great country, Canada.

Linda visited the Ontario Science Centre near Don Mills and Eglinton, which was quite close to her. She was amazed to see the wonders of Science demonstrated in there. She took a picture of her upright hair when she held a charged metal ball in her hands. That was hilarious. This was a must-see for any visitor to Toronto.

Next on her list, was Ontario Place near the Lake Ontario and the CNE Fair. The Summer Canadian National Exhibition fair was crowded and noisy while Ontario Place was serene and scenic. Linda watched a movie about the Himalayan mountain range of India at Cinesphere in Ontario Place on an amazing huge screen. She had never seen an IMAX movie before. It seemed so real; she actually felt she really was on top of the Himalayas.

Linda went for a picnic to Toronto Island with her colleagues by crossing a ferry and the scene from there overlooking the city was just stupendous, just like a picture on a post card. A week later she joined her colleagues and drove up north to Wasaga Beach, Midland. The beach was long and sandy. This reminded her of Calangute Beach in Goa. They stayed in a motel overnight. The next day they drove to Parry Sound, where Linda took a boat tour of Thirty Thousand Islands. She had never seen anything this spectacular in her life – a view of the greatest collection of beautiful little islands and channels in the world. There were many cottages on those islands and sailboats and motorboats all over the Georgian Bay. Canada was truly a blessed country, Linda decided.

About a month later Linda and some friends went to Thousand Islands in the St. Lawrence River, and again went on a boat tour, where they saw the famous Boldt Castle. This place too was scenic and beautiful. The same weekend, Linda attended the huge Thousand Island Picnic organized by the CanOrient Christian Association with members who were Goans and other East Indian Christians from Montreal and Toronto. Here they celebrated a Mass and organized lot of games. The whole place smelled of barbecue, sorpotel and pulau and everyone was having a great time talking loudly. It was just like the Friday Bazaar at Mapusa in Goa. Linda even met Goans from Karachi there.

Linda was barely in her second year at Sunnybrook Hospital, when she was promoted to Microbiologist. This promotion was in appreciation of her great performance as an Assistant Microbiologist. Her career was really taking off now. Linda was in touch with many Medical labs in Toronto and attended Microbiology conferences in Toronto and Montreal. As a result, she came in contact with Microbiologists from all over Canada. She was also a full member of Canadian Microbiologists Association. They had annual gatherings and meetings. Linda knew almost every Microbiologist in Toronto.

Linda began to invest her money with the aid of her colleagues. She took some evening courses at a business school and learnt about stocks and shares, mutual funds and even futures and options in commodities. This was very interesting, she thought. With relatively little money, as low as a couple thousand dollars she could control even about $20,000 worth of investments using the option strategy. This was unbelievable, but risky too. Linda tried to test it out by doing her own paper trading for one month just to see if it worked out, and it did at least on two occasions.

Linda opened an account with a broker with a minimum amount of $5000. She lost $500 in two weeks. But later she made a thousand. Within a month, she had made $500. It wasn't that bad. Linda continued investing for a year and she realized a healthy profit of $2500, which was a 50% profit on her initial investment of US $ 5000.

Chapter 41

A lot of unexpected incidents had taken place in Linda's life, but this one changed her destiny significantly.

It was December of 1970. There was a private Christmas party for doctors, nurses and the lab staff of the Hospital at a hotel. Linda attended this party. She was enjoying herself and having a good time, when a gentleman, probably in his fifties, approached her with a smile on his face.

"Hi, I am Dr Phillips, I have seen you around a lot, but I don't know your name." The doctor introduced himself.

"Hi, I am Linda Cardoso and I am the microbiologist in the lab." Linda said.

"May I have this dance with you?" the doctor asked.

"Sure. I am honoured. Thank you." Linda said in her usual charming manner.

While they were dancing, suddenly Dr Phillips stopped and said suddenly "Can I make a proposal?"

Linda was taken aback and blushed, not knowing what to do or say. She hardly knew this man. Besides, he was a lot older than she was.

Dr Phillips must have read her mind and just as suddenly, apologized.

"Oh I am sorry, I did not mean that kind of proposal" he continued, "You see I have a Medical office building at St Claire and Bathurst where I have a vacant basement office. Perhaps you could open up your own Medical lab there?"

Linda was thunderstruck at the suggestion. At first she thought it was a joke. But the doctor seemed serious and honest. She could not think for a second. She stood there for a few seconds not knowing what to say. A lot of things were going through her mind. Was she ambitious enough for such a commitment and risk? Could she go through with it?

"I really don't know what to say at this time, Doctor. I'd have to think about it and let you know."

"Of course, do think it over and let me know then," he handed her his card and continued - "You don't have to worry about the rent for a while. The place was vacant for over a year. It is big enough and perfect for a lab because there are five other doctors in the building, and there is not a lab nearby. I can help you too, though I am one of the partners of this Medical Centre. I will put in a good word for you. Why don't you just give it a try? It's definitely worth it."

Linda thanked the doctor for his suggestion and promise of help and she assured him she would get back to him soon.

The next day Linda told Anil about this business proposition. She asked Anil if he wanted to join her as a partner in this business. Anil declined, and said he was satisfied with his salary and would not want to try anything that was uncertain and risky.

Linda thought it over for a couple days and talked to a few fellow microbiologists in the industry. Most of them were warm and receptive to the idea and promised their support for her venture. But no one wanted to be her partner; they had their own excuses.

Linda decided it was worth the risk. What could she lose? She had only a cheap car and no major assets or liabilities. At the most she would have to declare bankruptcy. She would go ahead with her maiden venture. She called Dr Phillips and fixed an appointment to talk it over. Dr Phillips stated the terms of the lease and promised help in the financing of the lab. He also recommended she discuss the business matters with his accountant,

Gary Greenberg, who could help her develop a business plan. The good doctor was also ready to co-sign her bank loan.

Linda met with Gary and discussed the business plan. She made an appointment with her bank manager to discuss the financing. The bank manager looked at the business plan and approved it. Linda called her contacts and doctors in St Claire area to promote her business. She called the Ontario Health Insurance (OHIP) to discuss billing and other formalities and within two months, Linda was ready to open her lab. She incorporated the lab under the name 'Allied Labs' and became its President. She liked the title. It had a nice ring to it. She actually wanted to name the lab 'LI Labs' but people would be inquisitive to know what LI stood for. She did not want to disclose her secret, that it was an acronym for her child's name 'Lus-India.' So she called it 'Allied Labs'.

Linda resigned from Sunnybrook Hospital in February, giving them more than three weeks notice. They were very sorry to let her go but wished her well in her new venture and promised her their help and support. The staff gave her a farewell party and every one had only good things to say about Linda. February 28 was Linda's last day at Sunnybrook Hospital.

On March 6th, 1971 Linda inaugurated her lab. The big neon sign read 'Allied Labs'. A local Catholic priest was brought in to bless the lab. She had invited Dr Phillips to do the honours by cutting the ribbon and he was her very first client. The first day began very well; it looked like her luck was in. She had two hundred and twenty seven tests from the Medical centre. Later, the courier she hired brought in five hundred and twenty six tests from Hospitals and various doctors in the neighbourhood. Linda was very happy with the response on the first day.

She had hired one Medical technologist and one lab assistant. She also helped in the tests. Linda was very busy the first few days, as she had to help out in the lab and at the same time was on the phone promoting her business with the local doctors. The lab processed the tests and sent the results as soon as possible. The doctors were very happy with the speed of the test results. After a month the business increased so much, they could not keep up with the pace. The lab staff worked even on Saturdays.

Linda hired another Medical technologist. The work was still increasing rapidly. A month later, Linda hired yet another Medical technologist and a lab assistant. Now the work was steady and they could manage it well, but they still had to work on Saturdays. At the end of three months, Linda asked Gary to come over and help her with the accounts to find out how they were doing. Gary looked at all accounts receivable and payable and concluded Linda was doing exceedingly well, much better than the business plan projected.

Linda hired an accounting clerk to do the accounts, filing, mailing and payroll. Things got more organized and Linda did less of testing and more of business promotion. She sent letters to all doctors and thanked them for their business.

Soon the mailing list of doctors increased and they had to update it every day. At the end of six months, the lab business really prospered. Dr Phillips was happy that the idea worked and he got a steady income from his basement office space. Linda signed a two-year lease with Dr Phillips' consortium. Linda kept getting more and more tests but could not add more staff as the space was limited.

Within a year, Linda decided to open one more lab. On the fourth of July 1972, Linda opened a lab in Eglinton/Keele area to cover the West of Toronto. She hired two Medical lab technicians and a microbiologist and two lab assistants. She offered the job of microbiologist to Anil but he would not take it, saying it was not good idea to work for a friend. Linda realized he could be right.

The Allied Labs by now were known all over Toronto. Linda advertised in the Medical journals, Medical conventions and Medical magazines. Linda did lot of business with the Ministry of Health, Lab section at 81 Resources Road, Etobicoke. Most of the hospitals were her clients by now.

Linda was very busy now, supervising her labs. The increasing business meant expanding the staff and more time was required for supervision and control. In late 1973, Linda opened another lab in Etobicoke South. In 1974 she opened a lab in Scarborough and one in Rexdale, Etobicoke North. She had five labs by 1975 and the turnover was over two million dollars a year.

Linda was an overnight success. She became rich. Her staff increased to around one hundred. She moved to a nice posh area in Thornhill, where she bought a big, new, executive home. Now, she had it made and could relax. She had a general manager who took care of all the business and each lab had its own manager.

Life in Canada was great for Linda. She was lonely but there were a lot of activities and sights to keep her busy and occupied apart from her business. She loved the Caribbana Parade that had just started in the City of Toronto. A lot of colourful Caribbean floats took part in a huge Mas Parade with huge masks and big bands, curvaceous bodies gyrating to the groovy sounds of Trinidadian Carnival Calypso Bands. The brass bands played soka, reggae and samba tunes as the Carribana Parade slowly made its way down Yonge Street and ended on Toronto Island.

Linda just loved the multicultural face of Canada, when she visited the Caravan cultural festival held in Toronto. You had to buy a Passport to visit all the cities of the world featured at this festival. Here you could learn about great cultures from all over the world, like Ukraine, Poland, India, Portugal, Philippines, China, Japan, Greece, and most other countries of the world. You could even sample the foods from each of those countries and see their cultural performances. Linda loved the Ukrainian jumping dancers and the Filipino bamboo dancers in particular.

Chapter 42

Carlos had worked for the Portuguese Embassy for a whole year. When the flow of workers from Portugal had come down, Carlos had quit his job at the embassy in Bonn in July 1963 and started a small construction firm in Frankfurt employing Portuguese workers.

Carlos subcontracted for the big real estate developers. He was very busy developing his business. Soon it was one of the best-known construction firms in the Frankfurt area and he became quite rich. Heidi acted as his secretary.

As years went by, Carlos' business got bigger and better until in 1973, the Arab Oil Embargo had an adverse impact on business and industry in West Germany. Carlos' business was doing badly and in 1974, there were almost no new contracts at all.

Right at this time a tragic accident took the life of his young wife, Heidi. She was driving on the Autobahn, when a car hit hers from behind while she was changing lanes. Her car burst into flames and she died instantly.

This was too much for Carlos to take on top of his business debacle. He wound down his operations in West Germany and decided to go back to Portugal in November of 1974.

As he packed, he saw Heidi's old suitcase from Goa still in the closet. "No point in keeping that old thing. I'll throw it away," he thought while mechanically checking to see that it was empty.

To his surprise, his hand felt something in the inner pocket. He unzipped it and pulled out two envelopes. They were in his handwriting! He couldn't remember having written any love letters to Heidi that she would want to save.

As he unfolded them, his heart almost stopped beating. They were the two letters that he had written to Linda in Panjim, Goa years ago.

"O Meu Deus!" he said to himself and swallowed hard. It did not take him long to realize what had happened. Heidi must have intercepted his letters and lied to him all along. It must have been a lie then that Linda had married and gone to East Africa.

"Oh my God! How could I be so gullible," he muttered to himself.

"How could you do this to me, Heidi? You took my true love away from me. Where are you now Linda? Where are you?"

"No wonder my marriage to Heidi never felt right. Somehow there was always something holding me back. Heidi and I were never meant for each other.

"Linda, my darling, my soul-mate, I am sorry I betrayed your trust in me, by listening to Heidi's lies. How can I ever make it up to you, Linda? Please tell me?" Carlos murmured to himself with guilt.

"What is she doing now? I must find out what happened to her," he thought and could not sleep that night. He decided to forget about his life in Germany and proceed to Portugal right away.

When Carlos went to Portugal, he found a lot of changes had taken place there since he had left for Germany. Politically, Portugal had made a turnabout. The Socialists succeeded in bringing about the Revolution in Portugal in 1974 and Mário Soares was at the helm. There seemed to be chaos everywhere with the death of the old dictatorial system.

Carlos rented an apartment and settled down. His mother's house had been sold. He went to see his aunt, Teodora Cabral in Lisboa, who gave him a trunk full of his mother's valuables including the jewellery box, some documents and some mail.

When he went back to his apartment, Carlos opened the trunk and sifted through the valuables. His mother had left him a lot of money including the proceeds of the house. Carlos went through everything in the trunk. The jewellery box, he had laid aside not even bothering to open it. But as he lifted it to shift it, the rusty old hinges gave way and out fell ...a letter

Wasn't that Linda's writing? It had to be! How well he knew it still, even from a distance! He hurried to pick it up and was shocked to see a letter from Linda dated January 5, 1962 from Goa. Carlos read the letter with trembling hands, afraid of what it might say...

Panjim, Goa,
January 5, 1962,

My darling Carlos,

I hope you are well and happy in Portugal. My darling Carlos, I wanted to write to you much earlier but somehow I could not find the courage to write. My hands are still trembling as I write this letter.

I am sure you would like to know what happened to me after you left. I am also sure you had to leave Goa for a very important reason. I was deeply hurt because you left without seeing me and saying a last goodbye. After you left unceremoniously, I did not know what to do. From the time you left, I went through real hell.

The day I received your letter I was shocked that you had left me for good. I went berserk and was very sick. The doctor examined me and found me pregnant, which was yet another shock to me.

Those days were terrible especially since you were not there to hold me and comfort me. Darling, this was a time in my life that I would have given anything to be with you. I will never forget this time, when I felt so helpless, unwanted and abandoned. I felt my life was not worth living. I wanted to kill myself, as I did not want to live without you. But I had to live at least for this baby, the only legacy left from our love. The next few days were a living hell for me. I was only seventeen, pregnant and unmarried. How was I going to explain this to my mother and my people back home? They had warned me that I was going to be abandoned, humiliated and treated as an outcast.

To make things worse, the day after I received your letter, the war started in Goa and I was all alone and desolate. I could not even see my mother. There was chaos, confusion and suffering all around. I felt relieved knowing that you were safe in Portugal, especially during the days of the invasion.

Then, I went to see my mother. She was shocked that I was pregnant with your child and that you had gone to Portugal leaving me helpless and without any future. Anyway, I am going to have this baby whatever happens. I know you are in Portugal and maybe you will never see me again. But I want you to know I will always love you and I do not for one-minute regret the love we knew and experienced even if I now have to suffer as a consequence.

Now, my darling Carlos, tell me what to do. What should I do with my life? What should I do with my baby? I am all confused. My mother tells me to give the baby up for adoption. Should I? Please let me know. Is there any way you could take me to Portugal, where we could marry and have a normal family life? Please let me know. I will be waiting anxiously to hear from you. It would mean a lot to me, knowing that you still care for me and want to be with our baby and me.

Please take me with you as soon as you can and bring an end to my life of shame, misery and hopeless desolation here in Goa. I can't take this any more.

Please write to me at any of these two addresses:

Instituto Piedade   *Cuncolim*
Rua Afonso de Albuquerque   *Moddemaddem*

Panjim, Goa, India.   *Salcete, Goa, India.*

Your reply will bring great solace in these agonizing moments.

Yours,

Always in love,

Linda

Tears ran unchecked down Carlos' cheeks. He was shocked to learn that Linda had been pregnant and he had not even known. How stupid of him not to have persevered in getting in touch with Linda. If only he had received this letter on time! Though, he could not have entered Goa then; he would have been able to console her with his reply and made some other arrangements and bring Linda to his side. How could Linda forgive him?

What could he do now? He was pacing up and down like a madman. Shock after shock seemed to hit him. It looked as if his life was spinning out of control with the shocking lies and betrayal by Heidi, and now this long overdue letter from Linda. Heidi must have known all along that Linda was pregnant with my child. Why did she do this to me?

Then Carlos spotted a bundle of mail in the trunk. He looked them over one by one. Most of them were official letters addressed to his mother. But Carlos was in for yet another shock. He was thunderstruck to see another airmail envelope from India with Linda's name on it. With his heart throbbing even faster, Carlos quickly ripped the envelope open and started reading:

Panjim, Goa
July 16, 1962,

My Dearest Carlos,
I hope everything is all right with you. I still have not received your reply to the letter that I wrote to you on January 5th, 1962. I am at a loss as to understand why you have not written. I hope you are not angry with me.

In case you have not received my previous letter, I want you to know that I was pregnant but realised it only the day I received your last letter, after you left Goa.

Here is the good news. You are the proud father of a baby girl. She was born on the fourth of July 1962 at Escola Médica Hospital in Panjim. She looks just like you. I named her "Lusindia", because she is the fruit of our Luso-Indian blood. I have decided to give her for adoption to the Provedoria Assistência Pública. I made arrangements with the Provedoria to keep the names of the parents of the baby secret. Enclosed please find the photo of our newborn baby and her birth certificate naming you as the father and a copy of a document that allows you or me to claim the child back if the child is still with the Provedoria.

As I wrote in my previous letter to you, I found out that I was pregnant on December 17, 1961 when I received your last letter. I had terrible time since then, carrying the baby and going through a life of shame with no one to care for me or offer any kind of help, advice or comfort. But now everything is behind me. I also had asked for your advice in my last letter, but since you did not reply, I decided to give the baby up for adoption to the Provedoria Assistência Pública in Panjim. I hope you will realize I would not be able to bring her up myself, as I am not married and a single mother would be a big scandal here in Goa.

I hope you will agree with my decision. I do not know what is going to happen to me. I am going to College to pursue my education. I have not thought about my future. Once again I request you to write to me as soon as possible. It will give me some consolation and comfort to know that you are aware of what happened to me after you left me.

Please write to me at either of the following addresses:

Instituto Piedade   *Cuncolim*
Rua Afonso de Albuquerque   *Moddemaddem*
Panjim, Goa, India.   *Salcete, Goa, India.*

Please reply this time at least. It would mean a lot to me. I spent so many months crying over you. If you just write once, all my troubles will seem worth it. I am much better now. Waiting to hear from you one last time. Please let me know what is on your mind.

Yours,

Always in love,

Linda

Carlos cried softly and wiped more tears. He could not forgive himself. His poor Linda! She must have gone through hell. It was now 1974. Twelve years had passed. And where was his baby Lusindia? He was going to get her at any cost. He had all the necessary papers and all the evidence. It was just a matter of going to Goa and getting her back officially.

Thinking of Goa, it just dawned on him that now after the Portuguese revolution, there might be official recognition of Goa as part of India and that there might be the resumption of diplomatic relations between India and Portugal soon.

He called the foreign affairs department in Lisbon and they told him Mário Soares was already in the active process of resuming diplomatic relations with India real soon. Carlos was now relieved. He called some colleagues he had known during his tenure in Goa and said he was going to arrange a trip to Goa.

Chapter 43

In the weekend edition of all the national papers in Portugal, Carlos inserted the following advertisement:

Attention lovers of Goa!
We are a group of ex-Portuguese servicemen who served the military in Goa during the war in 1961. Many of us had friends, lovers and companions there whom we loved, but had to leave behind suddenly on account of our duty to the Fatherland and because of the displacement due to the Indian invasion.

It is estimated that there are hundreds of orphans of European blood in the orphanages of Goa. They are now teenagers and have no parents. The Provedoria Assistência Pública has adopted most of them since the time they were born.

We do not know anything about these kids. It is our responsibility to take care of our own. We appeal to one and all to please lend your support in any way you can to this great humanitarian cause. We plan to go to Goa soon.

There will be a meeting on November 14, 1974 at 4 pm in the Biblioteca Central, Lisboa to discuss all issues.

For more information call the number below.
All are cordially invited.
Carlos Soares
Convenor
Tel: 4539765 (Lisboa)

Carlos received a good response from the ad. Many people called to lend their support. Only eleven made commitments to go to Goa. As soon as Portugal resumed diplomatic relations with India, this group went to Goa on February 14th, 1975.

It was wonderful to be back in Goa after so many years. They enjoyed the fresh Goan air and the freedom. The last time, they had been here in

December of 1961 as prisoners of war. Now they were tourists, enjoying the hospitality of the Goan people.

The place had not changed much, but there was a lot of improvement. Most of the Goan villages had electricity now. There were new roads, new concrete homes and buildings all over. But overall Goa looked still pristine and natural. It brought back nostalgia of the years gone by.

Carlos had made contact with representatives of *Cultura Latina* in Panjim to book accommodation and make other arrangements for their visit to Goa. They needed a few investigators, translators and lawyers in Goa. The group stayed in Hotel Mandovi. The local representative welcomed the group and took them around. The first thing they wanted to do was to visit the *Provedoria*'s orphanages in Panjim, Goa Velha for girls and in Cuncolim for boys.

Carlos went to Goa Velha PAP orphanage for girls, a half an hour's drive from Panjim. He was hoping to recognize his Lusindia himself. The girls were all lined up – white Europeans, a couple of black Africans and brown Goans. Carlos approached one of the white European girls. He asked her name. She said it was Rosa. Carlos checked each one of them. None of them was called Lusindia and none had his or Linda's features.

Carlos went to see the manager of the orphanage. But, the manager knew no one by the name of Lusindia. He had been running the orphanage for the past six years. He asked all the supervisors, the servants and cooks in the orphanage. No one knew about Lusindia. All the staff from 1962 had been either transferred or retired. The nuns no longer ran the orphanage now. The manager told Carlos to check the records in the *Provedoria*'s head office in Panjim.

Carlos went to the head office in Panjim. The director himself helped. They delved into the files from the archives and at last found the required records. It seemed one Mr Romaldo and Mrs Cassiana Rodrigues had adopted Lusindia on June 21 1966. Their address was given as *Battim, Orlim, Salcete, Goa*.

Carlos took a translator with him, hired a taxi and went to Orlim, near Margão in Salcete, South of Goa. When he reached there, he went to Romaldo's house near a convent in Orlim. But the house was locked. The neighbours told him they now lived in Belgaum, which was east of Goa on the Western Ghats. After asking around, Carlos got their address from one of the neighbours.

The next day Carlos took the translator and boarded a bus from Panjim early in the morning and reached Belgaum in the afternoon. They took a taxi from the bus stand and went looking for the house. After about an hour of asking around they found the place they were looking for.

Carlos met Romaldo and Cassiana, introduced himself and with the help of the translator told them his sad story. "I am the natural father of your adopted child, Lusindia. I beg of you, please let me have my child, back." Carlos pleaded with the adopted parents.

Romaldo and Cassiana were plainly shocked at this new development. They did not know what to say. How could they give up Lusindia? What about the bond built over years of loving and sharing all those little everyday joys and sorrows? Surely she was more their daughter than his? She had not even set eyes on this father to feel anything for him.

Romaldo turned red with anger at the thought of having his daughter snatched away. Cassiana's heart felt drained. They could not imagine life without Lusindia. She had brought joy and fulfilment, replacing the loneliness and desperation that had consumed their lives before they adopted Lusindia.

Romaldo and Cassiana were adamant. "I am sorry, but the child is legally ours. We have raised her since she was four. She has been with us for the past nine years now and we love her. How can you ask this of us? Besides we do not have any other children. We are definitely going to keep our child." Romaldo explained, "Now please go away quickly. I do not want Lusindia upset. She has suffered enough, don't you think?"

As fate would have it, while they were talking, the front door opened and in walked a young girl with her schoolbag. She looked at the visitors. Carlos looked at her transfixed. He could not believe it. She was the exact copy of his Linda, but with his colour and some of his mannerisms!

Before anyone could stop him, Carlos got up and embraced his little girl and said, "My darling Lusindia, I am your unfortunate, natural father, Carlos."

Lusindia stopped dead in her tracks. Did she hear right? This man must be crazy! She always thought Romaldo and Cassiana were her parents though she had wondered why people in Belgaum pointed at her and called her '*gorie*'. She did not know that they had adopted her when she was four. She could not quite remember anything before that. Except that there had been plenty she had wanted to forget.

Then from the innermost recesses of her memory, she faintly recalled what the nun had said at *Provedoria* years ago, "Lusindia you are leaving us and going away with your new mom and dad to your new home." So she did have an old mom and dad after all! If this man was her real dad, then who was her real mom?

She still had that most precious of her possessions, the doll, which the nurse said was a gift from her mother. She also knew that though she was known as Lucy, she had to use Lusindia when her official name was required at school. These and other memories came flooding. Lusindia stood rooted to the spot – silent, perplexed and confused.

Lusindia's foster mom Cassiana hugged her tight and whispered "*Baai*, I'm sorry we did not tell you the truth so far. Yes, we adopted you nine years ago from the *Provedoria*'s orphanage. We did not have children of our own. We are not your natural parents, but you were always the heart and soul of this family."

Romaldo came too and hugged Lusindia "We never thought of you as our adopted child. We always loved you as if you were our own. And *baai*, this man is your real natural father."

Lusindia hugged them both and cried, "Thank you so much *Mãe* and *Pai*. I always believed you were my real parents. You gave me so much love I never had any reason to complain. You are my real parents; you brought me up and gave me a home." She stopped to look with accusing eyes at Carlos before continuing "All I ever wanted was to be loved and to belong. They made that happen. I will never forget that. Without them, I would have languished in that orphanage with no one to call my own."

Then turning to her anxious foster parents she said, "Oh my *Mãe* and *Pai*, how can I forget that you were and are my real parents, even if you are not my natural ones?" Then turning angrily to Carlos, "Besides, I don't think abandoning your child in an orphanage is very natural."

The white man looked at the girl with entreating eyes, slowly approached her and said "Oh my sweet little wise girl. My Lusindia! You have suffered so much. It is only natural that you feel this way. It was a result of the unnatural situation at that time, the unavoidable circumstances. Please let me explain. Give me just one chance."

Tears rolled down Carlos' cheeks as he recounted the story. "So my darling, please understand that your natural mother loved you with all her heart. She suffered even more to give you what she thought was a better chance at life. As for me, my heart yearned to find you from the moment I knew of your existence. Please try to understand! Won't you help me find your mother?"

There was not a dry eye in the room when he finished. Everyone looked anxiously at Lusindia for her reaction. She looked uncertainly from Carlos to her foster parents and back again unable to decide. Yet, inexplicably, she could not bear to see Carlos weep anymore. Impulsively she ran to him and an overjoyed Carlos held her in his arms. Lusindia had understood! A miracle! He thanked God for His tender mercy. Father and daughter were in each other's arms. Tears of joy trickled down their faces. Anyone could see that they were father and daughter.

"*Mãe* and *Pai*, can I be with my natural father? Just for a while, till we find my natural mother?" Lusindia pleaded. Romaldo and Cassiana felt sorry for Lusindia and Carlos. They looked at Lusindia's face, excused themselves and went to an inner room to confer with each other.

Both of them discussed what would be best for Lucy. They accepted the fact that Lusindia was Carlos's daughter. They knew Lusindia could have a better life abroad with her natural father than they could offer here. She would always be 'gorie' here and much as they loved her as their own they could not protect her from these taunts. They agreed as true parents would, to sacrifice their own happiness for the sake of their darling Lucy.

Romaldo and Cassiana returned to the room and faced Carlos and Lusindia, who looked at them expectantly.

"All right Senhor Soares! We have decided that Lucy should be with her natural father. We agree to sign the appropriate papers for her sake." Romaldo said quietly.

"Thank you Senhor Romaldo and Senhora Cassiana. God will certainly bless you for your great sacrifice. I can't thank you enough for taking care of my little girl all these years."

Lusindia hugged them both and said, "Thank you very much *Mãe* and *Pai*. I will always love you. I knew you would not refuse me. Your *morgada* is the happiest girl in the world today because she now has two sets of parents. Not many can boast of that! Thank you so much for giving me the chance to have both!"

They decided to keep Lusindia in Belgaum with them for the last few days until all the official paperwork was done. After all, this was all the time that they would get with her.

Carlos hugged and kissed Lusindia goodbye and returned to Goa. His lawyer filed the required papers and got all certificates in order to annul the adoption by Romaldo and Cassiana.

The next week, Carlos went to Belgaum, handed the necessary papers over to Romaldo and Cassiana and gave them a cheque of one lakh rupees as a token of appreciation for what they did for his daughter. Lusindia said goodbye to Belgaum. Her friends and teachers at St. Joseph's Convent and her neighbours were all sad to see her go. But parting from her foster parents Romaldo and Cassiana caused her the most anguish.

"I feel so awful to leave you, Mãe and Pai. Thank you very much for raising me up as your very own child. I will never forget what you have done for me. I know you came to Belgaum just to give me a good education. And now I am going away. I hope you understand why I have to. I will write to you regularly. I will always remember you. Always!"

After a final hug with both eyes streaming so she could hardly see, Lusindia picked up a framed picture of Romaldo and Cassiana, and holding it close to her heart, lifted her hand in a reluctant gesture of farewell.

Romaldo and Cassiana were deeply touched by her words but the pain of losing their daughter left them bereft of words. Weeping copiously, Romaldo and Cassiana, rosary in hand, made the sign of the Cross. "*Bapachem, Putrachem ani Espirit Santachem Bessaum tujer poddom baai. Devan tuka sodanch sukhi dovorchem, baai.*" Their blessing would always go with her.

Carlos and Lusindia got into a taxi with the translator and she waved goodbye to everyone in the neighbourhood who had gathered along the way. For the last time Lusindia looked at the house that was hers for the past few years and her heart ached.

Romaldo and Cassiana did not sleep that night. Now, there was no need to live in Belgaum. They decided to pack up and go back to Goa. They could live off the interest from the money they received as settlement from Carlos. But they would never forget the loving girl who had brought so much joy into their lives. Time and again they would look at Lusindia's smiling photograph and wonder what she was doing at that particular moment.

When they left Belgaum, Carlos and Lusindia boarded a bus bound for Goa, travelled through the Ghats and finally reached Goa. They were in Panjim rather late that evening. Lusindia liked the Hotel Mandovi. She had never been in a posh place like this before. They went to a fine restaurant in Panjim. Lusindia was in another world now, the one she could call legitimately her own.

Chapter 44

The next day Carlos took Lusindia to the *Provedoria* and the Court for the completion of the formalities and the paperwork. They went around Panjim to Dona Paula, Campal and Miramar and *Instituto Piedade*. Carlos wanted Lusindia to know all about her mother and himself before her birth in a Goa of another era.

Carlos booked tickets to go back to Portugal in two weeks. But before that he had to take care of certain things. He had to take Lusindia to Cuncolim to see her grandmother, and find out from her the whereabouts of her daughter, Linda. At the same time he had to do this discreetly. Linda could be married by now. He did not want to give rise to gossip that might ruin Linda's life.

Two days before leaving Goa, they went to Cuncolim at dusk to avoid being noticed. From the bus stand they walked to the house, as a taxi would give the neighbours some material for new gossip. When they went there, the house was closed.

"Is this my Mama's house, Papa?" asked Lusindia.

"Yes, Lusindia, isn't it a nice house? I wish you could see it during the daytime." Carlos knocked on the door, but no one came to the door. Carlos knocked once more. Still no one opened the door. Carlos noticed there was no light inside. Obviously no one was home.

"I guess your grandmother is not home, we better go back," Carlos said to Lusindia. Carlos wanted to ask the neighbours about Joanita. But he knew that would arouse suspicion and give rise to gossip about Linda. Carlos and Lusindia walked back to the village market area. As they were returning to the bus stand, they passed by the *Provedoria Assistência Pública's* orphanage for boys. There were several boys of Lusindia's age playing in the verandah.

They went in and Carlos introduced himself to the manager. "Do you know the whereabouts of your rear neighbour, Joanita Cardoso? Her house seems to be locked." Carlos asked the manager.

"I really don't know anything about it. But wait a minute, and I can ask Mário if he knows anything, as he sometimes helps her with household chores." The manager excused himself and shouted "Mário Pequeno, come here." And at once a skinny little white boy appeared from nowhere.

"Mário, do you know anything about Joanita auntie?" asked the manager.

"Yes, sir. She told me she was going for her annual *mudança* at Mobor in Cavelossim for a couple of weeks. She just left yesterday." Mário Pequeno responded and went back to play in the verandah.

"Does Joanita live alone in the house?" Carlos asked the manager.

"Yes Joanita lives all by herself. But someone told me she has a daughter, who went to London years ago." confided the manager.

"Thank you very much for your help, sir." Carlos thanked the manager and left with Lusindia.

"Lusindia, I think your Mama is in London." Carlos said to his daughter.

"Yes, I heard that, but if only I could see my grandmother today, she would have told us more about my Mama," Lusindia lamented.

Dejected, Carlos and Lusindia walked to the bus stand and were on their way back to Panjim. It was night now and they were still in the dark about Linda's whereabouts.

Carlos wanted to go to Mobor to see Linda's mother, but Mobor in Cavelossim, they said, was not accessible by motor transport. Not many people knew about the place. Besides, where in Mobor would he look for Joanita? There would be so many people on the beach, and it would certainly arouse suspicion if he were to ask for Joanita. Carlos had only a day left in Goa anyway and knew that the attempt to locate Joanita was futile. Carlos gave up the idea of going to see Linda's mother in Mobor. Now at least, he knew that Linda was in London. But he wondered whether Linda was married by now.

The next day Lusindia and her dad did some shopping in Panjim. She collected the items that she liked best from Goa. They bought a couple of Goan recipe books too.

Lusindia got to see her buddies from the *Provedoria*'s Goa Velha orphanage, but she could not remember anyone in particular. Carlos gave the girls some gifts and food and he instituted a scholarship at the *Provedoria* in Lusindia's name.

The group from Portugal left. Only three others found their offspring in Goa: one boy, Remedios Silveira, who was in the *Provedoria*'s Cuncolim orphanage and two girls Clara Sequeira and Belivia Flores from the *Provedoria*'s Goa Velha orphanage. When the news of these three orphans hit the Goa newspapers, Belivia's mother came out of the closet and joined her ex-lover Ricardo Flores in Portugal. The mothers of the other two were not found even after the investigators tried in vain to locate them.

Carlos and Lusindia went to New Delhi to finalize the papers and complete the processing of Lusindia's passport at the Portuguese embassy in New Delhi. They managed a grand tour of Delhi and saw the Taj Mahal. After getting Lusindia's passport, they flew to London. At London's Heathrow Airport, Carlos made some inquiries and called the operator to get the telephone number of Linda Cardoso in London. But the operator said there was no such person listed in the directory. Disheartened, they took the next flight to Lisbon on April 2, 1975.

Lusindia had never seen such places and cities before. It was like heaven to her. When they reached Portugal, Lusindia loved it, but could not speak Portuguese. It was the only language spoken there. She was registered in a private school for foreigners, who spoke English, and no Portuguese.

But Lusindia picked up Portuguese in no time from her school friends and practised it diligently with her father. Within two months she knew Portuguese very well, although at times she used Konkani or English words to fill the gaps. Her father spoiled her rotten. He would take her to school daily in a brand new car. They would eat out most of the time. Lusindia was too young to cook, but she knew how to cook some simple Goan dishes. She tried rice and chapattis. They went to a Goan store in Lisbon to buy ready-made pickles and spices. Lusindia tried her pork *vindalho* with the masala they bought. It was not bad for a first attempt.

Times were changing in Portugal. Politically it was unstable; prime ministers and deputies kept changing party affiliations and things were getting expensive. Portugal was going to be part of the European Community. Only real estate was booming because the North Europeans were buying real estate in Portugal. With spiralling inflation, the crime rate was rising. Carlos decided it was better for him to move out of Portugal with Lusindia. He did not want to go back to West Germany because it held painful memories for him. Ultimately he opted for Canada, the country of his birth and on October 11, 1975, Carlos and Lusindia migrated to Canada.

Carlos and Lusindia lived with a friend in Toronto at College and Ossington. Lusindia liked Toronto. Everybody spoke English and there were Portuguese-speaking people around the College area. Within a week they found a house on rent in the Bloor/Dundas area. Lusindia went to St Anne's School. She found it quite easy though the school system was quite different.

Carlos started a small construction business in the Toronto area and named it *Lusindia Custom Homes*. When they were not busy, he would subcontract to the big real estate developers in the Greater Toronto Area, which was developing fast. His business did well and so did his daughter at school. The teachers liked her and she was good in French, Portuguese and of course in English.

→❖◇❖◇❖◇❖←

Chapter 45

Linda was now very rich and well settled. She had enough people to supervise her business. A PhD in Microbiology headed her Technical Division and an MBA attended to the Business Division. She had acquired a Xerox machine and a brand new computer to store and process her complex database.

Linda loved Canada for it turned out lucky for her in many ways. Linda was now a Canadian citizen and she decided to go to Goa after a long time. Now she could afford to take it easy, and she wanted to see her mother. Her main goal was to get her daughter back at any cost from the *Provedoria*, now that she could afford to raise her herself. She could hardly wait to see her long lost child Lusindia, who would be the sole heir to her little empire.

Linda obtained her Canadian passport and went to India on November 1, 1975. She arrived at Bombay's Santa Cruz Airport. It had changed a lot. She remembered it as it was in 1963 when she took her first flight out of India. She smiled to herself. She took a connecting Indian Airlines flight to Goa. When she came out of the Dabolim airport, she took a taxi to Cuncolim. Everything had changed. New concrete houses had mushroomed all over the villages, built from the Middle East petrodollars. People crowded in the village markets. Clouds of smoke, noise and smells polluted the once clean and quiet village environment. It was not the same old peaceful Goa she had left behind in 1963.

She arrived in Cuncolim. Everyone was staring at her. Very few people could recognize her. She was home after about twelve years. Everything around her house had changed. Her mother opened the door hearing the taxi pull up.

"How are you, Mama?" Linda ran to her mother, hugged and kissed her.

"It is wonderful to see you *baai* after so many years," Joanita said through tears of joy, clinging on to her daughter as if afraid to let go.

They said a short prayer of thanks in front of the oratory and they talked and talked only to be interrupted by intermittent visits from excited neighbours. Everyone said Linda looked very beautiful. She had short hair now and still had an elegant figure. She looked fairer now and young for her 31years.

When the last neighbour left, Linda went to have her bath. Her mother had boiled some hot water and mixed it with cold water in a *baldi*, bucket. Linda found it strange after so many years to have a bath in the old style bathroom. She had to take water in a *tambio*, a little copper pot, from the bucket and wash herself in the smoke-filled bathroom in the kitchen, by the dim light of a kerosene lamp because the intermittent *apa-lipa* electric supply had gone off as usual.

After her bath, Linda ate some *chouriço* sausages, rice and curry with mango pickle licking her fingers with relish, after many years. They talked and talked about everything and everyone – those who had died, had babies, and got married. Linda's questions were never ending. How were all relatives doing? What were the neighbourhood children studying? Who went from rags to riches? Who were the priests in the church? What was the state of affairs in the village? How about the politics, the *panchayat*, the schools, the teachers and the postman? Where were Miguel and Saudina? Who was winning the elections – the Hand or the Rose?

"Mama, have you heard anything about Lusindia?" asked Linda suddenly, voicing the one that was uppermost in her mind. She waited till after she finished all her trivial queries almost as if she were afraid to know the answer. Sure enough, it was, as she feared. No news at all.

"Nothing *baai*. The people at *Provedoria* discouraged me from making visits to Lusindia after she grew up and so I stopped going. They would not tell me anything about her. They said they had to be secretive about the adopted children. I went to the *Provedoria* in Panjim once a month when the child was small. I took her some clothes, dolls and chocolates. But the manager told me not to visit her anymore as the child began to grow up. The last time I saw Lusindia, was when she was three and a half years old in Navelim at your uncle's house."

Two days later, Linda took the birth certificate, the certified option paper, the adoption papers and Lusindia's baby photo and went straight to the *Provedoria* in Panjim. She told them, she would like to see the daughter she had given up for adoption to the *Provedoria* in 1962. The lady in charge said all the girls were now in their orphanage at Goa Velha and boys were in Cuncolim. Linda requested to see the Director at the *Provedoria* to check the child's records.

"I am looking for my daughter, Lusindia Soares given for adoption in July 1962," Linda said to the Director.

"The name *Lusindia* seems to ring a bell. Yes, I remember now quite clearly." The director rang the bell and a peon came into the office.

"Rosario, bring me the file on 'Lusindia Soares' from the Archives cabinet." The director said to the peon.

The peon brought the file and the director made copies of the documents and gave them to Linda.

"Madam, I am sorry to inform you that Baby Lusindia has been taken away by her father, Carlos Soares recently, to Portugal. Here are all the documents," the Director said.

"Oh my God! Really? When did this happen?" Linda could hardly believe what she had just heard.

The director told Linda the entire story how Carlos came looking for Lusindia, and had to go to Belgaum to get her back from her foster parents Romaldo and Cassiana Rodrigues, who were now living in Orlim.

Linda was astounded to hear this. She pressed the Director for more information about Carlos and Lusindia but he only knew that the natural father had legally taken his daughter Lusindia to Portugal. Linda looked at the file and found Carlos's forwarding address in Lisbon and his phone number.

Linda went to the Post office and phoned the number in Lisbon, Portugal. The telephone operator said the phone number was disconnected since October 1975. Then Linda sent a telegram to the address in Lisbon and asked Carlos to please contact her in Goa either by telegram or leave a message at the Post Office in Panjim. She also left her phone number in Toronto, Canada as an additional precaution.

Linda went home to Cuncolim and told her mother the amazing story about Lusindia and Carlos. Suddenly Joanita remembered something.

"I remember now, the last time, I went to Mobor for mudança, Mário Pequeno from the *Provedoria*'s orphanage, who helps me sometimes, told me a white man and a teenaged girl were looking for me. He said they were asking questions about me and talked to the manager at the orphanage. Could they be Carlos and Lusindia?" wondered Joanita.

"I am sure they were Carlos and Lusindia. Carlos must have come here to show Lusindia her grandmother and maybe find out about me."

"Oh my poor granddaughter, Lusindia." Joanita sighed.

Linda immediately took off to the *Provedoria* orphanage and introduced herself to the manager.

"Hello, I am Linda, daughter of Joanita Dias Cardoso, your neighbour."

"Nice to meet you, Linda, what can I do for you?"

"Do you remember, sometime ago when my mother went for a *mudança*, there was a white man and a teenaged girl looking for my mother?" asked Linda.

"Oh yes, I do remember. The man introduced himself as Carlos Soares from Portugal and he introduced the girl as Lusindia," the manager recalled.

"Yes, that's the one. Do you remember what he asked you?" asked Linda.

"He just wanted to know where your mother had gone. Mário Pequeno told him that she had gone for *mudança* to Mobor for two weeks. Oh, yes, he also asked me whether your mother lived alone. I think I told him that Joanita had a daughter who had gone to London years ago."

"Thank you for your help. You have a good memory. Here is something for the kids." Linda opened her purse and gave him a thousand rupees and headed home.

So Carlos was still interested in her. He wanted to know what had happened to her. Linda realized that Carlos thought she lived in London. He must have come to Cuncolim to show Lusindia her grandmother and to find out about her too, she thought. It was strange how fate played games with everyone's lives.

Five days passed by and still there was no word from Carlos in Portugal. There was no telegram and no message in her Toronto office. Linda wanted to go to Portugal and find out what had happened. She could not concentrate on anything. She could not enjoy her vacation in Goa.

But Linda had to make a quick visit to Orlim, where Romaldo and Cassiana Rodrigues had retired.

"Is this the house of Romaldo and Cassiana?" Linda asked a woman outside the house.

"Yes *baai*. I am Cassiana. Who are you?"

"My name is Linda. I am the unfortunate mother of the little girl you adopted years ago, Lusindia." Linda introduced herself.

"Come inside *baai*. It's nice to meet you. Come," Cassiana opened the door and went inside taking Linda with her. "Romaldo, look who's here? It is our baby Lucy's Mama."

"Nice to meet you. You look just like our Lucy. Sit here, *baai*."

Cassiana went inside and got a glass of cold Coca Cola for Linda.

"I came here to thank you both. You adopted my poor helpless baby and brought her up like a princess. You protected her, pampered her, educated her and gave her everything you had. You loved her more than I ever could. For that I am ever so grateful. How can I ever repay you for all this and for your generosity in giving her up after all you had done for her?"

Linda took out a bundle of American Express Travellers' cheques and gave them to Cassiana and Romaldo.

"This is nothing compared to what you did for my Lusindia. You have no idea how much it means to me to know that my child had the best parents in the world in you." Linda said. "Please accept this for my satisfaction."

"*Baai*. No. No. We do not want anything more. Senhor Carlos gave us one hundred thousand rupees already and it was too much. Lucy was our daughter too and a joy to us always... no trouble at all. She was such a lovely daughter, our little *morgada*." Tears flowed down Cassiana's eyes.

"Please do not reject my small token of gratitude. Please keep it for my sake," Linda entreated.

"Oh my God. Why do we need so much money? We have very few needs. May God bless you *baai*," Romaldo said, as she pressed the cheques into his hand.

Cassiana and Romaldo were very happy to meet Lusindia's mother and they told Linda all about their beautiful Lucy. Linda was happy her

Lusindia had a nice childhood with them. "I have to leave now, Mr and Mrs Rodrigues. May God bless you both. I hope I see my Lusindia soon. Pray for me. Thanks a lot and *Adeus*!" Linda said goodbye.

Linda stayed in Goa for two weeks, and left for London. From London, she flew to Lisbon, went to the given address, but did not find Carlos there. She hired a private investigator to find out about Carlos Soares. The private investigator found out about the ad in the national newspapers way back in 1974 and about the trip to Goa. The next day, he put an ad in the national papers and asked for information about Carlos Soares.

The next day, the investigator received a phone call from Ricardo Flores, who told him that he knew Carlos had brought his daughter back from Goa to Lisbon and that he had mentioned wanting to emigrate with her. He wasn't sure if they had gone somewhere. So the investigation ended right there. The investigator told Linda that Flores had told him that Carlos had spent most of his time from 1962 to 1974 in Germany. So that's where Carlos had been living, and not in Portugal.

Linda felt very dejected as she was getting nowhere with her search for Lusindia and Carlos. After a couple of days in Portugal, Linda left for Toronto, Canada.

Linda arrived in Toronto on November 28th, 1975. She went back to her office and checked for messages. There was still no message from Carlos. She went back to her old routine in her office.

Chapter 46

It was the month of December 1975 and Linda looked at her year-end finances. Her accountant told her she was paying too much in taxes. He advised her to invest her money in real estate, where her value could grow without having to pay huge taxes. Linda thought a nice change in environment would help distract her from her immediate family worries. Linda decided to build a custom-designed home north of Toronto. She called her accountant and asked him to provide her with a list of custom homebuilders.

Linda received a list of plots for sale in Kleinberg, Woodbridge, Richmond Hill and Markham. She called the number in Kleinberg and she went to see the plot. It was a lovely big plot, secluded and peaceful with a marvellous view and the Humber River running down just below it. She bought the plot right away.

The next day, the accountant called three prospective custom homebuilders to Linda's office, so they could make their presentations and Linda could decide what she wanted. Linda came to the boardroom. The three builders introduced themselves and showed her samples of their recently built luxury homes along with references. Linda told them what she had in mind.

After a week, Linda received some sketches from the builders. Linda did not like any of their designs and wanted to see more designs from other custom homebuilders in the Greater Toronto Area. In the next few days, Linda received many designs from various homebuilders. As she went through some of the designs, a name on the letterhead caught her eye.

The letterhead read '*LUSINDIA CUSTOM HOMES*' and she recognized Carlos's signature below. Linda gasped and sat transfixed. Then she recovered and opened the folder. She read the covering letter in detail. She at once pulled out the card stapled to the folder. It had his name, address and the telephone number of his office. That's was all she needed.

Galvanized into action, Linda freshened up, picked up her car keys and bag, told her secretary she was going out and left. She was still not herself as she sped towards Carlos and her daughter. The car could not match the speed of her thoughts. She stopped at a red light, but her mind kept racing.

Was he married now? Was his wife with him? Did he have any children of his own? Where had he been all this time? When did he come to Canada? Did he know she existed? Would he be glad to see her? If he were still single, she could thank God for that. But if he were married and had commitments, then it would break her heart. She had waited for him for so long hoping he would come back one day like in those romances she had read to keep her hope alive. Even if he were married, at least she could see him and find out all about him.

Suddenly the lights turned green, she accelerated and turned on to Bloor Street. She had reached her destination. She pulled over and parked her car without even checking if she could park there or not.

Linda rushed out of the car, hurriedly smoothing down her hair, ran up to the address shown on the card and rang the bell. A young lady opened the door.

"Is Mr Carlos Soares in?" she asked.

"I am sorry he is not in right now. Can I help you? I am his secretary."

"Oh please, I need to see him right away," she entreated, "Can I have his residence address?"

"I am sorry Ma'am I can't give that out."

"But this is personal and very urgent, dear. Please, I can't wait any longer. It's very important. A life or death situation, please!"

The young secretary could see in her eyes an anxiety that she couldn't quite fathom. She went into the inner office, wrote the address and phone number on a piece of paper and handed it to Linda.

"I hope my boss doesn't get mad with me for breaking the rules."

"No, he won't. You are a darling, sweetie! Thanks a lot!"

Linda took the paper and ran to the car, her heart still throbbing heavily.

She had to go Dundas Street at Roncesvales. Linda got behind the wheel and sped towards Dundas Street. Again her thoughts kept her busy. What would he say to her? What would his reaction be?

The worst that could happen was that he might want to be left alone. She could leave him alone, if he so wanted. She loved him that much. And she could still have Lusindia!

Linda finally reached the address near Dundas Street West/Bloor area. She went to the house and rang the bell. No one came. She tried again. Still no one opened the door. She went to her car and waited. It was 3 p.m. and she had not eaten yet. She walked to a Bloor Street McDonalds and picked up a hamburger, fries and a coke. She went back to her car and saw a parking control officer take out his pad to write a parking ticket for the car next to hers. Linda got into the car and drove around the block, came back after ten minutes and parked the car just next to the house.

After what seemed an eternity, a young girl of about thirteen with jet-black hair and a face that looked just like hers, walked happily toward the house. The girl slowly took out her key, unlocked the door, opened it, walked in and closed the door.

"Oh my God!" exclaimed Linda. "It must be her. My Lusindia! What a beautiful child! My baby!" Linda could not wait any longer. She swiftly went to the door and rang the bell. Lusindia opened the door and looked inquisitively at the woman outside. Linda looked at Lusindia intently. She noticed that Lusindia had some features of Carlos and his skin colour but otherwise looked just like her.

"Can I come inside, young lady?" Linda asked.

"I am sorry. I don't think I know you," said Lusindia.

"Oh you do, my dear. Just look at me carefully," Linda said

Lusindia peered at Linda's face for a minute.

"Don't I remind you of someone?" Linda asked her

Lusindia kept watching her as she spoke. Yes, the lady did remind her of someone. Who could it be? Lusindia frowned in concentration. Suddenly her brow cleared and she looked like a thunderbolt had hit her.

"Oh my! It's me you remind me of. You're not…you can't be…" Lusindia's voice trailed off in shock.

"Is your name Linda?" she asked tremulously, wanting to be sure. Linda nodded as if she could not speak. Indeed, she did not trust herself to do so. Both mother and daughter needed time to let it sink in.

"You are my Mom!" Lusindia screamed out and leapt into her arms.

"Mama please hold me in your arms and don't ever let me go. You don't know how much I prayed and yearned for this moment," Lusindia whispered in her ear, through her hair. They clung to each other for a long time, holding hands and catching up on so much of lost time. The telephone rang. Lusindia picked up the phone.

"Hi Lucy, what are you doing sweetie?" It was her father, Carlos.

"Hello Papa, please come home right now, I have a big surprise for you." Lusindia hung up the phone. A minute later the phone rang again. It was her father again.

"Darling, I called to say an important business meeting has just come up and I will be late," said Carlos.

"Papa, I want you to come home right away. This is an emergency and it can't wait. Forget the business meeting, come home right away."

"Darling, this is a very important meeting with a client. I might not get the contract if I don't make it now," her father pleaded with Lusindia.

"No, no, no. I won't take no for an answer. Papa, I've never asked you to break your business appointments before, have I? So please come home right away. See you soon. I love you."

"Okay. You win, my little rascal! I'll come home right away." Carlos cancelled his appointment and was on his way home.

Lusindia went to the kitchen, brought some orange juice and cookies for her mother. Linda kept asking Lusindia about her life and her father. She wanted to know everything.

"Tell me honey, is your Papa married?"

"No Mama," Lusindia giggled. Linda felt so relieved that she hugged her little angel once more. She had an impish giggle, this daughter of hers.

"I can't tell you how happy I am today, darling. All those hard times and sacrifices were worth it. Finally, I am in heaven, honey," and Linda began to cry again, shedding sweet tears of happiness.

"Wait Mama, I want to show you something." Lusindia went upstairs to her bedroom and brought something with her, which she hid behind her.

"Now close your eyes Mama." Linda closed her eyes obediently. "Okay. Now open your eyes Mama and look here. Remember this?"

Linda couldn't believe it. Lusindia had the doll in her hand – the one Linda had given her so many years ago.

"Oh baby, you still have it?"

"Yes Mama, the nurse told me you gave it to me."

"You kept it all these years?"

"Mama, this was the only thing I could remember you by. It was the most precious thing I ever owned."

Linda kissed and hugged Lusindia all over again.

They had talked about an hour, when they heard the key turn in the front door. Linda quickly darted and hid herself in a closet and peeked in through the gap. Carlos walked in.

"Honey you had better have a good reason to get me here in such a hurry. What's the emergency? Where are you, Lucy?"

Linda's right eye focused on Carlos. He was still young looking and handsome. He had put on some weight, but was still very attractive.

She could hold back no more. She dashed out of the closet and hugged him tight, burying her face in his chest.

Carlos got the shock of his life. He did not know who this woman was; he did not even have a chance to look at her face.

Slowly Linda looked up at his face and their eyes met again for the first time after fourteen long years of agony and separation.

"O *Meu Deus*! My darling Linda, where were you all these years? I have been looking for you. How did you find us?" Carlos exclaimed.

"Please stop, darling Carlos," interrupted Linda with her hand on his lips, "Don't say anything. I am so happy now. Nothing matters anymore. It's like heaven all over again."

"See Papa, I told you the surprise would be worth it? It's fantastic. We finally found Mama or rather she found us. All that matters is that we're together now."

They hugged and kissed and cried. It was such an incredible reunion. Carlos and Linda held each other for what seemed to be an interminable length of time. It was 7pm and they were still in each other's arms, when the doorbell rang. Practical Lusindia opened the door for the pizza she had ordered. Her parents could survive on love and fresh air, but a growing girl like her needed sustenance.

"Here's to us, our little family and the future." Carlos raised a toast with some champagne and Linda said a short prayer of thanksgiving.

Linda excused herself for a moment and went to the living room to be by herself. She needed to be alone – to close her eyes in heartfelt thanks and express her regret for her earlier anger directed towards God.

The day December 21, 1975 was a milestone in their life. What a Christmas present, it was for them! Carlos and Linda told Lusindia not to go to school the next day. That night the conversation never stopped.

Linda and Carlos, whispered and kissed and made torrid love during the remainder of the night. They had missed each other for fourteen long years. They wanted to make up for all those years. Linda was in paradise again. It reminded them of that fateful night in Hotel Mandovi, where they had first made love. They slept in each other's arms like babes until they were awakened by a noise in the kitchen at ten in the morning.

Lusindia was the first one to wake up and started to make coffee. Linda heard her and woke up. Carlos slept with his hands around her. She quietly lifted his hands, got up from the bed, put on the robe she had borrowed from Lusindia and went to the kitchen. They hugged each other and whispered good morning.

Linda went to the washroom, brushed her teeth with a new toothbrush, which Lusindia had kept for her on the counter, and sat at the breakfast table. They began to talk about school and other things. Both of them prepared a sumptuous breakfast of bacon and eggs, toast and coffee. While they were talking, Carlos also woke up, hugged them both, went to the washroom, brushed his teeth and joined them both at the breakfast table.

At about 11:00 a.m., Linda called her office and said she would not come to the office that day and gave Carlos' phone number to contact in case of an emergency. Carlos did the same with his office. Linda made reservations for three at her favourite restaurant in downtown Toronto, where they could have their favourite food and relax quietly.

They kept talking non-stop and drove to Linda's place in Thornhill. Linda opened her remote controlled garage door and parked her car. They entered the house and Lusindia was overwhelmed by the majestic interior of the house. The house was huge, with a sprawling lawn, and a big backyard with trees and shrubs.

In the main bedroom there was a big picture of Linda with Carlos and another picture of baby Lusindia. The house was just too big for just one person. Linda rang for the maid, who had her own quarters, above the triple garage. The house was over 3000 square feet and the basement was finished in wooden panelling. There was a pool table, a bar, a TV set, a large hall, a huge sitting room, a washroom, and a hot tub in the basement.

In the backyard there was a swimming pool and a barbecue. Lusindia liked her mother's huge house. She asked her father if she could live there. Carlos said they had lots of time to talk about the future. Right now they wanted to talk about the past.

They had a delicious lunch at the restaurant near Kensington Market. They ordered a bottle of Mateus Rose and enjoyed the delicious Portuguese food, which included barbecued chicken and seafood. Afterwards they went for a ride around town. Later that night they dined at Bombay Palace Restaurant and tried Indian food. Late at night, they returned to Linda's Thornhill residence.

That night they talked till eleven. The next day was Saturday and Lusindia did not have to go to school. Lusindia went to sleep in her bedroom. Linda and Carlos ceremoniously entered the master bedroom and soaked in the Jacuzzi. Then they made love until they were exhausted and went to sleep in each other's arms. Another night well spent!

On Saturday morning, they woke up at ten. They had a good rest. Rosy, the Goan maid that Linda had hired cooked a hot breakfast. She had prepared hot homemade chapattis, fried some eggs and bacon and Goan sausages with fries, onion and eggs. Linda made some cappuccino for Lusindia.

They talked again at the table. They would not go anywhere today. Now, they could talk about their plans. But before that, Carlos related the entire story of Heidi and their ill-fated marriage, her deception and betrayal.

"Oh my God! I can't believe Heidi did this to me. How could she steal my letters? You can't trust anyone. Thank God it ended this way. I want to forget everything and put the past behind. There is no point in holding grudges any longer. Besides, justice has already been meted out by God and He has brought us together," said Linda.

"I agree. We are going to start a new life from now on," added Carlos, reassuringly.

Then Carlos knelt down on his knee, kissed her hand and posed the inevitable question to Linda. "Will you marry me, my dearest Linda?"

"I thought you would never ask. Sure my darling, anytime. I have waited for so long to hear that," replied Linda.

"We will marry right away then," said Carlos.

Linda called her priest and arranged to have the wedding within a month at St Michael's Cathedral downtown. It was going to be a modest affair with a simple church service. Then there would be a reception for their close friends at Casa Loma. Linda made arrangements for her mother Joanita to come to Canada for her wedding.

They decided they would all live in Thornhill now. They transferred Lusindia to a private school nearby and moved all their belongings to Thornhill on Christmas Eve. They had the best Christmas that year. They went to the church for midnight Mass. On Christmas Day, under the Christmas tree they had placed together a symbol of the best Christmas present they would ever receive – a loving family. It was a simple Nativity scene with Mary, Joseph and the child Jesus in the crib.

Chapter 47

On January 15, 1976 Linda and Carlos were married in St Michael's Cathedral in Toronto, Canada with their child Lusindia by their side. Linda's mother Joanita also was present, her heart bursting with happiness. She was extremely proud of Linda who persevered, prayed and worked hard to be reunited with her family.

The story of this memorable reunion and wedding reached the media. An American network signed a deal with Linda and Carlos to portray them on their forthcoming North American TV Show debut of *Here They Meet At Last*, a show about happy reunions after years of separation, which would premiere on February 14, 1976, St Valentine's Day.

Linda and Carlos had a grand wedding at Casa Loma with their good friends invited for the occasion. On January 16, they left for their honeymoon to Curaçao and enjoyed their honeymoon on the secluded island, appropriately named after the heart. They stayed there for a week, enjoyed the sights and sounds of nature and each other. They came back to Toronto to join their daughter Lusindia, who was with her grandmother Joanita. The family was complete now. Or was it?

On February 14, St. Valentine's Day, they sat in front of the TV set to see their show. A week before, the TV crew had almost turned their home into a studio, shooting scenes everywhere with blinding lights and huge cameras. The shooting ended after two whole days.

They looked fabulous on TV. Their story was very tenderly dramatized. Linda and Lusindia felt tears running down their cheeks. These TV professionals were very talented. The entire show was taped on their video recorder. They had informed their friends about the show and they all watched it. After the show was over, Linda felt some discomfort, felt sick and threw up. Her mother wanted her to call a doctor. But Linda told her not to bother. She had felt the same way on December 18, 1961 at *Instituto Piedade* in

Panjim, Goa. This time however it was not a shock.

"I am pregnant, mother," Linda announced.

Carlos and Joanita just hugged her. There was no need for words. "I hope it's a boy, Mama," exclaimed Lusindia excitedly hugging her mother.

After their appearance on TV, their phone was inundated with calls from their friends and journalists. The Toronto Star won a bid for the story on their Saturday Star Special. So on Saturday, the exclusive photo of Linda, Carlos and Lusindia graced the front page of the Saturday Star. The Soares family became quite famous and both the Goan and Portuguese communities were proud of them.

On September 19th, 1976 a baby boy was born to Linda at St Michael's Hospital. They named him Shawn Glenn Soares. Joanita's visa was extended so she could be there until the baby was born. Joanita took care of the baby for a month until his Christening. Though they wanted her to stay on, it was too cold for Joanita in Canada. She left Canada on November 3, 1976.

Life for the Soares family was wonderful. Linda wanted to devote her time to her family. She went public with her company and retained the largest shareholding with 60% ownership. She made a lot of money out of this transaction and remained a director on the Board with majority voting rights.

Linda never had to work again. She deserved the rest after her hard, hectic life. Carlos continued his custom home building business. Lusindia went to high school and Linda devoted her time raising her new baby Shawn full time. Linda was satisfied with her life. She finally had made it. She was a fulfilled young woman.

Was the Goddess Sottvi satisfied? Were the prophecies she made for her baby Linda on that fateful night of November 1, 1944, fulfilled?

Linda's mother certainly thought so.

******